PRAISE FOR THE NOVELS OF STEPHANIE MARIE THORNTON

"*And They Called It Camelot* is the book club pick of the year. Stephanie Marie Thornton brings an American icon to life: Jackie the debutante, the First Lady, the survivor who at last becomes the heroine of her own story."

—Kate Quinn, *New York Times* bestselling author of *The Rose Code*

"An extraordinary profile of the courage and grace of the indomitable Jacqueline Bouvier Kennedy Onassis, *And They Called It Camelot* is impeccably researched and richly drawn. . . . An unputdownable, unforgettable read."

—Chanel Cleeton, *New York Times* bestselling author of *The Most Beautiful Girl in Cuba*

"Addictive, dishy, and emotionally haunting, this novel paints an intimate portrait of a tumultuous marriage that played out on the world's stage and ended in national tragedy. . . . Vivid, engrossing, and utterly unforgettable, *And They Called It Camelot* is Thornton's best work yet."

—Stephanie Dray, *New York Times* bestselling author of *The Women of Chateau Lafayette*

"Jacqueline Kennedy Onassis leaves an enduring (and intimidating) legacy; for a writer, finding something new and meaningful to say about her is a daunting task. Thornton harnesses her immense talent for historical fiction and combines it with a biographer's immersive research to create a rich portrait that is both intimate and thoughtful while also wildly addictive. I tore through these pages and you will too. Thornton gifts her readers with a fresh appreciation for the indomitable woman behind the iconic sunglasses."

—Steven Rowley, author of *The Editor*

"Stephanie Thornton has compellingly and sympathetically humanized an American icon. Well researched and beautifully written, *And They Called It Camelot* is compulsively readable historical fiction!"

—Laura Kamoie, *New York Times* bestselling coauthor
of *My Dear Hamilton*

"In her rich, fascinating account of Jacqueline Bouvier Kennedy Onassis's life, author Stephanie Marie Thornton effortlessly transports us back in time. . . . A powerful and uplifting portrayal."

—*Woman's World*

"Thornton captures a celebrity with whom the world mourned in November 1963, but her down-to-earth approach has given us the opportunity for a more intimate and less sensational look at Jackie, the wife and mother. Highly recommended."

—Historical Novel Society

"Even if you think you know the story of Jacqueline Bouvier Kennedy Onassis, you're in for a rare behind-the-scenes look at the former First Lady's life. . . . This book is nothing short of magical."

—Renée Rosen, author of *The Social Graces*

"This book grabbed me from page one and wouldn't let me go. A multidimensional imagining of the trials and triumphs of Jaqueline Bouvier Kennedy, *And They Called It Camelot* will make you rethink everything you thought you knew about this remarkable First Lady." —Kerri Maher, author of *The Girl in White Gloves*

"Students of history will appreciate Thornton's exacting research and convincing portrayal of the First Lady and style icon, and Kennedy aficionados will feel as if they have an unparalleled access to Camelot. Thornton's magnificent portrayal of Onassis will delight fans of Kennedy-related fiction."

—*Publishers Weekly* (starred review)

"*And They Called It Camelot* is a sumptuous, propulsive, scandal-filled peek behind the curtain of American royalty. Thornton gives the reader a fascinating look at the masks worn by those who live in the public life."

—Erika Robuck, national bestselling author of *The Invisible Woman*

"Simply spellbinding. . . . A tale of love and devastation, greatness and sacrifice, this remarkable novel will grip readers until the last page." —Kristin Beck, author of *Courage, My Love*

"Readers will enjoy this heartbreaking story of a wife's fierce pride and loyalty to her president and country, despite years of marital loneliness and loss." —*Library Journal*

"Tackling a larger-than-life person such as Jackie Kennedy is a daunting undertaking, and Stephanie Marie Thornton handles that challenge splendidly. Thornton's decision to have Jackie narrate her own story lends an intimate feel to the tale . . . a fascinating and personal portrait of one of America's most iconic women."

—*Bookreporter*

"As juicy and enlightening as a page in Meghan Markle's diary."

—*InStyle*

WRITING AS STEPHANIE MARIE THORNTON

American Princess
And They Called It Camelot
A Most Clever Girl

WRITING AS STEPHANIE THORNTON

The Secret History
Daughter of the Gods
The Tiger Queens
The Conqueror's Wife

A MOST CLEVER GIRL

A NOVEL OF AN AMERICAN SPY

STEPHANIE MARIE THORNTON

BERKLEY
NEW YORK

BERKLEY
An imprint of Penguin Random House LLC
penguinrandomhouse.com

Library of Congress Cataloging-in-Publication Data

Names: Thornton, Stephanie, 1980– author.
Title: A most clever girl : a novel of an American spy /
Stephanie Marie Thornton.
Description: First Edition. | New York: Berkley, 2021.
Identifiers: LCCN 2021006680 (print) | LCCN 2021006681 (ebook) |
ISBN 9780593198407 (trade paperback) | ISBN 9780593198414 (ebook)
Subjects: GSAFD: Historical fiction.
Classification: LCC PS3620.H7847 M67 2021 (print) |
LCC PS3620.H7847 (ebook) | DDC 813/.6—dc23
LC record available at https://lccn.loc.gov/2021006680
LC ebook record available at https://lccn.loc.gov/2021006681

Printed in the United States of America
1st Printing

Book design by Tiffany Estreicher

To my grandparents:
Carolyn Christler, Marge Hintz, and Don & Billie Paulson

Was Elizabeth Bentley telling what really happened? Now, forty years later, one issue still resonates: Did Elizabeth Bentley tell the truth?

—Hayden Peake, *Out of Bondage*, Afterword

The gun in Catherine's Pucci handbag bumped reassuringly against her hip as she double-checked the address of the Connecticut apartment building.

The scrawled numbers refused to snap into focus until she blinked a few times; her eyes were still raw from yesterday's news of President Kennedy's assassination, from seeing photos of a tearstained Jackie Kennedy—whom Catherine sometimes glimpsed while giving tours of the White House—wearing that blood-spattered pink suit while Lyndon Johnson took the oath of office aboard Air Force One.

Yesterday had been the final straw.

One week ago, Catherine's entire world had fallen apart. One day ago, the country.

But today, armed with a crumpled letter and the Smith & Wesson revolver her father had carried when he was shot down at the Battle of Saipan, Catherine was going to right some very old wrongs.

Two bullets, she thought to herself. *One for her and one for me.*

The building hunched in front of her was nondescript, shabby, and run-down; even the wood of the stairs underfoot felt rotten. Catherine—Cat to everyone outside of her mother, who had called her Cathy—had probably watched too much James Bond in *Dr. No*, but she'd expected a former spy to have a more impressive abode than this two-story mud-brown building with sagging gutters and peeling paint.

Probably fallen on hard times, she thought to herself as she knocked on the door of number 201, wishing she could break it down instead. *She's damned lucky she's not in jail.*

Cat waited, then gave a second sharp rap with the heel of her fist. She was about to start peering inside windows when a squat woman with snuff-brown hair cracked the door wide enough to reveal a rusted chain lock. She looked more run-down than the building itself, save for her painted red lips. Not just any red—vicious, violent, poisonous *red*.

"Hello, my name is Catherine Gray." Cat smoothed the flip of her Jackie-esque bob, every rebellious blond strand lacquered into place with half a can of Aqua Net. Given the way the blood was pounding in her ears, she was impressed that her hands didn't shake. "I'm here to see Elizabeth Bentley."

The door slammed in her face.

Cat raised her fist again, this time ready to break the door down, but stopped at the unexpected rattle of chain. The door reopened, wider this time. The dumpy woman's gaze swept the empty street, making Catherine wonder what—or who—she was looking for.

"I'm Elizabeth Bentley." Her voice came out slightly nasal with that East Coast finishing school polish Catherine had grown accustomed to hearing after three and a half years at Trinity Washington University. Elizabeth Bentley's face was the sort no one would notice in a crowd. *The perfect face for a spy*. The image was only marred by a small mole below her left eye and a scar that streaked beneath her lower lip.

This was the face of the woman who had destroyed Cat's life.

It's now or never . . .

In one swift movement, Cat aimed the Smith & Wesson revolver straight between Elizabeth's eyes. The gun made a satisfying *click* as she cocked the trigger. "You ruined my life, you Communist bitch. And now you're going to pay for it."

She'd thought she'd be able to just pull the trigger, to end all this and escape the lethal undertow of pain. But when the moment came . . .

Cat hesitated.

Can I really end someone else's life? Am I capable of that?

To Elizabeth's credit, she merely blinked. Was she really so accustomed to staring down the muzzle of a gun? "Well, Catherine Gray, unfortunately, I ruined a lot of people's lives. Why don't you come in and we can discuss like civilized people what I did that was so heinous that you want to kill me?"

Whatever Cat had been expecting while she rehearsed this scene in her head on the train ride up from Washington, DC, a civilized chat was decidedly *not* it.

Except Elizabeth was already turning around, the open door an invitation to follow her.

Cat worried that perhaps Elizabeth was going for her own weapon, but the former spy merely looked back at her. "Are you coming? Or are you really going to shoot me?"

Cat could pull the trigger—at such close quarters she could hardly miss, despite the sudden tremor in her hands—and exact a quick and easy revenge. Except it was difficult to think with her heart beating in her ears and the foundations of her plan crumbling beneath her very feet. It might be easier to follow Elizabeth Bentley inside. Maybe inform this criminal exactly why she was here, and see if Elizabeth Bentley would confess to crimes that had led a twenty-one-year-old college student to her doorstep with murder on her mind?

Then Cat could shoot her. And be done with all of this. Right?

Gun in hand, Cat stepped over the threshold.

She'd half expected encoding machines or telegraphs inside, found instead merely a plain apartment decorated in every shade of brown. A clock ticked somewhere, and the lone decoration on any of the oak-paneled walls was a tacky wooden crucifix with a resin Christ nailed to the cross. A stack of leather-bound books tottered on a battered end table, and a long-haired ginger cat stretched out lazily on a mushroom-brown sofa as if he owned the place. The thing opened one eye, then howled piteously before rolling onto his back. "Hush, George Washington," Elizabeth chided him. "Catherine here has a gun, and you don't want to upset her with your caterwauling." She turned to Cat, arms open at her sides as if giving her one final opportunity to take the easy way out. *Talk or shoot?*

When Cat didn't move, Elizabeth gave a tiny nod. "It's almost one o'clock, but I'll put on a fresh pot of Folgers. Or I have gin, if that's your preference. Pick your poison, as it were."

"No coffee, no gin. I don't want anything from you." Certainly not a glass laced with poison, which Cat wouldn't have put past this woman who once took orders from the NKVD. "Except a confession."

Elizabeth sighed, gestured toward the Formica table inside the thimble-sized kitchen. "Do you mind if we sit? Standing is hell on my knees these days."

The last thing Cat wanted to do was to sit across from this woman in some cozy tête-à-tête, but she heard her dead mother's voice inside her head. *Manners, Cathy. And respect your elders.*

Except she didn't owe Elizabeth Bentley one iota of respect. She gestured with the gun toward the kitchen. "Let's get this over with."

And then I'll shoot you.

Elizabeth settled into a floral vinyl-upholstered chair—brown, of course—and tugged on the garish suntan-hued pantyhose she wore under her brown rayon dress that was better suited to World War II fabric rations. The woman was plain as mud, not even a stitch of jewelry save for a golden ring studded with a ruby on her left hand. Quite the juxtaposition to Cat, who wore a black button-up jumper dress on the cutting edge of fashion—the only black dress in her closet—out of mourning for President Kennedy, her one splash of color a scarlet ascot at her throat.

Elizabeth sat, folded her hands before her. "Why don't we start with you telling me exactly what I did to ruin your life."

Cat, refusing to sit, remained standing at the kitchen door. She didn't say a word, merely retrieved from her pocket her mother's final letter, which she'd discovered two days ago while sorting through Joan Gray's belongings in a neighbor's garage, their house having been sold—unbeknownst to Cat until that horrible week—to pay an ever-increasing mountain of bills. That innocuous piece of flowered stationery had sent a fresh shock wave through Cat's previously calm life. Joan Gray had fought a good fight, but she'd done it alone. And in the end, she'd lost.

And now, Cat was alone.

Cat tossed the bombshell letter on the table. "Read it."

Elizabeth Bentley frowned when she had to reach across the table for the letter, apparently more perturbed by the breach of etiquette than the gun still pointed at her. She perched a set of unfashionable reading glasses on her nose, and her eyes flicked back and forth over the paper—it seemed to Cat that she read the entire thing at least three times before she finally folded the glasses back up.

"My condolences," she said. "I can see why you sought me out."

"My entire life has been a lie." Rage seethed at the edges of Cat's words, protecting her from the dark maelstrom of grief that churned beneath. "Because of you."

"And that's why you've come to kill me."

"Your life for the one you stole from me."

"That seems fair." Elizabeth rubbed the scar on her chin. "Although I'm not sure a jury would necessarily agree. Life in prison is a long sentence for someone your age."

Cat tapped the chamber of the revolver. "Two bullets," she said. "Yours. And mine."

A deep V formed between Elizabeth's brows. "Your solution does seem terribly *permanent*. Also, as a patriotic American, I'd like to remind you about my right to a fair and speedy trial."

"Patriotic?" If Cat had been closer to Elizabeth she would have laughed in her face. As it was, she fisted her hands and leaned over the table. "You were a goddamned Russian *spy*, Elizabeth, the furthest from a patriot as they come. All I want is to hear you admit your guilt so I can kill you."

Elizabeth narrowed her eyes until Cat couldn't help the shiver that rippled up her spine. "Here's my counter to your proposal." She set aside her reading glasses and pushed the letter back toward Cat. "You hear my side of the story—the *real* story, from start to finish—and then you can decide my fate, and your own. Judge, jury, and executioner, if you will. For both of us."

Cat hesitated long enough that Elizabeth shrugged. "I've found that the best way to keep from drowning in grief is to find a distraction." She retrieved a golden cigarette lighter from her skirt pocket. Cat waited for her to light up—the apartment smelled of stale smoke, and there was already an overflowing ashtray on the table—but instead Elizabeth only flicked the lighter a few times, causing sparks but no flame. *Click click click.* "Consider my story a distraction."

"A distraction from the truth, you mean? I read enough old articles trying to track you down to know that you lied in your testimony to the Senate. *And* to the press. And God knows where else."

"Haven't you ever heard of shades of truth? That's the problem with being an accomplished liar—no one believes you even when you *are* telling the truth." Elizabeth sighed, pointed toward the sink, silently requesting permission to move. At Cat's nod, she shuffled to a drawer, hands up in that universal gesture of *don't shoot*. "Spy stories are rarely encumbered with something as mundane as the *truth*, but just in case you feel tempted to doubt me," she said—then handed a slim pile of old envelopes from within to Cat, all bound with a frayed piece of twine—"here's proof that although I *am* a Communist and I *was* a spy for Russia, there's far more to my story than just that. Namely that I'm a patriot blessed with the gift of making spectacularly shitty decisions."

Cat fingered open the first envelope to find a letter typed on official FBI letterhead and marked in capital letters: PERSONAL.

Dear Miss Bentley,

Your cooperation with this Bureau is a matter of public record and a commendable service to your country. I am happy to provide the same statement that I made before Congress in 1953: All information furnished by Miss Bentley, which was susceptible to check, has been proven to be correct. She has been subjected to the most searching of cross-examination, her testimony has been evaluated by juries and reviewed by courts and has been found to be accurate.

Sincerely yours,
J. Edgar Hoover

There were several more, all from the director of the FBI. The golden cigarette lighter clicked again. *Click click click.*

Elizabeth resumed her place at the table, tilted her chin in defiance at Cat still standing sentry across the room. "I suppose it's time someone heard the truth, even if that someone also happens to be threatening to kill me. So, I'll tell you everything—about how I fell in with the Communist Party and became their spy, about my involvement with your mother and all my lies, everything. It won't be a short story, but hell, I'll even tell you about the three people who died because of me."

"You killed three people?" *Dear Lord.* Cat shook her mother's letter. "And how many more lives did you ruin? Aside from my mother's?"

Elizabeth held up her hands. "All I ask is that you listen. Then you can decide if I'm worth going to prison for. I guarantee, I'm certainly not worth *dying* for."

The matador-red flag of Cat's rage was still there, but it no longer consumed everything, merely fluttered at the edges of her vision, biding its time . . .

Cat gestured with the revolver before crossing her arms. "It's one o'clock now. I'll give you an hour before I decide whether to kill you."

Because honestly, I'm not even sure whether I can go through with it, no matter how much I might want *to.*

Elizabeth snorted, an indelicate sound. This time she lit a Lucky Strike with her golden lighter—it seemed embossed with some sort of design—and drew a deep drag before releasing the smoke toward the ceiling. "I'm fifty-five years old, Catherine, and I was a *spy*, for God's sake. It's going to take longer than one hour to recite my entire life's story."

"One hour and not a minute more—set the kitchen timer. I'd start talking if I was you, Scheherazade."

And so, with the timer obstinately ticking down the seconds of her life, Elizabeth had no choice but to begin her tale . . .

ТОВАРИЩ

THE COMRADE

Perhaps you don't have too much of a personal future, I would say to myself, but at least, with your small efforts, you are contributing to a worthwhile cause.

—Elizabeth Bentley, *Out of Bondage*

APRIL 1933

I stood before the open casket, freshly orphaned.

(Before we go any further, Catherine, I ask you to hold on to this image in your mind. People always wonder how I could become a spy, how I could trick people into believing one thing when the exact opposite was the truth. Easily, I always respond. Because humans see what they want to see, hear what they want to hear. Right now, there's a good chance you are imagining a child version of me, wearing ruffled socks with polished patent leather shoes, maybe even a cowlick unsuccessfully smoothed by the licked palm of some maiden aunt, and perhaps a pinafore over a quaint gingham dress. Or perhaps you're envisioning me as copy of yourself at your mother's funeral. Now do this properly and picture the real me in this scene. Not some child orphan but a twenty-five-year-old version wearing a black silk purgatorial getup that's too tight across my ample hips, a wilting bouquet of spring pansies clutched tight in my fist. Let this be my first lesson to you: words matter. Use them carefully, like bullets.)

My silent, stoic father had died two days earlier of a heart attack, my art-loving teacher of a mother gone four years prior following a bout of peritonitis and late-stage intestinal cancer. I stared down at my father's closed eyes, his jug ears and long Protestant face, found myself fixated by the map of broken blood vessels around his nose and the way the undertaker had combed his hair all wrong.

The head of the funeral home cleared his throat: a standard social cue that my time was up, compounded by the man's gaze flicking to the grandfather clock on the cold fireplace mantel.

"Good-bye, sir." I forced myself to squeeze my father's stiff fingers, to remember this last physical connection. Given our constant cross-country moves as he'd chased one job after the other, without him there was no one left, no family or even friends.

I glanced around at the empty parlor, wondered if my funeral one day would also be a service for one.

The coffin lid closed, and that was the end of it.

It was 1933, the height of the Great Depression, and I had no job or connections. Unlike most women my age, I was unmarried, no well-positioned man to lean upon like all the other Vassar graduates from the class of 1930, nothing. Just me.

"I'll make you proud," I promised my father. "Both you and Mother."

I would tell many lies in this lifetime. I won't say that was the first or even that it was a lie, for back then I still thought I was capable of good.

Certainly, all the best villains do.

USE YOUR MIND, *do something good and important with your life, Elizabeth. Help people and make your time here count.*

That had been my mother's last bit of wisdom imparted from her deathbed, the same promise my father had made me repeat to honor her even as he lay dying. From my mother I'd inherited an appreciation of art and literature; we'd pored over library books on every art style going back to the Renaissance, and my weekend memories were filled with museum excursions. With my master's from Columbia in fourteenth-century Florentine poetry, I'd thought that perhaps I might follow in her footsteps and become a teacher. Except . . .

"It's difficult to use my mind and do good when I'm constantly getting my backside pinched," I muttered from my desk at the windowless insurance company where I'd finally landed a low-level temp job. I had moved to New York City following my father's death and had barely survived the past two years by living off the small settlement my father left me; now I spent my days mindlessly pecking away at a Royal typewriter with an *E* key that stuck. Inevitably, it would be the most commonly used letter in the English language that I'd have to write in each time.

"What was that, Miss Bentley?" The head underwriter, a middle-aged man with eyes that bulged like a dead trout, leaned over me in his plaid sports coat and licked his fleshy lips. "Have you reconsidered my offer for lunch yet?"

One glance at his cheaply made trousers and I saw that his eyes weren't the only thing bulging. His offer for lunch had been to share the ham sandwich his wife had made him. This, after his hand had somehow found its way to my breast and given it a painful squeeze.

Darkness pressed on my eyelids. I tried in vain to block out the way his roving eyes made me feel like something lower than the ugly things found under a rock. "I'm eating at my desk today."

I knew I should be thankful for any sort of work, given that America was still in the throes of the Great Depression. The last of my savings from my father had finally dried up after nearly two years of ill-paying jobs including temporary stints as a Macy's telephone operator, temp work at *Cue* magazine, and typing manuscripts. Still, it was difficult to be truly grateful when it felt like the only job I could look forward to over the next twenty years involved writing mindless shorthand, taking someone else's dictation, and dodging my male boss's wandering hands.

(Remember, Catherine, this was a woman's lot in the '30s. And we were supposed to be grateful for the moldy crumbs tossed to us.)

After yet another miserable day, I anticipated another evening spent hunched over a can of cold beans—heating up the hot plate required too much effort—in my echoing boardinghouse room that smelled of cabbage and despair. The only sign of life there was my African violet barely clinging to its leaves. I'd named the violet Coriolanus after Shakespeare's oft-forgotten tragedy that I'd recently checked out from the library. Along with a book on how to care for violets.

"'Thus I turn my back. There is a world elsewhere.'" I sometimes quoted the Bard when I pruned back Coriolanus's dead leaves and blossoms. "Except it feels like the world has turned *its* back on *me*."

Unfortunately, Coriolanus wasn't much of a conversationalist.

Lately, I found myself so lonely that I wondered whether any of this was worth it. No one would miss me if I died suddenly, probably wouldn't even notice until the smell from my room got too bad.

I was so very weary of being invisible.

Except, as I approached my boardinghouse that evening after work, I had the distinct impression that I was being watched. I stopped more than once to glance around—only to find that no one paid me any attention—and the back of my neck still prickled by the time I let myself in and trudged up the three flights of narrow stairs to my floor.

There was a surprise waiting on my doorstep: an anonymous basket.

I glanced around, but seeing no one and being unable to get into my room without passing the thing, I hesitantly nudged its lid with the toe of my shoe.

It jiggled.

I shrieked.

Half expecting a tongue-flicking python, I yelped in happy surprise as the lid flipped open and the most adorable furry face I'd ever seen popped above the rim.

I scooped the scraggly little terrier into my arms and noticed the note pinned to the side of the basket, written in a feminine hand.

Our dog had puppies a few weeks ago, and it looked like you could use a friend. Please don't say no—I have a whole litter to give away!

Your neighbor down the hall

Perhaps the world hadn't turned its back on me. I didn't socialize with anyone in the boardinghouse, and I'd never considered taking care of any living thing more demanding than Coriolanus, but one look at the squirming ball of fur in my arms had me reconsidering.

"Well, I don't suppose you can stay out here, now can you?" I asked the brown-and-white pup, straightening his floppy ear that had gotten flipped the wrong way. I was rewarded with sloppy kisses on my chin and couldn't help laughing as I shut the door behind us.

Me, laughing? Now *that* was a sound I hadn't heard in a long time.

I expected the puppy to find some cozy spot on the rug to settle down or maybe to explore his new surroundings, but instead, he followed me like a furry shadow, tripping over his own feet several times.

"Are you hungry? What a silly question. Of course you're hungry." I rubbed behind his floppy ears with one hand while I cut up some precious leftover Polish sausage from the icebox and let him nibble it from between my fingers.

Enamored, once the sun started to set, I popped outside to let him explore the pavement from the safety of a lead I fashioned from the tie of my mother's old housecoat, then sat on the cold stone stairs of my building and pulled out my lavender dime-store journal with the intent of taking down a few more entries. I was fluent in French and Italian, but as the awkward, introverted child of a traveling businessman who never stayed more than a few months in one place, I'd never had a steady group of friends. Most of my life I'd viewed people's behavior as if through a kaleidoscope, broken and indecipherable. So, I'd started this journal, had learned to untangle the unruly syntax of gestures and facial expressions by filling its pages with sketches of people and notes on their behaviors. Until finally I'd started to decrypt the nuances of their actions: the surprised lift of an eyebrow, the uncomfortable tug of an earlobe, the nervous drumming of fingers. Watching people had begun so I might learn to emulate them; now it had become a game to predict their stories based on everything they *didn't* say.

(Body language screams across a room, Catherine, as does tone of voice. It's facial expressions that can be trickiest, as humans are masters of deception. Or at least they like to think they are.)

"You there." I startled and glanced behind me to see a familiar woman striding out of my building. She might have been a pocket Aphrodite in the manner of Botticelli's *Birth of Venus*, barely reaching five feet despite the pale halo of blond hair piled high on her head. "You're Elizabeth, right?" One hand held a freshly rolled cigarette, but Aphrodite thrust out her free hand at me in a way that belied the softness of her features. Her friendly blue eyes flicked over me, assessing. "I'm Lee Fuhr, your neighbor from down the hall. Two doors down, actually." When she grabbed and pumped my hand, I flinched—an ingrained habit, considering I came from good Puritan stock that didn't believe in hugs and physical touch. Or smiling, really. But she dropped my hand just as quickly, struck a match, lit the cigarette, and inhaled a long drag. "Cute little mongrel you have there."

"Someone left him as a gift on my doorstep today," I said. "Any idea as to who the culprit might be?"

I'd have known the answer from the way her gaze slid away from mine, even if the puppy hadn't yipped excitedly and reached for her to pick him up. *Guilty.*

"Thank you," I said before she could demur. I hesitated whether to tell her how much it meant that she'd thought of me. Maybe she'd already guessed. "I've never had a pet."

She smiled, probably realizing she was off the hook. "Don't

mention it. Especially not to the landlady—she let me keep my daughter's dog when we moved in, but old Mrs. O'Sullivan would shit kittens if she knew we were harboring a clandestine litter of puppies. You're doing me a favor, really." Another drag on the cigarette as the sun finished setting. I chose to ignore her use of profanity. "What's his name?"

I hadn't thought of a name yet, although I supposed that was the natural progression of steps. "I don't know. Something tough—he *is* awfully small."

"The runt of the litter, but scrappy for his size." Lee cocked her head and frowned. "You'll need a new lead if you want him to look tough. Are those pink butterflies?"

"It's from a housecoat. I didn't have any rope."

She chuckled. "What about Vlad? After the Impaler, of course. No one would dare question him about wearing pink butterflies."

I laughed—the second time in one day—and watched Vlad introduce himself to a random passerby with a goofy doglike smile that had his tongue lolling out one side of his jaw while he rolled on his back with paws in the air.

"Vlad it is." I returned my journal to my purse and juggled Vlad's makeshift lead, feeling positively dowdy next to Lee. "Nice to meet you. Although I hope you don't always introduce yourself to strangers with gifts of puppies."

"Only sometimes," Lee laughed. "Listen, it's Friday night and I'm heading out for a bit. Care to join me?"

I started to make an excuse, but Lee's perfectly dimpled grin stopped me. Of course she had dimples. "I know you don't know me from Judith or Delilah. However, it can't be all that riveting spending every weekend alone in your room." I must not have hidden my expression very well, for Lee only laughed. "A boardinghouse is a small world, right?"

Too true—when I passed their door I could often hear Lee crooning off-tune Billie Holiday songs to her daughter, a girl with matching blond ringlets whom I guessed to be about four years old. I'd never seen evidence of a husband, and Lee didn't wear a wedding band, yet somehow, she'd managed to finagle a room from our strict and nearly Victorian boardinghouse owner. *What's Lee's story?*

"It's only for a couple hours," Lee continued. "Ms. Kowalski from downstairs is cutting out at nine o'clock, and I want to put Laurel to bed. Plus, it won't cost you a dime—you can even leave Vlad with them while we're gone. What do you have to lose, right?"

It would have been easy to demur with some sort of excuse—I had a new puppy and library loans that expired this weekend, after all—but I suddenly found Lee's arm linked through mine and her cigarette in my hand. In mere moments, Vlad had been deposited in Laurel's eager arms upstairs and I was choking on tobacco-flavored smoke while being swept back down the street the way I had just come.

Lee kept up a steady stream of rapid-fire chatter on the way to the subway: about the smart two-toned oxford heels she'd seen in the window of Macy's that she couldn't afford, that her boss at the garment factory was sleeping with his sister-in-law, that she had to remember to buy new silk stockings this weekend. It was only once we were on the crowded subway platform that I dared interrupt, "I don't suppose you'd be willing to tell me where we're headed?"

Lee removed a tube of lipstick from her purse, touched up her Cinderella-pink lips, and made a perfect moue. "A meeting of the American League Against War and Fascism."

Well, I'd be the first to admit that was *not* on my list of expected places for two young women to be on a Friday night. However, while it made me something of a crumb, an evening spent watching people discuss—and likely argue—politics actually sounded like good fodder for my journal.

Lee laughed, apparently misreading my expression. "Feel free to jump in front of the next train if you want."

"Actually, I was interested in Fascism while I lived in Florence last year," I said. "I even went to one of their meetings."

"Really?" Lee frowned. "So, does that mean you're a Fascist?"

I sensed that my answer was very important to her. Lucky for me, I didn't have to lie. "No, I just wanted to hear what they were all about. Politics is interesting."

"Even Communist politics?"

I shook my head. It had been nearly two decades since the Russian Revolution had broken out, but *Communism* was still a filthy word in America; I'd listened with my father to plenty of crackling broadcasts from our Zenith radio over the years that had espoused its litany of evils. "I wouldn't go that far."

"Well, are you coming?" Lee's hands were on her hips. "Or heading back?"

I'd be lying if I didn't admit that my quiet boarding room held some appeal, even with its stink of cabbage and beans. After all, Coriolanus and Vlad wouldn't judge me if I didn't understand a punch line or if I made awkward comments that stopped conversations in their tracks. *There's nothing wrong with meeting new people, no matter what they think of me. Who knows, I might even enjoy myself.*

So, I squared my shoulders and attended my first League meeting that night. I was prepared to listen, fully expected the speakers to be the down-and-outers I often saw gathered around Union Square.

Instead, in a night filled with surprises, what I heard in that cramped and stuffy hall filled with nearly a hundred people astonished me.

"People, we are witnessing the final death throes of capitalism!" the first speaker—a League organizer whose tomato-stained white coveralls were explained when Lee whispered that he was a food worker—exclaimed as Lee took a long pull from a communal bottle of gin being passed around. I declined when she offered me a drink. "There's no denying that there's something wrong with capitalism," he continued, "when my day begins by buying an apple from an unemployed architect shivering at the entrance to my building. Forty percent of New Yorkers are unemployed, and I've lost count of how many are sleeping in shacks made of oil barrels and cardboard along Riverside Drive."

I was intrigued. *Cautiously* intrigued, at least. Still, it was the next speaker who really piqued my interest.

I thought Lee was going to visit the ladies' room when she stood after the organizer's speech, but I gaped when she assumed the center of the room and stubbed out another hand-rolled cigarette beneath her heel. I realized when she began to speak that my neighbor possessed a serene courage when it came to public speaking. "The plight of America's women is a true travesty. Women should be liberated both in the workplace and in the bedroom, free to make their own destinies!" Her eyes were lit like an acolyte at the peak of religious thrall. "Instead, we remain shackled to the earnings of our husbands, with no options to earn equal pay. Our choices for work are limited—either a typist or secretary, or perhaps a nurse or teacher if we're so inclined. Any woman seeking to work outside those accepted boxes is ridiculed and rejected."

I found myself cheering with the rest of the League members once Lee finished her talk, answered a few questions, and resumed her place next to me. My fingers itched to pull out my journal, to make note of the various tics and behaviors around me, but instead I forced myself to commit it all to memory.

The best speakers—like Lee—make direct eye contact with their audience members.

Drop your shoulders and appear relaxed—people who squint while they talk seem tense and anxious.

A bit of self-deprecating humor never goes astray. (The tweedy college student who spoke after Lee had gotten a chuckle from the crowd when he joked that after graduation, he was looking forward to the perfect American life with a perfect job . . . but that anything was possible when you lied to yourself.)

"So, what do you think?" Lee asked when we left. I didn't like many people, but I *did* find myself drawn to Lee's enthusiasm and fervor. And I liked the fact that she chose *me*, of all people, to join her tonight. "Have I scared you off?"

"Far from it. I was impressed with everyone's spirit, especially given the times we live in. And you were amazing." I bit my lip. The League stated firmly that they were against war, but not exactly what they were *for*. Still, I'd liked what I'd heard, at least so far. "Truth be told, I'd like to go to more of those meetings."

"Really?" Lee stopped mid-stride so I had to stop walking and turn to face her. "You mean it?"

"I do." I liked the League's enthusiasm and their purpose. It was as if they'd taken all my discontent about America and my own situation, explained why I felt that way, and then offered a clear philosophy for how to solve all our problems. If only it weren't for a niggling suspicion that skittered around the dark corners of my mind . . .

(That whisper of conscience is one I'm only now admitting to for the first time, Catherine. In *Out of Bondage* I wrote myself the disguise of being a witless and dewy-eyed naïf who couldn't decipher the writing on the wall. I've been a lot of things in my life—a spy, an adulterer, a liar—but I've never been *that* dim-witted a fool. Young and naive, yes. A total fool, no.)

However, I quashed that murmur of suspicion like a cockroach underfoot, the main reason being that I *liked* Lee. It had been a long time since I'd found another person I actually enjoyed spending time with more than I did reading a good book. In fact, I found myself wanting to linger longer with her, to soak up her energy and ideas, especially on women's equality. To be *seen*. And *heard*. And so: "Is there anything I can do to help you? Or the League?"

Lee merely tapped her chin, a slow smile spreading across her face. "As a matter of fact, there is."

*   *   *

ARE YOU NOW or have you ever been a member of the Communist Party of the United States?

That was the $64,000 question that so many of us would be asked in later years. My answer, of course, was a resounding yes, but it didn't start out that way. Communism was insidious in the way it snuck up on me.

(Just like the men in my life, but that story is yet to come.)

My offer of help was how Lee and I wound up knocking on the door of the League's Manhattan headquarters the next morning. Whereas New York had once invigorated me, now each foray into the city's streets seemed only to reinforce the idea that something had gone desperately wrong in our society. The reek of abject poverty clung to the unemployed beggar sleeping under a week-old newspaper he'd pulled from the gutter, and the weight of homelessness bent the back of the old woman waiting for her daily ration from a Salvation Army soup kitchen.

After three flights up battered wooden stairs that moaned in protest and threatened to give way beneath my feet, I glanced at Lee. "Is this really the right place?"

"Just wait," she said. "It gets better." She pushed the door open to reveal bare light bulbs—half of which had gone out—and a stain of something brown across the ceiling. The only furniture of note was a couch with so much sawdust escaping from its cushions that I wondered how many rats had taken up residence inside.

"Don't mind the mess—we don't have the money to spend on fancy fronts." I startled to see a wild-haired man with an open smile straighten from where he'd been crouched down digging through file boxes, his shirtsleeves rolled up.

Lee only smiled at him as she gestured to me. "This is Elizabeth, the new volunteer I told you about."

Black ink stained the fingers of the friendly hand he thrust at me. "I'm Harold Patch, but everyone calls me Patch."

Roughly my age, Harold Patch was more shabbily dressed than the office, but I liked how his ears stuck out ever so slightly in a way that reminded me of my father, even if he *did* have a ridiculous nickname. I accepted the hand he'd thrust in my direction, hardly flinching this time. "Pleased to make your acquaintance."

"I've got my next League speech to write," Lee announced before sauntering toward a mostly empty corner with a pencil and legal pad. "Holler if you need me."

"I edit *Fight*," Harold Patch informed me, "the League's newspaper. It's a battle to get every issue to print—pun intended—so I can use any help you're willing to give."

"Sure." I set down my purse on the sorry excuse for a sofa and glanced at Lee's back before noticing the Underwood portable typewriters set against the far wall. I'd come all this way; I might as well do something productive. "What can I do to help, Harold?"

He quirked an eyebrow. "It's Patch, really. Only my grandmother calls me Harold. And she's been dead almost five years." Patch—I supposed it wouldn't do to quibble with a grown man about his name—gestured to what might have been a desk had its entire surface not been covered in a multitude of leaning towers of folders. "Want to organize these files?"

Alphabetizing wasn't high on my list of favorite things, but I was generally good at organizing things. So, I nodded.

Patch kept up a steady stream of chatter while we worked, informing me that he'd been a member of all manner of political organizations before he'd stumbled on the League: the Socialists and the Anarchists and even the American Association for the Advancement of Atheism, which I'd never heard of.

(Sounds nefarious, doesn't it? You'd be right to think that I should have run in the other direction, but again, I was young and naive and didn't know any better.)

Patch glanced up at me with a half-cocked smile on his face, rubbed the back of his neck. "Hey, how's your spelling and grammar?"

"Decent. It should be, after all the money I've spent on fancy degrees."

Patch grinned, handed me an article and a freshly sharpened pencil. "Great. I've never been able to spell my way out of a box. Take a stab at this. It's the lead article for our next issue."

I found a spot on the sofa that seemed least likely to either swallow me or introduce me to a nest of rabies-riddled rats. Then I began to read.

A decent job. A decent education. A decent chance for all.

Patch's article started out innocuous, then took a sharp left turn. As in to the *far-fell-off-a-cliff* left.

The Party understands the threat of Fascism, the equal threat of capitalism. Contrast the fall of the United States and the rise of Hitler and Mussolini with that of the Soviet Union. Stalin's economy is booming, and its industrial output is higher than ever before. The Russians are living in a paradise compared to the hell America has become for most of its citizens.

There is only one logical answer to the problem set before us. And that answer is Communism.

I set the paper down, my suspicions entirely—and irrevocably—confirmed.

Damn it all to hell.

"So . . . the League . . . is Communist?" My voice sounded resigned even to my own ears, the silent cursing justified given that I could no longer ignore what was written in plain sight. Of course, the signs had all been there—the violent rants against capitalism, the cries for equality for the disenfranchised, the demands for liberation—I'd simply chosen to ignore them. The pencil that twirled through my fingers failed to soothe my nerves.

Patch frowned. "Lee didn't tell you?"

Lee had stood, meandered her way back to us. "It must have slipped my mind."

Because Lee knew that I—like any good American—should have run the other way as fast as my legs could carry me if I'd known I was entering a hotbed of Communism.

Entering it *knowingly*, anyway.

Ignorance, or at least the illusion of it—because yes, I'd been suspicious after that first League meeting—had indeed been bliss, but in volunteering to look for missing commas on some Communist rag, I no longer had the luxury of pretending I was on friendly terms with Communists. And only suspected ones at that.

Hell's bells, but if I edited Patch's article, I may as well paint myself Soviet-red and run naked through Times Square chanting Marxist slogans. The Red Scare following Lenin's Russian Revolution had gone cold for nearly a decade, but Communists were as anti-American as they came. And I was a good, patriotic American, who wanted what was best for my country.

Lee's voice followed after me when I grabbed my purse and headed to the door. "Do you mean to tell me, Elizabeth, that you don't stand for what we stand for? Equality? An end to poverty? The downfall of Hitler and Mussolini and Fascism?"

"Of course I do." Emotions would get me nowhere; cold hard facts would serve better to solve this equation. If Lee and Patch thought I should turn my coat red, then let them alleviate my worries. "But you do realize that the Communists fomented a bloody revolution in Russia and murdered people in cold blood when they seized power? They terrorized and brutalized and persecuted anyone who didn't agree with them."

"No one is suggesting we start up a secret police force in America or make indiscriminate arrests or persecute anyone for free speech." Patch's hands went to his hips, elbows spread wide in a display of pure confidence. "Do Lee or I look like revolutionaries to you?"

No, neither Lee nor Patch looked like my preconceived idea of

Communists—no sickle and hammer banners or matching Party-issued overalls, no bearded terrorists with bombs in either pocket. They both looked wholesome and familiar. Heck, they looked like *me*.

Patch held up his hands. They were nice hands, strong looking, and somehow, I still found the ink stains on his fingertips rather endearing. "That was a different generation's Communism," he said, "in a different country. Trust me, I know the Communist label is an acquired taste. Think of it as a fine wine."

I scowled. "I don't drink."

"More like Russian caviar, then," Lee said. "Elizabeth, I swear that Patch and I are not the revolutionary Bolsheviks of old, looking to murder the czar and overthrow everything. We hate Fascists like Hitler and Mussolini, but we like FDR's New Deal—we just want to see the government do *more*, give every single American a fair chance. I mean, look around . . . this country still has a long way to go, right?"

I thought of the beggar and the woman in the soup kitchen line I'd seen just that morning. And although I didn't talk about it, during my time in Italy I'd witnessed the horrors of Mussolini's Fascist regime, namely when his feared Blackshirts poured castor oil—Il Duce called it the golden nectar of nausea—down dissenters' throats before publicly hanging them. From what I could tell, Germany's new dictator, Adolf Hitler, was even worse. Still, that didn't mean I was ready to start singing Lenin's praises.

But neither was I ready to turn my back on Lee's friendship.

"You want me to become a Communist," I said. *And I want us to be friends.* "That means you need to answer my questions. *All* of them."

Patch grabbed his jacket from where it was slung on a chair. "I'll let Lee answer your questions—she's better at that sort of thing, and I'm about to miss the deadline to get this copy to our printer."

He paused as he passed me, his light touch on my arm obviously meant to soothe. "If it makes you feel any better," he murmured, "I edit *Fight*, but I haven't yet officially joined the Party. If you decide to join, I'll submit my paperwork with you. All for one, and all that."

Lee arched an eyebrow at his quiet exchange and waited until the door closed behind him. "Well," she said to me, "what do you want to know?"

I spoke quickly, lest I lose my nerve. "I know you can't speak for all Communists, but can you promise me that the Communists here in America aren't violent? Because I'm not interested in assassinations or bloody revolutions."

"Any movement on a mission has extreme branches, but no one here pays them much attention," Lee responded. "Unless you count angry articles and fiery rhetoric."

"All right, and what exactly is Communism's *mission* here in America?" I bit my lip, plunged forward. "Because honestly, I'm having a hard time swallowing the idea that a patriotic American can also be a Communist. Aren't those two things mutually exclusive?"

"That's just what the government *wants* you to think. Communists *are* patriots, Elizabeth. We love America. We hate Fascism and are terrified that the likes of Mussolini and Hitler might spread here to the United States."

It was difficult to argue against any of that. Still, I doubted whether most Americans would agree.

"What repercussions should I expect if I joined the Party?" I found myself fiddling with a discarded pencil that was missing its eraser, made myself stop. "And don't sugarcoat it."

"If you join, it's not exactly something we suggest you broadcast to the world, at least not yet. So, I'd assume no repercussions, unless you do something stupid."

I never do *anything, Lee, that's the point. And I had no friends, until I met you.*

"And if I don't join?"

Lee shrugged. "I could still see you at meetings, but this afternoon I'm signing the papers on a little walk-up apartment on West 124th Street. It's just off Amsterdam Avenue, which is a bit of a hike."

Meaning it would be back to just me and Vlad and Coriolanus again. Lee, seeming to realize the downturn of my thoughts, reached out and squeezed my hand. "There's a whole world of opportunities open to Party members, you know. Just think of it, Elizabeth—this is your chance to have your hand on the throttle of history."

I unfolded my arms. I cared less for history than for my future, but I *did* agree with Lee's vision of equality for all Americans. "Fine. Where do I sign?"

Lee's eyes widened. "That's it? Just like that? I was expecting a full interrogation, not just a handful of questions."

"It's not as if my joining changes anything. I want to go to League meetings with you and maybe help Patch on the newspaper. If I have to sign a Party membership to convince you of that, then so be it—I'll sign with this pencil right here and right now. If that's what you want."

Lee wanted to recruit me, and I wanted to protect our friendship. It was as simple as that.

Lee studied me, then gave a satisfied nod. "I'll bring you the paperwork tomorrow. And a proper pen as well." She rose and enveloped me in a tobacco-scented hug that made me feel like all the soul-searching and philosophical grappling had been worth it. "Now can we get to work?"

"Sure," I said, then winked in a way I hoped looked natural. "Comrade."

|||||||||||||||||||

NOVEMBER 23, 1963
1:46 P.M.

"And you became a Communist?" Cat asked, giving a snap of her perfectly manicured fingers. "Just like that?"

Elizabeth planted a fresh Lucky Strike between her lips, lit it with the old one stained red from her lipstick—followed by the *click click click* of her golden cigarette lighter. "It wasn't *just like that*, Catherine. I put a great amount of thought and consideration into my decision." A deep drag on the cigarette, followed by a cirrus of acrid smoke. "Well, at least as much as I could at that tender age."

Cat crossed her arms, still leaning against the doorframe she'd refused to abandon. She didn't trust herself to get any closer to Elizabeth, certainly not with the gun she still held. "Unfortunately, I'm having a difficult time reconciling the shy, floundering woman you've described as your youthful self with this." She gestured with one sweep of her hand to the scowling, chain-smoking matron in front of her. "Also, my memory of cowering in an underground bunker during the Cuban Missile Crisis last year is still fresh. It's hard to believe that you would have taken up the red torch of Communism just because you wanted a few friends in your life."

Elizabeth exhaled in one big gust, set down the cigarette in its yellow glass ashtray, and stood, pruning a dead leaf from a potted violet on the kitchen sill that reminded Cat of Coriolanus. "If it were today, knowing what I know now about Stalin and Khrushchev and Castro, would I have done things differently, run away screaming from Lee?" Elizabeth leaned forward, hands splayed on the table before angrily stubbing out the cigarette. "I don't know. I still assumed that signing on Stalin's dotted line meant that I could merely playact at being a Communist. Go to meetings and sing their songs, but keep my head above their waterline."

Elizabeth opened up a deep drawer that sat slightly crooked on its track. Cat worried that she might pull a weapon, so kept her father's pistol aimed on the spy, but after a moment of digging Elizabeth retrieved with a triumphant smile her buried treasure from its depths: a bottle of Gordon's gin.

"I need a drink," she announced before retrieving two yellow plastic tumblers from an otherwise nearly empty cabinet. "Do you want one?"

Cat made a pointed glance at the clock, its ticking the only sound save for a couple of children playing outside on the sidewalk. "I don't think so. It's not even two o'clock in the afternoon. You have less than fifteen minutes left, you know."

Elizabeth didn't miss a beat, only poured an overly generous shot of gin into one tumbler and knocked it back. Followed by an Alka-Seltzer tablet dusted off from her skirt pocket and unceremoniously dunked into water in the second tumbler, which quickly followed the gin. "Getting old is hell," Elizabeth announced by way of explanation. "Take my word for it—it's a big decision, choosing to end someone's life. Not to mention what you'll do with yourself afterward. Shall we add some time to the clock? I have plenty more to tell."

Cat frowned as Elizabeth used her foot to nudge a kitchen chair toward her. "At least sit down," Elizabeth said. "You're making me nervous."

What the hell? What do I have to lose?

Cat gave the timer another turn—another hour added to Elizabeth's life—and leaned back in her chair. "You're going to have to work harder to convince me not to kill you. A *lot* harder."

To which Elizabeth only offered a Mona Lisa smile. "Oh, Catherine. For all you know, you'll want nothing more than to kill me at the end of all this."

3

"Elizabeth, I have good news." Patch offered me a jelly donut, which I declined. I didn't like to eat in front of people if I could help it, certainly nothing as messy as a jelly donut and certainly not in front of someone like Patch. The more time I spent with him at *Fight*'s offices, the more I enjoyed his ready smile and easy camaraderie, even his lame puns. And his Lucky Strike cigarettes, which he was keen to share and I was keen to smoke to avoid seeming entirely provincial. "I've got my Party paperwork ready. I meant what I said—we can submit at the same time, be comrades in arms together. Strength in numbers and all that."

I tapped a red pen against the article I was editing that praised the success of Stalin's Five-Year Plan to industrialize Russia. "Didn't Lee tell you? I've joined up—signed the paperwork this morning, actually."

(Catherine, given how we comrades were supposed to keep our membership secret from the rest of society, it still seems odd that there was actual membership paperwork. However, I suppose there's psychological weight to signing one's name on a dotted line, something that made one feel truly *committed*. Especially when signing beneath a red hammer and sickle emblem that reads *United Communist Party of America: All Power to the Workers!*)

"Really?" Patch slapped the newspaper he was holding against his desk, then crushed me into a hug so fast that I didn't have time to properly react. By the time I knew what was happening, he'd already placed his hands on my shoulders and admired me as if I were a fine canvas painted by Leonardo or Raphael. *Did I just imagine that?* "That's fantastic!"

I stepped back, tugged the hem of my fitted blouse. Wished it wasn't so snug across the chest. "So, you'll join up then?"

"Oh, yeah . . . Sure. Now that you have." He rapped his ink-stained knuckles against the desk. "I'll do it at tonight's meeting, as a matter of fact."

I frowned. "I won't be at the meeting; I have a class on shorthand tonight—my boss told me mine isn't good enough. Maybe we can celebrate afterward?"

"I wouldn't miss it for the world." Patch shocked the bejesus out of me by pressing a quick kiss to the side of my hair, just above my ear. "Congratulations, Elizabeth."

First a hug . . . Except a hug could have meant anything, could have been shared between siblings. But a hug *and* a kiss?

My notebook was very clear on the matter: Patch had been *flirting* with me. Which meant he was *interested* in me. Plain everyday logic backed up my notes, but I had absolutely no idea what to do with this land mine of information. I'd had one ill-fated rendezvous with a man during my fellowship in Italy—for the record, I do *not* recommend that college students succumb to the flattery of their faculty advisers—but aside from that and the harassment I received every day at work, I had no experience with the opposite sex. Certainly not with those who wanted more than a onetime tumble with a wide-eyed, gullible student who didn't realize that an invitation to discuss Fascism behind closed doors was also a demand to hike up one's skirt.

Right or wrong, for the rest of the day I thought of nothing save the pleasant press of Patch's lips against my hair, missed answering not one but two questions my teacher posed to me that evening. "Miss Bentley," the overworked and underpaid woman finally said, "I suggest you pull your head out of the stars and focus on the message before you."

You have no idea, Miss Brown, I thought to myself. *If only I could decipher a very different message.*

I was a fuse waiting to blow by the time I hurried to Lee's new apartment. In one twenty-four-hour period, I'd joined the CPUSA, cemented my friendship with Lee, and now found myself—*me*, who had been called a *sad sack* at Vassar—contemplating asking Patch whether he'd like to have dinner with me this week.

I doubted whether I'd ever had such a productive day.

"Welcome to the Party, comrade," Lee said to me over our celebratory dinner of frankfurters—my favorite, slathered with ketchup and relish—and ice-cold lemonades from the umbrellaed Sabrett's cart on the corner. I was accustomed to eating alone—or with Vlad now, who was currently seated at my feet awaiting tidbits—but today I was happy to share a triumphal hot dog with my best friend. We'd spread out the newsprint from an old edition of the *Daily Worker* as a tablecloth on Lee's scuffed kitchen table while her daughter, Laurel, alternated between playing jacks on the floor and petting Vlad. It was a perfect moment made even more flawless when Patch arrived, cheeks red from the chill outside. With a magician's flourish he pulled a bottle of apple cider from the paper bag under his arm. "For our newest comrade! I'd have brought champagne, but you mentioned that you didn't drink."

I set down the hot dog I'd been devouring, quickly scrubbing a fist over my lips to remove any embarrassing ketchup. I was touched that he'd thought of me, but that fragile joy quickly deflated.

"I can't stay," he said. "I just wanted to swing by to congratulate our new bona fide leftist. You're the real deal now, Elizabeth." Patch popped the cork to my cider. He was about to say more when little Laurel, already dressed in her pink flannel nightgown, tugged on his jacket.

"Can I have some too, Patch?"

He swung her into his arm, bounced her a couple of times until she let out a golden peal of giggles that started Vlad barking. "Of course. Anything for my best girl." He tipped cider into the Mason jars Lee pulled out of her cabinet, nudged one toward me and another toward Laurel. "Just be careful, Elizabeth. You know Communists aren't on stable footing in America, at least not yet. People think we're all bomb-toting terrorists."

There it was again: that feeling that Party membership was *forbidden*.

Which was of course why I'd joined under a false name. No one signed up for the CPUSA with their real name, the better to always hide one's tracks and instead assume the name of a favorite hero or a literary character that held general appeal. So today I'd assumed the first of many new names.

Elizabeth *Sherman*.

It was borrowed from my ancestor Roger Sherman, who had scrawled his name on the bottom of the Declaration of Independence. (At least that was the story my father had told me; I certainly wasn't going to set about disproving that now.) I'd joined the Party for selfish reasons, but before her illness, my mother had been a teacher, had instilled in me the idea that everyone needed to contribute something good to humanity before their time here on earth was over. I loved America, and this Depression had shown me there were so many obstacles yet to overcome. Those obstacles had felt insurmountable when I was on my own. But now . . .

Since meeting Lee, I'd nearly succeeded in convincing myself that perhaps, just by nature of becoming more politically active and joining the Party, I might find some opportunity to make a difference. To make my life mean something *and* build a better world.

Not on Sherman's level, mind you, but in some small, patriotic way.

(Surely, Catherine, you must know that Roger Sherman and those same signers of the Declaration had been accused of committing treason by the British government. Sometimes patriots really are deeply misunderstood individuals.)

"And are we?" My light smile and lifted eyebrows feigned levity as I faced Patch. "Bomb-toting terrorists?"

Lee laughed. "Of course not."

"The Communists in America are entirely benign. We're all idealists, you know." Patch checked his wristwatch, gave a lukewarm curse. "I hate to drink and run, but I'm late for a meeting."

"Are you joining up then?" I asked. The effervescence of the cider made me feel light, happy. Or maybe that was the brilliance of the company I now kept. "Tonight?"

Patch winked—difficult to tell whether it was directed at me or Lee, who seemed to be scowling now—before dropping a kiss on both of our heads. And then Laurel's. "Something like that. You girls stay out of trouble, all right?"

I frowned as the door shut behind him, turned to see Lee studying me. "Patch has been so supportive about all this," I said, then nearly blurted out, *I think I like him. A lot.*

"Patch is a wonderful man." Lee took Laurel's empty cider jar, wrapped her daughter snugly in a brown afghan from the sofa, and carried her to their bedroom. Laurel gave Vlad and me a little wave over her mother's shoulder that set Vlad's tail to thumping. It wasn't a full minute before Lee came back, removed a vodka bottle from the cabinet above her Frigidaire, and tippled a little into her half-empty bottle of lemonade. She toed off her shoes and curled up on her couch with the vodka-lemonade clasped between both hands as if it were a mug of coffee. "He helped me a lot when I joined too."

My memory wasn't photographic—not precisely—but it was

close. Once I heard or saw something, it was nearly impossible to unsee it. Or in this case, unhear it.

"But I thought you joined five years ago."

"Uh-huh. The same day as Patch." Lee pursed her lips. "He fed you that line about turning in your paperwork together, didn't he? I told him to stop doing that—his intentions are good, albeit misguided."

I tried to wave it away, the feeling that I'd been tricked. Still, it lingered.

(Let the record show, Catherine, that I'm not the only liar in this story. Not by a long shot.)

Lee gave a little smile. "The first time Patch kissed me was right after we'd signed our applications."

I reared back so fast I nearly spilled the remnants of my cider.

"I didn't realize . . ." I stumbled over my words, stood, and shuffled the crumpled hot dog wrappers and jars around the table, my back to Lee so she couldn't see my expression. My heart dropped to the pit of my stomach; I'd found Patch's boundless enthusiasm attractive, had even fantasized what it would be like to go on a date with him. "You and Patch, that is . . ." Suddenly, I gasped and whirled around. "Is he Laurel's father? He is, isn't he? But you're not married! Why aren't you married?"

And why didn't you tell me you and Patch were together?

To which Lee only laughed. "No, Patch and I aren't married, and no, he's not Laurel's father. I was only ever with Henry—my husband—before the mill accident that killed him. Patch and I have a very common . . . shall we say . . . *arrangement* within the Party."

My chin dropped, and I could feel the V that burrowed deep between my eyebrows. "What does that mean?"

"No petty bourgeois marriages for us. No relationship weighted down by legalities and tax codes." She must have read my confusion. "Drinking, profanity, and so-called loose morals are encouraged as ways to break down the old capitalist behaviors and etiquette. Patch and I are together when we want to be and not when we don't. He has lots of women he's friends with, if you know what I mean."

I struggled to take that in, feeling so very unsophisticated and provincial at the same time. Especially when Lee came around and bumped my hip with hers. "Don't look so shocked. The Party encourages us to *live*. You're just as young and unattached as we are— you should have some fun."

I'd tried to be free-spirited and fancy-free that one time with my faculty adviser in Italy, who I'd later discovered was married. I didn't care to repeat the experience.

"I'm not sure 'loose morals' are for me. And there's no one I'm interested in," I lied.

No one except Patch. Except I couldn't countenance going after my friend's lover, or even sometimes-lover, not even if Lee claimed that their arrangement was a common one. And I certainly wasn't interested in being another man's girl du jour. I thought of the way Patch had kissed both Lee and me tonight, and felt suddenly dirty.

Lee tapped her lemonade bottle against my jar of cider, then switched them so I held her vodka concoction. "You really are a stodgy New England daughter." I was prepared to be offended, but her lilting voice was full of sunshine. "Drink up."

"No alcohol," I said. "You know that."

"You mean, no *goddamned* alcohol, don't you?" She blew out a puff of air, a sign of exasperation. "No loose morals, no drinking, *and* no profanity? You've got to give me something, Elizabeth—I'm trying to be a positive influence."

I did just sign up to become a Communist, I thought to myself but didn't dare say the words aloud. Instead I cringed, hearing every one of my teachers' New England voices drill etiquette admonitions into my head. "Right," I said weakly. "No *goddamned* alcohol."

Lee clapped her approval, then reached down to roughhouse with Vlad. "For your next act," she said, "I know some handsome Party members, real gentlemen. I'll set you up."

"Absolutely not," I said, but Lee ignored my protests and pulled out her tattered address book.

I sighed. Perhaps I'd missed the fine print about "loose morals" when I'd joined the Party—I supposed it wouldn't kill me to curse on occasion.

But who knew having friends was this hard?

LEE SET ME up first with an Iraqi student and then a Greek worker who were members of my Party unit. When they invited me back to their apartments (one at a time, mind you—I wasn't a total hedonist, at least not yet), I thought, *The Party encourages equality and sexual freedom. Just do this, Elizabeth.*

It was only for kissing. I made sure of that.

"I hear you're eating pita in bed these days," Lee quipped one afternoon while we marched in a parade, our arms linked while belting out the Communist "Internationale" with other students. *Arise, ye prisoners of starvation, arise, ye wretched of the earth!* Party policy was that we could show ourselves publicly in large groups— CPUSA enrollment continued to swell following the Black Tuesday crash of 1929—so it was only when it came to a paper trail that we needed to be entirely anonymous, for our individual protection. Until public opinion toward Communism fully shifted, that was.

I took Lee's meaning, was adequately scandalized. "There's no bed about it. You mandated that I had to go on dates and so I have—"

Lee only wrapped her arm around my waist. "Good for you."

I wanted Lee to like me, which meant I was willing to make concessions—even those involving kisses and awkward fumbles I didn't always enjoy—for her. It was as simple as that.

(The bright side was that I'd started a whole new section in my lavender journal on human behavior: *Kissing & Loose Morals*.)

I'd thought being a card-carrying member of the Communist Party of America meant that I'd simply continue to attend the League meetings, but I was wrong. Apparently, I'd graduated to a new level of activism just by signing my name on a dotted line.

If the Communist Party of the United States possessed a patron saint, Lee Fuhr was her name. Lee constantly told me to do *more*. To say yes to everything and see what lit a fire in my belly.

So, I attended unit bureau meetings, volunteered for a fundraising party, and offered to become the financial secretary in charge of collecting party dues and keeping books for the unit. I wasn't always sure how to act or what to say, but I could manage those silent, behind-the-scenes chores that no one else wanted to do, and was surprised to find myself earning other comrades' admiration for accomplishing menial tasks. Perhaps I didn't have much of a personal future—it still seemed the highest job I could aspire to outside the Party was that of a shorthand secretary—but at least with my small efforts inside the Party I was contributing to a worthwhile cause. As an added benefit, I was so busy there was no time to be lonely or talk to houseplants; I was so immersed that there was no time to doubt the path I'd chosen.

This new Elizabeth Bentley, Elizabeth Sherman, whatever you wanted to call her—the one who finally had caught in her net that elusive feeling of *belonging*—merely lofted her hammer and sickle banner ever higher and sang herself hoarse.

SPRING 1938

Friendship and knowledge are all well and good, but a girl has to eat. Oh yes, and pay her rent too.

In a fit of ire following having my rather ample backside pinched one too many times, I'd quit my position at the insurance office and had landed a brief position at New York's Emergency Home Relief Bureau—a physically and mentally draining job I'd thrown myself into by walking from one end of Manhattan to the next to visit families in unlivable conditions—but I'd turned in my resignation after working myself to such a state of exhaustion that I'd fainted. Finally, my district leader informed me of a paid position with a highly placed woman within the Party named Juliet Glazer, who was doing research on Fascism and had requested my assistance translating Italian.

Fourteenth-century Florentine poetry had never benefited me much, but thank goodness I'd left the land of Mussolini with a brain stuffed full of Italian verbs and conjugations.

I forced myself to stop plucking errant bits of Vlad's fur from my jacket and twirling my fingers around its buttons—no pencil was handy to accommodate my nerves—when I showed up for my interview at Glazer's apartment building on West Seventy-Fourth Street, just off Riverside Drive. I expected an academic sort of woman and was instead surprised when a bearded man opened the door. "Juliet, the translator is here." He spoke with military precision in an accent that sounded almost German, and I felt the hot rake of his gaze as he gestured to a side room. After so much time spent in shabby boardinghouse rooms and run-down office buildings, the gleaming mahogany and plush Aubusson rugs jarred my senses, as did the silver candlesticks and oil paintings on the walls. "She is waiting for you in the dining room."

He took up a post at the near end of the long table while a tall and heavily built woman—Juliet, I presumed—already sat at the far end.

"Welcome, Elizabeth," Juliet of the toast-brown eyes and cultured New England accent said after she introduced herself. (Of course, Juliet certainly wasn't her birth name; as I mentioned was common practice within the Party, she'd swiped the name from Shakespeare.) Since she was a fastidiously dressed woman—her blouse's stiff neck looked tight enough to cut off her breathing—I expected Juliet to launch into the job requirements, but instead she spoke only of trivialities: the weather, the titles of my favorite books, and whether I enjoyed traveling. "Marcel and I have heard much about you through the Party grapevine," she said after she'd thumbed through my résumé and qualifications over a tray of afternoon tea. "Born in Connecticut, I see, although I understand you spent time in Europe. Please tell me you're not one of those puritanical New Englanders who don't drink and subsist off delusions that getting married and raising a brood of children is the only thing that matters in life."

Was this some sort of labyrinthine test? If she'd heard about me, wouldn't she know a thing or two about my background? "I spent a year in Italy and watched Mussolini's Blackshirts terrorize the Italians there. And I haven't given much thought to ever getting married."

Honestly, I could barely handle polite conversation. Raising children seemed about as likely as my suddenly developing a penchant for designing submarine engines.

I folded my fingers around my purse. "However, I don't drink."

"So, you *are* a Puritan." Juliet sighed. "Well, I suppose we're still pleased to meet a kindred spirit in this fight against Fascism. That said, I'll need your solemn oath that you'll never speak of anything we discuss within these walls. You see, I'm in constant contact with the anti-Fascist underground in Italy. I'm afraid you'd be punished if you ever revealed our meetings, given that you might wind up endangering those same operatives."

Was she serious? How on earth could I endanger people on the other side of the world? And what did she mean by *punished*?

"I promise?" I replied weakly, but even that timid vow seemed to placate Juliet. I was beginning to doubt my decision in coming here, and glanced at Marcel, still unsure of his role. He must have seen the question writ clear on my face, for he strummed blunt fingers against the table and gestured to Juliet. "Juliet means what she says. She and I have known each other since before the Ark."

"And you work together?"

He nodded slowly. I didn't miss the question in his eyes that was aimed toward Juliet. If only I'd known what the question was. "Yes, for an organization similar to the Catholic Church."

Juliet actually snorted at that. "Yes, except if you leave the Church, all you lose is your soul." I didn't have a chance to ask the question on the tip of my tongue as she tented her long fingers before her. "Miss Bentley, this is a rather immersive—and frankly, fairly lucrative—position I'm offering you. In addition to your translation work and duties in teaching me Italian, I'm interested in paying you for extra services rendered."

I shifted in my seat. "What sort of services?"

"All sorts. I could pay for a trip to Italy for you as well, although you'd be required to sleep with several high-ranking Fascists.

Think of it as a sort of mining assignment." My eyes bulged in their sockets, but Juliet and Marcel merely exchanged a glance before chortling with laughter, so I couldn't tell how much of what she'd said was farcical and what might have been true.

God and the angels. What have I gotten myself into?

I was the sort of girl who liked to know all the facets of any situation, but the facts of the matter were that my rent was due in a few days and my dusty cupboards contained a half-empty box of Saltine crackers, two cans of Campbell's celery soup, and . . . well, that was it.

(Let's be honest, Catherine. If Juliet had asked if I was willing to steal lollipops from babies or lie to old ladies in exchange for a decent wage, I'd probably have said yes. My banking balance was getting that desperate.)

Juliet suddenly grew serious. "One more question before we officially begin this new partnership."

I waited, counted almost to ten before Juliet spoke again. She certainly had a flair for the dramatic, this one.

"Are you willing to make certain sacrifices in the name of your country? We need someone who is passionate about the cause, who is willing to go even farther than the extra mile."

I felt that V forming between my brows again. If I wasn't careful, I was going to wind up looking like a woman twice my natural age. "So long as I don't have to do anything illegal."

(After all, Catherine, I still had *some* morals. Mostly.)

"Duly noted, my sweet little Puritan." Juliet gave a sly smile, crossed her arms, and tapped her chin. "But what about the gray area between legal and illegal?"

Rent is due in a few days. And you hate celery soup.

I ironed out the frown that threatened, rearranging my lips into a smile that was open for interpretation. "I suppose the gray zone is up for negotiation."

To which Juliet offered me her hand. "Glad to hear it."

* * *

Spit shining Mussolini's shoes would have been easier than working for Juliet. And less volatile.

Juliet was a late riser, so I showed up at her spacious, light-filled apartment every afternoon, eager to show off my translation skills and prove my worth to my new employer, whom I found to be a strong-willed, steely-eyed woman who smoked more than she ate. But I quickly discovered there was little work to be done. Sometimes Marcel was there, and instead of working, he'd take us out for dinner at Barbetta's, a quaint Italian place off Times Square that served decent meatballs, although not a word of Italian was ever spoken between the three of us. If I was lucky, Juliet had me translate a few sentences of Italian here and there, but she often spent long hours on meandering conversational tangents that I had a difficult time following. After several days of this, I realized that Juliet really only asked questions about me, yet never offered any substantive information about herself. Once, over scalding hot glasses of tea, Juliet asked my opinion on the Party's ideals of equality between men and women. "Can we women ever truly work equally with men? Or should we stick to our own kind?"

I had only been half listening—my mind had wandered to my latest worry, that Juliet wasn't even a real Communist given that no one outside of my district leader had heard of her when I mentioned her at my latest Party meeting—and offered some lukewarm response, prompting her to slam her teacup down on the table. "Are you a Trotskyite?" she demanded, pointing her cigarette in its tortoiseshell holder at me as if she might use it to gouge out my eyes.

I gaped, so gobsmacked that all the words I might have said rolled away like marbles. Calling someone a Trotskyite was one of the biggest slurs within the Party. After all, Leon Trotsky was an anti-Stalin ex-revolutionary who had split the Communist Party in Russia and had recently been sentenced to death in absentia for plotting to kill Stalin. According to current Party literature, he and his followers were unscrupulous terrorists who wanted to smash out the Communists in every land.

Pinpricks of panic dotted my shock when Juliet stood so quickly she almost knocked over her chair, leaning forward with both hands on her mahogany dining room table. "You know, I'm one of the powers behind the Communist Party here in America—I could make or break you. And I'd rather kill you here and now than suffer having a Trotskyite in my own home."

I almost bolted but forced myself to fall back on a Party maxim Lee had recently taught me: when you're in a tight spot and want to keep calm, think of a group of words—it doesn't matter whether they make sense or not—and repeat them over and over to yourself until you have drowned out everything else. Complements of my happy childhood moments spent studying paintings with my mother, I made a point to always think of art as a means to calm myself.

Tranquil. Garden. Pond. Water lilies. Monet. Peace.

It was only the fact that I desperately needed the job that kept me in my seat. That, and I didn't want Juliet to stab me with a teaspoon. No normal person talked this way. "Of course I'm not a Trotskyite." Now seemed a good time to employ a sanguine sort of smile despite the thunderstorm in my heart. I repeated an early entry from my journal that had helped me survive several social blunders at Vassar: *Calm face equals a calm mind, relaxed eyes denote comfort and confidence, eyes normally blink sixteen to twenty times a minute unless stressed or aroused.* "Would the Party have recommended me if I was smitten with that Socialist?"

Thankfully, that seemed to placate Juliet, and she sank back into her chair and started nattering about Mussolini's ill-advised invasion of Ethiopia, all the while pouring me a second glass of tea served in the Russian style—piping hot with a slice of lemon and a maraschino cherry. I tried to listen, but her next statement had me wishing I could flee for the door.

"You know, I think Marcel is interested in you," she said, suddenly seeming eager. "He's a very wealthy businessman and could offer you a very comfortable salary. I could tell he was taken with you from the start."

"Marcel?" I actually sputtered his name. "But I thought you and he . . . that he . . ."

The woman actually had the gall to laugh at me. "Marcel and me? Oh no, my dear. Certainly not. But *you* and Marcel, why that would be a different matter entirely."

This was the second time Juliet had propositioned me regarding men. Did I really seem to have no morals? Or was she teasing me somehow?

Did I really want to find out?

"I have to be going." I gathered up my things with lightning speed. "Good night, Juliet."

I swear that as soon as I closed the door, I heard her muffled laughter from the other side.

THE PARTY HAD gotten me the position with Juliet, so I couldn't very well complain to them. But I could complain to Lee—wasn't that what friends were for?

"I think she might be a counterrevolutionary," I confided to Lee that night after rehashing my ordeal. We'd just finished playing a new board game that one of Lee's coworkers had let her borrow— Monopoly—which Lee loved since its goal was to highlight the evils of concentrating wealth in the hands of the few. (Until I placed a hotel on Boardwalk and she started losing—then the game lost its allure.) The thought that Juliet might be a counterrevolutionary had occurred to me after I'd left her apartment for the day, what with how she was always trying to ferret out my opinion on everything political. Either that, or the woman was just plain unstable. "I've asked around the Party, and no one can tell me anything concrete about her—maybe she's spying on us. On *me*."

Lee started packing away the Monopoly pieces. "Or maybe she's part of the underground, trying to discern whether you're a suitable partner."

"Partner?"

"For some sort of secret project—the Party has those, you know. I don't know the details, but I've heard rumors—spying, gathering intelligence. With Marcel and the Fascists she wanted you to sleep with, it sounds like she's already felt you out for a couple possible jobs. Either that, or . . ."

"Or what?"

Lee gave a wicked smile, shook a stack of rainbow-colored play money at me. "Or she could be just a sapphist on the prowl, making sure you turn down all the men she throws your way." Lee dodged the couch pillow I threw at her. "It could happen!"

"I don't care which side Juliet butters her bread on—" Lee gave me an arch look, to which I only shrugged. "Really, I don't," I mumbled. (That much was true, Catherine. Who am I to fret about what people do in the privacy of their own bedrooms? I have far bigger things to worry about.) "I *do* care if she's somehow spying on me. And her threatening to kill me—even if it was hyperbole—creates less-than-ideal working conditions. I should quit."

"If Juliet Glazer *is* part of the underground, she might be so high-ranking that she could even have Stalin's ear." I snorted at that, but Lee only shook her head. "All right, maybe not, but you definitely don't want to upset her," Lee advised, so I wondered if she knew more than she was letting on. "Stick it out, comrade, or you might regret it."

I recalled Marcel's offhand comment, that leaving the Church meant only losing your soul. Had I gotten myself into something far bigger than I'd anticipated? And just how much did Lee know that she wasn't telling me? I'd joined the Party—and I stayed with it—because it built me a bridge to Lee and the sense of belonging and usefulness that I craved. I hadn't anticipated things becoming complicated like this.

I promised to tough it out, but my heart leaped a few days later when the Columbia University Placement Center informed me about a full-time job that had just opened up, this time at the Italian Library of Information on Madison Avenue.

I'd be surrounded by books and silence, my only job translating Italian texts into English. It was as if someone had asked my idea of heaven and then manufactured it, just for me.

(In fact, it was so perfect that you really can't fault me for inventing an enthusiastic reference from Juliet and fudging a few details on my application regarding the extent of my research during my year in Italy. I *needed* this job like a drowning woman needs air.)

I wasn't sure what I was going to do about my position with Juliet—it wasn't as if I was doing actual *work* there. I didn't have the wherewithal to hand in my resignation and face her wrath, wanted to wait until the time was right. Preferably when there were no sharp objects or blunt projectiles nearby.

"You'll work from here," explained the head researcher of the Italian Library on my first day, after she'd led me to one of the many desks huddled between the stacks. A few were occupied by women roughly my age whom I assumed to be fellow researchers, although none did more than scarcely glance my way. One even turned her nose up, so I worried I was covered in Vlad's fur. Again. (I simply couldn't resist those big brown eyes when I left every morning, made it a point to pick him up and let him cover me in a slobbery kisses to say good-bye.) "And here's your first assignment. It's imperative that these documents not leave the library premises, do you understand?"

My assignment was a crate of freshly printed newspapers from Italy, none of them more than a day old. Mixed in, I quickly realized, were also pamphlets, some of which were aimed at Italian Americans.

Each and every one was violently pro-Fascist, of course. A quick scan of their messages revealed that Mussolini might actually have turned water to wine *and* parted the Red Sea himself.

"Do people here read this stuff?" I asked the young woman at the next desk.

She glanced up from her work, peering at me through horn-rimmed spectacles. "Quite a few, actually." Her accent was a stew of Italian and the Bronx. "Including all of the employees here at the library. We're all impressed with Il Duce and the way he's improved Italy."

Oh, dear Lord . . .

Meaning I'd just stumbled onto a writhing snake pit of Fascism, right here in New York City.

Worse still, as I kept my head down and soldiered on, reading and translating, I realized that the rest of the literature I was meant to translate and file for readers was both virulently anti-Semitic *and* anti-Communist, going so far as to mention the CPUSA by name. And here I was: a registered member of the Communist Party of the United States. Meaning that every one of these people wouldn't hesitate to slip my head into a noose and cheer to see me dangle.

(Now, Catherine, I realize that no one was being hanged for Communist membership during this time. However, that doesn't mean that the sentiment wasn't there.)

My only consolation was that Elizabeth *Sherman* was a card-carrying member of the CPUSA, but Elizabeth *Bentley* had spent a year in Italy and possessed an advanced degree in fourteenth-century Florentine poetry. I'd taken this job under my real name, which meant that, according to my résumé, I was a perfect candidate for gobbling up Mussolini's propaganda like a freshly made tray of tiramisu.

Except that I wasn't interested in leading a double life. By lunch, I was gathering my coat, preparing to hand in my resignation.

Except . . .

I set down my jacket, licked my thumb, and sorted through the Fascist propaganda that glared back at me one more time. In one vitriolic article, Mussolini declared democracy—a solid American ideal that I held dear—was dead, and went on to claim that North America wished they had a leader like Mussolini in charge.

That will be the day . . .

My snort turned into a coughing fit when my new coworkers glared at me. Somehow, I doubted whether America wished for castor oil torture, weekend executions, or the OVRA secret police in their backyards, all of which I'd witnessed during my time in Italy.

Still, was it possible that my work here might somehow benefit the Party? Or America? Did anyone truly realize the extent of the Fascist propaganda that was infiltrating our very country? Or the extent of the harm it might be doing here, leading Americans to support the likes of Mussolini? Or even Hitler?

I wasn't sure, but I intended to find out.

How some of those newspapers and pamphlets made their way into my handbag just then remains a mystery, but once they were there, wasn't I duty bound as a patriotic American to show them to higher powers?

That's exactly what I did.

"I think this is something the Party should see," I said to Juliet that evening, feigning far more confidence than I felt. I'd considered taking the pilfered papers to Lee or maybe even Patch, but neither possessed the renown within the Party I was looking for. According to Lee, Juliet might well be high placed—not even I knew how high or what this woman really did—which meant she was my best bet for a straight answer.

Juliet took a deep drag on her foul-smelling cigarette, its extra-long tortoiseshell holder bestowing upon her a distinct veneer of class as she beckoned me inside. I followed her trail of fragrant smoke as if it were a trail of bread crumbs. I was possibly onto something, something *big*, and I wanted to hear her agree with me.

"Are these funny little papers connected to why you didn't show up this morning?" she asked after I'd upended the contents of my handbag onto her couch.

"They're from the Italian Library," I answered, avoiding eye contact. "They offered me a position as a researcher."

I pushed the story about Mussolini toward her, complete with my full translation. "Won't the Party want to know what's being said about them? This could damage their image here in America."

Wordlessly, Juliet perused the article. Finally, she tapped her cigarette holder against her teeth—which I noticed for the first time were stained from years of smoking—and nodded. "You know, my little Puritan, all this time I thought you were just a shrinking hothouse flower who would never make a good revolutionary. Perhaps I was wrong."

Being a revolutionary was near the bottom of my to-do list, but Juliet didn't give me an opportunity to argue. "Your position at the Italian Library is far more beneficial to the Party than the translation work I needed," she said. "Keep at it, scour everything that passes your desk for anything that might detract from our cause. Anything anti-Communist, or even anti-Semitic, you smuggle out to me in that handbag of yours, understand?"

Our cause.

I swear my already ample chest swelled even further with the importance Juliet had just bestowed upon me. I'd always felt like the most inconsequential of bit players in the drama that was the CPUSA, but this was a task that only *I* could do, something only *I* could contribute to the Party and to America. The logical bit of my brain knew that this was still only one bean in a very large jar, but it was *my* bean and no one else's.

I would become the Party's eyes and ears within the Italian Fascist propaganda machine, and I alone would expose them for the liars they were.

If I get enough data, I thought jubilantly, *perhaps I'll blow the whole works up.*

Of course, there could be steep consequences if I were caught. I'd definitely lose my well-paying job at the Italian Library, and the Italian government certainly wouldn't take kindly to their leaflets being stolen and distributed to their enemy. It was a chance I never would have taken when I lived in Italy, but this was America—I didn't have to fear Mussolini's Blackshirts dragging me out of bed into the dead of night.

I understood my meeting with Juliet to be over and started packing away the paraphernalia I'd borrowed. (Let it be clear, Catherine, that I never stole anything from the Italian Library. Each document simply went on a short tour of New York City in my handbag before making its way back to a librarian's desk.) Juliet cleared her throat. "There's someone I want you to meet. Tonight."

"Right now?"

"I already had the meeting planned—you're going to tag along." She waved impatient fingers until I ascertained that she needed the pen and notepad from the table behind me. Once she had them in hand, she scrawled down an unfamiliar address. "We can't arrive together—meet me in an hour and a half."

What the hell have I just gotten myself into?

THE RESTAURANT WAS Italian—its lights casting a golden glow on the changing autumn leaves on University Place in Greenwich Village. My stomach growled as I tugged my wool jacket tighter and peered inside at the patrons eating crispy breadsticks and spaghetti. Normally, I hated eating in front of other people, but I was hungry enough tonight to forgo my rule, even if it *was* for a messy plate of spaghetti. I glanced over my shoulder just in time to see Juliet striding toward me.

She approached but then strode past me, only paused and looked back when I failed to follow. A sharp jerk of her head had me falling into step next to her, walking toward Eighth Street. I struggled to match her pace. "Aren't we going in?"

"Basic Party training: never make your meeting location the same place you do business. And never, *ever* meet at any nightclubs—the FBI watches most of them," she said under her breath. I wasn't sure what sort of training Juliet had received from the Party, but taking courses on Marxist theory and hoisting banners overhead at rallies hadn't prepared me for whatever we were doing right now. "This contact is high up in the movement. Follow my lead."

The words made sense, but her meaning might have been in Swahili. I'd considered that Juliet orbited near the stratosphere of the Party's hierarchy, but here she was acting downright nervous to meet this contact. Of course, Juliet walked the knife's edge between sanity and lunacy on a good day, so I wouldn't have been surprised if this contact of hers turned out to be entirely imaginary. I might have excused myself, but the obedience drilled into me since childhood—and a strong dash of curiosity—meant that instead I followed her down the deserted street. I had to keep myself from balking when she grabbed my wrist in a vise. "That's him."

If anyone in those days was asked to imagine a high-ranking Communist, they'd surely have described a tall, imposing figure with a thick mustache and piercing eyes, probably stepping from the shadows in a military uniform or at least a crisp suit. Instead, the man who appeared out of nowhere and shuffled toward us was none of that: shorter than me and built like a cannonball, wearing an inadequate trench coat and scuffed brown shoes. With each step, one of the soles flapped loose, slapped against the pavement. His most distinct feature was the russet-red shock of hair poking out from under a battered tan felt hat.

And the icy blue eyes that lifted toward us and pierced me in place, like a moth to a specimen board.

Juliet's gaze dropped, and her entire body seemed to cave in, her manner suddenly subservient in a way I'd never seen. "Elizabeth, you can trust Timmy here with your life," she said by way of introduction. "Timmy, our usual tête-à-tête can wait; my dear little Puritan has information that might be of use to you."

"It is a pleasure to meet you, Elizabeth." His voice was rough and gravelly, sharp around the edges. He was terribly broad across, thick muscles straining the seams of his jacket shoulders, so unlike the professors and academics I was accustomed to.

More like a thug. Or a hit man.

Regardless of Juliet's instruction, I doubted very much that I could trust this man with my life, but I *did* know that if this man was named *Timmy*, then I was the Queen of Camelot. Honestly, Juliet had borrowed from Shakespeare, and I was fairly certain Marcel had pilfered his name from Proust. Surely, this bullish man whose glacial eyes brimmed with intelligence could have claimed a character from Twain or Thomas Hardy. Or even Tolstoy, whose grandiose and wordy novels I loathed with the fire of a thousand suns.

I didn't have time to make a quip—or respond at all—as Timmy-whatever-his-real-name-was and Juliet strode toward the corner, leaving me to follow like an obedient dog. It didn't escape my notice when they exchanged a white envelope between them, gone in a flash from Juliet's purse to Timmy's pocket. (I'd later learn this was called a brush-past.) I hustled to catch up as Timmy swung into the driver's seat of a gleaming beetle-black LaSalle sedan with white tires and polished running boards. Juliet held open the passenger door in a clear command to me. I clambered into the rear seat, wishing I knew what on God's green earth was going on.

She shut the door, leaned in its open window. "I'll leave you to it."

Then she was gone.

"There is a restaurant on Second Avenue where we can get a bite and actually talk." Timmy's eyes were firmly over the steering wheel as he eased the meticulously detailed car away from the curb. I couldn't quite place the residue of his accent, but it was certainly European, likely eastern from the way his *w*'s rolled into *v*'s. "Better than lingering on the street, I think."

"I didn't realize Juliet was planning to leave," I mumbled, my foot tapping nervously on the floorboard. We didn't have far to go—only a couple blocks—which meant I could still beg off. Or make a run for it.

"Why?" he asked. "Are you nervous?"

"Should I be?"

He didn't respond right away, which was the opposite of reassuring. "You know that Juliet is highly placed within the Party, yes? You can trust her."

Everyone kept saying that about these mysterious, high-ranking Communists, but I still kept my gaze on the door handle, just in case.

Timmy's eyes flicked my way, but I saw through the camouflage of his glance for its true intent: gathering data about me. I knew what he was seeing—a woman of an age where she could no longer rightly be called a girl, slightly plump with uncontrollable dark curls, wearing nondescript shoes and a belted navy jacket that was just on this side of fashionable. I didn't bother to hide my study of him—the powerful shoulders that strained his trench coat beneath a short, thick neck; the Slavic cheekbones and inquisitive eyes. I wondered if the loose sole on his shoe made it difficult to drive.

Our gazes met in the rearview mirror, but only for a moment.

Should I run? I asked myself. *I should definitely run.*

Yet, my new acquaintance pulled up precisely where he'd said, outside a Jewish deli with a jaunty green awning. "They have excellent Reubens here," he said. "If you like Reubens, that is."

The inside was bright and cheery with only a few tables open. Not exactly the sort of establishment where you expect someone to commit a violent crime, which meant I relaxed somewhat as we slid into a booth with cracked vinyl seats.

"Let us begin with any questions you might have." He handed me a laminated menu that was slightly sticky. "I will answer them as best I can."

I declined the menu. "I'm not hungry."

Which was now true, given the state of my nerves.

Timmy gave a gentle smile. "You must order." He gestured with his chin toward the restaurant. "To blend in."

The pieces clicked together in my mind—I realized it was precisely for the cover of the restaurant's hurry-scurry that we had met here. Still, my stomach was a writhing bundle of nerves, and not just because it seemed having to eat in front of other people was a hazard of the job. It struck me as a strange juxtaposition to be discussing potentially secret Party business smack-dab in the middle of an old Jewish couple arguing over what to order, a group of students debating their required reading over shared baskets of greasy onion rings, and the hustle and bustle of waitresses wearing ruffled white aprons as they hollered orders to the kitchen. Also, I wasn't sure why Juliet had asked me to meet this man, nor was I ready to talk to a stranger about my spying at the Italian Library. Still, I wanted to know what I was dealing with here. "Why do you do . . . *this*?" I dropped my voice. "Work for the Party, I mean."

"That is a question I will gladly answer," Timmy responded. "If you will as well."

That seemed only fair, although I recognized his tactic of getting me to reveal my motivations. "Honestly?" I asked. "I joined because it was the first place I ever felt like I belonged, like I had substance. Then I realized that maybe I could do something, contribute something worthwhile to help people, to help my country. One thing led to another until . . ." I waved my hand. "Here I am."

Timmy leaned back, one arm resting easily on the back of the booth. "Your story is not so unusual, you know. We are indeed a party of misfits and dreamers."

I loved that sentiment. In fact, I loved it a lot.

Timmy continued. "I contribute what I can to the Party because I have seen plenty of suffering and misery in my day, the greed and selfishness of a few who made life hell for everyone else. Yet, I like to believe that someday there will be a new society in which men—and women—will live like human beings and not animals." His might have been a canned answer, but he seemed so *sincere*, as if he'd just bared the innermost gears of his soul to me. "Next question."

Flustered at his naked honesty, I blurted out the first thing that came to mind. "What's your real name?"

His mouth settled into a firm line. "I cannot tell you that."

I gave an idle wave of my hand—a tactic I'd often seen deployed to cover someone's true emotions with a veneer of boredom. "Yes, yes, I'm sure it's classified and all that." I dropped my voice to a whisper, suddenly glad for the noisy chatter of the other diners around us. "But you look nothing like a Timmy."

He frowned, cocked his head to one side. "My first Party organizer gave me that name. From Dickens."

I skimmed through the character lists of *A Tale of Two Cities* and *Oliver Twist*. Then, "Do you mean Tiny Tim? From *A Christmas Carol*?"

"You do not approve?" he asked, and I waited for him to rail against me, but instead, a ghost of a smile quirked one corner of his lips, caused a one-sided dimple. (Catherine, there's a reason the eyes are called the windows to a person's soul, but most people also have a secondary window to their thoughts that is particular just to them. For Timmy—a man who had learned to temper the story his eyes told—it was his ever-expressive lips. After all, the human mouth is surrounded by ten intricately reflexive muscles, did you know that? They eat, drink, kiss, smile, laugh. Wonders, really.)

I wasn't sure whether to laugh or feel sorry for the man across from me—he *was* on the shorter side, but he was so muscle dense, like some specially bred eastern European bull, that one could never mistake him for the crippled Cratchit boy of Dickens's story. I didn't care for altering people's given names to nicknames, but either Timmy's first Party organizer had made a poor attempt at irony or he was deliberately making fun of Timmy's stature. And Timmy was a code name, not his *real* name.

"I just think a person should be able to choose their own code names." I fiddled with the tines of my fork. "I mean, Juliet obviously mined Shakespeare for her cover. You could be Romeo or Oberon. Even Lear."

"I fail to see how that improves my current name."

I glanced around the restaurant, gestured toward the group of arguing students near the door. "See that girl there, with the blond hair? She could be Katherina. From *Taming of the Shrew.*"

Timmy turned in his seat, then glanced back my way. "Why?"

"Look at the way she argues. One person gives their two cents and then she jumps in. Someone else interjects and then it's back to her again. She loves to argue, plus she never fails to interrupt the dark-haired boy at her right."

"Let me guess—Petruchio?"

"Look at the way she leans toward him when he talks. And every time she argues with him, she touches that pretty blond hair of hers. She *likes* him, but he doesn't know it. Heck, *she* might not even know it."

"You are an excellent read on human behavior." Timmy turned back around to face me. "What else should I know about you?"

"I'm fluent in Italian and French. And I have a box of worthless degrees under my bed."

"That explains how well-read you are." Timmy smiled. "While I have enjoyed our discussion of literary characters, my name has served me well for many years."

I snorted. The noise was in the *Socially Unacceptable* section of my journal on human behavior, but the sound of derision often escaped before I could stop it. "Even Sir Toby Belch or William Butts would be better than *Timmy.*"

He studied his menu, but I'd have bet my first day's wages from the Italian Library that he wasn't reading it. "I care little for Shakespeare," he said. "Too English."

"You're right. Not Shakespeare. We need something more apropos." I snapped my fingers. "I hate Tolstoy, but you'd make a good Levin, from *Anna Karenina*."

A noble hero made from the salt of the earth. It was an added bonus that his name was close to Lenin.

"Not my first choice." There was that smile again. "But better than William Butts."

I shrugged. "Then Levin you shall be."

Somehow, I'd finally relaxed enough to smile. And to order when a frilly-aproned waitress came to take our requests. Sadly, there were no hot dogs on the menu, but my stomach rumbled in anticipation of my bowl of chicken soup with kreplach. I felt more at ease, understood for perhaps the first time why people lauded the wonders of small talk. Usually my attempts to make chitchat—especially with people I'd just met—felt terribly awkward and stilted. Not so with this new Party contact of mine.

"So," I said after the waitress had trundled off with our orders. "Why did Juliet set up this meeting?"

Timmy—now Levin—steepled his fingers on the table. "She was impressed with your initiative at the Italian Library. What sort of work are you doing there? Juliet provided only the briefest summary over the phone before our meeting today."

Over steaming spoonfuls of soup, I spoke of the propaganda that crossed my desk, preened a little at the details I could recall. (My memory has always been both a gift and a curse; once I've read something it's difficult to shake it loose from my mind.) Then I told Levin how I saw an opportunity for the Party to counter the blatant lies being spread about them and convince America of the evils of Fascism.

"And you say all this was in pamphlets, articles, *and* political cartoons?" he asked once, followed shortly thereafter by, "What did the leaflets say about Mussolini's plans for the Fascists here in America?"

I found myself leaning forward and talking faster, unfurling in the warmth of Levin's rapt attention.

"You know, Elizabeth," he said when I'd finished, "your work at the Italian Library is vitally important—you must remain there at any cost and bring us as many documents as you can, anything on the Fascists' plans, their intentions, or their capabilities. Report on everything you see and hear, no matter how trivial it may seem."

"Report to whom? Juliet?"

He set down his Rueben. "To me."

"Then you're to be what? My . . . handler?"

He wiped the corner of his mouth with a napkin. Shabbily dressed, but with pristine manners. "I prefer the term *contact*, but yes."

"Why me? I'm just an ordinary woman."

"Are you?" He didn't smile. "You have shown the rare combination of intellectual curiosity and initiative, along with an intense desire to serve your country and the Party. In short, I think you would make an extraordinary spy. However"—he set his napkin on the table—"I must warn you that this partnership comes at a cost."

"What sort of cost?"

"By joining my cadre, you will no longer be an ordinary, run-of-the-mill Communist. You will become a member of the underground apparat, also known as the Center. Surely, Juliet warned you of this possibility."

"Not a word, actually."

In fact, I had no idea what he'd even meant.

I hadn't yet learned to regulate the emotions in my expressions, which must have made it easy for Levin to parse out my thoughts.

"If you join the underground, you must stop attending Party meetings." He leaned forward, making it appear to anyone who happened to glance our way as if we were simply two friends—perhaps more than friends—having a riveting conversation. "No more socializing or parades or demonstrations, just a clean break. Juliet tells me that your life is orderly and you are able to compartmentalize, that you have no husband and are not sentimental or romantic, all of which is ideal. That is the first rule of the underground: no close friendships and no unnecessary emotional connections, certainly no falling in love. However, if your friends ask where you've been—even Lee—you must tell them you have dropped out of the Party."

How does he know that I'm friends with Lee? It didn't even matter that he had just solved the riddle of Juliet throwing multiple men my way—the thought of spending every night in my lonely, cabbage-smelling boardinghouse room, cut off from Lee and the Party, made my breath hitch in my throat. *No close friendships? Not even Lee?*

"I'm not sure I can do that." I'd suddenly lost my appetite, pushed my soup away. "Or that it's even fair to ask it."

"Miss Bentley," he said, then corrected himself, "Elizabeth, surely, you must see the danger in actively participating in Communist activities while also stealing from the Fascists at the Italian Library."

To this day, I'm not sure if his slip with my name was to show me he knew everything there was to know about me—that my last name was *not* Sherman—or whether it was an honest mistake. "I didn't steal from the library," I said weakly. "I merely borrowed."

Levin lifted those colossal shoulders into a shrug. "You must choose—one or the other. After our discussion tonight, I believe you are too important to be a mere Party drudge—you can play a vital role in the building of a new world. We have all made sacrifices for the greater good, Elizabeth. Are you willing to do the same?"

To be singled out like this was a heady experience. I recalled Lee's exclamation about having my hand on the throttle of history. Perhaps this was my opportunity, one that would only come once.

I could build a better world. Have a life that means something.

For a brief moment, I wondered what sacrifices Levin had made. Or even Juliet.

"May I have some time before I give you my answer?"

"Of course," he said as the waitress handed him the check. He didn't even glance at it, just folded the receipt around a crisp five-dollar bill and passed it back to her. "Sleep on it if you would like. Of course, even if you choose to remain as you are, everything we discussed here must be kept entirely secret."

The meaning was clear. Yes, I could think about it, but not for long. And I'd pay a steep price for stepping out of line.

"Let me be direct." Levin's tone was a warm caress as he helped me into my jacket. "If you decide against working with me, you can still continue your comfortable life exactly as it is now. If you choose to accept, it will be one of the most difficult things you ever do. You will be completely alone except for me. Your old comrades may even believe you a traitor. But I promise you two things: first, the Party would not ask this of you were it not vitally important. And second, you will make a difference, Elizabeth. I swear it."

"It's a difficult choice." I hated the way my voice trembled.

"Indeed," he said. "One that only you can make."

Somehow, that failed to reassure me.

"I'D THOUGHT BETTER of you, Elizabeth." Patch's voice over the pay phone's crackling line was so fraught with anger and disappointment that I held the receiver away from my ear. I'd just finished a shift at the Italian Library and had a handbag stuffed with documents, yet my most difficult task today had been placing telephone calls. First the operator connected me to my Party organizer to resign as financial secretary in charge of collecting party dues, then to my professor at the Communist Workers School to withdraw from classes, and now to Patch, whom I hadn't spoken with in weeks. "I thought you understood the importance of our work for the Party. Never did I think you'd abandon it, abandon *us*. Does Lee know about this?"

Us? That was rich, coming from Patch. I still hadn't entirely forgiven him for making me think he was interested in me.

"I haven't talked to her yet." The next words tasted dirty coming out of my mouth, but I couldn't let my grand plan be derailed by my former friends' shock or their censure that would inevitably follow. "The Party just doesn't mean to me what it used to. What have American Communists accomplished over all these years except meetings and rallies and newspaper special editions? Nothing. CPUSA membership is up, but I can't spend my entire life tied to some quaint idea of a utopia that is never going to materialize."

A long silence. "I'm sorry you feel that way."

"I'm sorry too, Patch."

As I hung up the receiver, I *was* sorry, more than I'd expected. I'd worked so hard to create a circle of belonging for myself that this culling of that life left me emotionally drained.

I'd joined the Party out of loneliness. I wanted to build a better world, yes, but if I played my cards right, I could have my cake and eat it too. No loneliness required.

I'd scarcely finished my dinner of creamed chipped beef on toast when an angry pounding on my door nearly made me jump out of my skin.

It was Lee. And she was in a horn-tossing mood.

"Open this door, Elizabeth," she commanded. I opened the door to find my pocket Aphrodite purple in the face and locks of her hair straggling out from under her scarf like Medusa's snakes, as if she'd run the blocks between her apartment and my boarding room. "I left Laurel with a neighbor who happens to have a bridge group over right now. You have fifteen minutes to convince me not to wring your neck."

You don't waste any time, do you, Patch?

Of course, I'd expected as much, which was why I'd called Patch before speaking to Lee. (I actually felt rather smug that my plan was working precisely as I'd expected. Sometimes human beings really *are* predictable.) In order to convince Levin that I'd broken with the Party, I needed to put on a convincing show that made it appear that I'd successfully quarantined myself. Because while I could stop attending rallies and going to classes, it would be a cold day in hell before I gave up my friendship with Lee.

I gave a cursory glance down the hallway just to ensure none of my neighbors had gotten curious, then tugged Lee inside and slammed the door. Vlad gave a piteous whine at her feet, as if he could sense her ire.

"Talk," she ordered. "And do it fast."

"What I'm about to say can't leave this room." I scooped up Vlad. "You have to swear it. On Laurel's life."

It was dramatic and I knew it. But I also knew that running afoul of highly placed Party members was *not* a wise idea. There would be terrible ramifications for airing Party business outside approved channels—I had no intention of *ever* doing that—and there could be disastrous consequences if Levin ever discovered my current subterfuge. Except I had no plan of getting caught. Regardless, I wouldn't have chanced this verboten friendship for anyone less than Lee, who had single-handedly plucked me from the mire of my own loneliness.

She sighed. "I swear."

I was relatively confident that I could trust her. I mean, if I couldn't trust Lee, then who *could* I trust?

"I have a new handler." I rubbed Vlad's ears as a distraction. "He wants me to drop all my Party connections so I can work for the Communist underground."

Lee didn't move for a moment, then her eyes bulged and she burst out laughing, but not for the reason I thought. "That's all? My god, Elizabeth, I thought you'd gone and betrayed us to the Fascists you're working with."

Now *that* was sobering, since turning traitor had never crossed my mind. I felt mildly offended that my sudden desertion could be construed as a Judas move. "My blood is as red as ever," I assured her. "But you cannot tell *anyone*, not even Patch. You swore."

She cocked her head to the side, frowned. "He reads me pretty well, Elizabeth."

"It doesn't matter. The next time you see him you need to rant and rave about what a wretched cow I am for abandoning the Party. Call me every name in the book—the kinds of names that would make even Stalin blush—and win an Oscar statuette for your performance." I set down Vlad, clasped Lee's hands in mine. "It's important, Lee. I wasn't supposed to tell you—I'm supposed to be all alone, save for this new handler."

She bit her lip. "Who is this mysterious and all-powerful handler?"

Part of me wanted to tell her, but . . . "I'm not sure I should say."

She shrugged. "The Party keeps their highest operatives secret anyway." She slanted her eyes at me. "Be careful, Elizabeth. You're playing with fire—you probably shouldn't have told me any of this."

"I *definitely* shouldn't have told you." I fiddled with my sleeve, then stopped. "But I couldn't let you think I'd abandoned you."

My friendship with Lee was now forbidden, but then, so was stealing documents from the crates that passed my desk at the Italian Library. It seemed that Elizabeth Bentley, sad sack that she was, had suddenly become quite the rebel.

Lee wrapped her scarf around her hair again. "Watch your back, Elizabeth."

I gave her a fierce hug. "Of course."

After she left, I called the number Levin had given me—not his real number, of course, but a relay station—and left a message with the woman who answered. (Levin had instructed that I was to end the call if a man ever picked up.) My telephone rang a few minutes later, and when I responded, a man whose voice I didn't recognize relayed an address and a time an hour from then.

Despite my nervous exhaustion, apparently my work wasn't done for the day.

"You rang?" Levin said an hour later as he approached where I waited outside a Chinatown eatery, the very air fragrant with the soy-drenched aromas of chop suey and chow mein. My stomach rumbled, but this time we didn't enter the restaurant. "Sometimes it is best that we remain on the move: walking, driving, that sort of thing," he explained in a low voice. "The better to minimize other people seeing us side by side, save in passing."

"I have something for you from the library. Several somethings, as a matter of fact." I followed him a couple blocks to where he'd parked his boxy LaSalle. The tailoring on Levin's suits might be threadbare, but his car always—and I mean *always*—looked like it had just driven off the factory floor. "I don't care to sit on information for long—it's best if I return the papers the day after I borrow them."

"So you have decided to accept my offer?"

I forced myself to look askance, to let my gaze tangle with his. (Catherine, it's not true that people always avoid eye contact when lying, but they do it enough that I've learned to always look someone in the eyes when I'm not telling the truth.) "I have."

"I am pleased to hear it."

While we drove, I told Levin everything about my shift at the Italian Library, passed him papers from a thick envelope at the bottom of my floral knitting bag. (My handbag had proven too small to adequately cover the Fascist paraphernalia I borrowed, so I'd decided to take up knitting to have an excuse to lug the giant bag around. *Knit, purl, swipe.*) I might have just described everything from memory, but honestly, I still had no idea what sort of documents were helpful, so I stuffed everything that seemed of even passing interest into that bag. It had made me feel important somehow, as if I were taking my place in a proud line of patriotic American spies stretching back to George Washington's day.

Because I was doing this for America. So we could lift ourselves out of this Depression without falling into the trap of Fascism that so many other countries had stumbled into.

This was *my* contribution, however small it might have been.

"The Spanish attaché visited again," I said. "They requested the latest editions of *Il Travaso*. It calls itself the 'official organ of intelligent people,' but it's nothing more than a racist, anti-American rag. Oh, and did I mention it loathes Communists?"

"Franco's Nationalists are moving into position in Spain, and neither Britain nor France plans to lift a finger to help the anti-Franco Republicans." Levin strummed his fingers on the wheel in agitation.

I dug further into my bag, pulled out a crumpled package of Lucky Strikes that I'd bought weeks ago to smoke with Patch. "Cigarette? They're good for your nerves, you know."

Levin smiled, but shook his head. "Thank you, but I have a rule against smoking in the LaSalle. The smell is difficult to remove." Relieved that I wouldn't have to smoke the foul things, I put the pack away as he continued. "If I were a betting man, I would guess only Stalin will help the Republicans in Spain. Did the attaché ask for anything else? Weapon reports or anything similar?"

I'd never seen anything that important cross my desk. But I wasn't going to tell Levin that, not when I still needed to prove my worth to him.

"Not specifically, but another staffer took the copies of the full editions." Once again, I was impressed not only by Levin's far-reaching knowledge of world events, but also by how all the fiddly little pieces fit together. Suddenly, I wanted to show him that I was more than just a library researcher with sticky fingers. "I also eavesdropped outside the head librarian's door today. When he left for lunch I rummaged through his wastebasket."

A smile tugged at Levin's lips. "Did you find anything?"

"Not unless you count his receipt for dry cleaning."

He gave a muted chuckle. "No one digs through trash cans except in spy novels, Elizabeth. Important papers never get thrown away; they get destroyed."

Though gently delivered, his one-two punch lit my cheeks with a raging wildfire. "I'm sorry," I muttered. "I wasn't exactly born for this, you know."

"No one is born to do spy work—it must be learned." I was surprised when Levin reached over and gave my forearm a squeeze. "Focus your energies on impressing your library superiors with your trustworthiness. Extol Franco's many virtues and pen Mussolini love letters promising to name your firstborn after him."

My inhalation was a sorry attempt to douse the flames on my cheeks, although that was difficult to do considering I could still feel Levin's phantom touch on my arm. "Franco *is* my favorite Fascist leader." I batted my eyes a little. "Outside of Il Duce, of course."

Levin chortled and flicked off the radio with one deft movement. "So, tell me, how did your conversations with your friends from the Party turn out?"

"Fine." The lie tasted metallic and all wrong; I hoped Levin didn't notice the way I shifted uncomfortably in my seat. "My ears are still burning from the lashing Harold Patch gave me."

"He is one of our most fiery writers, you know." Levin's gaze remained straight ahead as he eased the LaSalle north along the Hudson. "And Lee Fuhr? I would guess you were not looking forward to that conversation."

"Patch told her the news."

See, that's not a total lie.

(They say when telling a lie to stick as close to the truth as possible. It's good advice, Catherine, not because you have less to remember but because then it's easier to justify being a liar to yourself.)

A heavy silence filled the cab. I recalled a vague instruction from Patch when I was copyediting one of his interviews to let silences linger so your interviewee would feel the need to fill them. I understood the logic there, just as I understood that I couldn't possibly let the silence stretch any longer.

"Lee was angry," I offered.

"And?"

"She said she never wanted to see me again."

Well, she would *have said that, at least. If I hadn't told her the truth.*

This time Levin waited until he'd stopped at a red light to look my way. And sighed. "I will never coerce you, Elizabeth, and I will never lie to you. I will work to gain your trust, day by day, until you realize that trust is the bedrock of our relationship. Unfortunately, right now this appears to be a one-sided relationship."

The full brunt of his gaze made me understand how Sodom and Gomorrah had felt. Fire and brimstone and pillars of salt were nothing compared to the raw power in that piercing blue gaze. *He knows I lied.*

"Elizabeth, I need operatives who trust me implicitly, who will report to me any mistakes they have made even if it is the dead of night. The strength of the Center comes from the fact that it is composed of men and women who care enough about their principles to subordinate everything else to them. You have done this in name only."

"I don't understand."

Except I did. All too well.

"You did not break ties with Lee." I'd expected his voice to be taut with barely restrained violence, but it was calm and cold. "I have been doing this for too long to be fooled by my newest recruit, clever though she may be."

I actually *cringed* at the recrimination in his voice. Perhaps I might have argued my innocence, but I understood that would get me nowhere. Or it might land me in a far worse position than I was already in.

"Does this mean I'm fired?"

"No, but it means you cannot see Lee again." Levin's tone brooked no argument. "We underground operatives work in isolation so as not to endanger anyone else. This quarantine is for your sake and hers, not to mention the Party's."

"May I at least write her a letter explaining all this?"

"Absolutely not," he answered. "Putting anything in writing—*ever*—is too risky. But you may call her. Once, and only to set this right." The light turned green and we rolled forward, the downturn of Levin's expressive lips informing me just how disappointed he truly was. "This is your one and only chance, Elizabeth. You have much potential, but I must have your full commitment now—no questions, no argument. Otherwise, I cannot trust you. And if I cannot trust you, you are a danger and I want nothing to do with you."

I fiddled with the handles of my knitting bag. I knew I should accept my punishment in silence, but I felt like I needed to help Levin understand my rationale so he wasn't so dismayed with me. "It's just that I was lonely for so long. And then I found Lee. It doesn't seem fair that I have to cut myself off from absolutely everyone."

"That is the funny thing about life." Levin's voice wasn't unkind. I was relieved to see the hard edges of his frown soften somewhat. "It is only fair because it is unfair to everyone."

I almost smiled at that. *Almost.*

Except I was terrified of being alone again.

Use your mind, do something good and important with your life, Elizabeth. Help people and make your time here count.

My mother's admonition reminded me of the need for courage and of what was really important. Throughout America's history, her citizens had suffered far more than lonely nights at home in order to leave their mark on our country. I recognized the rare opportunity Levin was offering me, to do something meaningful and fulfilling.

An opportunity like this didn't come along every day. Certainly not in the midst of this Depression.

I'd been alone before and lived to tell the tale. Surely, I could survive it again. And I wouldn't be totally bereft this time: there would be Levin, at least.

Whether the man next to me was my friend or enemy, I couldn't quite tell, yet, more and more he reminded me of the dark central figure in Jacques-Louis David's neoclassicist masterpiece *Oath of the Horatii*, willing to sacrifice everything, even his own sons, for the cause of patriotism. It would be good to have a person like that—a David facing down the Goliaths of the world—in my corner.

"You can trust me," I promised. "Or may lightning strike me down."

To which Levin offered a half smile as he pulled up at my arranged drop-off point. "Nothing so dramatic as that. Just the NKVD coming after the both of us."

(Catherine, think of the NKVD as the predecessor to today's dreaded KGB. A secret police agency created to protect the security of the Soviet Union, complete with foreign espionage, kidnappings, and assassinations. Not people you want to upset, especially considering their kindest form of punishment was banishing unruly citizens to the windswept Siberian gulags they created.)

Clutching my knitting bag to my chest was involuntary—I was going to have to work on my reactions. "Really?"

He gave an unconvincing half laugh. "Let us not find out, shall we?"

A moment later, I was standing on the sidewalk beneath a streetlamp, shaking my head in consternation as Levin's polished La-Salle turned a corner. I enjoyed Levin's company—his enigmatic quips and inquisitive nature, the streak of kindness that I suspected hid a spine of steel.

It's a damned good thing you like him, I thought as I turned up my collar and started toward the metro station. *Given that he's your only friend in the world now.*

5

Levin and I met every Wednesday evening for the next few months. Naturally, Wednesday had become my new favorite day of the week.

While Levin and I only ever met in diners and restaurants—after first meeting somewhere a few blocks away—we never ate at the same place twice. I fancied that I might someday boast that I'd eaten at every restaurant in New York City.

"I'd never tasted Indian food before tonight," I said as Levin paid the bill of the *palak paneer*–scented hole-in-the-wall that he'd suggested we meet at that night. I'd savored every last morsel of cold curry, the better to draw out our meeting even longer. Once, partway through, I'd even caught myself playing with my hair as other women did when trying to attract a lover. I forced myself to stop immediately, pinned my hands under my legs.

Tonight had been a longer-than-usual meeting that began with my usual presentation of materials filched from the Italian Library, followed by a discussion of world events.

Levin was fired up about Germany's blatant destruction of Jewish lives and property from Kristallnacht and that the Third Reich was now requiring the registry of all Romani people over the age of six. I'd sat with rapt attention—commenting only on the anti-Italian protests that had broken out in response to Italy's demands that France hand over their North African colony of Tunisia—before steering the conversation toward my new favorite pastime: a heated debate about our favorite artworks. Levin championed Otto Dix's *War Cripples*, which the Nazis had recently destroyed, while I preferred Pablo Picasso's masterpiece *Guernica*.

(Catherine, some say a strong set of shoulders or a chiseled jaw are the best sort of aphrodisiac, but I say give me a man who can argue symbolism in art and debate the merits of international foreign policy—any woman worth her salt will be slack-jawed and tongue-tied. I certainly was.)

Only when the waiters were pointedly stacking the restaurant's chairs did Levin and I bundle ourselves into our wool coats and hand-knit scarves (he was the recipient of some of my constant knitting from my breaks at the Italian Library—my room was crammed with all manner of hats and afghans, and I'd even knit Vlad a dog-sized sweater), before bursting outside to find New York tucked deep beneath a winter quilt of more snow than I'd seen in my entire life.

"Your car is buried," I exclaimed. It seemed impossible that we hadn't noticed the snow coming down, but I knew where my attention had been. A firebomb might have dropped on Yonkers and I'd have been oblivious. A common snowstorm didn't have a chance.

Except Levin was my handler. I was still young, but I knew better than to believe he'd ever get involved with me. Still, that didn't stop my mind from pining for the strength of his arms as he pushed the mass of snow from the LaSalle's windshield or noticing the way his lips quirked into a smile at the sight of the winter wonderland laid out before us and borrowed straight from a page of some Russian novel.

Levin shook the snow from his sleeve, fisted his hands into his pockets. "This could take a while. It might be quicker if you took the subway home."

Going home and claiming a decent night's sleep before my morning shift at the library would have been the responsible thing to do. And I'd always been responsible, mostly, at least.

Levin had bent down and started using those marvelously strong hands of his to shovel out his car. Now, I knew it was infinitely more acceptable to let my gaze flick to and from someone rather than stare at him like I wanted to devour him. So I caught stolen glimpses of Levin as I packed snow between my palms—enough for a modest-sized projectile—before launching it at his back.

Bull's-eye.

Levin exclaimed something in what might have been Russian, whirled around with tiger-quick reflexes as if to attack. His eyes widened when he saw my snow-covered hands. "I never thought my sweet Elizabeth capable of such a dastardly sneak attack."

My sweet Elizabeth . . .

(Catherine, if only he'd known the impure thoughts I'd been having about him, he'd have realized that I was certainly *not* sweet.)

I adjusted my scratchy woolen hat more firmly on my head, bent down over the snowbank to hide the flush stealing over my cheeks. "Woodenheaded Russian." I shook my head and *tsked* under my breath while I scooped snow away from the LaSalle. "As anyone can see, I'm helping dig out your car."

Which I was, just before I kicked a spray of snow his way. It wasn't ladylike, but then, I've never claimed to be a lady.

"You know, I am not actually Russian." He dropped the offhand bit of information while he used those strong and capable arms to compile a snowball—more like a snow *cannon*ball. Levin never spoke out of turn, so I saw this bit of truth as what it was: a small gift. "Also, you asked for this."

With that, he hurled the cannonball my way.

I sidestepped the missile, and gave a triumphant laugh even though I suspected that he'd missed on purpose. "Truce!" I plunged my now-frigid hands into the snow berm and pushed it away from his car's wheel. "This time I really *will* help!"

Levin answered by delving deep into the snow berm to manufacture another snowball. That was the moment our hands touched and suddenly, hidden out of sight, his bare fingers entwined with mine. Our eyes met and we stayed like that. One, two, maybe ten breaths. Pupils widening, lips parting, breath mingling. An entire conversation in that single gaze. Until . . . "Your hands are cold," he said.

Wrong, Levin.

Nothing was cold about me at the moment. Quite the opposite.

I wanted him to pull me closer, to kiss me, to do *anything*. And *everything*.

Instead, he released my hands and stood statue still. The snow fell around us in perfect silence, the streetlights casting a Dickensian glow.

Then the moment melted away like the most fragile and perfect of snowflakes.

Levin bent back over the snow berm and returned to digging out his car. I stooped to help, searching for words and finding none. I mentally flipped through the pages of my journal on human behavior, found absolutely nothing helpful there either. Levin seemed absorbed in his task, yet every so often I felt his gaze scorching the back of my neck.

My hands might have been frostbitten by the time we'd freed his car from its snow prison, but all I could think of was the fever-hot blood thrumming through my body.

I want him. I want Levin.

Because of course, *of course*, I would have feelings for the one man on earth that I could most definitely *not* have feelings for.

(Catherine, it's my duty as an older woman to inform you: love and lust are inconvenient at the best of times. Deadly at the worst of times. Consider yourself warned.)

I straightened, dusted off my jacket with stiff hands that felt simultaneously frozen and on fire. I hadn't realized that in my exertions that two of my coat's buttons had come open, and now set my only partially working fingers to remedy that situation. "Well, I'll be off to the subway then," I said in a stilted voice. "Good night."

Levin's hand caught my wrist. Again, that volt of power that stole my breath, muddled my thoughts. "Stay." He brushed a few crystalline snowflakes from my hair. It wasn't a command or a question, but a request that I could see somehow cost him dear, from a man I desperately wanted to spend more time with.

Stay and we'll kiss right here beneath the streetlight.

Stay and then come back to my apartment.

Instead of saying any of those things, Levin only opened the La-Salle's well-oiled passenger door. "Stay. And we'll go for a drive."

I hesitated, made no attempt to disguise the desire in my eyes, made sure he had seen it before I slid onto the cold leather bench. Usually, when we rode together, Levin meandered aimlessly through the city while peppering me with questions about the Italian Library. This time, the very air between us was alive as he navigated slowly through the hush of the snow-laden city along the Hudson, driving in a straight northern line until we'd passed Riverdale, Yonkers, and Dobbs Ferry.

There were so many things I might have said as our breath fogged up the windows, but what was there that could convince a self-sacrificing, disciplined, and revolutionary man like Levin to want a woman like *me*—selfish, undisciplined, and mostly inexperienced?

When he finally broke the silence, his words brought me teetering to the precipice of breathless exhilaration. "I need you, Elizabeth." His voice sounded unused, speckled with rust. As if each word was difficult to shape.

But his next words pushed me off the edge, plunged me deep

into the frigid waters of despair. They were a bucket of cold water over the fire in my chest, so I was left with only its charred remains.

"You're young and idealistic, the perfect compatriot and a true comrade. Essentially, you are the perfect apprentice."

I dug my fingernails into my palm to focus on that pain instead of the one being carved into my heart. Levin parked the car and let the engine idle. We were facing east, the Hudson at our backs and the weak winter light barely bruising the horizon.

"I know what you feel for me, Elizabeth." I startled at his bluntness and opened my mouth to explain, stopped when I saw his raised hand, the anguish clear in his eyes. "I feel it too."

I turned to face him, feigned insouciance with one leg tucked underneath me as I gestured between us. "Boy likes girl, girl likes boy . . . This should be simple. Instead, I feel as if I'm about to be lectured by a professor who caught me cheating on an exam."

He almost smiled—his lips moved, but the expression didn't meet his eyes. "And did you ever? Cheat on an exam?"

"A woman can't tell all her secrets."

(Of course I never cheated on a test, Catherine. I'd never done anything remotely interesting in my life. Until I'd joined the Party and met Levin.)

He sighed, ran his hands through his hair, the red gone nearly black in the dim lamplight. "This is not just boy meets girl, Elizabeth. I am your *handler*. We are not simply two comrades looking to have a good time; we are undercover agents. Emotions are liabilities, and they make *this*"—he gestured between the two of us—"whatever *this* is, very complicated."

"You're making things more complicated than they need to be." *Please*, I wanted to plead. *Don't push me away.*

"Elizabeth, I can't even tell you my real name. I've done things . . . things I can never tell you." Something in his face shuttered at that. "I swore an oath to the Party, I've made promises—"

"I don't care about any of that. All I care about is . . . you."

He shook his head, eyes tight and those lips I desperately wanted to kiss drawn into a firm line. "I should assign you another handler. Immediately."

"Don't you dare." I forced him to look at me. "I gave up everything to work with you. I turned my back on everyone, even Lee, who was the only friend I've ever had. You don't get to dump me like a bag of midweek trash just because your feelings have become *inconvenient*."

"Cheeky girl." His voice was rough as his thumb traced the line of my jaw. I caught the scent of him, a Siberian pine on a cold winter's night. "Assets are not supposed to reprimand their handlers, you know." God, it was such a small thing—that tiny connection, skin to skin—but I leaned into the touch until he was cradling my face between both his hands, his blue eyes ablaze.

"I must have missed that lesson," I murmured. "But perhaps you can teach me a thing or two." (Who was this daring woman who spoke with my voice, Catherine? I have no idea, but I'm forever grateful to her.) I luxuriated in the glorious heat of him, the way both our breaths hitched when he looked at me.

Closer. I leaned ever so slightly closer . . .

"I want you so badly, you have no idea," he murmured, his voice anguished. "This is a mistake . . ."

"Indeed." We were so close. "The best kind of mistake."

That first kiss was a bonfire, no gentle teasing or calm testing, just a riot of heat that ignited my entire body. Suddenly, I understood what all the fuss was about, why operas had been sung and masterpieces sculpted and poetry written, all odes to this glorious hot-honey feeling that spread from the crown of my head to the tips of my curling toes. I moved to brush a hair from my cheek, and his strong hands framed the sides of my head in a convincing argument. *Stay here*, they said. *Stay right here where you belong.*

"This will lead us nowhere good," Levin managed to say once

we'd finally parted, our foreheads touching and both our chests heaving. His hands were still fisted in my hair, and mine had found their way inside his jacket, seeking *more*. "I am the last man on this earth you should get involved with. I should walk out of your life forever. But I cannot."

"Then don't." I touched his lower lip with my thumb, reveling in his shiver. A thrill ran down my spine—he wanted me and I wanted him; it was that simple. "All I care about is that you're *mine*. No one ever got anywhere by following all the rules."

Levin groaned, tugged me close for another kiss. One that felt like I was being told a secret.

LEVIN AND I danced the most delicate of dances in the months that followed.

We could never live together—Levin insisted for my own safety that I not even know his address—but there were no chaperones, no steady progression of approved dinner dates and dancing venues, only the undeniable, magnetic attraction that we gave in to.

We were breaking every rule—written and unwritten—in the Communist underground playbook. *No close friendships and no unnecessary emotional connections, certainly no falling in love.*

Were we falling in love? I had no frame of reference, at least not for romantic love. And I didn't dare ask Levin for fear that I was merely an excuse to indulge in loose morals, like the men I'd once allowed to kiss me. Perhaps Lee could have told me the answer, but I'd kept my word to Levin and had ceased contact with her.

(In case you're wondering why Lee didn't visit me again, demanding answers, that would have been difficult since I'd upgraded to my own tiny apartment in the three months since that snowy December night. Levin said I was too well-known to the Communists in the Columbia University area, so I was happy for the change of scenery to Greenwich Village.)

Sometimes Levin visited my apartment on Grove Street. It wasn't much, what with its constant smell of fried onions from Mrs. Vitkus's Lithuanian *kugela*, pipes that banged relentlessly, and the stain of black mold that ran down the ceiling in the kitchen. But none of that mattered when Levin was there, even if he never stayed the night. Vlad adored him, would wag his tiny tail and give an eager bark as soon as Levin's signature knock sounded on the door. Red cheeked in front of the radiator that clanged, and sometimes dressed only in our underclothes, we played card games while he sipped Hennessy cognac—fine brandy and the LaSalle were Levin's only extravagances in life—and sometimes we'd listen to Roosevelt's latest address on the radio.

Other times we escaped the city—and the rest of the collapsing world—in Levin's freshly waxed car, wending our way upstate while I concocted fanciful stories about the people and houses we saw along the way. A yellow clapboard with a spotty yard packed with rusting bikes housed a woman who had taken in children abandoned during the Great Depression, a mansion in Oyster Bay with peeling paint contained an old Dutch pair of spinster sisters fallen on hard times, and a haggard woman towing four children behind her had once had dreams of being a Hollywood actress. Sometimes we laughed together; other times we grew somber, realizing how difficult it was for many Americans to make ends meet.

Sitting next to Levin on those car rides, I realized I was one of the lucky ones. Which only made me more resolute that the work I did would count for something. That I could help bring America one step closer to realizing Levin's—and the Party's—dreams of equality and a good life for everyone.

With all the time Levin and I spent together, bit by bit, I was putting together a picture of who he really was. Intensely knowledgeable and generous, with obsidian-sharp attention to the details of any situation. His favorite color was an unassuming navy blue, and he harbored a secret passion for listening to opera. He loathed mushrooms in any form and preferred to sleep on the right side of the bed. I could know these current preferences and dislikes, but those wonderfully expressive lips of his turned downcast whenever I nosed about his past: his favorite childhood memory, whether he'd spent any time in Russia, how he'd gotten the lightning-shaped scar on his right forearm that I so loved to kiss. "You know I cannot talk about these things, Elizabeth," he would say.

"For my own safety," I would grumble. "So you keep telling me."

"It is better that you do not know me. At least not that part of me, anyway."

My consolation prize of stepping on those conversational land mines was always worth the frustration: as many greedy kisses as I wanted, plus far more when we'd stumble our way back to my apartment, drunk on lust. (Levin's generosity and knowledge continued all the way into my bedroom.)

Not that his name was even Levin, of course. The irony of that fact wasn't lost on me. I'd asked again for that one little gift, but he'd only shaken his head. "To hear a man's name is to truly know him, Elizabeth. And there are parts of me I hope you never know."

"I'm not scared. Of your secrets."

He'd merely brushed a thumb against my lips, his eyes infinitely sad. "You should be."

I WALKED IN for my shift at the Italian Library one sunny morning with my brown-bag lunch in hand and a little extra joie de vivre in my step, my curls still in disarray after parting from Levin with plans to see him again tonight.

There was nothing in my journal on human behavior to explain the way my heart stuttered whenever I heard Levin's voice on the other end of the telephone, how—no matter the number of people between us—I could hone in on his steady approach from the far end of a New York City block before we met outside another new restaurant.

I found myself wanting to impress him, planned to bring home more items than usual from the Italian Library. Except today, I rounded the corner to find the library's main secretary standing at my desk.

Not standing, per se. More like rifling through my desk.

I watched her as I'd watched so many people over the years. That's the one good thing about being invisible—you become an excellent spectator of all aspects of humanity.

First, she inspected my planner, followed by my pencil cup, and then my top drawer. My heart stuttered as I racked my brain to remember if I'd left anything important there, but of course I hadn't. That was the first rule Levin had hammered into my head—never write sensitive information down and never, *ever* throw away anything that might be incriminating. It went without saying that important documents shouldn't be left in desk drawers for busybody secretaries to discover.

That same busybody secretary scowled through her horn-rimmed glasses with such heat that I thought perhaps my spare steno pad might go up in flames.

I walked on silent feet behind her, set my lunch down with a thud. The woman would make a terrible spy, given the way she jumped halfway out of her skin. "Can I help you?" I asked.

"Oh, Miss Bentley." At least she had the decency to look chagrined. Until she sniffed and squinted through her thick lenses at me. "The library director wishes to see you. *Immediately.*"

So much for joie de vivre.

I'd only met the library director—a bookish man (imagine that) with a disdainful, high-nosed manner like one of the pope's guards—when I'd interviewed for the position; the rest of the time he remained closeted inside his office, probably memorizing verses from Dante and waxing poetic about Castiglione's *Courtier* in scholarly journals. The fact that he wanted to see me meant one of two things: either my work had caught his attention or the steady stream of paperwork that left the library each night tucked in my knitting bag had been noticed.

I bit my lip and knocked at his office door, straightened at his terse, "Enter, Miss Bentley."

I waited for him to offer me a chair or perhaps even a coffee, but he merely sniffed and folded his hands over the aging manuscript he'd been reading. "I'm afraid it has been brought to my attention that you entered into employment here at the Italian Library under fictitious circumstances."

That, at least, was unexpected.

"Pardon me?"

He removed a folder from beneath the manuscript. "This article from the Columbia University student newspaper discusses scholarships awarded by the college for that semester." He removed the offending article and passed it my way. "*You* are mentioned in the article." Using two fingers, he pulled the article back toward him. "And I quote, 'I'm attempting to complete my master's degree in Italian, but the college denied me because of my affiliation with the American League Against War and Fascism.'" The glare he leveled at me might have frozen the Hudson. "You are *anti-Fascist*, Miss Bentley, which means you are no friend of Italy or this library."

I vaguely remembered being interviewed for Columbia's paper, couldn't recall ever actually reading the article itself. My mind raced. I *had* to keep this job, for Levin, for the Party, for myself. "That was written in 1935, four years ago. Things change—"

"Please pack your personal belongings, Miss Bentley, and leave the premises immediately."

"You can't fire me." As soon as the words left my mouth, I knew how wrong they were. Of course he was within his rights to fire me. Any argument I might have made stood on ground less stable than quicksand. Worse, if he knew what I'd been doing during my time at the library, he would be justified in pressing charges.

"Ms. Smith has your wages ready. Please do not cause a scene."

Instead of further argument, I made a rude gesture as I left his office, stopping only to fling my steno pad, some paper clips, and my meager salary check that Ms. Smith handed me into my lunch bag before storming out the main entrance and back into the balmy spring air.

"What am I going to do now?" I asked myself. My sole purpose in supporting the Party had been supplying Fascist documents. Without that position, I'd never have met Levin.

I served no purpose now. There was nothing I could offer the Party.

And Levin?

What use would he have for me now, unemployed and without a single connection that would benefit him or the Party?

Maybe he just wants me.

I knew better than to trust that quiet voice that whispered in my mind. After all, I'd lived long enough to realize that people only tended to keep you around as long as you were useful to them.

"I'M NOT FEELING well—I might have the flu." I coughed dramatically for emphasis over the telephone line once I'd finally returned to my building and had the operator connect me. I was looking forward to the day when I might have a phone in my own room— Levin and I no longer communicated through a go-between— instead of having to use the shared one in the hallway, especially as wizened Mrs. Vitkus from downstairs gave me a hand motion to hurry my conversation. "I'll let you know tomorrow if I can meet as planned."

Tomorrow would give me an entire day to formulate an idea for where I was going to find gainful employment *and* a way to benefit the Party and Levin. Not enough time, but better than the few hours I had now.

I must have paced at least a mile back and forth across my apartment but still hadn't come up with any solutions, when there was a vehement knock on my door. I thought at first it was Mrs. Vitkus, come to borrow another egg for her Lithuanian *kugela* (which I was convinced was the only recipe she knew), or perhaps my landlady, although rent wasn't due for another few days.

Either would have been preferable to reality.

"Open the door, Elizabeth," Levin said from the other side. "Arguing will only waste your breath."

I considered pretending I wasn't home, but that seemed childish. Especially as Vlad gave an excited yip from his sentry position at the door, his head cocked in question: *Why aren't you letting him in?* "Don't you ever listen?" I asked Levin as I undid the latch. "I told you I was sick."

Levin stepped inside and refastened the latch behind him. "I *always* listen; I did not believe you." He held up a brown sack. "I did bring chicken soup, just in case. Perhaps you can tell me the real story while we eat."

I crossed my arms in front of me and perched on the couch with a scowl. Normally, I wanted to spend every moment with Levin, but not when I hadn't had time to concoct a plan. "The story is I'm sick."

He pressed a dry hand to my forehead. "There is no fever. And you did not sound sick on the phone."

"Really? With all that coughing?"

"Yes, your performance would have put Vivien Leigh to shame." He sat opposite me, leaned forward with elbows on his knees even as Vlad hopped up next to him. "Never fib to a spy. What is going through that head of yours?"

A dozen tall tales unspooled through my mind—that a maiden aunt of mine had died, that I had female troubles, that I'd been tailed on my way home from the library—but I didn't want to lie to Levin.

Not anymore. Perhaps I could lie to others, but I wanted him to be the one person who knew all there was of me, the good *and* the ugly. Who knew it and still accepted me in spite of it.

Everyone needs a person like that.

"I was fired from the library today, for being an anti-Fascist." I couldn't look him in the eyes. The words tumbled out, faster and faster. "I know that means I no longer have anything to contribute to the Party, but if I could just have some time, I'll figure something out. I'll go back to working for the Party, writing the newsletter, cheering at rallies . . . whatever they want. Only please don't be upset with me."

And please don't break off this—whatever this *is—between us.*

This was it, the test of why Levin was with me. Was it because I was useful to him as a Communist or was I merely a Party-sanctioned dalliance? Or, hope against hope, was it because he simply wanted me?

I waited for him to rant about this setback, but instead he leaned in and clasped my face between his hands in one surreal moment. "Why would I be upset with you? You silly, wonderful, clever girl. Now this means you can work for me. Would you be willing to do that?"

(Would I have been willing to crawl over shards of broken glass for this man, Catherine? You better believe it.)

Still, I didn't want to seem too eager. This agreement I had with Levin was still feather delicate. "I need to know the job parameters first."

"Of course." He leaned back, draped one arm over the back of my sofa as if he were enjoying this as much as I was. Which I suppose he probably was. "Well, you will have to see your favorite Communist much more often than you do now."

"A hardship," I interjected. "But one I'm willing to bear."

He rolled his eyes heavenward toward the black stain of mold on the ceiling, winced. I was fairly certain it was spreading until soon it would be creeping down the walls. "Second, you will have to give up the comforts of this palace. I found a brownstone at 58 Barrow that you might like. With a fireplace, which is essential. Without mold. It allows dogs, provided they are fiercely loyal like this little man here." He ruffled Vlad's ears, cut his gaze to me. "How does that sound?"

"Well, I was rather attached to the leaky faucet and the window that doesn't latch, but with time I can overcome my sorrows." I found I enjoyed sarcasm, at least with Levin. Then a new concern occurred to me. "What exactly will I be doing? For you, I mean?"

I half expected him to say I'd be his kept woman, and wasn't sure how I'd respond, not when I had a box of degrees sitting under my bed. Levin's arms fell to rest on the back of the sofa, the fingers of one hand idly playing with my curls. "I need someone who can do research, but also more important tasks. Would you be willing to act as my mail drop and courier, receive mail and cablegrams for me? Travel to Brooklyn to retrieve messages sent from international Party contacts?"

To hell with sounding too eager.

"Yes." My heart pounded against my ribs. I felt there was some invisible line here that I was crossing. That I *wanted* to cross. "Yes, to all of it."

"Elizabeth, we could build a network the likes of which have never been seen before. At least not here in America." Levin got up, began to pace. It was the same compact pattern as always: six feet forward, followed by six feet back. Neat, sparse, and barely contained, just like the man himself. "I will need to train you," he continued. "Things like how to avoid bugs on phone lines and how to store documents, how to lose a tail. How to fight your way out of a corner, use one-time pads to make radio transmissions back to the Center. To be a real spy."

(Catherine, I look back and hear the warning in his words. Except back then they only made me want to dance with glee.)

"Do you accept, Elizabeth?" he was asking, looking down at me. "Will you be my apprentice?"

I need you, Elizabeth. You're young and idealistic, the perfect compatriot and a true comrade . . . You are the perfect apprentice.

Apprentice, lover, compatriot . . . I'd have been his chief confessor, his exorcist, and his whipping post if he'd asked.

I tugged him back to the sofa and moved closer, hitched up my skirt and sat astride him, reveling in the way his eyes went molten. "Just say the word and it's done," I said.

(And that, Catherine my dear, is how I started my career as an honest-to-God Russian spy.)

ШПИОН
THE SPY

||||||||||||||||||||||||||||||||||||||||||||||||||||||||||||||||||||||||

There is no peace for a revolutionary except in the grave . . .

—Elizabeth Bentley, *Out of Bondage*

6

"Am I supposed to be impressed?" Cat asked.

It had been less than three hours since she'd knocked on Elizabeth's door, and the kitchen timer had dinged nearly fifteen minutes ago, yet Elizabeth had ignored it and kept talking. Cat was weary of sitting, weary of the stale smell of Lucky Strikes. Most of all, she was weary of Elizabeth Bentley beating around the bush. Was she really trying to make Cat sympathize with the way she'd fallen in with the Communists? "I know you were a spy." She'd inched her chair closer to the kitchen table during Elizabeth's recitation, now tapped on the table with the barrel of the gun for emphasis. "That doesn't change the fact that you tormented my mother and ruined my life. Or other people's lives."

"Perhaps not." Elizabeth's lips drew so tight they almost disappeared, save for the poison-red lipstick that had bled into the spiderwebbing around her lips. She was hand-cranking a can of tuna for George Washington, who enthusiastically wove his way through her legs. It seemed ridiculous that a traitor had named her pet after one of America's greatest patriots, but then Cat supposed that was probably why she did it—perhaps for the irony or maybe to try to convince herself of a rabid case of patriotism. "But I hope now you have some understanding for why I chose the path I did."

Cat stood and rolled her shoulders, the gun still cocked in her hand. "You can justify and prevaricate all you want, but it doesn't change the despicable things you did. You said it yourself—all villains think they're good. I like Levin, but I sure as hell don't like *you*."

"I've scarcely scratched the surface about Levin," Elizabeth said. "And you came here ready to kill me, so I suspect you're biased. It's hardly fair to pass judgment before my tale is told."

"You may be right." Cat shrugged. "But I'm the one with the gun."

Not that I'm sure I could use it. Or that you've convinced me not to.

She stopped for a moment, imagined what her mother would think to see her now. Hell, even what her best friend Shirley would think to see her pointing a gun at another woman. *What the hell do you think you're doing, Catherine Gray? Put that thing down this instant!* Of course, Cat wasn't exactly on speaking terms with Shirley, given the knock-down, drag-out fight they'd had just before the funeral. If only Shirley hadn't married such a worthless excuse for a husband, and then made it worse by rationalizing the bruises he gave her. *God, I wish I could call you now, Shirley, just to hear a friendly voice. Maybe I'd even apologize for making a scene at the funeral and demanding that you leave that miserable son of a bitch.*

"What's stopping you from ending all this right now?" Elizabeth dropped the tuna can on the ground so hard that George Washington jumped back. "Put a bullet between my eyes and be done with this. Spend the rest of your life in a federal penitentiary or six feet underground. What do I care?"

Cat hadn't expected that. "Do you *want* me to kill you? Because it would certainly be faster that way."

Elizabeth exhaled, the sound laced with exasperation as George Washington slunk forward and tucked into his tuna, eying both of them warily over each bite. "God, Catherine, you're so *young*. There are worse things than dying, you know. And more unpleasant ways to go than being shot."

Cat had to work to keep her expression neutral. Once again, nothing with Elizabeth was happening the way she'd rehearsed. "No one calls me Catherine," she said, buying herself a few moments to get her mind in order. "Just Cat. Or Cathy."

"Catherine is a perfectly respectable name. If you want me to butcher it to some ridiculous nickname—one that you'd share with George Washington's species here—you may as well shoot me now."

Was there anyone else in the history of humankind who, when threatened with the loss of their very life, became *more* bossy and cantankerous? It was almost as if Elizabeth was *trying* to goad Cat into taking the easy way out.

Of course, that didn't make any sense.

"What happened to you and Levin?" Cat tilted her chin toward the living room's fireplace mantel, where a silver frame enshrined a faded black-and-white picture of a man matching Levin's description. Dark hair, boxy jaw with the hint of a one-sided dimple, expressive lips. It was the only photograph in the entire apartment. "Is that him?"

"Yes, that's Levin." Elizabeth's golden lighter was suddenly in hand. *Click click click.* Cat tried to make out the design—some sort of eagle, perhaps—before it disappeared again into Elizabeth's pocket. "Everything in its time, Catherine. Unless you have somewhere to be?"

They both knew she didn't.

Elizabeth took it upon herself to wind the kitchen timer this time, then raised a hand to the photograph of Levin and stroked a thumb across his jawline. "God, but I worshipped the ground that man walked on . . ."

|||||||||||||||||

SPRING 1939

I'd spent my life being invisible. Now I used that invisibility to become a spy.

"Any tail is cause to abort a mission," Levin often warned me. "You must either bore your tail to tears—walk slowly enough for him to keep up, stop at every red light, and convince him you're up to nothing . . . or you must find a way to disappear."

It had taken weeks of practice, but today I'd finally done it—I'd lost Levin after ducking into the women's waiting room at Grand Central Station and emerging out its second floor. Now I waited for him on a bench in Madison Square Park, filled with triumph, and lit a cigarette and enjoyed the gentle breeze of the pleasant spring. I was a city girl through and through, but even I had to admit there was something peaceful about green spaces: the smell of the grass and the rustle of leaves overhead that were punctuated by a child's cry of delight over the sudden discovery of a ladybug.

Levin found my bench, sat next to me with his eyes closed and his barrel-like legs stretched out in the dappled sunlight. It would have been a perfect image to paint had I been an artist—Seurat's pointillist masterpiece *A Sunday Afternoon on the Island of La Grande Jatte* came to mind—and I found myself wishing for my lavender notebook to sketch a few lines and forever capture such an idyllic image. Except that I'd stopped carrying the notebook with me, hadn't sought the comfort of its entries since becoming Levin's apprentice.

The idyll, and my feeling of triumph, didn't last long.

Levin didn't congratulate me. He just said, "The Soviets have made a pact with the Nazis."

Mouth agape, I stubbed out my Lucky Strike. "Why would Stalin do that? Why would he sign a treaty with that mustachioed little Fascist?"

"Little? Actually, Hitler is taller than Stalin," Levin said, yet his tone and expression were far from joking. He opened his eyes, stared at the sky's blue dome while the gears of his mind processed the new game board that made up the globe, the pieces familiar but in all the wrong places. "Uncle Joe must be trying to keep the wolf at bay awhile longer. It is no secret Hitler wants Poland and Russia's western frontier for lebensraum."

German living space. Hitler had written as much in that terrible Fascist tome of his, *Mein Kampf.* I wasn't a proponent of book burning, but *that* volume would do well to be consigned to the trash heap.

"Even so, I don't understand how Stalin could get into bed with the Nazis!" Guilt surged in my conscience—I'd signed on as a Communist because I believed in a better world. Hitler and the Nazis didn't fit in with that picture, no matter what treaties Russia signed.

"Just wait." Levin drummed impatient fingers across his leg. "Our Man of Steel might be paranoid, but he is not stupid. Stalin is using Hitler, just as Hitler is using him. The pact will crumble quickly, and when it does, Stalin will be aligned with the US again to bring down Germany. And Russia—vast, limitless Russia—will win."

Still, I was dubious. "How can you be sure?"

"I feel it in my gut, and I understand how Russia works. Uncle Joe is stalling to give the motherland time to build up her resources. He knows a war of aggression is coming."

Still, I felt absolutely decimated to be helping a country that was allied with our erstwhile enemy. Yet, I told myself to trust Levin, to be patient as we played a long game. As if I had a choice. "We'll see."

He glanced at the docket I handed him, today's research notes from the New York Public Library along with several unopened letters from Canada postmarked to me but meant for him. "Any important research today?"

I wished I could say yes—Levin had asked me to dig up anything I could find on a leading Canadian Communist, but compared to the colossal events unfolding in Europe, Canada seemed relatively docile. "Nothing much."

Levin thumbed through the packet before tucking it into his inner jacket pocket. He retrieved a slim envelope from within, handed it to me. "Show tickets for later this week. I cannot make it, but I thought perhaps you could take a friend."

I tilted my head. We both knew I didn't have friends.

He smiled, pressed a kiss to my temple. "A neighbor, perhaps."

I unsealed the envelope, found two tickets for the *Only Angels Have Wings* showing at the Loew's State Theatre for Thursday night. The adventure drama with Cary Grant looked entertaining—like any American woman at the time, I'd have watched Cary Grant read from a phone book—but what was even more interesting was the word scrawled in capital letters atop the tickets. Not a word, a *name*.

GOLOS.

My thumb on those five letters smudged their black ink. "Golos?" I asked softly.

I knew what this was—what a gift it was—but I'd have given several years from my life to know whether this was a slipup. Or was Levin sharing this with me on purpose?

I understood the answer from the way Levin's entire face blanched a sickly white.

Not *Levin*, not *Timmy*.

Golos.

His real name—his last name, his family name—was the first true glimmer of summer sunlight on the mysterious dark winter of a man who had become as important to me as the air I breathed.

Or perhaps that wasn't quite fair. I honestly believed that the man I'd come to know these past six months *was* the real man, not a carefully constructed facade. But I knew none of the bedrock that formed who he truly was: not his background, the names of his parents, nor how he'd come to America, what he really did for the Communists. The barrier he'd built kept me from knowing his past, his purpose. It was meant to keep me safe.

Except, this one word—this one name—was a sudden chink in that barricade. Because from those five letters, I could learn *more*.

My friend, my mentor, my lover . . . He suddenly stood up, his movements wooden as I'd never seen them before. Eyes bulging and flicking toward me, one hand rubbing the back of his neck. His jaw opening and closing. Then again.

The signs were unmistakable: *panic*.

Then, before I could say anything, he strode away, steps disjointed like a broken marionette, as if he had been thrown off course for the first time in his life.

"Levin, wait. *Wait*, goddammit." I hated the way my heart turned leaden when he didn't respond, how I jumped to my feet and called after him. "Where are you going?"

No acknowledgment. As if he suddenly had to put as much distance between us—and his mistake—as he could.

I knew the same thought was churning through both our minds as he left me standing in Madison Square Park.

Shit, shit, shit.

I'D WANTED TO know Levin—*Golos*—for so long, and now that I finally had his name, I wished I could shove that information back in that show-ticket envelope and return it to wherever it came from.

Any self-respecting woman, a woman like Lee, would expect Golos to come to her after that scene in the park. If I were Lee, I certainly wouldn't go to Nathan's Famous, where we'd planned to have a quick hot dog supper, and wait for him to appear.

But if I didn't go . . . And he didn't call . . .

Levin—and the underground work I did for him—was my *life*.

So, I reapplied my raisin-toned lipstick, tugged straight the lines down the backs of my silk stockings, and marched myself down to Nathan's. The tiny restaurant was packed, but I managed to finagle a seat at the counter and ordered a five-cent frankfurter and a ten-cent ice cream soda. (A woman facing her own personal apocalypse deserves ice cream, after all.) The hot dog tasted of ash, but I'd make myself swallow every last bite, even if it killed me. If Golos hadn't appeared by the time I was finished, then and only then would I admit defeat and return to my empty apartment.

Three bites of my hot dog remained when I felt someone at my side. "I am an ass," a familiar voice murmured so only I could hear. "A complete and utter ass."

The gravelly sound of that wonderful voice made my heart soar, but I forced myself to count to ten before I swiveled on my counter stool to face him, gave him a steely glare even Stalin would have admired. "I never took you for a man who would run when he was scared."

Because I recognized his reaction today for what it really was: *fear*. But fear of what? That he'd failed somehow, or that by letting me in, he had somehow endangered me? Or that his name was the key that would unlock all his secrets?

Those colossal shoulders sagged. "I know and I am sorry." His voice was so low I could barely hear him over the din of the restaurant. "I was taken by surprise, that is all. I did not look at the tickets before I gave them to you."

"I had to learn your name by accident." My scowl was black. "I wish you trusted me enough to tell me."

"Keeping my name secret was an added layer of protection for you." He flicked a dark curl from my shoulder. "I have never made a mistake like the one I made today. I think something—some*one*— is distracting me."

I sharpened my gaze. "There's a simple solution for that. Two, actually." I stiffened my spine, recited in my head one last time the ultimatum I'd rehearsed so many times as I ticked off his options on my fingers. "One: Trust me and be with me. Two: Don't be with me."

Why did I say that out loud? My lungs burned as I waited for him to exit the restaurant, leaving me behind forever. This moment sat poised on a knife's edge: either we would push further into our relationship than I'd ever gone with anyone—*ever*—or we would throw it all away. The choice depended on the man standing in front of me.

Golos tapped the gentleman in a bowler hat seated on the stool next to me, gestured for him to move down. Once seated, Golos placed both his hands on my knees. That simple touch was a lightning rod that sent an electric current straight to my heart. "It is no choice that you give me, Elizabeth. I must be with you."

I nearly sagged with relief. "Then stop being sloppy."

He smiled. God, I loved that smile.

I'd come here expecting my entire world to return to the dark abyss of loneliness I never wanted to face again. Instead, I would leave with Golos at my side, perhaps with a relationship forged stronger than before.

If I got the next few minutes right, that was.

"So," I said. "What do I call you, O-Man-of-a-Thousand-Names? Timmy? Levin? Golos? I assume the latter is your surname, correct?"

His voice was so low against the din of the restaurant that I could barely hear him. "It means *voice* in Russian. Does the name sound familiar?"

"Should it?"

"That depends on how much you learned of Russian history before you abandoned the Party."

I gave him a side-eye glance. "You mean the Party that my handler demanded I leave?"

He winked. "Your brilliant handler, yes."

"Never heard of him."

His eyes sparked as I popped one final bite of hot dog into my mouth and he paid my bill, then that blue fire guttered. "Golos," he started, "Jacob Golos helped found the Communist Party of America and was one of the three-man Central Control Commission. A *rezident* here in the United States."

I nearly choked on my last bite of hot dog. Felt those hands that I'd trusted—hands I'd let wander all over my body—thump me on the back.

Bent over, I held up a palm to stop him, needed to pause and catch my breath.

I'd been dating—and sleeping with—one of the behind-the-scenes manipulators who had given the orders in Russia's Communist Party.

"Elizabeth, I understand if you want to walk out that door and never see me again." Even I could see that those words cost him dearly. "But if you want to hear the rest of my story, you will find me on the sidewalk."

I watched the man I loved disappear out the doors of Nathan's Famous, felt him take a piece of me with every step. It was frightening to imagine what orders a man like Jacob Golos had given and perhaps even carried out himself.

It is better that you do not know me. At least not that part of me, anyway.

But I didn't want to imagine anything. I wanted to know the truth. And I wanted to hear it from the man himself.

I met him on the sidewalk.

His eyes lit when he saw me, and the stiffness of his posture melted away. I knew then that this thing between us was no casual Party arrangement, that his feelings plumbed as deep as my own.

He actually feared I would let him walk away.

Together, we strolled in the settling twilight while he spoke of himself, the words coming slowly and deliberately, as if they had long ago taken root somewhere deep within him and were only now being brought to the surface.

"I was born Jacob Raisen," he began, his fingers twining with mine. "But no one has called me Jacob in so long I doubt I would even answer if I heard it on the street. I was born to a Jewish family in the Ukraine, but I hardly remember them, was arrested for the first time at eight years old for distributing anti-czarist literature. My parents died soon after, and I was cared for by a printer. It was both the best and worst place for me—that Ukrainian Gutenberg was a rabid Bolshevik and I helped operate his press, soaked up every clandestine screed and bit of bile against the czar. At seventeen, I was discovered and sent to a Siberian prison camp."

"Like Lenin." Gooseflesh rolled down my arms, and my heart ached for the young man Jacob Raisen had been, the horrific conditions he had surely endured while in prison. I'd thought my youth difficult, what with the constant moving and my parents' deaths, the crushing loneliness, but that was nothing compared to the suffering this man before me had survived. I wound my fingers tighter through his, and we continued walking, no destination in mind save the past.

"Two years later, I escaped on foot into China. My feet were bloody ribbons from walking by the time I arrived, but I had decided what I wanted to do. I could not return home, not with Czar Nicholas still on the throne, nor could I stay in China and wait for him to be overthrown. So, I worked a boat to Japan and from there, to America."

"Land of the free and home of the brave," I whispered. Just then, a taxi down the street blared its horn and made us both jump, the sound reverberating up the budding skyscrapers. America certainly wasn't perfect, but it was a far cry from czarist Russia.

"America was better than Russia under the czar, and I became naturalized—and changed my name—while the Great War raged.

However, when Nicholas was deposed during the February Revolution and Lenin returned, I knew it was time to return home. I became the foreman of a Siberian coal mine. No medals, but I received this during a cave-in." He pointed to the jagged lightning streak scar on his arm. He glanced at me, his expression pained. "Are you sure you want to hear the rest?"

I imagined keeping such truths buried for so long—more than two decades—and knew there was only one answer.

"Tell me everything," I said. "Every last bit."

He hesitated, the same emotion I'd seen earlier in the day flickering deep in his eyes: *fear.* Whatever he was about to tell me terrified him. "From there," he finally continued, "the Party took notice and asked if I would serve them as a member of the Cheka."

I felt his gaze on me, shook my head for him to explain. "The Cheka was Russia's secret police," he said. "It is dissolved now—thank goodness—but they were infamous for persecuting deserters with tidy nape-of-the-neck executions at point-blank range. The better to minimize the bloody aftermath of executions."

I barely stopped from gasping, my worship of this man flickering for the first time. What terrible crimes had Jacob Golos—my lover and mentor and friend—committed in the name of something larger than himself?

I held up a hand, a universal gesture: *stop.*

"Tell me one thing." I felt myself waver, forced myself to plunge ahead. "Do you still do the things you did in the Cheka here? Do you hurt people?"

An emphatic shake of his head. "My days in the Cheka are over, and I never want to repeat them. I am a different man now, Elizabeth. I swear it." His eyes carried another layer of that message: *Please don't ask me what I did back then.*

I'd commanded that he tell me everything, but *this . . .* ?

Honestly, I had no idea how much more I could bear to know.

"I was part of the Cheka," he continued, "but I got out as quickly as I could. After years at home working for the secret police, I followed the Party's order that I return to the United States and found the Communist Party of America." He paused, inhaled as if steeling himself for more. But how could there be *more*? "And then . . . I was married."

"Married?" I reared back. How had I not known this, not thought to ask? I took a step back, needed the sudden distance between us. "And are you still married?"

His eyes were infinitely sad. "I am, but not in the way you imagine. I have no excuse for keeping such a thing secret. Celia was a fellow comrade in my unit. We were matched by the Center."

"What does that mean?" I ground out. My fingernails dug into my palms. "You were *matched* by the Center?"

His shoulders slumped. "It is a common practice, especially with the Center's most valuable members. Sometimes it is done to balance personalities. Other times, two people are paired so one can keep an eye on the other."

"You'd spy on each other?"

"The Center is a well-oiled machine with many cogs. It recognizes that sometimes the machine requires a matched pair to keep those cogs operating properly."

That seemed so cold, so clinical. "And where is Celia now?"

"In Russia." He rubbed an overlarge hand across his haggard expression. "It has been years since I have seen her, Elizabeth, and I swear on everything I hold dear—my beliefs, my homeland, my love for you—that our marriage was in name only. I never thought I could have this happiness I have with you, thought I was born and would die to serve the Party. But now . . ."

"Wait . . ." I stopped, forced him to turn back. "You love me?"

His lips turned up, palms open at his sides. "I thought it was obvious—I am a fool for you, Elizabeth Bentley. *Da, ya lyublyu tebya.*"

Then he surprised me once again, kneeling before me on the

sidewalk, his hands in mine and face turned up like a supplicant. Suddenly, I didn't know what to do. "Get up," I whispered, but he refused.

"You deserve far better than me, Elizabeth—I have done terrible things and I will never, *ever* deserve you. But if you walk away from me right now, I will go to my grave loving you. You are my other half, the wife of my heart."

In that moment, with his eyes shining up at me with such naked honesty and hope, I might have absolved him of any and all sins. I'd never been loved like this, had never dared hope I'd find someone who worshipped me like this. It terrified me, yet so did the thought of spending my days without him.

"I love you, too, you big Soviet ox," I managed to choke out. "Now stand up and kiss me."

He did. By God, he *did*.

Until a passing businessman whistled and we broke apart, my cheeks flushed and Levin's eyes glazed in that way that told me exactly what would have happened had we not been standing out on the streets of New York.

Once recovered, we kept walking, this time at a more languorous pace. Levin's arm draped around my shoulders, and mine was around his waist, each of the two edges of our bodies seeking the perfect fit and warmth of the other. "Now I know what you did in the past," I finally managed to say. "But what is it that you do these days?"

He ran his thumb over the back of my hand in a way that sent a delicious shiver up my spine. "Today I control the entirety of Party contacts here in America and collect all of the information gathered by our domestic targets."

Dear God in heaven . . .

I stopped walking, gaped anew at the man beside me.

I wasn't in love with a highly placed member of the early Party. I was with the man still *in charge* of the Party.

(Catherine, I would learn later that Jacob Golos was so highly placed that he attended all the top Communist meetings here in America while hidden behind a black curtain to keep his identity secret. Like a Bolshevik Wizard of Oz, only instead of smoke and chimera, he was masterminding intelligence gathering, covert operations, and espionage.)

He offered a sheepish smile. "As an American citizen I am uniquely placed to carry out a different sort of operation that no one else is suited for. Are you familiar with World Tourists?"

"You mean the travel agency on Fifth Avenue?" The only reason I'd heard of it in a city this large was because it was the lone American company allowed to make travel arrangements in Russia, which meant that every Party member I'd encountered who had traveled to Russia—or hoped to one day make the trip—had gone through World Tourists.

"Ah . . ." He patted my arm. "You only *think* it is a travel agency." Suddenly, he raised his hand and hailed a yellow cab. "After tonight you will know everything. Come."

It didn't take much to guess that we were headed to Fifth Avenue.

Part of me wondered how I'd react after he let us into the empty agency—the business had closed for the evening, although there was still lukewarm coffee to be had—if he showed me a hidden basement or a secret passage. Or perhaps a room full of listening devices or a chest full of encrypted letters.

Instead, after thanking the elderly elevator operator and locking the office door behind us, Levin merely offered me a chipped mug of lukewarm Folgers followed by one travel brochure after another. "A one-month tour of Russia complete with three-day cruise down the Volga River," I read between sips of mediocre coffee while he scribbled something. Levin handed me a fresh brochure, this time with a slip of paper bearing his handwriting tucked inside. It fluttered to the ground.

Ya lyublyu tebya.
Ti amo.
I love you.

I smiled, pocketed the paper. No matter the language—Russian earlier tonight, now Italian and English—there were no sweeter words. I still couldn't believe this man had chosen to say them to *me*. "You're distracting me."

"I know not what you mean." Yet the playful light in his eyes said otherwise. "Keep reading."

"The 'Great City' tour or a one-week package sightseeing in Leningrad. 'From the moment of his arrival, the visitor from abroad comes across entirely new human relationships and realizes he is in a society that has never before been known, a society whose members are bound together by the common idea of refashioning their own backward fatherland.'" I gestured to the travel posters and stacked brochures on every desk. "I'm going to have a difficult time believing you if you try to convince me this is a NKVD interrogation site, or even a Party headquarters."

Golos took the brochures from me, left them fanned out on a desk. "This is all real and the profits are substantial. World Tourists supports all the Party's East Coast enterprises, including the *Daily Worker*."

I tapped a finger against my chin. "Let me guess . . . It's also your cover."

He winked. "Clever girl. Indeed, the front of World Tourists helps me secure American passports for Party members and the Comintern."

Comintern. Also known as Communist International, which advocated world Communism. The connections this man possessed were staggering.

"To what end? Why do you do this?"

"My mission is simple: to build a better world. And the foundation of that goal is ensuring that Russia and America never fall to the Fascists."

"But some people must know you're a Party member. A high-ranking one at that."

Golos started organizing the pamphlets, by both size and color. I could see his personality reflected here at World Tourists just as it was in his own appearance—his shoes might be worn and the linoleum scuffed, but everything was orderly and in its place.

"I admit, it is an untenable position," he finally said, turning to look at me. "That is why I need you, Elizabeth, to know all of this and perhaps learn some of what I do in case . . ."

I didn't like the way he trailed off. "In case what?"

"One day my past catches up with me. It would not take much for the FBI to learn what I do here, if they only thought to look."

I shuddered, unwilling to think of what could happen if the FBI came knocking on Jacob's door. Spying on one's country was treason, and no matter what nation you hailed from, there was only one sentence for traitors: death. That Jacob trusted me of all people meant that I hadn't been wrong in choosing him—there was no question that I would do as he asked.

"Is that everything?"

His gaze plumbed to the very core of me. "Everything important."

I bit my lip, set down my coffee. "You said earlier that Jacob doesn't feel like you anymore. If that's true, then I will call you something different." I leaned against the desk and thought to my limited knowledge of Russian diminutives, mostly gleaned from slogging my way through Tolstoy and from what I'd picked up from Party members who'd adopted Russian monikers. "Yasha is the familiar form of Jacob, right?"

He nodded. "It is."

"Then you shall be Yasha, but only to me. It will be my code name for you."

"Yasha?" His smile this time reached his eyes. "Yes, Yasha and his *umnitsa*. I approve."

"*Umnitsa*?" The Russian word tasted delicious on my tongue. "What does that mean?"

"It means *clever girl*. For you are my most clever girl, the only one I want by my side."

He leaned over me, dipped his head. The kiss between us this time was hesitant, questioning. It left me wanting *more*. "Are you sure my story has not scared you off?" he asked.

"It will take far more than that to scare me off you." In fact, I wanted nothing more than to be *with* him, right here and right now. I fisted his shirt, parted my knees, and tugged him so he had to stand between them, felt the crinkle of the love note he'd written in my pocket. "But no more secrets, Yasha. At least not important ones about who and what we are." After all, I was under no illusion that Yasha would be able to tell me every specific about his operation's day-to-day activities. "Those are my terms."

His lips touched mine again, teased them open in a way that made me glad there was a sturdy desk to lean against. Finally, he pulled me into the solidness of his body, that place where I fit so perfectly with my legs wrapped around his. "*Da*, my clever girl. I accept your terms. For now, and always."

MAY 1940

The Nazis invaded Poland, plunging the world into war, before striking Denmark, Belgium, and finally France with the terrible lightning of Hitler's blitzkriegs, but still, Russia kept its uneasy pact with Germany. In the meantime, Yasha began my spycraft training in earnest, although he warned me its principles would often be different in the field. He taught me to check for intruders at my apartment by numbering scraps of paper in a random order known only to me and slipping them into the doorframe, how to use one-time encryption pads to transmit messages back to Russia, and to open doors with a lockpick disguised as a Catholic prayer card that he'd given me for Valentine's Day. Above all, he informed me of the need to always appear entirely *ordinary*. (After all, a spy who *looked* like a spy would never get very far.)

"Normally, I would spend time teaching you to read people, to understand their body language so you can tell if they are lying or what they are really thinking," Yasha informed me after we'd spent the entire afternoon analyzing people's behaviors in Central Park. "But this is your gift—you have a natural instinct that is sharper even than mine."

It was no natural instinct but one I'd honed through years of writing in my lavender journal. I'd pieced together that my main tasks would be gathering information from and about Yasha's contacts. It seemed like a job tailor-made for me, given that I'd spent much of my life researching, taking dictation, and scrutinizing people. My patience had paid off, and I was finally doing something useful. Now, I was on constant alert everywhere, keen to prove to Yasha that I was serious about being a spy. And that I could be a good one.

It was an overcast Wednesday morning when I stepped out of my new apartment, a unit that was part of a furnished brownstone at 58 Barrow that Yasha had helped me find. It was a step—or maybe seven steps—up from the dismal boardinghouse and dreary apartment I'd occupied (not lived in, for I felt as if I hadn't truly started living until now) in New York. I hadn't had much to move, just my clothes, a few mementos, and my violet, Coriolanus, who—although I no longer talked to him—occupied pride of place on the windowsill. As instructed, I carried no identification on me—not a driver's license or even a ticket stub. Just Yasha's latest love note in my pocket (this one in Ukrainian: *Ya tebe lyublyu*) and Vlad, who tugged excitedly on the lead. My first stop was the World Tourists building to pick up Yasha's latest instructions from where he'd hidden them—coded, of course—in a pamphlet meant to appear discarded atop the mailbox. The door was propped open to let fresh air inside, and as I picked up the pamphlet, I overheard the exchange between an elderly man inside and the World Tourists clerk who was helping him. "The Nazis killed much of my family back home in Lithuania, but I am trying to track down those that might have survived," he said through a heavy accent as he wiped his nose. My heart went out to the gentleman, then startled at his next revelation. "And now the Russians have pushed in," he continued, his hand turning to a fist, "lying and promising to 'liberate.' Except Stalin is even more ruthless than Hitler—there will be nothing left of my people when he is through. You Americans don't realize what a paradise we are living in here across the ocean."

I paused, trying to make sense of what the gentleman had said. Except no matter how I turned it over in my mind, his words didn't make sense, but must have been the ramblings of an old man's grief. No one—absolutely *no one*—was worse than Hitler.

Once back on the sidewalk, I followed Yasha's instruction and picked up the pay phone to call him, waiting for any telltale clicking sounds that would mean the line was bugged before asking the operator to connect me.

(Perhaps everyday life had been easier before I decided to become a spy, but it had certainly been far less exciting.)

Yasha's telephone line—his real line and not the Party headquarters I'd called in the early days of working for him—rang and rang until I finally gave up. My nickel jangled in the coin slot, and I tucked it into my pocket as I checked my wristwatch.

Ten o'clock. Just as Yasha had instructed.

I shrugged. Perhaps he'd had an unexpected meeting with a contact. For my own safety, Yasha kept me separate from the rest of his ring of spies, many of whom I'd been told were highly placed in the echelons of American government. It would be faster just to meet Yasha at his apartment on West Thirteenth Street, the address of which he'd finally revealed along with the truth of his identity.

I had forgotten my umbrella and was trying to keep Vlad from excitedly greeting everyone on the street while I nabbed a newspaper from a stand pulling in its wares from the threat of angry gray clouds gathering overhead. All around me, harried businessmen hustled home in woolen Chesterfield trench coats, hoping to beat the onslaught of rain.

TROTSKY IS DEAD, screamed the front headline of the *New York Daily News*.

Leon Trotsky—the same man Juliet Glazer had once accused me of following—had been Vladimir Lenin's closest compatriot and the leader everyone assumed would take over Party leadership back in Russia before Stalin seized power. I stood speechless, eyes bulging at the gruesome photograph of Trotsky's bandaged head and ruined face; the image below that showed the Mexican police holding a short-handled alpenstock pickax. Aghast, I skimmed the rest of the story.

"'I will not survive this attack,'" Leon Trotsky, exiled Soviet leader, whispered last night shortly before he died from injuries after a serious pickax attack. Resigned to death, Trotsky added, 'Stalin has finally accomplished the task he unsuccessfully attempted before.'"

"Mother of God."

Vlad whined, but I shushed him, my mind reeling as the downpour began in earnest.

How can Yasha and I support a man who would order such a cold-blooded killing? What have we gotten ourselves into? And why would we continue working for his party?

Fifteen minutes later and still with no answers, I emerged fully drenched into the brightly lit second-floor hallway of Yasha's building, which smelled of sugar and yeast, compliments of the European bakery on the bottom floor. The key Yasha had given me a few weeks ago still felt shiny and full of promise as I turned the lock and deftly collected the numbered pieces of paper from where they were wedged between the door and its frame before they could fall.

1, 1, 1, 9, 0, 8.

He'd set the numbers to my birthday, would know I was inside when I'd set them in reverse order and tucked them back between the frame from the other side. A secret code between the two of us.

His apartment was nondescript, and everything inside served a purpose. In the living room, the old wooden Truetone radio was always on, a low hum of static or whatever program was playing meant to muffle conversations. Thick curtains hemmed by Yasha's capable hands all ended at least six inches from the ground—the better to eliminate a possible assassin's hiding place.

"Let's get some towels," I said to Vlad as I picked him up. "No dirty paw prints anywhere, all right?"

Towels were in the immaculately scrubbed washroom; the rest of the rooms were neat and efficient, masculine and unexceptional. At least on the surface. The bowl on the kitchen table was full to the brim with walnuts—the shells were perfect for concealing rolled-up sheets from one-time encryption pads before passing them off to other Center agents. And the lime juice and red wine in the cabinet weren't used for drinks but instead as invisible ink and its revealing agent. I also knew that a suitcase at the back of Yasha's wardrobe next to the bed we'd happily rumpled yesterday afternoon—now remade with precise military folds—held a clandestine radio that he used to communicate via Morse code with the Center.

"I'd wager you've been gone almost an hour," I murmured as I toweled off Vlad—who now smelled of wet dog—and noted Yasha's coffee mug and breakfast plate drying on a still-damp towel. At ease in the home of this man I'd come to trust and who I loved for his steadfast certainty in a better world, I let Vlad curl up on the towel while I perused the leather-bound books stacked atop Yasha's freshly dusted fireplace mantel. I knew that the wooden bookends contained hidden cavities that sometimes hid forged passports and other secret documents before Yasha delivered them. Those beautiful books were the one extravagance in an otherwise austere living space—a hefty collection of philosophical tomes in both English and Russian ranging from Karl Marx's *Das Kapital* to John Stuart Mill's *On Liberty*. I picked up Sir Thomas More's *Utopia*—Party approved, as they believed King Henry VIII's adviser had been previewing a Communist paradise—and thumbed through the pages crammed with Yasha's notes in the margins. To my surprise, a key sounded in the lock and Yasha stepped inside, dropping his black umbrella into the stand by the door.

"Elizabeth." He scrubbed a hand over a haggard face, didn't respond to Vlad's tail-thumping greeting. "Now is not the best time."

Yasha had never greeted me—or Vlad—with anything less than enthusiasm. "Are you all right?"

"Please, Elizabeth."

His tone was pleading, vulnerable enough that I had to stop myself from smoothing the worry lines that formed on his forehead. Until he saw the newspaper that I'd left on the kitchen table. Then all the color drained from his face.

"You saw the news?"

"I did," I said. "How could Stalin do such a terrible thing? And more importantly, why are we helping him?"

Yasha's expression twisted, turned suddenly ravaged. "Not Stalin," he whispered as he collapsed into one of the kitchen chairs, head in his hands. "Me."

"What?" That didn't make sense—Trotsky had been killed in Mexico, for God's sake.

"What I am about to tell you cannot leave this room." Yasha glanced up and waited for my nod before continuing. "You understand, as part of my position here in America, I am a courier of all manner of information, often highly classified and potentially volatile if it fell into the wrong hands."

"Information from your American sources?"

"Yes, but also my international contacts."

I waited as he rifled through his inside jacket pocket. "Read this," he commanded.

I knew Yasha burned any incriminating message immediately after reading—it was one of the reasons he'd insisted I move to an apartment with a fireplace. (He'd once told me about an agent who had been ordered to either burn documents or flush them down the toilet; once he became confused and crammed a mass of flaming papers into the toilet, which only resulted in setting the wooden seat on fire.)

So why had he saved this one?

Yasha started pacing, six feet in one direction, followed by six feet in the other—the habit I now knew he'd picked up while locked in the cell of a Siberian prison camp. I was overcome with sudden waves of pity and love, but he only shook his head when I started toward him. "The letter."

It was a crisp envelope without a return address, but the stamp was from . . . Mexico?

I flicked it open, read the missive within.

Greetings, Timmy,

The weather here in Coyoacán is sunny, not a cloud in the sky. Tell your uncle that we found the duck he had mentioned and will make sure it is taken care of within the year. We don't want Starik to have any further worries.

Also, we hope to see you next time we're in New York. How does this August sound?

More to come,
Tom, Raymond, and Mother

I looked up at him. "It's obviously coded. What does it mean?"

Yasha stopped pacing, kept his hands clasped behind his back. "Tom, Raymond, and Mother are NKVD agents working on Operation Utka. The word *utka* means both *duck* and *false news* in Russian. Leon Trotsky—who they see as both a sitting duck *and* a disseminator of false information—is Starik. The word means *old man*." He waited, as if to make sure I was following. "That means the uncle is . . ."

He waited for me to provide the answer, but my eyes merely widened as the entire puzzle snapped together. *Uncle Joe* was common slang in the news these days. "Joseph Stalin."

Yasha gave a terse nod. "Stalin has tried to make Trotsky disappear in Russia for years, removing him from photographs of the revolution and even exiling him. This letter alerted me that the NKVD was planning to assassinate Trotsky. They were only waiting for Stalin to respond in the affirmative once I passed along the message."

"And did you?"

His eyes were raw when he looked at me. "I still believe that supporting Stalin will mean the fall of Hitler. That is most important."

"The lesser of two evils," I whispered, feeling the horror of it froth inside me. Yasha had sworn he'd left this life of violence behind him.

"I would understand if you wanted to leave," he said. "Right now. The safe thing to do would be to leave all of this and never look back."

I contemplated it, really I did. Yasha had warned me that night of the snowstorm that he was the last man I should want to be with, but I hadn't listened.

I deserved a life that was meaningful and that would make a difference, wanted to do my part to help win this war being fought all over the world. I'd never in a hundred million years get that if I went back to working as a secretary surrounded by leering men with wandering hands. A life of drudgery wasn't for me, not when the door to excitement and the man I still loved was wide open.

Despite his past, Yasha was the *only* man I wanted to be with. And I *did* still want to make a difference, to do my part to take down Hitler.

It wasn't the first time I'd had to choose between the lesser of two evils. And it wouldn't be the last.

Pick your poison, as they say.

"You once asked me if I wanted to build a better world," I said slowly. "My answer then was yes, and it hasn't changed. I choose you, so long as you choose me. Safety be damned."

I needed Yasha like I needed air in my lungs, but I also needed him to trust that I shared his mission. I was under no illusion that we'd ever take wedding vows, but still, the words *for better or worse* floated into my mind.

"Always, Elizabeth." He threaded his fingers through mine, placed our fisted hands over his beating heart. "I will always choose you."

"I SEE VLAD has been taking good care of you," Yasha said from where he waited in the hallway of my apartment. He'd taken extra time with his appearance today, his shirt crisply pressed and a pair of new shoes I'd insisted he buy freshly shined. Yet, he'd declined my offer to come inside. Had seemed *nervous*.

"That's because Vlad is my good boy, aren't you?" I asked as I dropped a kiss onto his furry forehead and received a thump of his tail in response. "Yuri from down the hall will check on you tonight, all right?"

Silence stretched as I locked the door and Yasha and I walked downstairs. My nerves were taut after learning that we were scheduled to visit Earl Browder—current head of the Communist Party in America—at his summer home in Monroe. That tension stayed tightly coiled when Yasha unlocked the passenger side of his La-Salle and held my door open.

I smoothed my skirt as Yasha slid onto his seat and rolled down the window to let the breeze combat the sweltering August heat. The sounds of the city passed us by—two people arguing, stray dogs barking, cart sellers hawking nuts and hot dogs and newspapers.

"So, we're meeting with Browder today," I said. "Then what?"

Yasha cleared his throat. "We will meet a new contact—William Remington—an eager student of economics from Dartmouth who has been a Party member for some time and has begun work for the US government. I have not seen him yet, but Browder believes with proper training we can move him into a more productive government agency. Earl wants me to feel him out over lunch tomorrow. However, I was hoping you would help me."

The unhurried way he looked at me made my toes curl in my shoes. Slightly. All right, more than slightly.

"What manner of help?"

"Bill is young and nervous. He is bringing his wife tomorrow, but she does not know about her husband's interest in our covert activities. I hoped you could entertain Ann while I discuss the details of undercover work with Bill."

In other words, sit around and make idle female conversation while Yasha took care of the actual job. "I'm worth more than mollycoddling some wife, Yasha, and you know it. I have no desire to spend an evening chatting about the best way to organize forks for a dinner party or how to make a stockinette stitch."

"Some jobs are more interesting than others, Elizabeth. We do as the Center asks."

I cocked my head. "Do you? Do as the Center asks?"

"What do you mean?"

"Telling me about Trotsky? Bringing me to this meeting with Earl Browder when I know full well that, for everyone's protection, people in the underground are supposed to meet one contact and one contact *only*? You're shattering rules right and left, Yasha. What I want to know is *why*."

"You are my *partner*, Elizabeth. The regular rules don't apply, not to us."

Well. The rush of pleasure at his words made me grin, even though I quashed it quickly. "Then don't make me waste time gossiping with some clueless woman. Give me something *real* to do."

"I will. Afterward, I am taking you with me to stake out a Russian diplomat who fled Moscow to the United States with fifty thousand dollars. We will record the license plate number of the car he is using, probably stolen."

I perked up at that, somewhat appeased, and pulled from my knitting bag a pair of fake bifocals and an ash-blond wig, donning both as my soft disguise for the day. (A soft disguise was a simple facade, always recommended when meeting new contacts, be they up or down the underground ladder. People saw what they wanted to see, and after a life spent studying people and taking notes on their every action in my journal, now I *became* them. I preferred to age myself older—few suspected women of spying, and certainly no one expected a middle-aged knitter to be surreptitiously gathering intelligence. It was easy to slip into someone else's skin for an hour or so—I enjoyed the disguises and playacting and being a woman whom no one suspected was strong enough or smart enough to manipulate a man. Oh, how wrong they were.)

Browder's new summer cottage on a lake near Monroe was a perfectly elegant hideaway in which Yasha told me the CPUSA leader planned to rest and do some writing following his recent release from prison for passport fraud. (Apparently, Browder had thoroughly enjoyed playing chess with the other inmates but didn't relish another term.) The cobblestone drive was framed by graceful flowering trees and possessed a lawn so flawlessly manicured I wouldn't have been surprised to see a gardener measuring each blade of grass with a ruler. I forced myself not to gawk when a butler answered the door, the first time I'd seen such a thing outside novels or the occasional movie. Having servants didn't quite scream *equality*, but my stomach was tied in too many nervous knots to quibble over philosophical matters.

"Comrade Browder," Yasha said cheerfully once we'd moved beyond the entrance foyer. "This is Umnitsa."

I couldn't help beaming with pride just then. Yasha's term of endearment—Clever Girl—had become his code name for me.

"I realize how important you must be to Jacob here and the Party," Browder said to me between puffs on his pipe after he'd ushered us into the dining room, where a large table had been loaded with salads, meat, and cheese. Earl Browder was a big man well on his way to becoming corpulent, with a sort of Santa Claus appeal and a Kansas twang to his voice that made it impossible to find him threatening. Still, in spite of his general air of weariness and flabbiness, I sensed a deep current of vitality and energy pulsing beneath the surface. Yasha called him a good guy, but I suspected he was sharper than freshly shattered glass, given that he was the head of the entire CPUSA. "In all my years," he continued, "Jacob has never introduced me to one of his operatives. Everyone else is just a code name on paper."

There was no mistaking the pride in Yasha's smile. "Umnitsa would do anything to help the Party in our quest to crush Hitler and the Fascists."

I crossed one leg over the other. I'd worn new heels and had clipped a pair of fresh-out-of-the-package silk stockings to my waist-nipping girdle today. I would never be a heart-stopping beauty, but I had a passable—albeit a very upside-down-pear-shaped—silhouette and decent legs. "I would do anything, including helping with this Canadian job. Tell us what needs done and we'll see it through, Mr. Browder."

"Eager *and* enterprising." Browder laughed. "I like this one, Jacob."

"As do I. Umnitsa is very special to me." Yasha looked at me over the rim of his gin and tonic, which I noticed he was only pretending to drink, the better to keep his wits. Plus, if it wasn't pure Hennessy cognac, it may as well have been curdled milk to Yasha.

"I insist you call me Earl—Mr. Browder sounds like I have one foot in the grave. Still . . ." Browder rubbed his chin. "Normally, my wife is home to help me entertain, but I'm afraid she's out organizing a benefit luncheon. I hope you'll understand, my dear, when I ask you to wait in the garden. We've only just met, and I have sensitive information for Jacob."

The request stung a little, but spies and secrecy and subterfuge were my life now.

"Please don't be offended." Browder showed me to the garden after asking if Yasha needed anything else for his comfort. I marveled for a moment at Yasha's importance; Earl Browder was the head of the CPUSA, yet he was treating Yasha with a shade of deference. "I have the highest opinion of Jacob. Any man who can survive a firing squad at the age of eight by playing dead and then walk out of Siberia while still wearing his gulag chains has my utmost esteem."

My heart stuttered and I didn't know what to say, for I hadn't heard those sobering details from Yasha's youth. I suspected he was in no hurry to relive them.

"Jacob Golos is the best man I know," Browder said. "And it's clear he's absolutely besotted with you." I flushed with happiness, but the pleasant feeling didn't last. "However, I have to wonder if this new liaison with you is making him sloppy."

"In what way?"

"Jacob may not tell me your real name, but bringing you here today is a flagrant breach of procedure. Not to mention the Party's first and foremost rule—"

"No relationships," I muttered, having accused Yasha of breaking Party rules on the very drive over here. I fisted my hands in my pockets, where I'd taken to keeping Yasha's love notes. *No falling in love.*

"Where do your loyalties lie?" Browder asked. "To Jacob? Or to the Party?"

"Both."

Browder made a sound deep in the back of his throat. "In my experience, that's not possible. A spy has only a single loyalty."

What could I say to counter Browder's accusation? The truth, I supposed. "We're stronger together, Jacob and me. And together, we serve the Party."

Browder rubbed his chin, seemed to ponder that. His expression wasn't unkind, merely a mixture of concern and curiosity. "I hope that's true, for both your sakes."

Rolling the tension from my shoulders once he'd returned inside, I sat on one of the benches and forced myself to relax into the heat of the day and the scent of summer roses. Five minutes passed, then ten. The afternoon had exhausted me, and I was just considering stretching out along the bench when Yasha rejoined me.

"Are we all finished?" I asked.

"Earl has asked us to stay overnight. I told him it was up to you." Yasha perched on the bench next to me, but I could see his mind was a thousand miles from this pleasant little garden.

Our legs were almost touching, and I scarcely resisted twining my fingers with Yasha's. Except when I looked up, his expression was troubled. Glowering, actually. "What is it?"

He plucked a rose petal from its blossom, shredded the poor thing into angry strips that made the air heavy with its fragrance. "Browder needs sensitive information from one of the Canadian operatives I am meeting next week. Which means I must lure the man away from the rest of his ensemble. They believe they are coming to New York to make a routine handoff of information."

"So? Follow him to the men's room or something. Or get him drunk to loosen his tongue."

"It is not so easy. Browder suspects the man knows more than he is saying. He works for the Canadian War Department, which is actively recruiting for Britain's Royal Air Force. This man might know about the Luftwaffe's capability—perhaps even their weaknesses—now that they are bombing Britain." Yasha shrugged. "Or he might know nothing."

Even without a declaration of war, it was obvious that America was against Germany, which meant we needed to be willing to do anything that would help defeat Hitler. That was what I'd signed up for, and I was willing to see this through. *We're stronger together.* "This information will help us determine Hitler's weak spots?"

"Correct."

"I'll help separate this man from his group. Then you can question him."

I expected Yasha to smile at least. Instead he turned colder than a marble statue. "It will not work quite that way. You understand, this man has a certain susceptibility. To women."

"A susceptibility to women?" I nearly choked on my laughter. "Isn't that every man alive?"

Yasha's face told me this was no laughing matter. "What's wrong?" Ice crackled in my veins. "Why don't you want me on this job?"

Because it was obvious that Yasha was regretting the moment he'd gotten in the car this morning and driven me upstate.

"Browder believes you, not me, could get the information we need." "How so?"

"Because only you can work as a honey trap."

I wrinkled my nose at the unfamiliar term. "What does that mean? A honey trap?"

Yasha held himself so still, so erect. "It means you would sleep with this man in order to get the information we need."

If I hadn't already been sitting, a breath of wind could have knocked me flat over. *No close friendships and no unnecessary emotional connections, certainly no falling in love.* "What?"

Now Yasha dared look at me, his voice tightly leashed. "Men will spill all sorts of secrets across a pillow. It is a common practice among the Party. Even Browder's wife is a former GPU operative whose duty it is to keep him in line and report on him to the Center if necessary."

My very skin crawled, and when I spoke, my voice was strung tighter than a piano wire, each word falling flat. "And have you ever forced one of your contacts to be one of these . . . honey traps?"

"Never." Yasha must have read the doubt in my eyes. "I swear on the soul of my father. I have one contact who chose that line of work, but I would never, *ever* force such a thing on anyone."

Still, my stomach roiled to learn that this was the task of some women in the Party, the same Party that crowed about equal rights for women. No matter how many rights women won or how many amendments were passed, our bodies were still exploited. And what happened when that commodity stopped being beautiful or desirable?

I folded my hands in my lap so tightly my knuckles went white, wondered whether Yasha could hear the coded message my thudding heart pounded out. "And do you want me to go through with Browder's plan? To be a honey trap?"

Yasha's eyes were hollow wells when he looked at me. Not for the first time, it amazed me that I was looking at one of the Party's top operatives in America. Perhaps I would never know everything about Yasha—that mystique might be one of the reasons I loved him—but in that moment I could read every emotion on his face as if I were looking into a mirror. "How could you even ask?" he said to me. "I will never make choices for you, Elizabeth, but you must know that watching you with another man would kill me."

My hands framed his face, my heart pounding into my throat as I pulled him near so I could breathe in the crisp, clean scent of him. The pine-and-snow scent that told me I was *home*. So long as I had Yasha, I would always have my true north, my compass point. "You silly Soviet fool," I managed to gasp before I claimed him in a storm of a kiss that unsettled us both. "Then we'll do things our own way. Like we always do."

"Earl gave us two rooms for the night," Yasha murmured between kisses that shattered my very breath, his insistent hands roving in a way that lit a devastating bonfire deep in my soul's core. "Very proper—two beds."

"Then we should use both of them." I dragged a wanton hand along his thigh. "Unless you were planning on sleeping tonight."

I'm not ashamed to say that we barely made it to the first room.

And yes, we used both beds that night.

Several times.

8

The meeting with the Canadians wasn't for a few days, which meant that Yasha and I tailed the Russian diplomat who had stolen fifty thousand dollars all the way to Hoboken and got his license plate number, which led to his eventual return to Russia. Next, I did my bit meeting with the Remingtons, smiling sweetly when Yasha introduced us as Timmy and Myrna.

The Remingtons were a nice couple, really, perfectly middle-class Americans who blended in like beige at Schrafft's restaurant on Fourth Avenue. Bill might have been a lanky high school football player, save for the thin wire spectacles he wore shoved close to his eyes and his penchant for clearing his throat whenever he was nervous, which was all the time. Bill's wife, Ann—whom he called Bing—was short with hair the shape and color of a brown football. She seemed the steadier of the two.

"So, Ann," I said when the waiter arrived with our plates of egg salad rolls and sliced liverwurst and tomato. (I'd lobby for a place that served hot dogs and hamburgers next time. Choosing the restaurant was a handler's prerogative, after all.) While I stifled my envy as Yasha drew Bill into a far more interesting conversation about troop movements and munitions, I asked Ann, "What are your hobbies?"

"Well, Bill and I were just married a few months ago, so I particularly enjoy crocheting doilies for our new apartment." *Yawn.* I might have carried a knitting bag with me everywhere I went, but that didn't mean I wanted to spend an evening discussing garter stitches and crochet needles. However, the first part of my job was to distract Ann, to allow Yasha to hammer out the finer details of this new partnership with Bill. I contemplated bringing up recipes for homemade bombs, decided that topic was perhaps too avant-garde.

"So, is it true?" Ann leaned forward as if we were swapping recipes. "Are you really a Communist? And Timmy too?"

The way she looked at me, I might have been the bearded lady in a circus freak show.

It was one thing for Ann to know that her husband was supporting the hammer and sickle, another for her to learn that we were recruiting him to spy for Uncle Joe. Still, Yasha hadn't said exactly *how* I was supposed to distract Ann. I took a sip of my water, entirely nonchalant. "Guilty as charged."

"You must be clever, to be involved with that." She gave a simple shrug. "I'm afraid I've never had a head for politics. Although Communism seems so . . . forbidden."

She was waiting for a response, but I gave a carefully orchestrated titter of laughter. "Oh, it's not as exciting as people want you to think. Mostly we just want everyone to have an equal shot at a good life. Rather dull, really."

Says the woman who this morning learned how to forge American passports. Dull as watching paint dry, darling.

Thankfully, Yasha chose that moment to interrupt. "Bill and I have agreed that you'll meet him on your trips to Washington, Myrna, bring him current Party literature and collect his dues. He's especially interested in Russia's aircraft production, allocation, and performance. So he can inform the War Production Board, of course."

Yasha's entire statement was coded and encrypted in double-speak: *dues* meant data that Bill would smuggle out for *us*, and he would be the one informing us of *America's* aircraft production, allocation, and performance, not the other way around. I reminded myself that this information would better inform Russia of where to funnel their massive resources, given that we would all unite in our shared goal of taking down Hitler.

"The War Production Board?" Ann's perfectly plucked eyebrows drew together. "But, Bill, you work for the National Resources Planning Board."

To which Bill offered his first genuine smile of the evening. "Except Timmy here has just found me a promotion. It's perfect timing, what with the baby coming and all. We can certainly put the extra money to good use, right, Bing?"

Ann's pregnancy wasn't showing yet, but her hand stole to her flat belly anyway. I felt a pang of some foreign emotion and didn't have a chance to ponder that before I lifted my water glass in a toast. "I suppose congratulations are in order, then."

Yasha tapped his glass to mine, then to Bill's and Ann's. "To a long and fruitful partnership. May we enjoy many years working together."

(Catherine, sometimes you look back on some innocuous moment in your life and see it for the ticking time bomb it really was. If I could go back and push Bill Remington in front of a bus when he stepped off the curb that night, I would. But I'm getting ahead of myself.)

A FEW NIGHTS after meeting with the Remingtons, I managed to lure Yasha's Canadian spy away from his dinner party at the Soviet pavilion at the New York World's Fair. It was easy—I merely discovered over pickled herring rollmops (the man had a yen for Russian food and Vat 69 scotch whiskey) that he had a penchant for stamp collecting, which had been a hobby of my father's. Or at least, that's what I told him.

After ten minutes discussing the value of a Warren Harding full face perforated stamp versus a Canadian London to London flight stamp—no horizontal mambo necessary to interest *this* man—it was easy for Yasha to corner our mark and persuade him to part with information about the Luftwaffe's aerial capabilities.

Now *that* felt good. Both the intelligence we passed on to Earl Browder about the Germans but also the knowledge that Yasha couldn't have completed the job without me.

In fact, I was doing so well that Earl Browder had taken to singing Umnitsa's praises in his official cables to Yasha. And to Russia.

Umnitsa. Clever Girl.

I loved everything about it.

So, it came as a terrible surprise when Yasha called my apartment one morning before I'd even had my coffee, demanding in hushed tones that I come to World Tourists.

"Immediately, Elizabeth," he whispered. "I need you."

Then the line went dead.

I was just getting out of my taxi—a horrific expense justified only by Yasha's urgent and rare demand—when I balked at the scene before me.

Two uniformed US Marshals exited World Tourists, both lugging heavy brown filing boxes to two waiting trucks, which already contained at least a dozen other haphazardly stacked wooden crates. Four guards stood outside. *Armed* guards.

Shit shit shit shit shit.

Yasha kept all his contacts' information coded and their identities secret from everyone—including the NKVD. Still, I wondered for a panic-stricken moment if one of those boxes contained a file labeled with my code name, whether the FBI would soon be breaking down my door. I'd been to World Tourists several times since Yasha had first exposed the inner workings of the Soviet front. My one relief at being seen there while the place was crawling with federal agents was that I'd had the wherewithal to don a black-haired wig, this time with sunglasses and a fashionable crimson scarf tied around my neck.

But what about Yasha?

What should I do? All the training Yasha drummed into me rumbled around my mind.

Any sane person in this situation would turn tail and walk the other direction. No one would expect a spy whose cover was potentially being blown to stride straight into the eye of the storm.

Except . . . *Never do what they expect. The best offense is an attack.*

"I'm sorry, miss." The first guard stationed at the entrance was built like a solid rectangle, his boxy frame blocking the door. His lined face screamed Sicilian, but his accent was a cauldron of the Bronx. "You can't go inside."

"*Porca miseria,*" I cursed in flawless Italian and bit my lip, waved my hand in imitation of the way so many Italians talked with their hands. I'd freshened up my lipstick and pinched my cheeks before I left the taxi, knowing I could pass for a wide-eyed young secretary. "I took a long lunch so I could get information on a trip. To Russia. It's for my grandparents for their anniversary—the entire family is pitching in."

"You're Russian?"

"Second generation, Russian and Italian," I lied, motioned to the people all around us. "America, you see?"

"You'd do best to find a different travel agency, miss." His gaze slid over my shoulder to the street behind me. "This one is being investigated by the US government."

"Really?" I leaned in, my mouth a perfect O. (Catherine, I swear I could have won an Oscar statuette—*Elizabeth Bentley lands the award for best supporting role as a local secretary who dished up juicy tidbits back at her desk over ham on rye.*) "Whatever for?"

A second agent cleared his throat, gave his companion a pointed look.

"Nothing that would concern a pretty girl like you," the boxy Sicilian answered. "There's a decent travel agency on Broadway—check there."

I recalled Yasha's instruction that I needed to look like everyone else and never appear too inquisitive. That was enough. For now. So, I thanked the agent and headed toward Broadway, let my hips sway just a little. What the guards didn't realize was that I'd walk the entirety of Fifth Avenue as many times as I needed until the feds packed up and left. In the meantime, my thoughts were a tempest.

Has Yasha been taken away? Is he still inside the agency? And how much do they know?

Ducking into an alley, I tore off the wig and dropped it behind a trash can, shoved my crimson scarf into my purse and replaced it with a dull navy one around my natural hair so I might have passed for any Russian babushka. It wasn't a full costume change, but, with a tweak of mannerisms, it was the best I could manage on short notice. On my next perusal of World Tourists, I walked with the hunched shoulders of a woman twice my age, stiffened one of my legs so it dragged a little. When the US Marshals finally left half an hour later, just for good measure, I forced myself to duck into a sandwich shop and waited another twenty minutes. Yasha had said to come immediately, but I had to be smart about this. For both our sakes.

"You sure you want to go up there, Miss Myrna?" Ernie the elevator operator squinted and actually took off his hat when I entered. I suddenly wondered whether it would have been less conspicuous to take the metal fire escape stairs outside. Except Ernie had never been told my real name and I wouldn't match the description of any woman the FBI would be looking for—I'd made sure of that. "I've taken the feds up and down at least a dozen times today." He leaned closer to me, dropped his voice. "It was a *raid*."

"Thank you, Ernie. I'm just here to help. Second floor, please."

Upon arriving at World Tourists, I breathed a sigh of relief to discover the door unlocked, then panicked to realize that meant perhaps there was nothing left inside. For all I knew, Yasha could be locked in a prison cell somewhere.

The interior of the agency was a mess, as if a German howitzer had gone off.

"Yasha?"

I found him at his desk, head cradled in his big hands and his expression distraught. I knelt next to him, afraid to touch him and shatter the relative calm he'd gathered around himself. "What happened?"

He could barely look at me. "The US Marshals subpoenaed me. They had all the necessary paperwork. I was trapped, Elizabeth." He ran his hands through his russet hair and gave a sigh that shook his entire frame. "They must have been planning the raid for weeks, perhaps longer. They are turning everything over to a grand jury."

"Oh, God." I dared touch him now, placed both my hands on his knees. "They have everything?"

"Everything except the names of my American assets. I destroyed or coded every scrap of evidence that might identify them."

Thank God. "At least they're still safe. That's something."

"Some of the material is going to involve our comrades badly. Very badly." His free hand was on his forehead, half covering his eyes as if he couldn't bear to meet my gaze. An entry from my journal came to mind: *hand on forehead to ease tension or to hide eyes after a shameful experience.* "The US government now knows everyone who has ever used World Tourists' services—all of my Party connections, even my friend Browder. My carelessness is going to send him back to jail."

My gut clenching to see him so distraught, I said, "Browder is a grown man—he can take care of himself. What about *you*? What happens now?"

"I committed treason—"

"How? Your spy ring was meant to bring down Hitler and Mussolini, America's enemies. You have *not* committed treason."

For that matter, neither had I.

But Yasha only shook his head, looking forlorn. "No American jury will see it that way, Elizabeth, not while Russia is still allied with Germany. It is only a matter of time before I am indicted. After that . . ."

I couldn't stop the image of Yasha pacing a six-by-six cell, this time not in some Russian gulag but in Sing Sing. Or worse . . . sentenced to a firing squad or the electric chair.

"Let's just think about this." Desperately, I took both Yasha's hands in mine and suddenly needed to hold on to him. "What are we going to do?"

"There is no *we*." Yasha's words sent hoarfrost coursing up my veins. "To the United States government, my clever girl never existed." He looked at me with bloodshot eyes. "I put you in danger just by calling you here today—I did not think, did not know what else to do. But we must be careful, Umnitsa. You must be safe or I would never forgive myself."

"I'll stay invisible," I promised. "Except with you."

I was rewarded by his crushing me into his chest. "You have never been invisible to me," he murmured into my hair. All the power in his embrace suddenly ebbed away. "What am I going to do?"

I merely hugged him tighter. "Whatever it is, we do it together, all right? Every step of the way."

All that remained was to put our heads down and stay one step ahead of the FBI.

We may as well have been trying to dodge a meteor.

BROWDER GOT LUCKY. He was arrested for passport fraud, which is what happens when you have multiple passports under a variety of fictitious names. However, it was a small offense, and he was soon released, free to return to his comfortable life on his lovely Monroe estate.

My Yasha, on the other hand, couldn't wiggle free of the FBI's net. As soon as he finished one testimony, he was dragged back to the New York field office to repeat the ordeal.

He was called before grand juries at least twenty times.

With each one, I watched the strong and confident man who had courted me during a snowstorm slowly unravel until his skin took on a waxy, ashen pallor and a tremor started in his hands. He was like a man going through the motions of life, and not even my kneading the tension from his shoulders each night and forcing him to eat borscht from his favorite Russian deli could ease the way his breath hitched when he walked the stairs to my apartment or how often I caught him rubbing his chest with the heel of his palm.

"Just a twinge," he answered when I asked what was wrong. "It will pass. It always does."

I wanted to be there when the final jury handed down Yasha's sentence, but we both agreed that wasn't wise.

"If I am sent to prison, you must be free of any association with me," he said that fateful morning as I helped him with his tie. The air of his apartment smelled of baking bread from the bakery below, and the sun outside was shining. However, the radio was on to block the sound of our voices just in case his apartment was bugged. His hands were shaking so he couldn't force the knot on his striped rayon tie. It pained me to see such a vibrant man laid so low. "You should be safe in your apartment," he said. "Not here, with me."

It was a risk, being in Yasha's apartment, which was undoubtedly being surveilled. But I'd entered through the bakery on the ground floor and worn an excellent disguise. My hair was wrapped under a vivid purple scarf, and a certain little terrier whom I'd bribed with several sausages and trained to curl up and hold still under my jacket gave me extra bulk. One hand looped underneath and another balanced atop gave the perfect approximation of a woman nearly ready to give birth.

No FBI agent—especially given that they were all men—would expect a woman to enter a bakery immensely pregnant and then exit sans baby. Or for another much older woman to leave later while leading a scraggly rapscallion of a terrier on a leash. I didn't care if they noted the incongruity and wound up confused, only that they couldn't properly identify and then trace me.

"Hush," I said as I helped him tie a proper Windsor knot. "There's nowhere else I'd rather be. Vlad either—he told me so."

Ever so gently, Yasha rested a crooked finger beneath my chin, tilted my face so I had to look him in those damned intelligent eyes. "I can't walk into that courtroom knowing you're at risk. Promise you won't come to court today."

So, against my better judgment, I agreed not to accompany Yasha. "Vlad and I will be here waiting when you get home."

The kiss he gave me lingered an extra beat. One extra moment. To say *good-bye*.

Yasha rubbed Vlad behind the ears. "You be a good guard dog for Elizabeth, yes?"

Vlad cocked his head in question, then scratched at the door just once after Yasha closed it with such cold finality.

"Come, Vlad." I suddenly needed to bury my face in his fur, to let out all my worries and anxiety. And dear Vlad, noble little soul, let me howl until there was nothing left, even licked up the salty tears that had slipped down my chin.

Then, together, we sat down to wait.

If Yasha was found guilty, we would be separated by the cold iron bars of Sing Sing. If, by some miracle, he was acquitted, he'd stride back through his door a free man.

I wrapped my arms tight around myself; my stomach tied and untied itself into knots. I turned off the radio, marveled at the unfairness of it all as life went on as usual for most of New York outside—taxis blaring, people yelling, and pigeons fighting for scraps outside Yasha's window.

By ten in the morning, I'd already knitted an entire scarf.

At noon? I'd taken Vlad out for a walk and bitten my nails to the quick.

When the clock tolled three, I'd worn blisters onto my heels from pacing. (Vlad had decided to take a nap by then, his little feet twitching with innocent dog dreams.)

By five, I'd exhausted myself from jumping at every sound in the stairwell, hoping it was Yasha.

Heartsore and imagining the worst, I finally kicked off my shoes and curled on the couch with a knitted blanket that smelled faintly of Yasha's aftershave. The sun was nearly down, and I'd started to doze—Vlad on my chest—into a fitful sort of half sleep.

Until the door opened.

I laid eyes on the endless tunnels of Yasha's eyes and those wonderful lips I'd kissed countless times.

This time I flung myself at him, couldn't get close enough even as Vlad yipped at our heels. "Not guilty," I breathed. "They found you *not guilty.*" I didn't question the miracle; it was only after I'd pulled him inside and shoved the door shut that I noticed the shadows beneath his eyes and the way his shoulders slumped when he should have been as elated as I was.

He ran one index finger under his eye, a Romanian secret code he'd shared with me that meant *Be careful, we don't trust everyone who is listening.* Once the radio was turned on to mask our conversation, he continued, his voice soft. "The jury never had a chance to decide," he said, and I could see what the words cost him. "I confessed. They indicted me on counts of espionage and violating neutrality laws."

"But . . . they let you go?"

He shook his head. "My attorney orchestrated a plea bargain, and the Party ordered me to accept. It was a fine piece of bribery, really. I pled guilty to failing to register as an agent of a foreign power, and in return the other Party organizations escaped scrutiny. I received a five-hundred-dollar fine. And World Tourists is ruined."

I could only stare, trying to make sense of this new unfathomable reality. All his life, this brave and noble man had been a silent hero first to Russia and then to America, working tirelessly and without credit for the betterment of his government and his comrades, even the world. He had done nothing wrong, yet he'd been accused of being the most despicable manner of criminal. Now he'd confessed. And condemned himself.

I wondered whether he would have been so lucky had he been in Russia, was relieved we would never have to find out.

"Your American assets?"

"Safe. I am grateful for that at least."

His entire empire, toppled in a matter of days, save for his ironclad list of secret contacts. One man's life destroyed; it was only a matter of time before the ripple effects might be felt within the Party, as if one of its hands had suddenly been cut off. But the Party could survive without a hand.

"You were the scapegoat?"

"The Party sacrificed me to protect itself. It is as it should be." He rubbed his palms over the dark stubble on his cheeks, then squeezed his hands into fists as if that might keep me from seeing their tremors. "No one—American or Russian—will come near me now. I am ruined."

Every fiber of me hated what had been done to Yasha, but on some deeper level, I understood the cold logic there. What happened to an individual Communist was unimportant compared to the welfare of the Party. Yasha had understood the risks, just as I did.

"Now what?"

"By now, the NKVD has already discussed with the Center what to do with me. When agents are exposed or they become too visible to be of use, the Center will do one of three things. Recall, arrest, or execute them."

I reared back, appalled.

"Arrest?" I swallowed hard. "*Execute?*"

"I no longer serve any purpose; worse, I am a liability." Yasha's voice was strangely cold, detached as he began pacing his usual six-foot square. I could only thank God and the angels that he wasn't pacing an actual prison cell. "If they deem me too large a threat, I will die of mysterious circumstances. Or, if they feel creative, they may recall me to Russia and then kill me. It is easier to kill a patriot on home soil than on enemy ground."

I was receiving a lesson on international politics that I'd never wanted to learn, realized that while the Party may have given me a purpose in life, there was an entire side to the organization that I'd been blind to. But we were in America, not Russia. And Yasha was an American citizen, which surely gave him more than just a veneer of protection. "Then you won't return to Russia, period. No matter what statues or parades they offer as enticements."

Yasha's chuckle was wry. "But this face would look so fine in bronze, yes?"

Part of my heart grew light to hear him jest—his first joke in weeks—but this situation was too terrifying for real humor. A schematic of sorts began unfolding in my mind.

Could I do it? I thought to myself. *Am I willing to take the risk?*

"You're not useless." I held up a hand to halt his pacing, let the final details fall into place. "Not at all."

It surprised me that Yasha missed this finer point, but then he'd just been through an ordeal that would have broken a lesser man. "You still have your American assets," I said. "So long as you continue producing accurate intelligence, you serve a critical purpose to the CPUSA. *And* to Moscow."

Was that hope that flared deep in Yasha's eyes? If so, it flickered and died before it could smolder to life. "I am a tainted man, Elizabeth. I cannot so much as call my assets without the FBI jumping on them like a pack of rabid dogs." He tapped a finger on the table, the movement growing more rapid, on the cusp of the solution.

"It's true." I waited for him to see the solution to the puzzle. "*You* can't call your assets . . ."

Understanding dawned, but he shook his head. Vehemently. "Absolutely not. You promised to be invisible."

"That was before all this. *I* could call them, meet with them . . . Not right away, of course, but eventually. Once this dies down and the FBI gets distracted with something else. Let me do this for you, Yasha."

I would crawl on my belly through every crackling flame in hell for him. This new challenge seemed minor by comparison, exciting even. I'd gone from surveilling the Italian Library to becoming Yasha's apprentice and was now poised to become a full-fledged handler.

He scrubbed a hand over his face. "You make it sound as if I have a choice. What can I do to dissuade you?"

"Nothing. But you *can* promise to take me out tonight to Moe's for celebratory meat loaf. To celebrate my brilliance."

Yasha let out a bark of laughter, and suddenly, I was in his arms, every last bit of air being squeezed from my lungs. "I love you, Elizabeth."

Yasha's life was in shambles, but I was a glorious crusader helping him find hope amid the rubble. "You'll be careful, understand?" I said. "You'll stay close to home, and I'll do your shopping and take care of whatever is left of World Tourists." I shook a finger at him as he opened his mouth to protest. It was a good idea for Yasha to lie low after his trial, but it was also a perfect excuse for what I really wanted: for him to *rest*. "Then—and *only* then—will I take on your contacts, one by one. This is *not* open for negotiation."

He frowned as if ready to argue, then sighed his acceptance and rubbed his temples. "I accept your terms, dictator though you may be."

"*Benevolent* dictator," I corrected, and was rewarded with a distracted sort of smile.

"I have one further favor to ask you."

"Let me guess . . . You want me to disseminate propaganda to the masses? Rob the Federal Reserve? Kidnap a Supreme Court justice?"

"Nothing so nefarious as all that." He disappeared into the bedroom, and something scraped across the floor. Perhaps a loose floorboard coming up. Yasha returned with a plain filing box and lifted a slim packet of documents from inside. "Take these to your apartment and burn them?"

"Of course." Fortunately, my knitting bag could be pressed into service. It shut after the packet had been dumped inside, but barely.

"The US raided World Tourists, but not my home," he answered, as if he could read my thoughts. "It is only a matter of time. Go now," he said. "Leave through the bakery. Moe's meat loaf will have to wait until Friday. I will send word when it is safe."

That was the moment when I wondered whether I'd made the right choice, whether I truly wanted to live this saber-toothed life of moves and countermoves. It was the same life that had pinned Yasha between its jaws and nearly devoured him.

I didn't waver long. I would do this, for Yasha.

And for myself.

In a world that wanted to turn me into a secretary, I would instead help in some small way to take down Hitler and usher in an era of freedom and equality here in America.

I took a circuitous path home through every theater and subway station on the way—and even a couple out of the way—until my shoulder ached from the weight of my knitting bag. *All clear.*

Once back in my apartment, I started a fire before I'd even taken my coat off.

The obliging kindling caught right away until a cheerful fire crackled and popped in my hearth. I'd thought at first that I'd just feed the flames without reading what Yasha had given me.

In the end, my curiosity got the better of me.

Most were blank forms signed and stamped by New York City, used to obtain birth certificates and passports for Russians as American citizens. But then . . .

Yet another secret. The love of my life was a member of the NKVD.

AFTER READING THE rest of the documents, I now understood that Yasha had been a founding member of the OGPU, the predecessor of the NKVD.

"It's true," Yasha said when I called him from a clean pay phone and confessed that I'd read his files. *No secrets.* "But I steered clear of the worst of NKVD's violence. No secret arrests or executions. Why do you think I came to America when I did?"

It didn't matter if Yasha had fled to America to escape the worst of the NKVD's excesses. The Center had eaten its own. Without even a second thought.

To my mind, this only lent further credence to Yasha's suspicions that they might have put out a hit on him since the raid at World Tourists. In the following days, I took it upon myself to surveil his apartment and World Tourists, donned my frumpiest dress in the dullest shade of mud brown, and tacked a pair of horn-rimmed glasses to the end of my nose. Hair pulled back into a no-nonsense bun at the nape of my neck completed the look I'd stolen from memories of a particularly stern librarian I recalled from grade school.

People see what they want to see . . . Or better yet, what I want them to see.

Which today happened to be a somewhat matronly woman emerging from World Tourists. I'd spent the afternoon taking care of tasks for Yasha, mostly filing the remainder of his dwindling accounts, but I still had one more job, a meeting with the editor of *Hemisphere*, a pro-Communist Latin American newsletter.

To my surprise, on my way to their offices, I discovered it was me—not Yasha—who was under surveillance.

It hadn't been a matter of *if* I would ever find myself being followed, just *when*. This was a risk I had always been willing to take.

Two men in dark suits loitered on the corner across from World Tourists—no briefcases, only cigarettes almost burned down to stubs in their hands. One block later, they were following me, keeping the same distance between us no matter how I varied my pace. I stopped at the next corner and pretended to check my lipstick in my mirrored compact, snuck a look at them, and committed to memory one's bulbous nose and the other's knifepoint chin, both traits it would be nearly impossible to alter. They might be with the US Marshals or even the FBI, but there was also the distant possibility that they were NKVD.

(Catherine, I know that the Ian Fleming instinct would be to run or give chase, but that's idiotic. Either of those mistakes would obliterate any remaining cover I might have had, make me more useless than a trapdoor on a raft. Plus, my particular brand of spycraft wasn't well suited toward sprinting down New York blocks, not given my love of processed meats and not even if my one-inch black pumps *were* my most sensible shoes. No, I had to use my head to get out of this one.)

Four blocks later and in front of World Tourists once again, they were still following me.

It was one thing to read about dodging pursuit, as all the heroes in the murder mysteries did, quite another to find that you had to do it yourself. On instinct, I slipped into the pay phones outside a nearby candy store, determined to remain coolheaded despite the staccato beat of my heart, when one of the tails entered the booth next to mine. *Bold. Which means they're either stupid, or very, very dangerous.*

To buy myself a few moments to think, I dialed a series of random numbers that led to nowhere and ignored the operator. Instead, to steady my thoughts—and my hands—I stared into the rainbow-hued candy store and thought of words, any words.

Candy. Colors. Van Gogh. Sunflowers. Irises. Starry Night.

Steadier, I hung up and collected the nickel that jangled back into the return slot.

I focused on keeping my face neutral while I pulled up a map of the city in my mind, did my best to ignore the roaring in my ears and the way my heart threatened to break free of my ribs.

Broadway to Penn Station. I can lose them by ducking into the ladies' room from the upper level.

Trying to appear nonchalant and even pausing to check my wristwatch, I slipped out of the phone booth and wound myself through the busy maze I'd mapped in my mind, then doglegged to the public library on Forty-Second Street and Fifth Avenue, going in one entrance and out the other.

And heaved a shaky sigh of relief when I confirmed I'd finally lost them.

"Probably FBI," Yasha said when I arrived late and informed him what had happened. "You will never see the NKVD unless they want to be seen. Or unless it is too late."

I wanted to roll my eyes heavenward at his dramatics, but something told me he wasn't jesting. Instead, he came around to massage the muscles that were corded tight around my shoulders. I glanced up when his magical hands stopped, found him pressing the heel of his hand against his chest, his eyes tight.

"What is it?"

"Only a bit of heartburn and a sour stomach. I had pastrami for lunch."

"I'll make you a doctor's appointment tomorrow."

"No. I hate doctors."

"No one likes doctors." I stood and poured his usual tumbler of

Hennessy, neat. Paused, then poured a second. I wasn't a drinker, but today had done a number on my nerves.

Yasha arched an eyebrow. "Sometimes I worry I have corrupted you."

"Why do anything halfway?"

He lifted his glass in salute. "To you, Elizabeth. The woman who outsmarted the FBI today."

I took my first sip of cognac, grimaced and sputtered as it scalded its way down my throat. Yasha thumped my back as if I was choking, then handed me a starched handkerchief from his pocket to wipe the tears leaking from my eyes.

Well, that settled it. Alcohol was *not* for me.

"What are we going to do about World Tourists?" I finally asked once I'd recovered. It had taken nearly a gallon of water to wash down the terrible taste, and my throat still felt raspy.

Yasha swirled the brandy in his glass, meditative. "You finished the accounts today?"

"I did. All loose ends have been tied up."

"Then it is time to move on to the next phase of a very old plan."

"Explain."

"I have thought for a long time about creating a business to handle not just passengers but also freight between Russia and America. It is perfect timing now that World Tourists is too well smeared to function."

"Yasha, that's insanity. You can't think the FBI won't be watching you—"

He drummed his fingers along the table. "All I need is one businessman whose reputation is beyond reproach, who sympathizes with the Party but has no connection to it."

"So . . . you need a leprechaun."

He smiled. "One with a pot of gold. And I've found one. His name is John Hazard Reynolds. Social registerite, millionaire Wall Street broker who got out before the market crashed in '29. Married to the heiress of Fleischmann's yeast fortune. Old money family, with a New York Supreme Court justice for a father. Reynolds himself served in World War I. And best of all?"

"Yes?"

"He contributes to the Party and has agreed to invest five thousand dollars to start United States Service and Shipping Corporation."

I blinked. "Is five thousand dollars enough to start an entire shipping business?"

"No, but Earl Browder will finance another fifteen thousand—anonymously, of course—to make it look like it is all Reynolds's cash." Yasha rubbed his chest, fingers fanned out like a bird's wing. "And there is one more thing."

I rose to make some tea. Cognac was out, and I was still too keyed up from being tailed, craved a comforting mug of something warm between my hands while Yasha unboxed this new scheme. "What's that?"

"We want you to run USS&S. To be the vice president, actually."

I almost dropped the teakettle. "What?"

"Reynolds is the sort of person who likes to sit behind a desk and look important—he is the face of the company—but we need someone trustworthy to do the real work. No one else has the right background. Except you, Elizabeth."

I came around the table, pressed my palm to his forehead, then mine. "I'm not sure which of us is having a fever dream. Or did you hit your head this afternoon? The FBI tailed me today, remember?"

"But you shook them. *And* you covered your tracks; they will lose interest in you soon enough." He held up a hand and started ticking off his fingers one by one. "You have a family tree with roots to the colonies, degrees from Vassar and Columbia, you were educated abroad, speak multiple languages—"

"All true, except most importantly, I don't know anything about running a freight business. Christ, Yasha, I don't even speak Russian."

"It is not running the business, not really. That is mostly a front for running my contacts. You will be the woman behind the curtain, Elizabeth; the center hub for the largest spy ring in North America."

His words sent gooseflesh rolling down my limbs. "It has to be you, Umnitsa," he continued. "I've already rented the company space—the nineteenth floor of 212 Fifth Avenue. With a postcard view of the Hudson over to the New Jersey shore . . ."

An office with a view . . . Only a block from where World Tourists had been. For a job I was totally unqualified for.

Yasha covered my lips with one finger before I could say no. "Say you will think about it."

So I promised—what else could I do?—and followed Yasha to bed. Once the lights were off, he stared at me across the pillow, our noses nearly touching in the moonlight. His face was relaxed, his pupils dilated in the manner of a man who likes what he sees. "You are a rare woman, Elizabeth Bentley." I wished the long kiss that followed would never end; it was the kind that had my every nerve tapping out coded messages to the rest of my body. "I cannot comprehend how I ever lived without you."

I'd never been an easy sleeper, and it took longer than usual to drift off that night, my mind still turning over and over the question of whether I could actually run United States Service and Shipping as Yasha believed I could. I was hovering somewhere between dreams and reality when Yasha's gasp shook me awake.

I rolled over to see him sitting up and panting, beads of sweat at his temples and his face twisted in agony as he clutched his chest. "Help me, Elizabeth."

Then that bull-like body of his crumpled forward onto our bed.

NOVEMBER 23, 1963
4:03 P.M.

Against her will, Cat found herself on the edge of her chair—the backs of her legs peeling away uncomfortably from the brown floral vinyl—as if leaning forward would somehow help her better hear Elizabeth's next words. She wouldn't care less if Elizabeth got struck by lightning in front of her, but somehow, over the course of her tale, Cat had grown attached to Yasha, despite the fact that she suspected she was about to hear his death story.

Except Elizabeth merely fell silent and rubbed her eyes, the skin there worn down to the thinnest crepe. Elizabeth Bentley was only fifty-five, but she looked like a woman well into her sixties. She flicked that ever-present golden lighter a few times and fiddled with the knobs on the Zenith portable radio, which crackled to life.

"President John F. Kennedy's funeral will be held two days from now. Tomorrow, his body will be moved to the US Capitol to lie in state and his casket will be available for viewing by the public."

Cat winced at America's grim new reality, an intrusion she'd been able to temporarily forget, at least while Elizabeth had been talking. "I knew him, you know," Cat said once Elizabeth had flicked off the broadcast. "Well, not *knew* him, but I saw the president once when he came through the Visitors Foyer. On Saturdays, I sell guidebooks at the White House with some of my sorority sisters. I met Mrs. Kennedy a few times—she wrote the official guidebook, of course. I got the position through my school's Catholic Newman Center—I'm Catholic, the Kennedys are Catholic . . ." She sighed, felt the tears prick her eyes. "One more thing destroyed this past week."

She stopped herself, wondered what the hell she was doing. Was she *confiding* in Elizabeth Bentley?

For God's sake, Cat, pull yourself together.

"Nothing good lasts," Elizabeth said. "Don't trust anyone who claims otherwise."

"And Yasha?" Cat knew she was prodding a hornet's nest, but couldn't find it in herself to stop. She was angry and hurt and wanted to lash out. And by God, Elizabeth *deserved* it. "Did he die?"

Elizabeth stood suddenly. "I don't want to talk about Yasha anymore—I never should have mentioned him."

"That's not how this works, Elizabeth. You talk, I listen. You're going to tell me all about my mother, but first, I want to hear about Yasha."

Elizabeth gave a frustrated exhale. "You might as well just shoot me and put me out of my misery."

The timer chose that moment to go off, its strident ring making both of them jump.

Cat picked up the cheap plastic timer. "You tell me about Yasha, and I add half an hour to your time."

Cat held her breath, for she could *see* Elizabeth wrestling with her inner demons and wondered what they were whispering in her ear. Had Elizabeth spun Yasha's tale just to pique Cat's interest? To buy herself more time?

Did it matter, when the outcome of all this was going to remain the same?

Finally: "It's been a long time since I've talked about him."

"Now's your chance." Cat used her foot to nudge out Elizabeth's ugly brown-flower chair in invitation. She felt like she was encouraging a wounded animal not to bolt. "Maybe your last chance, come to think of it."

Elizabeth sat—more like deflated—as if her very bones had been built from hot air and bluster that suddenly evaporated. "Yasha didn't die," she said. "Not that night, at least . . ."

|||||||||||||||||

JUNE 1941

The doctor proclaimed Yasha's sudden collapse was a heart attack. Likely brought on by stress.

Even walking up a flight of stairs now exhausted him, and the sound of his beleaguered lungs kept me awake each night, straining my ears to ensure there was always a next breath. Sometimes I would run a hand over the stubble of his jawline at night and marvel at how brittle even that had become. I had almost lost him and was suddenly terrified at what our future might bring.

I would have moved heaven and hell to make things easier on Yasha. So, of course I agreed to run United States Service and Shipping.

I hired top-notch accountants and impeccable lawyers to write the initial contracts getting the company off the ground and made arrangements directly with the Soviet government through Earl Browder. John Hazard Reynolds was its president on paper, and I was listed as vice president to the tune of two hundred fifty dollars per month, more than three times what I'd earned at any of my prior jobs. Except I wasn't just taking dictation or writing shorthand—I learned all the practical aspects of the business until I could type up a Soviet import license on a Russian typewriter and make up a document package and wrap it myself. Not a single piece of evidence connected Yasha with the company. And because of that faultless conception, the State Department decided USS&S didn't even have to register as an entity of a foreign government.

The only problem was that Russia was still allied with the Nazis.

"Give it time," Yasha murmured into my hair while he held me one dark night. He'd woken to find me staring out the window at the electric-illuminated city, had risen and gently closed the curtains, plunging us back into ink-black darkness. Despite my worries over Hitler and Stalin and Mussolini and Yasha's health, it was nice to feel Yasha stroking my hair and to pretend that he was taking care of me instead of the other way around. "Be patient," he whispered. "We are playing a long game, my little dove. You and me and Stalin. Together, we are going to beat Hitler—just you wait and see."

Then, on June 22, 1941, our usual evening radio broadcast was interrupted with news that Hitler had breached the Soviet frontiers. Apparently, German food shortages and the Führer's immediate desire for lebensraum for Deutschland had overridden any qualms about torching his nonaggression pact with Stalin. Yasha and I held hands as we listened to Molotov's angry proclamation over the radio that this was "an act of treachery, unprecedented in the history of civilized nations. But have no doubts: the enemy will be crushed and victory will be ours."

"See." The triumphant gleam in Yasha's eye that I'd missed these past months returned as he poured us two tumblers—one of Hennessy cognac (despite the doctor's orders, I didn't have it in me to deprive him of this celebratory toast) and mine with apple cider. "I knew Russia would land on the right side of history. To the health of Stalin and Molotov, Churchill and Roosevelt."

We clinked our glasses together and tossed back the drinks, but I hushed him when Washington followed up with a special announcement that the United States would give economic assistance to the Soviet Union to help in its struggle against armed aggression. Uncle Sam and Lady Liberty were determined to beat Hitler and were prepared to do whatever it took to make it happen.

"Which must mean supplying Russia with whatever it needs." I felt suddenly lighter as the twin vultures of guilt and worry finally took flight from their roosts on my shoulders. "Including intelligence."

"*Da*, my very clever girl." Yasha's lips were soft on mine, teasing even. "I do suppose you are right."

In one fell swoop, Yasha and I had seen our positions as secret patriots solidified, albeit patriots that the American government would never know about. In the days and weeks to come, US Service and Shipping was jammed with patriotic Americans sending to Russia presents that ranged from vitamins to shotguns. (The latter had to be rejected for obvious reasons.) America still watched the war from the safety of the sidelines, but everyone rich and poor wanted to help the besieged Soviet Union.

So long as America was in bed with Stalin, we were in the clear.

YASHA AND I had taken Vlad out to romp in Central Park—my energetic bundle of fur had a difficult time being cooped up in my apartment, and Yasha didn't often have the strength to walk him while I was out, although I knew from the fur on my pillow that he let Vlad sleep on my side of the bed when I was gone. It was a fizzy, incandescent sort of July morning where everything seems possible, and I'd brought my knitting bag and a large leather valise with me, placed both on the ground next to the Bethesda Fountain. (Catherine, like the shape of snowflakes, the sound of falling water is totally unique. This means that even as sound filtering inevitably improves—especially on recordings—a fountain will always provide the perfect cover for spilling secrets.)

"Well, Miss Wise," Yasha said. "Are you ready for your trip to Washington, DC?"

My latest code name was a play on Clever Girl, which I enjoyed far more than the prosaic Myrna that I also sometimes used. I looked at him through my dark glasses and tugged tighter the knot on the black scarf at my neck. "As ready as I'll ever be."

You see, Yasha and I had decided it was time I met alone with my contacts; being the freshly minted vice president of US Service and Shipping gave me reason to travel to Washington without the need for convoluted excuses. Not only that, but since America and Russia were now allies, the FBI had lost interest in surveilling Yasha and me.

(Catherine, I will go to my grave singing the praises of the FBI, but even I have to admit that wasn't their finest decision. Even if they had only ever followed me while I was disguised.)

Yasha's *konspiratsia* he'd built up over the years included informers from the Treasury Department, State Department, Office of Strategic Services, even the Army and Navy. I'd spent weeks listening to Yasha describe each of them until I could parrot back with crystal clarity their likes and dislikes, their idiosyncrasies, and the motivations—patriotism, medical bills that needed to be paid, a desire to end this war before America entered it—that led them to spy for him. There were no written records on any of these contacts, not even a sentence on a scrap of paper that could lead the authorities to them. Now I was to be their sole link to the Center.

Yasha beckoned so he might kiss me from the park bench where I'd commanded he remain while I tossed a stick to Vlad. My shaggy little beastie had a penchant for tearing off after sticks, often returning with a new one twice as long as himself. "First, you will meet with William Remington," Yasha instructed, beaming like a proud papa. "And then today, Miss Wise will officially take over the contact of Miss Mary Tenney."

I smiled, the flush of pride warm as sunshine on my skin. Never again would I be a lonely woman eating alone over a hot plate. Now I was working the largest Russian information network in America. And that was something.

"Code name Muse," I said about Mary Tenney, gingerly tossing Vlad his slobbery stick while pulling out the imaginary drawer in my mind that contained Mary's file. I'd met her once in New York during her final meeting with Yasha, but back then I'd been merely a silent observer. "Graduated from Chapel Hill and now works as a secretary for *New York Herald* journalist Walter Lippmann. Relies on her kickbacks from the Party to finance her expensive lifestyle." I knew I had my facts straight, yet memorizing dossiers was different from actually interacting with the people in the field. After all, no matter what my journal said, years of observations taught me one uncomfortable fact: people are unpredictable. I swallowed hard and barely avoided wringing my hands by clasping them in front of me. My flush of pride was replaced with cold worry. "I hope I'm ready for this."

Yasha pressed my palm to his cheek and then kissed my knuckles, his eyes utterly adoring. "Elizabeth, you were born for this. Just be careful with Mary. She is . . . delicate."

Buoyed by Yasha's steadfast confidence in me and with my totes in hand, I kissed him and then Vlad for good luck. "Don't let the dog sleep on my pillow."

"I would never." Yasha's water-blue eyes gleamed with his poorly kept secret. "Although if I *did* let him sleep on your pillow, it is only because I miss you."

When I arrived three hours later at the station in Washington, DC, I knew from studying maps and schematics exactly which exit to take onto the street. And the best route to William Remington's apartment.

"I'm afraid I don't have the full amount of the dues I owe to the Party," he said in a statement that I knew from Yasha was his usual greeting. Beyond him, a baby dressed in only a cotton nappy played with wooden blocks on the floor with Ann, who lifted a hand and wiggled her fingers at me. I wondered how Ann dealt with a husband who seemed perpetually broke. I wasn't sure how much Bill's promotion to the War Production Board paid, but apparently, he had never learned how to write a simple budget when taking his fancy economics classes at Columbia. He held up a finger. "But I do have this for you."

I only pursed my lips. Bill had refused to make a carbon copy of the document, had instead scrawled something or other on the scrap of paper he now pressed into my hand. "It's a formula for making synthetic rubber out of garbage," he whispered. "Please make sure it doesn't fall into the wrong hands."

I have no idea how I managed to keep a straight face. We'd asked Bill to report on aircraft production, and instead he gave me a fantastical, nonsensical formula for *rubber*? Made from *garbage*?

Still, I waved to Ann and thanked Bill, admonished him to pay his dues in full next month, plus this month's shortage. Made a mental reminder to suggest to Yasha that we return Bill to the open Party. The man was more trouble than he was worth.

That out of the way, I took several taxis to get to my next destination. The roundabout journey made getting there more laborious, but it meant that I'd be more difficult to track, although I didn't spot anyone surveilling me. A frisson of excitement rolled up my spine when I left my final taxi two blocks away from the brick office building and walked to the rendezvous point on the second floor.

My knock was quick—four hard raps followed by two taps.

The woman who greeted me was a wintery sort of beauty with a figure to make Claudette Colbert weep with despair and cause men to step off a curb into oncoming traffic, an angelic halo of soft blond curls framing her pale heart of a face, with lively blue eyes and a complexion fresher than newly fallen snow on Christmas Eve. And, yes, her looks were exactly the reason why I had taken extra care with my own outfit this morning—a black-and-white houndstooth day dress with a Valentine-red belt and matching hat—before meeting her. Not that it mattered—I still felt like a

back-alley mongrel next to her pedigree. (The bit of mud and slob-
ber on my hem gifted by Vlad didn't help.)

"Come in, Myrna. It's been so long since I've seen you!" Even
though we'd met once before, Mary Tenney enunciated her prear-
ranged verbal bona fides to reconfirm her identity as she pulled me
inside the office, although no one else was currently in the hallway
of the building. Our cover, should anyone come knocking, was that
Mary and I were old school friends. I'd come to visit her during
work—which would never have been allowed if her boss were present, a fact that added a little clandestine verisimilitude to our story—
and was staying the night with her to catch up on old times. I didn't
miss the way she glanced down both directions of the corridor before she pushed the door closed. And locked it.

Tightly wound, this one.

Yasha had warned me that the NKVD's greatest fear was that an
agent would crack and land in a psychiatrist's office, where they
would spill all their secrets; if there was even the slightest hint of
this, then he—or she—was dropped like a hotcake.

However, in Mary's defense, I might also be high-strung if I'd just
opened the door to the woman who was going to help me pilfer my
boss's office for interesting tidbits on Anglo-American relations and
the war effort. Mary Tenney worked as the personal secretary to the
indomitable powerhouse that was political commentator Walter
Lippmann, the lone wolf who maintained an office in Washington,
DC, and wrote the syndicated "Today and Tomorrow" newspaper
column and who seemed to know everything about international
politics. In the past, she'd memorized data and then rushed home to
write it in shorthand before she'd passed it off to Yasha. This week,
however, Lippmann was out of town, and I was here to help Mary
avail herself of anything the Center might make use of.

"Gorgeous pocketbook." I gestured to a coral-red ruched scallop
bag—its calfskin was the exact same shade as her impossibly high

heels and the fashionably thick bracelets at her wrists—in an effort to put her at ease. "Is it Dior?"

"Louis Vuitton." She fingered the bag like some women would a small child. "I have a weakness for purses."

"I'm jealous." I laughed, held up my unwieldly floral knitting bag. "Hazard of the job, I suppose."

One glance at the office told me I might need an even bigger bag. Papers and files formed several snow-covered Matterhorns on every surface that would hold them.

"Where do we begin?" I asked.

"I started pulling everything Mr. Lippmann has on Operation Barbarossa." Mary thumbed through several yellow files. "Stalin gave a radio address on July 3 regarding Germany's plan to restore czarism and the rule of landlords. Do you really think they plan to obtain slaves for German princes and barons?"

I thought for a moment. "If by princes and barons he means Nazi officials, then yes, I think so."

"And this memo claims that Stalin plans to move Lenin's body from Red Square and put it into storage."

I read over her shoulder and between the lines of the terse message. "That's not good. In fact, that's really bad."

"That they still have Lenin's body on display seventeen years after he died?" Mary blew at a perfectly coiffed curl that had fallen over her forehead. Her breath was tinged with the delicate scent of mint. "I'll say. Can you imagine how bad he must smell?"

"Lenin is mummified," I murmured, deep in thought. "No, it means that Stalin believes Germany will take Moscow."

Mary and I took turns hunched over the typewriter making copies of Lippmann's papers until our backs ached, furiously transcribing any and all documents that looked even minorly interesting. (At least all those mind-numbing typing classes of mine hadn't gone to waste.) Into my knitting bag each paper went; I only paused to smile at Yasha's latest linguistic love note hidden within—*Je t'aime*—before I tucked our treasures deep beneath several skeins of woolen yarn and my latest scarf for Yasha.

But the job wasn't done.

"Had enough for today?" Mary asked once the sun had hit the horizon.

I glanced around at the trove that was Lippmann's office. The opportunity to plunder its secret depths wouldn't come again for a long time—the man rarely took a vacation. "We can come back tomorrow."

"Agreed. After a good night's sleep," Mary said. "My apartment isn't far from here."

Of course, I already knew that: she lived on Olive Street in the Georgetown area. I wished I could go home to New York tonight and off-load the scalding-hot intelligence now burning a hole in the bottom of my bag, but it was too far, plus I couldn't risk registering at a Washington hotel (which Yasha had warned me always to avoid since the FBI kept a strict watch on them). So, I followed Mary, both of us laughing when our stomachs grumbled loudly as we stopped off to pick up cartons of Chinese food. A chicken egg roll and roast pork fried rice for me, chop suey chow mein for Mary.

Her apartment was spacious and well-appointed; the oil paintings of Moscow and Paris that framed an ormolu timepiece and matching candelabra on the mantel screamed of easy money. I glanced at the leather sofa, gave it a poke with my finger. Soft on the eyes, but harder than a park bench. So, Mary cared about appearances.

Which meant she shocked the hell out of me when she sat and pried off her fashionable slingbacks, gave a groan better suited to a sweaty bricklayer after a hard day's work. "I call these my fuck-me shoes." Her grin was mischievous when she caught my look. "Not because they compel men to such action, but because that's what I say every night after I take them off."

I didn't bother quashing my smile. I had a feeling I was going to like Mary Tenney. She reminded me of Lee, except without strings attached to her camaraderie.

"It must be nice having this lovely home to settle into after a long day," I said. In pride of place in the curio cabinet was a beautifully carved wooden cross, breathtaking with its intricate floral design. "It's so peaceful."

Mary followed the direction of my gaze and smiled as she rubbed her stockinged feet. "My father made that—he liked to dabble in woodworking when he wasn't at the office. He didn't survive Black Tuesday—took his own life after we lost everything." She poured me a glass of merlot that I pretended to sip before setting it aside and opening our cartons of Chinese food. "It *is* a lovely apartment, but I always wanted a home full of children with toys everywhere and handprints on the walls. Someone to give that cross to."

That image was so at odds with this luxurious suite of hers that I almost laughed. But this was my first time with a new contact, and I didn't want to offend her.

"What about you?" Mary pointed her chopsticks at me, chow mein noodles pinched tight in their grip. "Do you want the typical American family? Husband, two kids, a dog?"

"Just the dog part, I think." I chewed my egg roll, felt like a bit of a troll at the grease that slicked my fingers and lips. Somehow, Mary was eating her chow mein without even mussing her coral lipstick. "I've spent plenty of time being alone."

"But not anymore."

I cocked my head in question.

"You and Timmy, I mean." Mary gave an elegant wave of her hand. "It was obvious when I met you both in New York that you were . . . *together*. And I saw the love note he left in your bag before you hid it away."

I shouldn't have startled at her perceptiveness—Mary *was* a spy after all—but I hadn't anticipated that she could discern people as well as her boss's memos.

(No good ever comes of underestimating people, Catherine. Take it from someone who knows.)

"Timmy and I trust each other," was all I said. "That's important in this line of work."

"Well, I think it's nice," Mary said. "Everyone should have someone special in their lives. A parent, lover, child . . . We're not engineered to be alone."

Her eyes were so sad then that I felt a sudden urge to embrace her. But I'd never been given toward outward displays of emotion, and I wasn't about to start now.

Instead, I changed the subject.

We chatted about the war—briefly—then the warnings of gasoline rationing and electricity shortages that were planned as American factories began to convert to military production. I tried to imagine Mary Tenney in coveralls with her angelic halo of hair hidden beneath an olive-drab kerchief, drilling rivets or pounding nails. And failed miserably.

In the background, a radio newscaster informed us that Britain was making appeals for Americans to conserve food, the better to export more to support the Allied war effort. It seemed we were tiptoeing closer and closer to the war with each passing week.

Finally, Mary and I yawned our way to bed.

"There's an extra pair of pajamas in the bureau," she said when I'd turned out my valise and realized I'd forgotten mine. Mary had already changed into a billowy candy floss–pink nightgown, her arms and shoulders bare. She'd taken off her coral-red bracelets from earlier, revealing bracelets of an entirely different sort. Slashed across her wrists were scars that spoke of loneliness and veins opened—one raw mark on her left wrist looked only days old. I suddenly understood Yasha's warning that Mary was delicate, and wanted to curse him for his obtuseness. Instead, I caught her watching me and found my throat dry and my tongue a knotted mess. Fumbling for words, I instead opened the bureau's oak drawer to find a pair of men's silk pajamas in deep burgundy. And atop them, a whole package of French letters, the same brand that Yasha used without fail.

I grabbed the pajamas and slammed the drawer as if burned, found Mary studying me with a sad little smile on her face. "Timmy didn't tell you, did he? That I'm a honey trap?"

I recalled Yasha asking at Earl Browder's summer cottage whether I wanted to sleep with the visiting Canadian Party member, how he had mentioned his lone contact who had chosen that line of work. The subject had been dropped and had never rematerialized.

Because I'm with Yasha? Does he shield me?

And I knew then that the answer was a resounding *yes*. I felt a sudden sunspot of anger at Yasha, for *no*, he hadn't told me, and *yes*, that seemed like an important detail. One he must have known I'd ferret out for myself.

"You must be very valuable." I managed to recover my aplomb, setting aside my ethical pangs about the situation. If Yasha knew of this, there must be a reason why he allowed it. And why Mary did it. Who was I to judge her or the Center's methods, which I knew served the higher cause of defeating Fascism? "To the Center, I mean."

She gave me a silver screen smirk. "I might know more than the *rezident* himself. I've been with virtually every spy and Party member since the crash of '29—I could write a book on their secrets, weaknesses, and fetishes: who had a hand in Trotsky's death, which agent needs a triple shot of Stolichnaya to loosen his tongue, who prefers to rough up his women before he has them. Of course, that makes me dangerous, which is why Timmy keeps me his secret—to protect me."

"Is it your choice?" I asked her. Her answer was critical. "The men, I mean?"

"There's a saying my father often said: Sinners make the best saints. I know what I'm doing isn't strictly right, but it's not wrong either. Because it's for a good cause." The ruffled strap of her pink negligee slipped off her shoulder when she shrugged. The rest of the peignoir draped her every curve like she was a fleshy Renaissance model, so it was easy to imagine eager-to-please lovers spilling their secrets in an attempt to impress her. "My father lost everything in the crash of '29, made himself a sinner when he put a revolver to his head and left me alone. I didn't have a lot of options, joined the Party out of youthful optimism, and then a government official I was seeing boasted of intercepting a memo about the failure of the Smoot-Hawley Tariff over cigarettes one night. I thought the information might be valuable to the Party, further proof that America needed to change her ways. Timmy intercepted me—it was my choice to join his underground—and he created an entire legend for me."

(Catherine, a legend is a sophisticated, artificial life story meant to hide a spy's true identity, although it's usually used for illegals operating without diplomatic immunity. Those of us who operated without legends were more exposed, but also had less to hide.)

Mary continued. "I'm two women, you see: Mary Tenney, who works in Walter Lippmann's office, and also glamorous Helen Price, who meets with high-placed international Communists and convinces them to part with their best-kept secrets. All to help my country." A shy smile. "Timmy tells me all the time that I'm his most important asset."

I gave her what I hoped was a reassuring smile. "Which means that now you're *my* most important asset. I'll run things just as Timmy did, with one exception: I don't want you doing anything you don't *want* to do."

She removed the silk throw pillows from the bed, turned down the coverlet. "Don't worry about me. Timmy always let me turn down jobs—men—I didn't want, no questions asked. And he let me take time off when I need to take care of certain things." She gave the French letters a meaningful look, and I caught the way she touched her wrist. "My precautions aren't always fail-safe, you know."

Certain things. God above . . . *she means abortions.*

I knew such things happened—illegally and often in back-alley operations—but suddenly I felt very sheltered from the harsher realities of the world.

Were these choices, those of Lee's mind-numbing factory work and Mary's pillow jobs, really the only options open to regular salt-of-the-earth women? Did it even matter what type of government was in charge?

I was proof that there were other choices, but I was also proof that such exceptions were a rarity. It didn't seem fair that some of us had to get down in the mud and wallow in it in order to build a new world, that we couldn't all stay in the open Party, where the air was clean and wholesome.

Mary planted her hands on her hips and gave me a Hollywood starlet sort of smile. Only this one didn't fool me. "It's a good gig, Myrna, for a woman like me. Plus, it pays for this fabulous apartment."

She was beautiful and broken. No wonder the men flocked to her.

"Call me Elizabeth." It was an utter breach of the rules, but I didn't care. I wanted Mary to have something—one thing—she knew was real and trustworthy. "Please."

"My bed's big enough for the two of us, *Elizabeth*," Mary said breezily as she slipped beneath the lavender-scented coverlet. "The bathroom is down the hall if you want to change."

When I returned, I was in the borrowed pajamas—smelling of detergent and not men's cologne as I'd feared—and Mary's hair was in pink foam curlers that made her look ten years younger. Like the little sister I'd once hoped for. "I have a present for you," she said. "It's not my color, but it's perfect for you."

She surprised me by tossing a small gold cylinder from her bedside drawer my way. The Bésame lipstick I caught gleamed dully in the lamplight, delicate flowers vining their way up the lid.

"Victory Red," she said when I uncapped it to reveal an eye-numbing shade of scarlet. "Men have their army camouflage and their suits of armor, but lipstick is women's war paint, you know."

Actually, I didn't know. "That color looks like sin itself."

She laughed. "It might be. But repeat after me: Sinners make the best saints."

I did as I was told, prompting Mary's glorious smile. On the surface, I may not have agreed with Mary's line of work, but she was a perfect example of how the world refused to operate strictly in black and white. It was becoming clearer to me that everyone who wanted a better world had to sacrifice something in the name of that higher good, be it their morals, their friendships, or their rose-colored view of humanity. (Or maybe that's just what I told myself back then so I could sleep at night?) "Excellent," she said. "Remember to wear that the next time you have to do something that isn't strictly right. So long as the ends justify the means, you're on the proper side of the war."

I was touched by the gift, even if I doubted whether I could really wear so shocking a color. I preferred dull raisin tones or nothing at all, but perhaps I'd use this to become a new, bolder version of Elizabeth Bentley. "Thank you."

Mary lay on her side, pillowed her head with its awkward bunch of curlers on her hands. "You know, there's a new secretarial position opening at OSS. I was thinking of applying."

OSS. The Office of Strategic Services, the new wartime intelligence agency here in America. Also sometimes sneeringly called *Oh So Secret* or *Oh So Social*, especially by our Soviet contacts.

"Is that what you'd like to do?" I asked. "Work at OSS?"

Mary gave a little nod. "Is that all right?"

It was typical to run an asset in place—spy speak for remaining in their current position to continue passing information—for years and years. Having a spy in Walter Lippmann's office was like gold in the bank. However, planting a spy in the OSS would be better than printing money from inside the federal mint.

A surge of worry temporarily overwhelmed my giddiness. Having such a strategically placed asset would also mean it would be harder for me to shield Mary or to preserve her legend. But neither would I shut the door of opportunity in the face of this woman who had already sacrificed much in the name of patriotism.

I reached over, turned off the bedside table lamp, and plunged the room into darkness. "Mary, I think whatever you want would be perfect."

THINGS PROGRESSED FAST and furious after that, like a snowball careening down the Swiss Alps.

I'd come home from Washington, DC, sporting the new Victory Red lipstick Mary had gifted me, along with papers from Walter Lippmann's stuffed into both my knitting bag and a Bloomingdale's hatbox Mary had given me for the job, and even tucked a couple documents into my brassiere when it became apparent that I needed more space.

"What treasures did you bring home today?" Yasha asked when I'd returned. This was, unfortunately, after I'd asked about putting William Remington out to pasture and he'd gently reminded me that Remington's work often corroborated intelligence from other sources, which meant we couldn't siphon Bill back to the open Party. And who knew, Yasha said, but maybe one day he might catch something big for us.

(He'd catch something big, all right, but not quite what Yasha was hoping for.)

In response to Yasha's question, I merely turned the radio to the jazz station and upended my knitting bag. There were political reports from the Treasury, the State Department, and even limited data from the Department of Justice, enough to keep us up all night encrypting everything with one-time pads before transmitting it all to Russia. I doubted if there were many people who were quite as well-informed as we were on what was happening in Washington. "Oh, you know," I answered Yasha with an impish grin. "Just the entire Pentagon."

In response, I received a rather enthusiastic kiss and the warm glow of Yasha's appreciation.

Well. I suppose we didn't spend the *whole* night encrypting documents.

"EARL BROWDER HAS a new contact for you. Nathan Silvermaster," Yasha said the following morning over bacon and coffee he'd made us for breakfast. "Code name Robert."

"Russian-born economist," I remembered. "Member of the Maritime Labor Board and the Department of Agriculture who recently asked to be assigned to the United States Treasury. The weekend parties and musical salons that he and his wife host are the talk of DC." I reached over and snagged an extra piece of bacon from Yasha's plate. All this spying really worked up an appetite for some cured meats. "Has he informed for us before?"

The invasion of Russia by three million Axis troops suddenly meant that all sorts of patriotic Americans were interested in doing anything and everything they could to help the Allies, especially since the United States was still dragging her heels about entering the war. We'd had a sudden influx of informers willing to share American secrets if it would help take down Hitler.

"Silvermaster has been with the Party since 1920 and worked closely with Browder before." Yasha picked up both our empty plates and took them to the sink to wash up. He was more animated than usual today—I'd planned to ambush him with a doctor's checkup by preparing a white lie that I had a sinus appointment and needed him to accompany me—but perhaps his health was turning a corner. "This is a big job, Elizabeth, one that *must* go off without a hitch if Nathan is to trust you."

"I have Mary Tenney in my pocket, don't I? I don't see why Silvermaster will be any different."

"That's because you haven't had to deal with Silvermaster's wife." Yasha's lips drew into a tight line as he glanced back at me. "Helen comes from a family tradition of Communism. Her father was known as the Red Baron back in Russia for his support of the Bolsheviks. She and Nathan have a rather . . . interesting relationship."

I waited for him to elaborate. When he didn't, I only stood and wrapped my arms around his middle, leaned my cheek against the solid wall of his back while he scrubbed the frying pan. Sometimes, at moments like this, I could pretend that we were any normal couple, rather than two spies living double lives.

"I'm sure I can handle the Silvermasters," I finally said.

"Nathan is the hub of a huge network of informers, with access to potentially critical information to help Russia deliver Germany's death knell." Yasha set down the frying pan, planted his thumb in the middle of it before fanning out his fingers one by one as he ticked off Silvermaster's list of contacts. "He has Treasury agents in China, men in the Department of Justice, even contacts in the Air Force. There are rumors he has placed people in the Pentagon. They all report to him."

"And he'll report to *us*." Recent accounts of Hitler's war of annihilation against Russia included hushed reports of special *Einsatzgruppen*, killing units deployed behind the lines in mass-murder operations targeting all of Russia's Jews and Communists, no matter their age or gender. Such atrocities had to be stopped, no matter the means. "I'll take care of it, Yasha."

"I know you will." He touched his nose to mine. "You are going to need a bigger bag this time."

* * *

"You must be Miss Wise." Helen Silvermaster's voice still held a delicious hint of the Old Country, richer and deeper somehow than any Yankee drawl. She immediately made direct eye contact with me, and held it. *A direct challenge after I've known her for all of five seconds. Impressive.* "Do come in."

It's no secret that women scrutinize every aspect of each other upon first meeting, searching for the slightest blemish or fashion faux pas to determine our ranking in some invisible but all-important feminine hierarchy. This woman I needed to win over wasn't classically beautiful, but her face constantly enticed the eyes back for a second look. With a profile like an Italian greyhound, Helen Silvermaster—code name Dora—might have passed for a statuesque version of Katharine Hepburn, so tall and stately it wasn't difficult to imagine the branches of her family tree reaching out to Baltic barons and counselors of the czar. Just the tilt of her head screamed the fact that, had she been born a hundred years earlier, this woman would have been feting kings and dukes in her drawing room. I could feel Helen Silvermaster passing judgment on my sensible one-inch heels, my bulky floral knitting bag, and even the feathers of my Sunday hat. There was no doubt from the way her nostrils flared ever so slightly that she outranked me.

I should have at least worn my Victory Red lipstick, I thought with an inward wince as she offered to take my wool jacket. *Let's hope her spouse is a different case.*

"This is my husband, Nathan Silvermaster." Helen gestured to a dapper-looking gentleman with a Charlie Chaplin mustache, then toward a second, sallow-faced man in his mid-thirties who entered the foyer. "And this is Lud Ullmann, who lives with us."

"It's a pleasure to meet you," Silvermaster offered, speaking slowly and with a pronounced British accent, which made sense given that he'd attended an English school in China in his youth.

"I'm at the Treasury Department." Lud Ullmann offered a dead fish sort of handshake that made me instinctively recoil. He was of average height with receding brown hair and no distinctive features— the perfect face for a spy. (Much like my own, Catherine—I didn't even have this damnable scar on my chin back then.) "Although I'm hoping the Party can maneuver me into the Pentagon."

I avoided wiping my palm on my dress. "I appreciate a man who knows what he wants."

"I assure you, I do." It wasn't my imagination when Lud's gaze flicked to Helen and lingered there a beat too long. How had Nathan Silvermaster not noticed the way his friend looked at his wife as if she were on tonight's menu?

"Please, make yourself comfortable." Nathan gestured toward the spacious living room that was tastefully appointed with chintz lounges and perfectly polished oak end tables.

"So." Helen crossed one slim ankle over the other after Nathan had shaken up martinis for everyone else, a plain tonic water for me. "Miss Wise?"

I waited for the question that didn't come and sipped my drink to have something to do. Her tone told me to be on guard. "Yes?"

"Is that the best you could do for a code name? You don't think it seems too much like a tasteless sort of pun?"

And don't you think you might have learned some manners in the overpriced boarding schools you surely attended?

I offered her a saccharine smile. "We must take our laughs where we can find them. I actually have several names, but you may call me Miss Wise."

This is a big job, Elizabeth. I could hear Yasha's warning in my head. *One that must go off without a hitch if Nathan is to trust you.*

I wasn't worried about Nathan. Helen, on the other hand . . .

"Do you have any children?" I asked Helen, searching for a safe topic of conversation. My question was a risk, but mothers *did* love to talk about their children, although Helen was obviously no ordinary woman. I realized I'd chosen poorly when Helen slanted her Russian-blue eyes at me until Nathan finally answered.

"One," he said, offering a small framed photograph of a blond infant with Helen's curls. "Spitting image of Helen. Yourself?"

"Just me," I responded.

"Lud here is a photographer." Thankfully, Nathan steered our chat into calmer waters. *Bless you, Nathan.* "If things go according to plan, we're hoping to set up a darkroom in our basement. We're not always able to smuggle out intelligence—top secret papers get noticed when they go missing—but photographs . . ."

Now *that* piqued my interest. "And you believe you'll have pertinent information to pass on that might assist the war effort?"

"I'm s-s-sure of it." When Nathan was excited, which I later learned wasn't often, he tended to stutter. "Estimates of German military strength cross my desk on a regular basis."

If I'd been one of Pavlov's dogs, I'd have been salivating as he rustled through his top desk drawer, retrieved a thin folder of papers. Especially when he handed them to me. "Secret estimates of Germany's current military strength. Oh, and it seems FDR might be willing to extend the terms of the Lend-Lease Act to Uncle Joe."

Helen cleared her throat. "Nathan, that's enough."

I maintained a placid expression when I really wanted to tear into the folder and devour every word. "Why do you want to help the Party?" I asked calmly. "This is incredibly sensitive information you're handing over."

If it's accurate, that is.

But my gut told me that Nathan Silvermaster was telling the truth. This first round of information would be carefully vetted, but any experienced contact would know that. Still, I wanted to understand his motivations.

(That's critical in this manner of business, Catherine, but also in life. Get to the bottom of a person's motivations, and you'll be a puppet master making them dance the polka. Or the bunny hop. Whatever dance you want, really.)

"You know, there aren't any medals for what we're doing, but I wouldn't want any even if there were," Nathan answered. "When I die I want to know that at least I've had some part in building a decent life for those who come after me. America and Russia are allies—Helen has a brother fighting for the S-S-Soviets." Agitated, Silvermaster paused when Helen rested a hand on his forearm, and took a deep breath from an atomizer of medicine he pulled from his pocket. Asthmatic, then. "Lud, my wife, and I are only doing what the US government should already be doing—sharing relevant intelligence with our ally. That's the only way the world is going to achieve its paramount goal: to take down Adolf Hitler."

Helen set down her drink and rose, my signal that I was being dismissed. "That's if," she said, "and I stress how big an *if* that is—we decide to move forward with this relationship. Because, Miss Wise, I, for one, have a feeling that you don't quite fit in the Communist movement like the rest of us. And my suspicions are usually right."

Helen's words were a gut punch, probably because she wasn't entirely incorrect. I *had* joined the movement for personal reasons first, but I also strove for a better America and had put my own neck on the line to keep my country from falling into the clutches of Fascism.

"Helen . . ." This time it was Lud Ullmann who nearly growled at Helen.

Just what is his role here? I swallowed an exhale of exasperation. *Gentlemen, tell your guard dog to back off.*

If the folder Nathan had so blithely handed over was any indication, there was a treasure trove of potential information here—documents *and* photos—if only I could make my way through the sticky morass of distrust Helen obviously held toward me.

As she said, that was a big *if.*

"I'll be in touch," I said over my shoulder as I buttoned my jacket and stepped into the entrance foyer of their apartment, Nathan's manila folder safely ensconced at the bottom of my knitting bag. I hated leaving without a promise from the three of them, but Helen stepped past her husband and Lud, hand on the brass doorknob.

"Good-bye, Miss *Wise*."

Then she shut the door in my face.

"WHAT THE HELL did you *do*?"

I'd scarcely stepped inside my apartment when Yasha accosted me, the radio already playing to mask his raised voice. I kicked off my heels and set down my bag. It was lighter than usual with only Nathan's folder hidden beneath my yarn and needles, but certainly that would change with future visits to the Silvermasters.

At least, I *hoped* it would.

"What do you mean, what did I do?" I took off my hat, a gaudy thing with gray feathers that had seemed perfectly lovely when I bought it but now appeared garish after Helen Silvermaster's understated elegance. I tossed the hat on the table. "I took a train down to DC and met with the Silvermasters and Lud Ullmann. What's their story, anyway? Some sort of ménage à trois?"

Yasha ignored my questions, started pacing his usual six-foot square. "Helen called here an hour ago. She is refusing to work with you and demands that the three of them deal only with me."

His words hit me like a bullet to the face. *That bitch.*

"She thinks you work for the FBI," he continued. "That you are trying to expose her husband and Lud."

"You must be joking." I almost laughed out loud. One look at Yasha's face caused my laughter to shrivel and die.

"Do I look like I am joking?"

"No." I swallowed. Hard. "You look like you want to wring my neck."

"These are important contacts, Elizabeth, *the* most important contacts in our cadre outside of Mary Tenney. Your job was to make them trust you—"

The Bolshevik self-criticism Yasha had steeled me with meant that I should be able to view my own actions impersonally and judge right or wrong. And realized that perhaps this time I had aimed too high.

"So Helen Silvermaster hates me!" I pulled the lone file from my knitting bag and flung it across the table, which it skidded over before crashing to the linoleum, spewing the papers that still needed encryption across the floor. To hell with it—Yasha could encrypt them himself. "Did it ever occur to you that I wasn't cut out to take over for you? Or were you too busy covering your own ass after the FBI cleaned you out?"

There it was. All my worries, all my insecurities and anxieties, laid bare for Yasha to see. Still, the ugly truth of my own words surprised me. Somewhere below us, my Lithuanian neighbors pounded a broom handle into their ceiling to demand that Yasha and I cease yelling.

"Did it occur to me?" Yasha's voice was taut, fingers opening and closing into fists. I'd never seen him this way and I didn't like it. "God, Elizabeth, if you knew how many sleepless nights I lay awake, staring at the ceiling and wondering what the hell I was going to do."

Yasha never believed in me. He knew I was going to fail.

"I can't believe you set me up like this." My tone was feral. I wanted to throw things into my bag and slam the door in his face, but this was *my* apartment. If anyone was leaving, it was Yasha. (And yes, Catherine, I realize this all might make me sound petulant, but remember that I was young and American, and neither of those traits are conducive to tolerating criticism.) "You sent me to the Silvermasters knowing Helen was going to hate me—"

"I most certainly did not." Yasha's tone was steel. "I put you in charge of this, Elizabeth—the Silvermasters, all my contacts, US Service and Shipping, *everything*—because you are the only person in this country who can run what has taken me years to build."

I gaped at him, my anger deflating as I struggled to make sense of this about-face. "Well," I said, scrubbing a sleeve across my nose, "I certainly proved you wrong today, didn't I?"

"You can do everything right and still not get the result you wanted." He placed those giant paws on my shoulders, anchored me. "That's all."

"That's *all*? I walk in and you start yelling at me and that's *all*?"

"*Mne zhal'*." His apology and the kiss he pressed to my forehead did little to calm my nerves. He gave a ragged sigh. "I should not have gone off like that. It is only that Nathan Silvermaster and Lud Ullmann must cooperate with us."

"*They* wanted to cooperate. It's only that bitch Helen who hates me."

In for a penny, in for a pound, it seemed. At least with the cursing.

"I will ring them tomorrow, inform them that it will be my final conversation with any of them—no exceptions." Yasha gave a deep chuckle in the back of his throat as he bent down and helped me pick up the contents of Nathan's folder. "And to answer your question, yes, Lud is having an affair with Helen. *And* with Nathan."

"I knew it." Helen Silvermaster had flustered me, but I was still a damned good read on people.

Except running the largest Soviet spy ring in the nation meant doing more than getting lucky guessing at a game of musical beds.

Right or not, I'd still failed. And I couldn't afford any further failures.

I'M NOT SURE Helen Silvermaster ever truly learned to trust me— we were never going to swap gossip like bosom buddies, but she grudgingly agreed to cooperate with me after Yasha's telephone ultimatum.

So I worked to prove myself to the Silvermaster ménage visit by visit, went out of my way praising the documents Nathan and Lud fed me while also rewarding them with bits of nonsensitive intel about how they were contributing to the war effort. I also relayed requests from the Russian Secret Police about subjects or people they were particularly interested in—from performance tests on airplanes to secret deals between the Americans and various governments in exile, anti-Soviet elements in Washington, and Communists the Center was interested in recruiting. Sometimes I passed along the messages via shorthand I'd jotted down, but I often gave over the original Russian instruction sheet so that Helen could feel important translating them over steaming mugs of fragrant Russian chai at the long, wooden table in their kitchen.

I'd looked at Helen Silvermaster as a puzzle to be solved, had realized that her self-importance was the key to finding her good side. So, I kept her busy and thus off my back.

Between Nathan and Lud, we had access to extremely confidential data, which, while it could not be abstracted from the United States government files permanently, could be "borrowed" overnight, then returned first thing in the morning before its absence was discovered. Even better, I provided the men with a clandestine Soviet camera that was hidden in a man's watch and able to produce eight exposures on a one-inch film disc, which they then developed in the darkroom that Lud set up in the Silvermasters' basement. Despite such intriguing gadgets—inevitably, when people think of spies they envision phones hidden in shoes and smoking umbrella guns—in reality, being a real spy entails a long slog of visiting contacts and sifting through so much static, like a television station gone off the air. But then, sometimes you hit the jackpot . . . And I squealed like a schoolgirl on Christmas morning to see the microfilm specs of the B-29 Superfortress that Ullmann was able to photograph once he was assigned to the Pentagon as a major in the Material and Services Division of the Army Air Corps.

It was a fragile détente between the Silvermasters and me, but one I could work with.

And there were more contacts. So many more.

Yasha had turned over virtually all of his contacts to me, but he still kept one or two tucked up his sleeve, which I accepted because I wanted him to feel useful. I remember one distinctly, believed the man at the time to be entirely inconsequential . . .

It was 1942, just a month or so after the sneak attack on Pearl Harbor that had finally plunged the entire country into war. Yasha and I were driving through the Lower East Side, and it was mostly dark—the Army had ordered a dimout since the city's lights silhouetted ships offshore and made them potential targets for enemy bombers—so Times Square and even the Statue of Liberty's torch had been doused. Yasha had hooded the LaSalle's headlights, and the streetlights were dimmed, but he still saw the contact hiding in the darkness. "Wait here while I meet with this one, Elizabeth," he told me, and for once, I didn't argue, given my exhaustion after running to meet contacts all day and so many other days prior.

I sat alone in the LaSalle once Yasha got out, my attention drawn to a government poster taped to a lamppost, a shadowed Uncle Sam shushing the viewer with a reminder: *Don't Discuss Troop Movements, Ship Sailings, War Equipment.* It would have been funny, given that was precisely the information we were gathering on that street corner. I watched as Yasha spoke at length to a tall man wearing a trench coat and spectacles. I recall the spectacles—they caught the meager light from the streetlamp.

"Who was that?" I asked Yasha when he got back in the car.

"An engineer." Yasha rested his arm on the seat back behind me, carefully reversed the LaSalle away from the sidewalk. "Julius is his name."

"Julius . . . ?"

"Just Julius. I'm not sure what will come of it, but I gave him your telephone number so he can always contact one of us."

(And wouldn't you know it, Catherine, but that man woke me out of a dead sleep in the middle of the night whenever he called—I always wondered if Julius could read a damned clock. And I never did learn his last name. Honestly, I've thought more than once that it would have been better if I'd never learned he even existed.)

A life of at the center hub of a spy ring was a life fraught with secrecy and half-truths, shadows and lies. Of always second-guessing everyone.

Mary Tenney was another story entirely.

I'd never had a sister, or a brother for that matter. Hell, not even a cousin.

Mary Tenney was all that plus my friend, the school chum I'd never had during all those years of moving around with my parents. I found myself counting the days until my overnight visits at her apartment, of carefree nights spent eating sweet pickles out of a jar followed by chocolate Jell-O cake afterward, or whatever strange culinary sensations she had in her mostly empty icebox. (Mary couldn't heat up a can of Campbell's tomato soup, so it was fortunate that her contacts were happy to treat her at swanky restaurants. Otherwise, the poor woman would have starved to death.) Sometimes we'd go to a picture show, or stay up far too late varnishing our nails until Mary proclaimed us to be absolute Mary Pickfords. But my favorite moments were when we played chess. She'd taught me to play the game on her scratched wooden board— she always played white, I had black. "It's just like spying, Elizabeth," she said during our first game. "Be nimble and stay several moves ahead of your opponent. And remember, the queen is the most powerful piece in the game."

Chess was like a mirror for my life. And I loved it just as much as I loved Mary.

So, I was worried when she called one Thursday afternoon and informed me she couldn't make our regularly scheduled drop that weekend in DC.

"I'm going out of town for a little bit." The pay phone's line crackled, but I'd just checked it for bugs. "There's something I have to take care of."

"Next week, then?" I was disappointed not to see her, but perhaps I could use the time to finally persuade Yasha to see a doctor. Or we could take Vlad for a drive upstate, stay at a bed-and-breakfast. Rest and relax for a change.

Mary hesitated. "Actually, I'm going to be indisposed for a little bit. Yasha usually let me take as many weeks as needed, but I'm not as young as I used to be. And things are a little more complicated this time."

Understanding dawned.

Mary was only in her early thirties, but I could guess how many times she'd performed this same exact scene over the course of her life.

"Of course," I said. "I'll send the Center a message that you're spending a while in Bermuda getting your health back." I'd need a good excuse, but perhaps I could play to Russia's fears and tell them that I feared Mary was cracking up following her rejection by the Office of Strategic Services. That rejection part was true, for OSS had somehow discovered Mary's "past Communist associations" and shattered her dreams by denying her the position she'd hoped for. This little twist of the truth, along with some concoction of personal difficulties while working for Walter Lippmann, should buy her some time.

"Will you be all right?" I asked. "Is there anything else I can do to help?"

Hold your hand and dry your tears? Just what comfort exactly was one expected to offer a woman about to do away with the child she carried?

There was a long pause. Finally, "Actually, there *is* something. But I'm not sure I could ask it of you . . ."

I waited for her to finish, realized she'd volleyed the conversation back to me. I'd promised her that she'd always have choices, and now she was extending me the same courtesy. Not only that, but I'd had to leave behind a lot of people over the course of this life. I didn't want to leave Mary behind, not when she needed me. "Name it, Mary, and it's done."

IIIIIIIIIIIIIIIII

NOVEMBER 23, 1963
5:37 P.M.

"So, which one was my mother?" Cat demanded. "Helen Silvermaster, Mary Tenney, or Ann Remington?" She picked up her mother's final letter, flicked it with an angry finger. By God, was she ever angry—at Elizabeth Bentley, at her mother, at the whole damned *world*. And yet, at the same time, she was so damned tired—holding so much anger was downright exhausting. "She claimed you sought her out, that *you* contacted her. And that you were the only one who could tell me everything. I've been here more than four hours, Elizabeth—my patience is running thin."

"You know what you need?" Elizabeth stood and shuffled to the cabinets, followed by a contrail of Lucky Strike smoke from the cigarette dangling between her fingers. "Dinner."

"No, what I need—"

"Well, you may somehow be beyond eating"—Elizabeth sounded snappish as she removed a fresh can of tuna from the cabinet and clamped a cigarette between her lips, fastening the metal opener to the can—"but I'm an old woman. And I'm hungry."

Cat scowled—she'd come here this morning not planning on seeing the sunset, hadn't even thought to eat breakfast. She'd never admit it, but she *was* hungry. Ravenous, really.

This time as Elizabeth cranked open the can of tuna, her hands shook—several generous pours of Gordon's gin into her coffee hadn't escaped Cat's notice, although it was still a mystery how the teetotaling young Elizabeth transformed herself into the grizzled gin-guzzler seated across from her. Cat resisted the urge to help when the half-opened can clattered to the ground, spilling tuna juice and bits of fish onto the scuffed linoleum.

Fortunately, George Washington made himself useful by cleaning up the mess.

"Catherine, I warn you, getting old isn't for the faint of heart." Elizabeth spoke around her cigarette as she picked up the can, suddenly sucked in a sharp breath as she touched the lid's sharp edge. "Damn!"

Her finger burst with a geyser of crimson blood.

Without thinking, Cat was on her feet, pressing a kitchen towel to Elizabeth's finger as she set down the can with its sharp metal edge. It was laughable really, given that she still planned to kill this woman. "Elevate and apply pressure," she commanded, hearing her mother's voice in her head. "Sit down and I'll make your damned tuna."

Elizabeth sat. "I usually just eat it with mayo on bread—it's easier to shop when George Washington and I eat the same things. But there's cream of mushroom soup and noodles if you want a casserole. Frozen peas in the freezer too."

You have got to be kidding me. Now she wants me to cook for her?

"Fine," Cat finally said when it became clear Elizabeth was serious. "I cook. You talk. About my mother."

"I'm getting to that, Catherine. But there are some important bits on the way. You can't go from point A to point Z without hitting all the spots in between."

"You're snapping my last thread of patience, Elizabeth."

"I see that. But you'll only hear all of this once, right?"

Cat sighed. In truth, Elizabeth's life seemed like something from a novel, and under normal circumstances, she'd have happily listened. Except these were far from normal circumstances.

"Fine," Cat said. "What's the next part of this saga?"

She expected some sharp-edged retort, but instead, Elizabeth's shoulders caved in and she grew suddenly smaller in her chair. Only her tilted chin remained defiant. *Defiance against what?* Cat wondered. *Me? Life? Her past?*

"Well, I suppose I'm going to tell you how the Party killed Yasha."

NOVEMBER 23, 1963
5:57 P.M.

"It started like any other day," Elizabeth began.

She and Cat had moved to her sparsely furnished living room while the casserole cooked, a jungle of plants on every table, piles of leather-bound books on the floor. Cat caught the titles out of the corner of her eye—*Das Kapital*, *On Liberty*, *Utopia*—and realized that these must be Yasha's well-loved volumes. "Any day when the world ended, that is," Elizabeth continued. "It was Thanksgiving and I was exhausted—I had more contacts than any handler had a right to. This was the golden age of spying, and I was smack-dab in the middle of its hurricane. Fatigue was my constant companion; I was so tired that I could fall asleep on buses, on trains, even standing up. And things were getting worse, so much so that I'd even tried dumping Bill Remington again, but Yasha still refused to cut the bastard loose."

Elizabeth flicked the golden cigarette lighter and then slowly—ever so slowly—set it down and folded her hands in her lap. Yet she couldn't quite sit still, fiddled instead with the gold ring on one of her swollen fingers, its ruby gleaming like the blood she'd recently spilled. "Despite the holiday, Yasha had been upset the entire day. In defiance of the volume of work we were producing—or perhaps because of it—his Russian superiors in DC and New York were pressuring him to hand over the names of his contacts. The Soviets had finally given him an ultimatum: turn over all his sources—now *my* sources—or leave the Party and be forever branded a traitor. He had three days to decide."

"And?"

Elizabeth scowled at Cat. "And what?"

"What was his decision?"

"Yasha fought like hell to keep our contacts, but he worried that the NKVD would lash out in retribution against him, maybe even against me. By that time, anyone with two working eyes—maybe even one—could have linked me to him. We should have been more careful, but we weren't."

"And what did you want?"

Elizabeth looked at Cat like no one had ever asked her that before. "To keep our contacts, of course. They were *ours*: Mary Tenney, the Silvermasters, Lud Ullmann, even nervous William Remington and so many others. We'd grown that network with our own sweat and tears. While the horrific Battle of Stalingrad raged and Russia kept Hitler bogged down in the bloodiest battle in the history of warfare, I systematically funneled to the Center all the sensitive information my contacts fed me: OSS diplomatic cables detailing efforts against Hitler by the French resistance and the Polish government in exile, United States aircraft schematics and numbers, deciphered intelligence cables that the Americans were on the verge of breaking every Russian code following the discovery of a half-burned Russian codebook on the battlefields of Europe."

Cat scowled. "So, you and your contacts all committed treason together."

Elizabeth's glare crackled with hoarfrost. "Listen well, Catherine, for I won't repeat this again: if you care very much for the well-being of your countrymen and you take steps to protect them and their way of life, then you are demonstrating great loyalty, *not* committing treason. For Christ's sake, all you have to do is look at the recent history of Auschwitz and Stalin's gulags to realize that blind obedience to authority is the exact opposite of patriotism."

It was the first time Cat had heard a single critique of Russia pass Elizabeth's lips, a lone sentence that compared Stalin's regime to that of Hitler. But she refused to apologize for her barbed comment. Not to this woman.

Still, Elizabeth scrutinized her so long that Cat nearly squirmed in her seat. "I loved those contacts," she finally said with a sigh. "Hell, I'd even bought them early Christmas presents: jars of Russian caviar and a bottle of scotch for Earl Browder, vodka and caviar for the Silvermasters, and a magnificent lingerie set for Mary Tenney that cost a whopping thirty-five dollars."

"And you loved Yasha."

Cat could see the truth shining in Elizabeth's eyes, especially when she blinked hard and scrubbed a sleeve under her nose. Elizabeth cleared her throat, slid a thick leather-bound book from the very bottom of its pile, and handed it to Cat. "Here."

Cat turned it over in her hands, read the title. "I'm afraid I never made it through *War and Peace*."

Elizabeth gave a sigh of exasperation. "You'd have made a terrible spy, Catherine. Open it."

It wasn't Tolstoy's novel at all—not anymore—given that someone had cut into the pages to transform it into a hollow book. Given Elizabeth's loathing of Tolstoy, Cat suspected she knew the culprit. Tucked inside its hidey-hole were several folded notes handwritten on yellow legal paper, creased and worn around the edges. Elizabeth's hands fluttered in her lap, almost as if she wanted to snatch them back. "You can read them in the bedroom," she said to Cat.

"I'll read them right here." Cat smoothed the pages on her lap. "Can't have you getting any ideas about leaving, right?"

Honestly, she was shocked that Elizabeth hadn't tried anything thus far. It was almost as if she *needed* to unburden herself in some sort of catharsis.

Elizabeth remained stone-faced, unreadable. Cat glanced down, took only a moment to realize what she held in her hands.

The story of Yasha's death.

* * *

We attended a picture show matinee of Sahara *with Humphrey Bogart—between bites of maple taffy I whispered to Yasha about the way Bogie tugged on his earlobes whenever pondering a question—but Yasha was silent, preoccupied. The movie and even a Thanksgiving dinner at a restaurant opposite the London Terrace failed to distract him from the Center's ultimatum. It was good to have meat again—a rarity in those days—but he merely pushed food around on his plate, left untouched his turkey and even his sugar-ration apple pie; this from a man determined never to waste anything.*

"Talk to me," I commanded. "You've hardly said two words all day."

"It is this ultimatum. I still do not have an answer." His hand strayed to his jacket pocket, and his eyes lifted to meet mine. He seemed about to say something, but then the moment was lost. Instead, he pressed the heel of his hand to its usual place above his heart. "I am sorry you are saddled with a broken old comrade like me. This is not what you signed on for."

"Yes, it is. I chose you, remember?" I tried to infuse my expression with nonchalance and happiness and concern. With an added teasing glint in my eyes. It was a difficult look to master in a single facial expression. But I did my best.

Still, I could tell from Yasha's wince that his pain tonight was worse than usual, more than just his heartsickness over the Center's ultimatum. I'd call first thing in the morning, finally schedule that doctor's appointment.

Once back at my apartment, Yasha ignored Vlad's eagerly wagging tail and instead stretched out on the sofa, one arm thrown over his eyes. I fed Vlad his own turkey dinner, then turned the radio to the jazz station and rinsed my stockings— my second-to-last pair, as I'd donated the rest for parachutes— in the bathroom sink. When I'd finished and hung them over the shower, it was to find Vlad curled up before the fireplace and Yasha snoring softly, still fully dressed in his worn gray suit. Not even sleep could smooth the fresh lines etched deep around my love's eyes.

It was nearly eight o'clock—7:58 according to the wristwatch I'd given Yasha as an early Christmas present, since his old one didn't keep good time—but I didn't have the heart to wake him, merely tugged my dress over my head and curled up next to him in just my slip and garters. Fitted my body alongside his and pulled the green-and-white granny square afghan I'd just finished knitting over us.

I kissed the sharp angle of his jaw and drifted toward sleep, my limbs entwined with his. That was always where I'd felt safest, next to Yasha.

All was right with the world.

Until an hour later, when I woke to the sound of the floor creaking. Disoriented, I blinked, saw a shadow in the murky darkness that solidified into the shape of a man. Masked and wearing black, as if he drew the shadows to him. Cold terror drenched me, made it impossible to cry out. Something moved— a rust-stained ice pick he held aloft over Yasha's chest. Like the one that had killed Leon Trotsky.

I screamed and, without thinking, tried to shove away the assassin and his blade. I may as well have been trying to stop a Soviet storm. Some faraway pain registered in my hand, but nothing could mask the thud of the cold metal spike splintering bone before it slammed into the meat of Yasha's heart.

His blood, spattering the white silk of my slip and the woolen afghan like a crimson hail of bullets.

I screamed.

Horrible choking sounds came from his throat as the assassin slowly stalked away.

I'll forever see the moment Yasha died, terrified blue eyes frozen wide open in a rictus of death.

* * *

CAT'S HANDS FANNED over her lips in silent horror, and she could only blink at Elizabeth's stark words as she reread them, the horror of Yasha's death forever searing itself into her mind. She found herself gaping in abject shock at Elizabeth's stoic back while the former Soviet spy stared out the living room window.

How do you go on living after that?

Cat couldn't force herself to form the question. Elizabeth's arms were crossed in front of her as if barely holding herself together while she stared fixedly at the opposite building. The only sign of her mood was the fingers of her right hand scrolling rapidly down her left arm.

Cat cleared her throat. "I don't know what to say."

She considered offering some bit of condolence. After all, no one—not even Elizabeth Bentley—deserved to see their loved one killed in such a brutal manner. Despite herself, Cat felt tears prick her eyes, told herself it was merely because Elizabeth's recounting was too close to the events of the president's assassination yesterday. Cat hadn't been at the White House when Jackie Kennedy returned, but she could scarcely imagine what that poor woman had endured, what Elizabeth Bentley had endured.

Elizabeth merely shrugged, a gesture meant to appear casual, but to Cat it seemed heartbreakingly brave, not that she'd ever admit as much out loud. Yet, Elizabeth's voice was frigid when she finally responded, crowding out any inconvenient pity Cat might have felt. "You're only on the first page. Keep reading."

Cat frowned and flipped to the next page, saw that the account continued. *I don't want to read any further*, Cat thought, *but then, I only have to read it. Elizabeth had to live it.*

So, Cat forced herself to plow through each word.

It was nearly eight o'clock—7:58 according to the wristwatch I'd given Yasha as an early Christmas present, as his old one didn't keep good time—but I didn't have the heart to wake him, only tugged my dress over my head and curled up next to him in just my slip and garters. Fitted my body alongside his and pulled over us the green-and-white granny square afghan I'd just finished knitting.

Cat frowned in confusion, flipped back to confirm that she'd already read nearly those exact words. She glanced at Elizabeth, but she remained a silent sentinel by the window. So, Cat kept reading.

I kissed the sharp angle of his jaw and drifted off to sleep, my limbs entwined with his and Vlad curled up asleep on his blanket in front of the fireplace. That was always where I'd felt safest, next to Yasha.

All was right with the world.

I woke to the sound of Yasha's moan, followed by a sudden thud. There was no moon that night, and I stumbled for the lamp, winced against the sudden electric glare before I saw Yasha on the floor, his every muscle spasming as the strychnine— the odorless, colorless powder surely dropped into his holiday apple pie by some NKVD operative at the restaurant—worked its way through his once-powerful body.

His neck and back craned like an archer's bow, arms and legs rigid, fingers splayed at painful angles as if they'd been shattered.

I screamed.

Horrible choking sounds came from his throat.

I'll forever see the moment Yasha died, terrified blue eyes frozen wide open in a rictus of death.

There was still one page left, also scrawled with Elizabeth's handwriting. That page started the same way, so, perplexed, Cat skimmed to where the story once again changed.

. . . All was right with the world.

I woke to the sound of someone breathing—not Yasha's ragged breath, but someone else in the room. Suddenly alert while still feigning sleep, I cracked an eyelid, made out a masked man seated on one of my wooden kitchen chairs, his Tokarev service pistol staring through one wide eye at me. My heart stopped before I burst into action, scrambled from the couch to stop him.

The gun exploded.

Except there was no bullet, only a translucent mist I realized too late was a cloud of cyanide gas. I covered my nose with my arm to avoid the death-fog I knew would smell like almonds. Couldn't breathe, couldn't think.

In my scramble, I had left Yasha unprotected, exposed.

The poison was fast. So fast.

Yasha's eyes snapped open and his body started convulsing.

I screamed.

Horrible choking sounds came from his throat as the assassin slowly stalked away.

I'll forever see the moment Yasha died, terrified blue eyes frozen wide open in a rictus of death.

"What the hell is this?" Utterly confused, Cat shook the papers at Elizabeth. "What sort of sadist writes not one, not two, but *three* variations on the way their lover was murdered? What game are you playing, Elizabeth? And what the hell really happened?"

Elizabeth didn't respond until Cat stomped over to the windowsill, stepped so close she forced Elizabeth to look at her. Elizabeth's eyes were twin lighthouses of pain, dulled by a fog of alcohol.

"They all happened." She waved a hand. "None of them happened."

The penultimate liar had returned, but against Cat's will, her heart cracked a little for the wreck of a woman before her. "Does it matter?" Elizabeth asked, more to herself than to Cat. "Yasha died and I lived. The world kept turning, just as it always does."

Except looking at her, Cat could see that the world hadn't kept turning, at least not for Elizabeth. Not since that night twenty years ago.

"Yes, it matters," Cat snapped. "I want to know what really happened."

It was as if Elizabeth could no longer hear her.

Cat recalled stories of couples where one person died and the other soon followed, supposedly felled by a broken heart. Here before her was evidence of a woman who had tried to keep living, had taken the thousand fragments of her shattered heart, painstakingly stitched them back together, and forced the patched-up mess to continue beating. Cat wondered briefly which fate was kinder.

Elizabeth sighed, stalked to the kitchen, and retrieved a fresh bottle of gin—off-label, not pricey Gordon's this time—from beneath the sink, where it was hiding among bottles of bleach and Pine-Sol. She cracked it open but didn't bother to pour a tumbler this time, just swigged straight from the bottle.

"Go away." Elizabeth's breath when Cat approached blasted her with a foul furnace of alcohol fumes. Elizabeth rubbed the bridge of her nose. It was threaded with tiny blood vessels, and her eyes were slightly bloodshot. "I don't have to explain anything to you. Kill me if you want—I'm done with this. It's too much."

Cat merely scowled at the gin bottle. "Old habits die hard?"

Elizabeth snorted. "Whoever came up with that was an idiot. Old habits lurk beneath the surface, patiently waiting for you to dip your toe in the water so they can drown you like a Russian *vodyanoy*. They never die."

"You're dramatic, you know that?"

"Catherine, my dear girl, I was a spy. My entire life was dramatic."

Cat considered holding back, but only for a moment. "Our deal included the truth about your life. The *relative* truth, anyway. The three stories of Yasha's death you fed me were hardly the truth."

Because Cat doubted very much that Jacob Golos had been assassinated via ice pick or strychnine or a Tokarev service pistol loaded with cyanide gas. Strychnine and pistols loaded with cyanide gas were ways the current KGB—formerly known as the NKVD—had assassinated Cold War dissenters in recent years. Of course, Cat already knew of their penchant for ice picks from Trotsky's unfortunate demise. Yasha's story would have landed in the newspapers if he'd been killed that way. "What's the truth?"

"The truth?" Elizabeth gave a strangled sort of chortle. "The truth is that Jacob Golos, a Ukrainian-born Bolshevik revolutionary and Soviet intelligence operative, died November 25, 1943. That was all his obituary said, you know."

Then Elizabeth was on the move again, this time back to the living room, where she riffled through a stack of books and retrieved not one of the beautiful leather volumes, but a dime-store paperback.

Out of Bondage by Elizabeth Bentley.

She flipped to the middle of the book, found the passage she wanted as if she knew the page number by heart. She held it out to Cat, hand still trembling. "Here's the one spot where I actually told the truth in this damned book."

Cat skimmed the familiar scenes, then began reading out loud.

I went to the bathroom, changed into pajamas, and set my hair in pin curlers for the morrow. When I returned to the living room, Yasha was sleeping peacefully. Completely exhausted myself, I stretched out beside him and must have dozed off for about an hour.

I awakened suddenly with the panicky sense that something was badly wrong. Then I realized that, although he still seemed to be sleeping peacefully, horrible choking sounds were coming from his throat. Frantically, I shook him.

"Wake up, Yasha," I cried. "You're having a bad nightmare."

He didn't respond but still lay inertly on the couch, the same choking sounds coming from his throat. Then my mind flashed back to my father's last moments. This was a death rattle that I was hearing . . .

Elizabeth sat on the couch when Cat finished reading. Her expression remained as cold and immovable as a northern glacier, so it was easy for Cat to imagine her dealing with her contacts—and worse, the NKVD and FBI—over the years. But Cat caught the way her knuckles went white as she clutched them together, the brief lightning streaks of pain that lit her eyes before she realized Cat was studying her.

"The NKVD didn't kill Yasha, did they?" Cat knew she may as well have been probing a wounded bear with a stick, and part of her felt awful for it. But she wanted to know. And she felt like maybe Elizabeth needed to say it, to purge herself.

"They may as well have, what with all the stress they put him through. But no, technically it was his heart that killed him. A second heart attack."

Thank God. Any manner of death was awful, but Cat couldn't imagine someone she loved dying so violently as Elizabeth's first three scenarios. Which begged the question: What could possibly have possessed her to write those three horrific versions?

"As it turns out, the NKVD had no interest in liquidating Ya-sha." Elizabeth sat with hands laced tightly around her gin bottle. Over the course of her coffee and alcohol, her Victory Red lipstick had faded, leaving her looking older somehow. Exposed. "Actually, the FBI's prior investigation of Yasha was the very thing that con-vinced the NKVD that he was firmly on Russia's side. The Russians were rather fickle about loyalty, you know. Still are, I'd imagine."

"Then why give me those three other stories? Why not just the truth?"

Elizabeth stared at the gin bottle. "Because I let a great man die. I should have forced Yasha to see a doctor, should have taken him to the hospital a dozen times over. Hell, I should have demanded he take a trip to Mexico to rest and recover on some sunny beach. In-stead, I let him die a meaningless death."

"You didn't let Yasha die, Elizabeth. Terrible things just hap-pen." Cat heard the truth of her words, even as her mind struggled to reconcile that with her own mother's death. She boxed the juxta-position away.

"This time I just wanted it to be the NKVD's fault," Elizabeth whispered. "Not mine."

"But you told the truth in *Out of Bondage* when you could have lied." Cat refrained from mentioning the discrepancies she'd noticed—her hair loose or in pin curlers, pajamas or a slip and garters—for she suspected that in her memoir Elizabeth was trying to project to America the image of a respectable older woman. *If only they knew . . .* "Why?"

"*Out of Bondage* was meant to prove the truth of my story, in key places at least." Elizabeth's shoulders slumped. The brash spy Cat had been listening to these past hours was now replaced with a woman infinitely more fragile than she'd imagined Elizabeth Bent-ley could ever be.

"I'm sorry," Cat said before she could remember how much she hated that trite platitude that she'd endured countless times since her mother's death. Or how much she hated Elizabeth. Still . . . "I'm sorry you had to endure that. Truly, I am."

Elizabeth heaved a sigh, worried at the gold-and-ruby ring on her left hand. Her only adornment. "Do you want to know the rest? After Yasha?"

"Will it be the truth?"

"You're like a bulldog with some stick of truth caught between your teeth, you know that?"

"Perhaps."

Elizabeth harrumphed—actually *harrumphed*—as Cat took the gin bottle from her, poured a single thimbleful into a civilized glass, and handed it back to Elizabeth. She didn't want her drunk, but there was a time and a place for liquid courage. "You might need this."

Elizabeth gave Cat the faintest glimmer of what might be considered a smile. "Now you're learning, girl."

11

One moment Yasha was there. The next, he was gone.

The horror I'd felt at the choking sounds Yasha had made during his last moments was nothing compared to my panic at the roaring silence that filled my living room once he went still.

No pulse, no breath. *Nothing.*

Frantic, I scrambled—still dressed only in my slip and garters—to ring an ambulance. Somehow, somewhere, Vlad gave a high-pitched whimper and nudged Yasha's hand with his nose.

No pulse, no breath. *Nothing.*

"Don't do this, Yasha," I commanded once I'd slammed the receiver back into its holder. Shaking him didn't do anything, and there was no response when I tried pinching his nose to force brandy down his throat.

No pulse, no breath. *Nothing.*

Somehow, I buttoned myself back into yesterday's dress before the ambulance arrived with its two white-jacketed medics from St. Vincent's Hospital. The taller of the two medics lifted Yasha's eyelids and stared into his engorged pupils, then listened to his heart.

He looked at his partner significantly, then picked up my telephone and dialed.

"Dead on arrival." The man's voice was cold and callous—bored, even, as he hung up and lit a cigarette—as if this happened every day. My own heartbeat was lost in the roaring of my ears, the sudden numbness that spread from the cavern of my chest. I'd known in my mind that Yasha was dead, but the medic's words were a thousand rusty knives piercing my heart.

Dead on arrival.

Despite being frozen in place, I must have made a sound.

"I'm sorry, miss." The second medic touched my shoulder, his hazel eyes kindly beneath a hairline that had receded years ago. "I'm afraid we have to wait for the police."

My eyes snapped open. The numbness receded. "The police?"

"It's standard procedure whenever there's been a death." He had the decency to look chagrined, took his white cap in his hands. "To ensure there was no foul play."

Foul play . . .

I hadn't murdered Yasha—that much was obvious—and the police and coroner would inevitably find that his heart had given out on him, but they'd also find much, *much* more than that.

Yasha kept coded telephone numbers of most of his—*my*—agents in his pockets, no longer trusting that they could be left anywhere but on his person following the raid on World Tourists. I'd long ago memorized them—a photographic memory comes in handy—but I silently cursed him and then myself for not emptying his pockets while I'd waited for the ambulance to arrive. What was done was done. Now that the US knew he had been a Russian spy, the police would turn over whatever paperwork they found on him to the FBI.

Every last one of my contacts, from Bill Remington to the Silvermasters to Mary Tenney, would be compromised.

There was no way in hell I could let that happen.

Yes, I was in shock, and yes, I wanted to collapse in a torrent of self-indulgent tears. But for Yasha's sake, for his legacy and for the safety of our contacts, I had to pull myself together and give the performance of a lifetime. And I wasn't going to play the role of a grieving and hysterical lover.

Lover, partner, confidante . . . You taught me to be all those things, Yasha. But first and foremost, you taught me to be a spy.

"Do you think we need to move the ambulance?" the first medic asked his partner. "There's no telling how long it will take the cops to get here, and you parked in front of a fireplug. I don't want to get in trouble again."

Yes, get the hell out of here.

I needed two minutes alone with Yasha. Just two minutes.

"You can go," I said, making a show of sniffing and wiping my eyes as I picked up Vlad and buried my face in his fur, gesturing to Yasha with a jerk of my chin. "I'll stay with him."

"That's very kind of you, miss." The second medic handed me a handkerchief from his pocket. It was plain but clean. "But I'm afraid that would go against procedure."

Of course. You can't leave someone with the body before you rule out foul play.

I drew a deep breath, made a show of calming my nerves. "Oh, please don't worry about me." I sniffed into the handkerchief, deliberately misunderstanding them. "I can handle being alone with a dead body for a few minutes."

"Well . . ." The egg-bald medic looked to his partner, his gallantry winning out. "I'm sure we can leave her for a minute or two while I help guide you in. To a *legal* spot this time."

The callous one frowned, glanced out the window onto the street. "All right," he said. "But we'd better be quick."

I gave myself the luxury of counting out ten precious seconds before locking the door behind them—it would be easier to explain why I made a habit of locking the door if they returned rather than why I was rifling around a body. Then I was on my knees next to Yasha, turning his pockets inside out.

The coded numbers were all there—a quarter sheet of tissue paper written in tiny, immaculate handwriting—and some addresses too.

"You damned stubborn man," I muttered to him through my tears as I tugged off his shoes, felt around his feet and ankles. The left side was empty, but tucked into his right sock against his ankle was a switchblade, which I palmed and shoved deep between the couch cushions.

A Russian House trick is infallible—fold papers into an accordion and then light them on fire within a toilet bowl, the better to minimize smoke.

I could hear Yasha's instruction in my mind, but I didn't have time for fancy spy tricks. Instead, I shredded the papers, and then, because it went against protocol to flush the remnants without burning them first and because they were written on tissue paper for this precise reason, I swallowed them.

It was only then that I realized Yasha's jacket was hanging by the door.

That was where I found the box.

The ring inside was simple, a golden band with a tiny Communist-red ruby. And tucked within the gold was a note written in Yasha's hand, the same message repeated in a dozen different languages—Russian, Italian, French, Spanish, German, even what appeared to be Chinese.

With an extra line this time . . .

I love you, Elizabeth. You are the wife of my heart.

I moaned to recall the way Yasha's hand had strayed to this same pocket over dinner, how he'd seemed ready to say something. How the moment had evaporated and instead he'd apologized.

I am sorry you are saddled with a broken old comrade like me. This is not what you signed on for.

My mind exploded with the enormity of all I'd lost.

A sob escaped my lips as I slipped the cold circle of gold over the ring finger on my left hand. I would never take it off.

Two minutes after the medics had left, I was sitting demurely on the wing chair across from the couch, the door unlocked and open. I'd powdered my face, rolled my freshly laundered stockings up my legs and snapped them into my garters, slipped my feet into the heels I'd worn to the restaurant with Yasha.

On the outside, I was a perfectly respectable woman who just happened to be sitting next to a dead man. On the inside . . .

In the battlefield of emotions, anger and rage are the infantry. Grief is the guerrilla fighter, waiting to lay ambush around every corner. Yet, in that moment—the last where I knew I'd be alone with Yasha—I held them all at bay with a single silent command.

Fall apart later. Not now.

A minute or two afterward, the medics arrived and stood around awkwardly once they'd covered Yasha with a white sheet— I ignored their attempts to make small talk, although I *did* accept the kindly one's offer of a Lucky Strike to calm my nerves—until two friendly Irish policemen arrived.

Play dumb, Elizabeth. You know nothing.

"Hello, Miss—"

"Bentley," I provided as I stubbed out the cigarette in my kitchen sink. It wasn't difficult to look stunned, but I reminded myself that this was the most critical performance of my life. I had to recite my lines perfectly, for myself, for Yasha, for our contacts.

"Can you tell us what happened here? Who this man is?"

(Catherine, remember the truism where I mentioned that when lying, to always tell as much of the truth as possible? Here it is again in action.)

"His name is Golos. Jacob Golos." The police would learn that themselves after a perfunctory search of his wallet. It was the next sentence that threatened to undo me. "He was an associate of mine at work, but I hardly knew him. I was on my way home from having Thanksgiving dinner at that place opposite the London Terrace"—the waitress there could confirm, although I was taking a chance that these two Pinkertons wouldn't waste more of their holiday by spending the time to verify that I was alone—"walking through the neighborhood when he recognized me, asked if I could help him."

I paused for effect. *Three, two, one . . .*

The first Irishman stopped scribbling in his notebook and gave a little frown. "Help him with what?"

Good man, I thought. They thought this was an interrogation, and it was, but on my terms. With any luck, they'd ask only the questions I guided them to, believe exactly the story that *I* wanted them to hear.

I bit my lip, nearly lost my composure when Vlad whined and nudged his damp nose into Yasha's hand that now dangled toward the floor, as if Yasha might suddenly wake from a nap and take Vlad to play fetch in the park. To keep the officers from witnessing my rising tears, I scooped Vlad into my arms, closed my eyes, and breathed in deep. Forced myself to bend and fold Yasha's arm so his hand rested over his heart beneath the sheet. "He said he was having chest pains. He was always nice to me at the office, so I brought him here so he could rest. He fell asleep, and I didn't want to wake him. Then he started making horrible choking sounds." The bedrock of my composure fractured then, and I looked at them, blinked a few times, and scrubbed a hand under my nose. "What killed him?"

The police looked to the medics for confirmation. The tall one frowned. "All symptoms match a heart attack."

One cop scribbled something in his report; the other reached out to squeeze my shoulder. I flinched.

Yasha had only been gone a matter of minutes, and already, I found myself reverting back to habits I'd thought were long since buried.

Except I'm not the scared, lonely girl I was before I met Yasha. He made me more than that. I made myself more than that. Because of the faith he had in me.

"I have to trouble you with a few more questions, miss," the first policeman said, then asked what Yasha did (sold vacations to Russia and abroad), who his doctor was (no idea, I lied), and whether he had any relatives or close friends (none I was aware of). Finally, the questions ceased. "I'm sure this isn't how you wanted to spend your Thanksgiving," the tall policeman said. "It's a helluva time to die."

The first policeman asked to use my telephone so he could place a call to the coroner. I nodded, didn't hear a word of the conversation. Because his partner was going through Yasha's pockets.

I held my breath, waiting . . .

What if I had missed something?

But the officer found only what I wanted him to. Yasha's wallet and identification. A crumpled pack of Wrigley's spearmint gum. One of Yasha's old business cards for World Tourists. There would be no doubt that Jacob Golos, convicted Soviet spy, had died of a simple heart attack, but there would be only the most brittle of ties linking him to me. I'd even removed the *Sahara* ticket stubs from the show we saw earlier in the afternoon so the police wouldn't go snooping back to the theater and asking questions.

"Will you be all right waiting for the coroner?" the first officer asked after he'd hung up my telephone. "My family is waiting for me to finish Thanksgiving dinner."

I bit my lip again. "Will it be long?"

"He said ten, maybe fifteen minutes."

I nodded. "I'll be fine."

(That was another lie, Catherine. I'd never be fine again.)

The police apologized, then they and the medics left, and I was standing in my living room, just Vlad and me.

Alone with Yasha for the last time.

"You have to tell him good-bye, boy," I said to Vlad. Some daft people claim animals can't feel proper emotions, but confusion and sadness shone bright in Vlad's wide terrier eyes. I could feel the farewell when I removed the sheet the medics had placed over Yasha's body and picked up Vlad so he could lick Yasha's face for the final time. Our dear little dog gave one long whine, one last baleful look at his friend who had always made a place for him on our bed. Then Vlad circled me, sat at my feet, and gave one thump of his tail. My brave little sentinel, who was all I had left in the world.

My unchecked tears splashed Yasha's cheeks when I kissed him for the final time.

"*Ya lyublyu tebya,*" I whispered to him in the Russian he had taught me. *I love you.*

Ten minutes later, I watched the coroner and his assistant from the International Workers Order cradle Yasha's stiffening body into a canvas sling and carry him down the stairs before placing him in the back of a dark hearse. Then they drove away, taking with them my best friend, the only man I'd ever loved.

One moment Yasha was there. The next, he was gone.

The hands of the clock moved relentlessly forward.

DAWN HADN'T YET risen by the time I was at Yasha's office.

I hadn't slept, had only lain in bed and stared at the night-dark ceiling listening to Vlad's soft breathing from where I'd let him curl up on Yasha's pillow next to me.

If I did *let him sleep on your pillow, it is only because I miss you.*

It had only been a few hours, and I already felt the void Yasha had left behind. So damned much it threatened to crush me.

Finally, I couldn't stand it anymore. I felt hollowed out and strung tight, and it wasn't yet five o'clock when I ran a brush through my snarled hair and buttoned a jacket over the first dress I pulled out of the closet. Who cared what I looked like on the outside when I was a bleeding mess on the inside? The entire city was still asleep when I strode out my apartment's double doors.

"You're up early this morning, Miss Myrna," the liveried elevator operator at World Tourists said when he closed the cage behind us. World Tourists had essentially closed, but Yasha had maintained a mostly deserted office here so he wouldn't be connected in any way to the new venture of United States Service and Shipping Corporation.

The FBI won't look for more evidence right under their noses, Yasha had proclaimed. *They won't think I'd have the wherewithal to return to the scene of the crime.*

Now he was gone and everything would likely be scrutinized with the finest-toothed comb. By both the FBI *and* the NKVD.

"It is early, isn't it, Ernie?" To buy myself time to think, I parroted the question back to the elevator operator. In my daze, I hadn't concocted a story to explain why I was here, and hadn't anticipated seeing anyone, since I had keys to what I knew would be an empty office. Of course, I'd forgotten about Ernie, and he'd spotted me before I could take the stairs. With my bad luck, the cleaning lady would still be finishing up too. "My alarm went off early," I answered with a wave of my hand. "I was already up and dressed by the time I realized it."

"They do say that the early bird gets the worm," Ernie said as the elevator chimed and he opened the door. "Have a good day, Miss Myrna."

No chance of that, Ernie.

Lucky for me, the rest of the office was tomb-dark and deserted. Still, I worked quick.

Wearing white gloves, I opened the safe—Yasha had set it to the date of that fateful New York snowstorm—and took out every document, returning only the ones I knew to be innocuous. Each incriminating paper was stuffed into a suitcase that Yasha had left in the office's broom closet for precisely this purpose.

True, if ever questioned, Ernie might comment that I'd arrived empty-handed and left with a bulging suitcase, but I planned to take the stairs and avoid his notice.

Also in the safe was a pristine stack of one-hundred-dollar bills. To the tune of at least ten thousand dollars.

My palm itched to pocket the money—my financial position was now precarious given that I could be released from USS&S at any time—but I didn't want anyone coming after me for something as pedestrian as theft. Yasha had given clear instructions that should anything happen to him, USS&S's assets should go to Earl Browder—he could shoulder some of this burden, given that he was the current general secretary of the CPUSA.

The cash went to the bottom of the suitcase.

I was down the stairwell and out the rear entrance before six o'clock. Back at my Barrow Street apartment with a fire roaring in the fireplace before my mantel clock struck seven.

I swirled a glass of Yasha's Hennessy to create an amber-hued vortex, took tiny, painful sips while I fed the stolen documents one at a time into the crackling flames. With Vlad as my only witness, I watched each paper until it had burned completely, nudged tiny miscreant pieces that tried to escape back into the all-consuming flames.

This permanent destruction was for the best—there would be no evidence that Yasha was anything other than an upstanding citizen following his conviction, certainly nothing to tie him to me or any of my contacts—but still, tears streamed down my cheeks as I watched fragments of his handwriting go up in fragrant clouds of smoke and ash.

I continued my vigil until there was nothing left.

Yasha was gone. But his legacy—his life's work—was not.

Because he'd entrusted it to me.

I was alone now, but I had one thing that would keep me going.

I was still Yasha's Umnitsa.

I was still Clever Girl.

NOVEMBER 1943

I met Yasha's replacement the day after his funeral.

I could say it was a chill and rainy afternoon, the sort that makes you wish you didn't have to venture out into the world, or I could claim that the heavens smiled down with soft autumn sunshine meant to soothe my grief, but I can't recall whether there was a biblical downpour or if a furious sun beat down upon our heads. I was still made of fragile flesh and brittle bone, but since Yasha's death, I'd gone hollow inside. I moved, I spoke, I ate . . . but nothing else.

Earl Browder, bless him, had made the arrangements at Gramercy Park Funeral Parlor on Second Avenue after I'd given him the cash from Yasha's safe and informed him I was taking over Yasha's contacts, a move he concurred with. There were no hymns or sermons inside the small chapel filled with Party members and wide-eyed comrades—no one from the underground, save me, of course—only a string of long speeches lauding Jacob Golos's dedication and achievements that were done all for the Party's benefit.

The same ungrateful Party who tried to edge him out.

Drugged with grief, I was still surprised at the sudden use of

Yasha's real name and the public litany of his many accomplishments, but then, now that he was dead, his cover was worthless to the Party and the Center too. It was even possible that this was a Russian ploy so Yasha's secret contacts would realize they'd been orphaned and come forward to request a new handler. What the Center didn't realize—but what all our contacts knew—was that they hadn't been orphaned at all.

They had *me*.

And I'd made sure they'd known it, had contacted every single one of them before Yasha's funeral via coded telephone conversations, a black chess queen mailed to Mary Tenney to let her know I was all right, and even a symbol drawn with Rolaids (Yasha always warned that being apprehended with chalk would look suspicious) on the mailbox outside Nathan Silvermaster's apartment requesting an intelligence drop.

I wondered who here at the somber service was NKVD—likely not the mourners, but perhaps the chapel attendant or even the hearse driver—and whether we were all being surveilled. If the NKVD was half as fearsome as Yasha had claimed, it was probable they already knew that one of their former top officials hadn't died in some random woman's apartment, that he and I had been more than just compatriots.

That I was more than I seemed.

But there was no point broadcasting that fact to the world. To that end, I said nothing and gave no eulogy, despite being the one person in the gathering who knew Yasha best. Perhaps the only one who knew him at all. I'd taken a calculated risk in coming here, had debated the wisdom of attending, but knew I'd never forgive myself for missing my last chance to say good-bye. Hopefully, in everyone else's minds, I had merely come to pay my respects to a Party legend. So, I listened to the speeches, and then, when everyone else filed out, I placed a Russian-red rose onto his casket.

The same shade of red as the ruby in his ring that I would never take off.

It was while standing before Yasha's casket, unable to truly say good-bye, that I felt a hand on my arm. "Elizabeth?"

I jumped at the unfamiliar touch. *Calm down, Elizabeth, and stop imagining the NKVD at every turn.*

It was almost more surprising to see Lee Fuhr looking the same as she had when I first met her, but this time with Harold Patch on her arm, his fingers still stained with ink from writing draft articles and presses, probably even some recent ones eulogizing Yasha. Lee's expression was open and warm; Patch's scowling reception was distinctly Siberian.

"Lee. Patch." I'd heard they'd spent time together in Spain working to undermine Franco's Fascist regime, couldn't muster the urge to truly care about that now. "It's been a long time."

"What are you doing here?" Lee glanced about, as if I'd just tagged along with someone else. Satisfied that I was alone, Lee frowned. "Surely, you didn't know Jacob Golos?"

Flustered, my mind skipped several ripples ahead, trying to see how the future would unfold if I answered her question honestly and welcomed the truth back into my life.

Except I had to remain underground and keep a safe distance from the Party if I hoped to keep my contacts safe and stay in control of the life I'd chosen to live. The only life that had ever felt worthwhile and that still kept me somehow connected to Yasha.

There would be no clear, clean air for me to breathe above ground. Not for a long time.

"Golos was a legend. It seemed proper to pay my respects." I smiled at them. "It was good to see you both. Take care."

Lee appeared as if she were about to say something more, but I turned my back on her and strode away before she could change my mind. Patch's angry murmur only strengthened my resolve.

"Let her go," he muttered to Lee, loud enough so we both knew I could hear. "She's not worth it."

Except I *was*. With Yasha's network—the largest in America— I'd built a *life*, had made myself into a legend, albeit an underground one. And I wasn't willing to give it up.

Yasha was gone, and I had to stay one move ahead of everyone else. I had to remain separate, removed. Above reproach.

I'd scarcely arrived home when my telephone rang.

"The newsreel theater on East Forty-Second Street," said a woman's voice. "Five o'clock tomorrow night."

Then the line went dead.

AFTER A SLEEPLESS night, I kept myself busy the following morning by crating up Yasha's apartment. The furnishings I left, but his beautiful leather-bound books, spy equipment, and clothes that still smelled of a Russian pine in winter . . . all those I took. And the Hennessy, which I tippled in a tiny toast to Yasha once I was safely back in my apartment. I couldn't bear to look at Vlad, who sat with his baleful eyes trained on the front door, faithfully awaiting the return of his beloved master. The cognac's woody aroma reminded me of happier times, allowed me to put my head down and pretend that Yasha was sitting across from me. But the illusion was a lie.

"He's not coming back, Vlad," I said when he whined once. "The sooner we accept that, the better."

Eyes stinging, I poured the Hennessy down my throat, swallowed it. Discovered that a single tumbler of scotch somehow sanded down the ragged edges of my pain.

Well. Who knew that alcohol could be quite so magical?

Warmed by the Hennessy, I dressed carefully for my meeting at the newsreel theater on Forty-Second Street. More one-sided phone calls from the Center had followed—I was to carry a copy of *Life* magazine and wear a red flower. The bruises under my eyes stubbornly refused my attempts to hide them, so I gave up and opted for a short-sleeved black dress and my last pair of silk stockings, ones with only a tiny hole in the toe that I'd dabbed with clear nail varnish. It wouldn't do to attend this critical Party meeting with runs, or worse, with lines drawn up the backs of my legs as some women did these days due to the silk shortages.

One step at a time: first, to the newsreel theater, and then to God only knew where. A nondescript go-between—this time a freckled boy probably hired straight off his newspaper run—awaited me outside the theater. With a sharp whistle, he flagged down a cab—which I paid for—before having us get out early and walk an extra block to Janssen's restaurant on Lexington.

Then he left me to my fate.

The restaurant was elegant—*too* elegant for a Party meeting—and the corpulent man wearing the signal panama hat and scarlet pocket square lounged like a czar of old in a dark corner booth. My spy's eyes missed nothing, not his double chin that bordered on a triple, his perfectly tailored white seersucker suit and the sheen of his silk tie, or the Brylcreem that slicked back his receding hairline, which was revealed when he removed his ridiculous hat. (Catherine, I've always believed hair to be a person's unofficial résumé—critical to dating and romance, used to inform, adorn, or shock. Mine has always been styled to conform, but my new contact's card shouted that he was oilier than a used mattress salesman.)

He even smelled of some designer cologne as he gave me his verbal credentials. "It is a nice day today." He spoke around rather protuberant teeth, but despite his excellent English, he couldn't quite camouflage the first word; *it* came out sounding more like *eet*.

"I hope you have an umbrella." I recited the second half of the key. "It looks like rain this evening."

Official identifications aside, he shook my hand—his palm slightly damp and smoother than a newborn's cheek—before moving the panama hat to the edge of the table and clearing a place for me. "I appreciate your timeliness tonight—I run several businesses here in New York that keep me very busy, although I am originally from Czechoslovakia." All lies, of course. "You may call me Al," he continued. "I shall refer to you as Myrna in all my correspondence with the Center, although you shall remain known as Miss Wise to your contacts."

Of course. Back to where I'd started, dancing to the tune of a contact who fed me a flimsy cover story and wouldn't even tell me his name. As my new handler, Al assumed it was his prerogative to choose my new name. Once Umnitsa, now I was to be plain old Myrna?

Whereas Yasha had been an honest-to-God revolutionary, this corpulent boulevardier who lit his cigarette with an expensive-looking gold lighter was better suited to being an uptown business executive for some foreign corporation. Al might have been an NKVD illegal, or even Stalin's favorite lapdog, but this vainglory was no Yasha in scuffed shoes and patched clothes, sacrificing for the good of all.

(Honestly, Catherine, his scarlet jacket pocket matched his socks and tie. No one should be that color coordinated.)

The Center might call me Myrna now, but that was just another disguise. I was still Umnitsa, professional spy and handler. I didn't owe Al—whoever the hell he was—a damned thing.

"Myrna is fine," I muttered.

"Excellent. I took the liberty of ordering us oysters and caviar. With broiled lobster as the main course." Al's idle gesture toward the menu made it easy to imagine him as some filthy rich landlord during the days of the Roman Empire. Lobster and caviar, in the face of wartime rationing . . . I found myself craving the comfort of a hot dog with ketchup and relish. And a man who let me order my own damned food.

"Very generous." I refolded my menu, pushed the useless thing away when the waiter arrived with oysters and drinks. Champagne, naturally, of some vintage more accustomed to kings and emperors. I set mine aside.

"Let's get straight to business, shall we?" The restaurant was full of chatter, and there was something harsh around Al's eyes that I hadn't noticed at first and didn't particularly care for. "We are still deciding what to do with Golos's contacts—sadly, it's only clear now that he is dead what colossal work he has done for us. However, due to the circumstances of his death, it has come to our attention that you worked far more closely with Golos than previously believed. It is imperative that you share what you know about his list of contacts. Especially the woman known as Muse—she must be handed over immediately. It's the Party's wish that she report directly to me."

Muse . . . The Center finally realized how critical Mary Tenney is. And how dangerous.

I was never so thankful that Yasha had kept his intelligence reports so well coded that not even the NKVD or the CPUSA knew their identities. The Center understood that Mary knew all their secrets, but if they learned the *full* truth about Mary and her trip last year, the truth that I hadn't even told Yasha . . . Well, then they'd hold a guillotine over her head. Or worse, a dose of strychnine or an ice pickax.

Despite the harsh thud of my heart, I didn't respond, merely pretended to sip my champagne. Here was the same demand the NKVD had made of Yasha, the stress of which had helped kill him. "Actually," I finally said, "Muse is in a highly nervous state and won't be any good to you now. Earl Browder and I agreed that she needs to stay right where she is. With me."

Here's your gauntlet, Al. Enjoy.

I could see from the way a vein throbbed in his neck that he hadn't expected resistance against what was supposed to be an easy turnover of contacts. Which made some perverse part of me enjoy this all the more.

"Perhaps the chain of command here is unclear, Miss Bentley." Al's use of my real name failed to intimidate. He stubbed out his cigarette and nudged his champagne glass aside, even pushed his oyster knife to the edge of the table as if clearing the way for some sort of tournament, one I planned to win. "You take your orders from me, not Earl Browder."

"Earl Browder is the head of the Communist Party of the United States." I kept my voice down and my expression playful. For all anyone at the next table knew, I was thoroughly enjoying a date with this arrogant, dandified walrus. "And he's always been my superior."

"If I was you, I'd do my best to distance myself from Browder. I can assure you that Moscow grows less and less enamored with him every time he opens his mouth about how the US and USSR are equal allies."

That was news to me, not that I planned to take Al's advice. Unfortunately, I wasn't in a position to ride into battle carrying Browder's standard while also fighting to protect Mary. "Be that as it may, Muse is fragile. She won't work with anyone else."

(To be fair, Catherine, if Mary was assigned to a different handler, there wasn't anything she could do to change things, save quit and spend the rest of her life hiding from the Center's possible retribution. After all, it wasn't as if you could file a formal complaint with the CPUSA or the NKVD. Recall, arrest, or execute, remember?)

"Muse is a honey trap, one we've been very patient with because she attracts so many well-placed flies." Al's casual tone at the Party's treatment of Mary made my every hair stand on end. Worse, it made me want to break my chair over his well-coiffed head. "We want Muse and we want her today. If Golos had possessed half a working brain in that head of his, he'd have turned her over ages ago."

Al's words sent an explosion on par with the *Hindenburg* over my entire vision.

"Let me ask you a question, *Al*." Voice dangerously level, I leaned back in my chair and slitted my eyes at him. "Explain to me precisely what roles you believe I've held in the underground all these years."

"You began by gathering low-level—mostly useless—intelligence from the Italian Library during Mussolini's rise—"

"A position I created out of thin air."

"Then you were assigned to Golos, worked as his mail drop and picked up documents for him, worked at US Service and Shipping and met with his contacts. An unorthodox arrangement at best, given that it breaks every NKVD rule for contacts to meet with more than one handler at a time. It's not difficult to see how Golos managed to compromise his own position."

(Catherine, I nearly eviscerated the tub of lard where he sat right then and there. Let the NKVD try to explain *that* to the news outlets. Or to Stalin. Instead, I committed a different crime of passion.)

"Let me fill you in on one or two details you might be missing." I ticked off each statement on my fingers, my voice growing tauter with each one. "First, you may tell your Moscow superiors that Jacob Golos wasn't just my handler. And yes, I knew his real name long before his funeral yesterday. In fact, I was his closest assistant, the one person in the world from whom he had no secrets."

I pressed on, not giving Al a chance to respond. "You think you're so wise, but you still can't figure out the names of Jacob Golos's sources. Well, I'm the one who ran all of Golos's contacts these past two years following his indictment. Muse and all the rest are *my* contacts, and you must be out to lunch to believe I'm going to hand them over to a shadowy organization that doesn't even have the wherewithal to pinpoint my existence all these years."

I wished I had a camera to capture the slack-jawed expression on Al's face. No self-respecting spy should ever let their eyes protrude in such a telling and unattractive manner.

"You're very sincere and passionate about your position, Miss Bentley." Al spoke slowly once he'd recovered and worked to crack open an oyster, one hand gripping his oyster knife so tightly that I worried he'd snap it in half. Suddenly, I wasn't so sure it had been wise to poke a stick in this particular hornet's nest. But what choice did I have? "If all you say is true, then it appears Jacob Golos fed the Party half-truths in order to preserve his own power. I've never heard of a case where an American citizen handled American contacts—as you can imagine, there would be far too many opportunities for one to turn double agent. I guarantee this won't sit well with Moscow."

His diatribe made me stop just short of rolling my eyes so hard they'd hit the ceiling. As if I'd suddenly turn double agent *now*, after I'd fully identified myself. Except, I'd just revealed that I knew too much. I would have to make that work out in my favor, convince the Center of my worth. "I won't be persuaded to stop what I've been doing these past two years," I said. "The intelligence my sources have gathered has been solid."

"Then it seems we are at an impasse. For now." Despite our lack of lobster, my new handler retrieved his bulging billfold from his jacket pocket and dropped a couple crisp twenties on the table. I'd never eaten such an expensive meal in all my life, not that I'd actually eaten anything. "I'll speak to Moscow about your contacts, but do *not* under any circumstances take on further sources. Do you understand?" At my nod, he continued. "In the meantime, we should meet again next week."

"So, everything remains status quo?"

"For now. You're an important asset to the Party."

My heart leaped. Had I actually preserved my contacts? In just one dinner meeting?

"Miss Bentley." Al's tone deflated my excitement like a child's week-old helium balloon. "Don't expect things to remain this way. I'm sure the Center will have plans for you."

"What plans?"

But the walrus merely left me sitting at the table, the detritus of a tray of half-finished oysters littering it.

I stayed and I ate every bite of that damned lobster.

I DOUBLE- AND then triple-checked that I wasn't being followed the next day when I headed for Greenwich Village, looping around the bohemian district's many theaters enough times that I was almost dizzy. Only when I was sure there were no NKVD shadows nipping at my heels did I approach Mary Tenney's new building, which was conveniently located near my own Barrow Street apartment now that she'd recently moved to the city. Tonight's was a surprise visit—I couldn't call ahead and risk being bugged—and I felt unsettled, still needed to wrap my mind around Al's threats last night.

What plans will the Center have for me? What will I do if I can't—or won't—carry them out? And how will I shield Mary from Moscow?

I recalled my early entrance into Communism, Juliet and Marcel insinuating that they'd lose more than their souls if they left the Party . . . Juliet had simply vanished without a trace shortly after she'd introduced me to Yasha, begging the question of whether people ever *left* the Party. Voluntarily, at least.

I heard masculine voices when Mary—in the glamorous guise of Helen Price tonight—opened the door of her ground-floor apartment, her svelte figure draped in a stunning Chinese silk wrapper. Her mascara-laden eyes widened to see me, and she put a finger on her lips. "I wasn't expecting you tonight," she whispered. "I'm entertaining two men from the Office of War Information. They dropped in by surprise."

"I need to talk to you." I glanced over her shoulder, recognized the pale, cold-looking man with a face like a sleepy fish from my old Communist unit at Columbia University. "I'll wait outside," I said. "Until you get rid of them."

It was two hours before Mary's visitors finally departed, during which I heard through the open window in great detail exactly what a honey trap did. Drinks, laughter, flirting . . . And then the party moved to Mary's bedroom. During which time I took a walk around the block. A *long* walk.

When I was sure she was alone, Mary answered my triple knock, then ushered me inside and bolted the door. It occurred to me that life as a spy often meant living as a rat, scurrying inside hidey-holes and cowering away from strangers. Those of us who worked in the underground had no respite, no rest, no relaxation.

"I'm sorry, Mary. This couldn't wait." I turned off all the lights save one and glanced outside before lowering the blinds and turning on the radio. Standard procedure. And it never hurt to be too careful, especially with Mary living so close to me now. "I just met my new handler."

She moved a plush pillow to her lap to make room for me on the overstuffed sofa next to her chess table, where a game remained in play. Her face was scrubbed clean, and I could still smell the tang of Noxzema cold cream. "I'm sorry. That must be difficult, so soon after Timmy."

I was touched that she was concerned for my feelings, but we had more important issues to face. Together. "They want me to hand you over. In fact, my new handler requested you specifically. They want Muse."

Mary's perfectly chiseled cheeks blanched the color of curdled milk. Suddenly, she was in front of me, eyes wide. The sleeves of her wrapper fell away, and, not for the first time, I winced at the pale scars slashed across her wrists, each bracelet telling a terrible story of heartache and loneliness. I considered it a wonder that she hadn't added to the collection since I'd taken over her case. "Did you tell them about me?"

"Of course not," I answered. "I came to warn you that they're hot for you."

"I don't care if they're chasing after me like bitches in heat. I'd sooner quit than have my strings pulled by the Center."

"Just like that?" I raised my hands to this new apartment's lush surroundings. "And how will you afford all this?"

"I'll give it up. I swear to God. I'll drop it all and go into retirement."

Now *that* was a surprise.

"Retirement?" I moved a black pawn on the board. "Or hiding?"

Because to the Center, it would be one and the same.

Mary's movements became jerky. "If the Center finds out what I've done . . ." She looked at me, her pupils wide. "You know my secrets, Elizabeth . . ." Her beautiful face turned blotchy, and I could tell by the rapid rise and fall of her chest that she was struggling—and failing—not to panic. Her hands fluttered by her sides. Mary had always been delicate and perhaps even high-strung, but I'd never seen her like this. "You know the Center would hold my mistakes over my head, what horrors they'd make me commit. No, I won't do it."

(Trust me, Catherine, when I promise that if I had much to gamble in standing up to the Center, Mary had far more to risk. But let's tell this story one problem at a time . . .)

"Mary, I'd sooner burn you than hand you over. I swear it."

To burn her would mean taking her out of commission as an agent: ratting her out to the FBI, turning her over to a psychologist, that sort of thing. She'd never, *ever* be able to spy again. The trick was doing it in such a way that the Center couldn't track her down and exact retribution. Against either of us.

A tall order.

Still, some of the tension melted from her shoulders. "You mean it?"

"I'll swear a blood oath if you want." I spoke in earnest as I touched my foot to her bare ankle. Even that part of her was graceful, sculpted like some ancient Greek statue. "Just say the word."

She gave a nervous laugh and tugged at the sleeves of her wrapper in a vain attempt to hide the ugly scars there. "You and Timmy are just the same." She moved the white queen diagonally to capture my knight. "Good people."

I might have swallowed the lump that rose in my throat then, but I so desperately wanted—*needed*—to unburden myself after days of carrying the load of Yasha's death and its fallout all by myself.

She turned to face me, one ankle tucked under her leg. "You must miss him terribly." Mary pushed a stray curl behind my ear. "Anyone with eyes could see how much you meant to each other. So, tell me what you miss most about him."

It was terribly personal, but then, I knew the worst of Mary's secrets. I wondered then what she would tell me if I posed the same question to her: whether she would describe the heavenly scent of someone's hair in the early-morning sunshine, the downy touch of their skin, the way their warm body felt curled into the safe harbor of yours.

"I don't know if I want to—"

"Nonsense." She cleared her throat. "Sometimes talking and remembering is the best thing you can do. The *only* thing you can do."

So, I began talking about Yasha—really *talking*—about our first meeting, where I named him Levin instead of Timmy, the magic of our first kiss, the way he'd curl up with Vlad on his lap on rainy days, how I missed the sound of his even breathing next to me at night.

"You were lucky," Mary said when I finished, a starched handkerchief of hers pressed into my palm at some point during the deluge. She'd poured us both glasses of scotch as we'd half-heartedly continued the chess game, and I'd indulged, wishing the burn down my throat could scorch away the pain that now haunted my every step. "You really loved him, didn't you?"

I snuffled into her handkerchief, wiped my nose in the most unladylike way. But then, I'd never been a lady, not really. "God, yes. I did. I *do*."

We sat in a companionable silence for some time afterward. I appreciated that she didn't bother to ask if I wanted to stay the night instead of going home to my empty apartment that might well be under NKVD surveillance but merely brought me a pillow and blanket that smelled of her lilac perfume. "So," I finally said, picking up the white queen and twirling it between my fingers. "If I'm going to burn you, we'll need a plan."

"Not just a plan," she responded. "We need to take control of the board."

I smiled. "A Queen's Gambit then . . ."

AL HAD COMMANDED that I not take on any new contacts, but how was I supposed to know that Earl Browder would request I meet with a tidy set of contacts he wanted me to take on after their current handler—some wishy-washy attorney for the CIO-PAC labor political action committee—had decided he could no longer be involved in espionage activities?

I could either play it safe *or* I could distract the Center from their obsession with Muse. If I proved my worth to the Center, I could also make them realize they couldn't afford to shunt me to the side.

I was damned good at what I did, and the sooner they realized that, the better.

For both Mary and me. For my entire ring, actually.

The sky when I buzzed my way up to an empty apartment on that dreary March morning seemed exhausted, as if it hadn't seen the sun in too long. A single light bulb hanging from the ceiling illuminated a fraction of the Perlo group, a set of nine highly placed government workers (three worked for the War Production Board and others were staff members for senators) named for their undisputed leader, Victor Perlo. I'd instructed only four to attend the meeting today—still unconventional, but having all nine spies in attendance would have been too risky. Even for me.

"Miss Wise." Perlo seemed to possess a frenetic energy as he bounded toward me, one slim hand outstretched beneath a face full of sharpened angles. (No fleshy Michelangelo or reclining Rembrandt, that one, just Picasso at the height of his cubist period.) "Thank you so much for agreeing to take us on," he said. "Our skill sets haven't been utilized in far too long, and we're eager to get you all the Capitol Hill gossip. Has Uncle Joe seen what I sent you last week?"

I took my time removing my jacket, needing to soothe some of Perlo's jagged enthusiasm. "I'm not sure what's hit Stalin's desk, but yes, the aircraft production specs were especially helpful with their distribution by country and theater of action." Perlo had sent Earl Browder documents he'd claimed couldn't wait in the interim before our introduction, and I'd looked them over before coding them and sending them off to the Center. Now I settled into the folding chair across from Perlo and crossed my ankles. "In fact, all intel suggests that the Allies will be making a big push against Hitler's western flank this summer. It's about time, don't you think, since the Russians are making inroads following their victory at Stalingrad?"

My question had two goals: first, to establish to these men I was fully abreast of the war. Second, to ask their opinions.

(All men love to be asked their opinions, Catherine, especially when it comes to war and politics. It makes them feel important.)

"The Russians won this war at Stalingrad, even if the other Allies won't admit it." Perlo tapped his twitchy fingers on his knee, and his compatriots nodded in unison. "So, you believe aircraft will play a large part in this new push?"

I smiled dotingly. I could already tell Victor Perlo was the fervent, revolutionary sort of spy who wanted to believe he held the key to turning the tide of history. All the better—the adventurers in it for the thrill were unreliable, and "bought" agents were dicey since a foreign intelligence service could always lure them away with more money. Without a doubt the best contact was motivated by patriotism or idealism. Just like Victor Perlo here.

"According to the intelligence you passed along," I said, "it certainly looks that way."

"And today, we have fresh information." Perlo's sharp nod prompted the three other men to shift on their folding chairs and make their offerings to me. I hadn't expected anything earth-shattering, but my head started reeling as one glorious tidbit after another fell into my lap, until I felt like a child in the largest candy store east of the Mississippi.

Dates on industrial production from the War Production Board along with minutes from its recent meetings.

Information from congressional investigations on multinational corporations.

Documents on trade policies following the war.

Reports on commodities in short supply in America.

OSS plans for the postwar occupation of Germany.

I gave a Cheshire cat smile once the men were done. "Thank you, gentlemen," I said when it was time for me to leave. "Every bit of this information is invaluable for the war effort."

Which in turn, I mused as I walked down the stairs from the apartment, my floral knitting bag bulging as it bumped against my thigh, *makes* me *invaluable*.

Or so I thought.

13

Hell hath no fury like a woman scorned.

That was a lesson both the Center and I would soon learn.

The Perlo specs—and a priceless photograph provided by Lud Ullmann of the schedule for D-Day—had been spot-on, and shortly after, the Allies successfully stormed the beaches of Normandy, which meant the whole of America—from sea to shining sea—was in a cautiously celebratory mood. However, Al didn't waste time telling me all manner of bad news when he arrived half an hour late for our rendezvous at Chase's Cafeteria.

"Due to the stupidity of one of my subordinates, I went to the wrong place. I am not used to such inefficiency—the man who committed this blunder will pay for his mistake." He glared around Chase's Cafeteria, which actually made his lip curl in distaste. My own lips that day were painted Victory Red—dealing with Al felt akin to marching into battle, so I'd decided to wear the color to meet with him. "I am also not accustomed to this sort of base establishment, Miss Wise."

I'd insisted on Chase's this time—I was sick to the gills of swanky restaurants where an entrée cost enough to pay my apartment's monthly rent—and had ordered the cheapest item on the menu: a glass of tap water and a BLT. (Sadly, no hot dogs were to be found.)

Whatever happened to the revolution, I silently asked myself when Al ordered both chopped liver *and* pork chops, *to ending bourgeoisie excesses and bringing economic equality to all?*

Not only that, but despite his cover Al was so damnably *Russian*—the caviar, the Tokarev pistol like Yasha's that I'd caught hidden beneath his jacket, and even an ushanka hat I'd seen him wear on one rainy evening—that he seemed to revel in being the bearer of a Dostoevsky-esque tragedy.

Al lifted a bite of chopped liver to his fleshy lips. "The Center has at last decided what to do about all the contacts Golos handled. You cannot, obviously, continue to handle them; the setup is too full of holes and, because of your connection to him, might endanger the entire apparatus. You will therefore turn them over to me; the Center and I will look into their backgrounds and decide which ones to keep."

Like hell you will . . .

I folded my hands in my lap. "I'll do no such thing."

Al set down his fork and slitted his eyes at me. "Miss Wise, I had thought you a rare breed—a Yankee with brains." He drew out the last syllable on Yankee: *Yank-eee.* "Now I see I was mistaken. I'll have you know that the Center just intercepted a letter that Victor Perlo's ex-wife recently wrote to President Roosevelt. You know Victor Perlo, of course, having recently met him against our wishes."

I stopped, my BLT suddenly suspended midair. How the hell did Al know about that? It didn't matter—Perlo was *my* contact, given to me by Earl Browder. "Oh? What sort of letter?"

Al took his time chewing, lips glistening with enough grease to make my stomach roil. "The sort that outlines in great detail all the espionage her husband has been committing. Also, the sort that mentions by name every single member of the Perlo group." He dabbed his lips with a paper napkin that was obviously beneath his dignity. "*And* a certain Miss Wise."

If that was true, it was likely only a matter of time before the FBI came sniffing at my door. *God damn it.*

My mind whirled, but I kept my expression placid. As placid as the eye of the storm in an impending hurricane, but all the same . . .

"Why would Perlo's wife do that? What's in it for her?"

(Because, Catherine, I'd learned that everyone—even the most heinous villain—has reasons for breaking the rules of life. Reasons that let them rationalize their wrongdoing and convince themselves they're in the right.)

Al dropped the wadded paper napkin on the table, lit a fresh cigarette with his trademark golden lighter. I noticed for the first time that it was embossed with a unique sort of double eagle, its wings spread wide. "Apparently," he said, "the Perlo divorce was very recent and *very* bitter. They're currently fighting for custody of their children. Victor's wife must have decided reporting on his espionage was the best way to destroy her husband."

I could have written Al's next lines myself.

"The Perlo group is dead in the water, Elizabeth. We're putting you on ice." He dragged in a mouthful of smoke, exhaled it with sensuous pleasure. "This is precisely why we frown on American handlers, especially the sort who don't follow protocols. Such irresponsible freewheeling on your part will not be tolerated in the future."

"Which protocols did I break?"

He leaned forward, tapped an angry sausage-thick finger on the table. "What protocols *don't* you break? You never vet your contacts before meeting with them, you refuse to clear new contacts with me and instead meet with multiple contacts at a time . . . Name it and you've done it, Miss Bentley."

Thank providence he didn't know anything about Mary Tenney

and all I'd done for—and with—her. Al would have blown a gasket right there on his stool at Chase's Cafeteria.

"So"—heart thudding in my throat—"does this mean that I've been burned? That I'm out?"

A tiny part of me almost wanted him to say yes, to end this sorry chapter in my life. But I recalled Yasha's steadfast dedication to his ideals and the intricate plan I'd made with Mary. I couldn't forsake either of them.

I had to stay with the Center, for now.

So, I forced myself to keep breathing while I waited for Al's answer. He shifted on his stool before deigning to respond. "Not yet, but you are barred from meeting with Perlo or anyone from his group ever again." He shook a finger at me. "I informed the Center that your life would lose meaning without this assignment, but I cannot help you if you don't start playing by the rules."

I couldn't help it—I let out a chortle of relieved laughter. Al gave me a look as if I was the village idiot before he continued. "This unfortunate episode has only reinforced in my mind the need for you to hand over the names of your other contacts. Muse, especially."

It was probably the firebomb that was the Perlo letter that made me less concerned, or perhaps I really was the loose cannon Al claimed. But I looked him in the eye, spoke more calmly than I had in my life. "Muse is retiring."

"Excuse me?"

"Retiring. As in, done with spying."

"Explain. *Now*."

I had only one shot to get this right. For Mary's sake, if not my own.

"With Golos gone, Muse feels that this is an opportune time for her to bid the Center a fond farewell. Exit stage left and all that." I hoped that line sounded natural, nonchalant even. "It's for the best, Al. She's unstable." I tapped my temple. "You know what I mean."

It was a gamble that was also patently false, but it was the best chance of killing the Center's interest in Mary by playing on their vestigial fear of a contact cracking and spilling everything to a psychiatrist. Better to eliminate the Center's interest so they would release her now than have them feel required to eliminate her later on.

Of course, that was banking on them having qualms about killing their own operatives. Which still remained to be seen.

I didn't so much as breathe while I waited for Al's demand that I turn Muse over anyway. Instead, he merely pulled out a dollar bill, tossed it on the table. "Fine. But before we go, you will hand over your contacts Robert and Dora, along with the Army photographer they work with, the one that gave you the specs on the B-29 Superfortress and the schedule for D-Day—we know that the three of them are connected. No questions, no arguments."

Now *that* I hadn't expected.

Robert and Dora were Nathan and Helen Silvermaster, and Lud Ullmann was the photographer who worked out of the darkroom in their basement. Between the three of them, they were my most prolific informants.

No arguments, my ass.

"I've controlled that ring since 1941. If you think I'm going to hand them over—"

"This is *not* up for negotiation." Al's eyes narrowed, and he gave a sharp inhale, the kind people give before delivering news of the fatal variety. "You think you're irreplaceable, Elizabeth, but the truth is, your contacts won't care if you're swapped out. In fact, they'll probably prefer someone who plays by the rules. Those three sources are too valuable to lose now that you have been exposed—"

"*I* haven't been exposed; *Miss Wise* has been exposed—"

Al held up a hand, nostrils flaring. "I smoothed over this Perlo business when I could have easily had you terminated. Now you tell me that Muse is out of operation, when I think perhaps you're hiding something. Maybe she's gone turncoat—"

"She hasn't—"

"Or is it *you* who has gone traitor? Do you perhaps wish to end up like your old comrade Juliet?"

"Juliet? Do you mean Juliet Glazer?" Ice-cold dread spiraled down my spine. "I don't know what you're talking about."

Except, suddenly, I did.

Al's grin was serpentine as he leaned forward. "Juliet Glazer was terminated, Miss Bentley. She is six feet under, by my orders, actually, after she decided to burn herself. Yes . . ." He nodded as the horrible truth of my new situation unfurled in my mind. "They never found her body, but I know exactly where her bones are buried. You see, I used to be the man behind the desk in Moscow, reading all Golos's reports. Before that, I was NKVD here in America, and one day I'm going to receive the Order of the Red Star for all I've done for the motherland. If you don't care to join Juliet and you don't want me tracking down your precious Muse, I want the real identities of Robert and Dora and that photographer. And I will have them before you leave this table."

Terminated. Six feet under.

If Al truly was as highly placed as he claimed—I was being forced to operate blind about him, but every fiber in my body screamed that he was telling the truth—then he could have me liquidated with a snap of his fingers. It went without saying that I could never voluntarily leave the underground, but it wasn't a stretch to imagine the alternative: that Al would have me killed, and then, with his single-minded focus, he'd track down Mary Tenney. If I refused to give in on this one thing, I would leave this restaurant forever keeping one eye over my shoulder.

And I would put Mary in terrible danger.

Perhaps Al was right—my newfound Perlo group had slipped through my fingers the moment Perlo's ex-wife wrote to FDR. And perhaps the Silvermaster trio wouldn't care one whit if they were assigned a new handler. Certainly, Helen would find reason to cheer.

And so, in order to save my skin—and Mary Tenney's—I offered up the Silvermaster ring on a freshly polished platter.

To make matters worse, two weeks later, I had to introduce Al to the Silvermasters and Lud Ullmann myself, which only rubbed lemon in the raw mess of my wounded pride, especially when Lud bragged about his coup regarding the date for the Allied invasion of Normandy. "I had a bet with one of my coworkers," Lud announced proudly to Al. "The poor sap owes me twenty greenbacks."

To which Nathan excitedly added, "And now we have the currency printing plates that the United States is preparing for use in the German occupation."

I couldn't miss the way Helen Silvermaster cooed like a Russian dove under Al's attention, as if she were some sort of predator who could sense my weakness and was happy to join the pack baying for my blood.

It didn't matter that I'd forever lost the Silvermasters. I'd bought Mary and myself some time. Except I hadn't heard from Mary in weeks.

Radio silence was *not* part of our plan. So, I went to her apartment.

There was no answer when I knocked and rang the bell, only a terrible feeling settling deep in my gut. It took me two minutes to jimmy the lock with the pick disguised as a prayer card Yasha had once given me for Valentine's Day.

The sight that greeted me made a sinkhole of my heart.

Every room: empty.

Each closet: bare.

Every wall: desolate.

I raced from room to room, praying I'd find a note or something, anything. But the only thing I discovered was the loose brick in the fireplace she'd shown me—her white chess queen.

The signal that she'd put our plan into motion. Except it was missing the rest of the message.

The queen is the most powerful piece, she'd repeated that night we'd crafted our plans and set up our codes. *This will be our Queen's Gambit.*

Mary had initiated our plan on her own, had cut me out of the opening maneuver and disappeared without a whisper of warning. Straight from plan A to plan Z.

I thought we'd been friends, confidantes. But now she was gone, and I had no idea where to find her.

I'm not ashamed to say that I crumpled down onto the kitchen linoleum right then and had myself a knock-down, drag-out cry, the sort that leaves your face blotchy and eyes looking like a bruiser's for the rest of the day.

I'd lost Yasha and now I'd lost Mary. I was truly, totally, and wretchedly alone.

Again.

Except this was worse than after my parents died. This time, I knew what I'd lost.

When I arrived back at my building, I checked the mail out of habit. Out of *hope*.

Nothing. No word from Mary.

In the hours and days that followed, I found myself slipping into dreary old habits, talking to myself or Vlad while my heart caved in on itself. My apartment echoed, and all the color had been leached out of life. It wasn't until two days later that I received a package without a return address. I held out hope against hope that it was from Mary, that she wanted to continue contact with me. Inside was the wooden chess set—all save the white queen—with the scratched board that Mary had taught me to play on.

It didn't make sense that she'd taken time while skipping town to mail this.

Unless . . .

I'd learned from Yasha never to accept items at face value. A jacket's button sometimes contained a coded message on its back, a shaving cream canister could conceal a roll of film, a spy's sketch of a butterfly might disguise plans on fortifications and positions of armaments.

A chess set might even hide a secret compartment . . .

Sockets had been drilled into each square for the wooden playing pieces.

What I needed was a toothpick or a paper clip. Lacking both, I rummaged through my knitting bag. My needles were too big, but the hatpin at the bottom was just right.

It was one of the center squares that contained the hidden mechanism, which released with a satisfying *pop*.

The base of the board separated from the top to reveal a secret compartment. I wondered if Mary had created this herself, or whether perhaps Yasha had helped her with it. Inside was a coded letter on tissue paper addressed to E.T.B.—the initials I always used on my personal correspondence—and clearly written in Mary's familiar handwriting. It took less than thirty seconds to retrieve the shared copy of the one-time pad we'd chosen that I'd hidden away in my hollow copy of *War and Peace*, less than two minutes to decrypt the jumbled mess of letters that made up Mary's message.

Dear Elizabeth,

I had to accelerate our plan. The boy will be in danger if they ever find me. I swear I'd sooner jump off the Golden Gate Bridge than allow anything to happen to the child.

Don't try to find me. I'll send word when I can.

The Center knows we are the most powerful pieces on their board. Stay nimble and always keep several moves ahead of them.

Just like that, I'd lost my last friend in the world.

|||||||||||||||||

NOVEMBER 23, 1963
6:23 P.M.

"Wait," Cat interrupted Elizabeth, shook her head as if to clear it. "Mary Tenney just packed up and left town? Didn't she trust you? And who is *the boy*?"

There was so much more to ask, but she found herself so caught up in Elizabeth's story that she could barely stop from rattling off more machine-gun-fire questions.

"Of course she trusted me, probably more than I trusted myself." Elizabeth spoke slowly, whether because she felt Cat wasn't picking up the story quickly enough or because she was still stung by Mary's betrayal after all these years, Cat couldn't tell. "But this was Russia and the NKVD, the same people who put an ice pick through Leon Trotsky and found poison an acceptable solution for individuals who became inconvenient. There was never any guarantee of safety, for any of us."

"All right, what about the rest of it? Who is *the boy*?"

Elizabeth folded her hands on the table in front of her—they'd moved back to the kitchen since the tuna casserole was nearly ready to come out of the oven—and leaned forward, an exact replica of the pose Cat had seen in a newspaper photograph of her hearings before the Senate and House Un-American Activities Committee. "Mary Tenney gave birth to a child while I was her handler."

"What? When?" Understanding dawned just as soon as the questions were out of Cat's mouth. "When she called you about fail-safes failing . . . and asked for your help getting things *taken care of*?"

Elizabeth nodded. "She didn't have an abortion then. The time she wanted to recuperate . . ."

"Was to have the baby."

Another nod. "A healthy baby boy. I was there when he was born. And I lied to the Center and told them Muse was in Bermuda, resting."

"Where was her son all this time? She couldn't very well keep a baby hidden in a kitchen cupboard every time one of her contacts came to visit." It didn't escape Cat's notice that Elizabeth had failed to mention him until now.

"A child would have put a damper on the pillow talk, wouldn't it?" Elizabeth gave a wry smile, one that seemed pained. Or forced. "She named him Jacob in honor of Yasha, which made me love her even more. And she found a family—a good American one in Tennessee—to adopt the baby. Still, I always blamed myself for not forcing Mary to retire after she had the child, for not clearing the way to raise the boy herself."

"So even though she always wanted a child, she gave birth, handed the baby over, and went straight back to work spying for the Center? What sort of mother does that?"

Elizabeth's gaze ossified into a glare. "You have no idea what Mary went through. Don't you dare judge her." She got up and poured herself a mug of now-cold coffee, laced it with a healthy shot of gin. All right, two shots. "She feared what sort of life her child would have, given that the Center never would have allowed one of its most productive honey traps to be burdened by a crying infant. If she'd kept the baby, she'd have faced one of the NKVD's three retirement options, and the child would have been at risk as well."

"As potential leverage against her, in case she ever stopped toeing their line?"

Another nod. "Once you've been a Soviet spy, there's always a hatchet hanging over your head, waiting to fall if someone exposes you."

"But you protected her."

Elizabeth shook her head. "I shielded her. It wasn't enough."

"And then Al demanded that you hand her over. And everything fell apart. Checkmate, right?"

Elizabeth looked at Cat with weary eyes. "Oh, Catherine, can't you see? Now I was alone on the board." She lifted her coffee mug to Cat in a tired salute better suited to a funeral. "And you should know this about me: I never, *ever* make good decisions when left to my own devices."

IIIIIIIIIIIIIIII

I'd been a *razvaluha* for a long time—that's Russian for a car that's falling apart as it goes. And I was about to hit a wall. A brick one.

Al showed up in my office at United States Service and Shipping for our next meeting. It was October 1945, and the war was finally over—Germany had capitulated, and then America had dropped two atomic bombs on Japan, hastening the end of the Pacific front.

With that, I felt vindicated in my wartime work, what with the Manhattan Project proving that America *had* been hiding critical information from her ally in Russia. I was just as patriotic as those scientists who had labored over the creation of Fat Man and Little Boy, all of us working toward an Allied victory.

Except now, just like America's wartime détente with the USSR, my own fragile alliance with Russia was crumbling to ashes.

I couldn't stop Al from visiting USS&S, but I wanted him in and out as soon as possible.

There was another reason I wanted him to leave.

I was drunk as a skunk. Boiled as an owl. Three sheets to the wind.

I'd spent my nights since Yasha's death and Mary's disappearance unable to sleep, pacing the floor as Yasha once had or surrendering to walk to Mary's old apartment in the Village until three o'clock in the morning. Last night, the straitlaced Vassar schoolgirl whose father had always warned her to steer clear of bootleg gin had needed something, *anything* to face the yawning chasm of loneliness and disgust and disenchantment that threatened to swallow her. So, while Vlad looked on with wide and confused eyes, I'd tippled one of Yasha's abandoned bottles of Hennessy cognac until the edges of the world went fuzzy. I thought I preferred them that way. And I'd helped myself again like a hedonist on holiday when I'd woken with a headache that felt like Satan himself was pounding a drum inside my skull.

Who the hell cared if I drank myself into oblivion?

No one. That was the tragic truth.

"Elizabeth, did you hear me?" Al had started off this visit at USS&S in a foul mood after trying to squeeze into a chair that wasn't suited to his walrus-sized frame, had given up, and now leaned awkwardly against my desk. His brow furrowed as if he had already asked the question more than once.

"I'm sorry." I rubbed the ache gathering at my temples. Wondered whether more cognac would soften that too. "My mind wandered."

"I said the Supreme Presidium of the Union of Soviet Socialist Republics has awarded you the Order of the Red Star." Al's announcement—with an exaggerated huff the second time around—made me stop everything. He gave me a filthy look as he pulled a paper clipping, in color, from his pocket. Had I not been so shocked, I might have laughed, given that this was the same award Al had once admitted to wanting. "This is a facsimile of the decoration—the original will arrive shortly. This profound honor is bestowed only upon the most devoted fighters to our cause."

I stared at the picture with its oxidized tin medallion over a crimson star, the embossed image of a Russian soldier wearing a long overcoat and hoisting a rifle over the sickle and star. I'd never heard of a spy receiving a medal of any kind, couldn't fathom why the Center would see fit to award me with anything so incriminating. Except . . .

I was a spy and therefore shouldn't fully exist, had ensured over all these years that my real name was not on a single scrap of evidence here in America. Perhaps deep in the bowels of Red Square there was a file with my name in Cyrillic. Something out of my control. And now, Russia wanted to publicly recognize me?

"This is a day to remember," Al finished with a puff of his chest.

A day when I realized the Russians were trying to frame me. Or buy me out.

Perhaps these cherished little bits of tin were being used to bribe Americans like myself, those who had become inconvenient for the NKVD. Well, the Center was about to find out just how inconvenient I could be.

"A great honor, indeed." And it might have been; had Yasha been alive or had Mary still lived around the corner from my apartment, maybe I'd have raised a glass of apple cider in a toast. Moscow, perhaps even Stalin himself, had taken notice of my efforts after all these years.

"The Order of the Red Star confers certain benefits." Al's unctuous monotone continued. "There's a comfortable monthly salary of fifteen hundred rubles per month, preferential living quarters in Moscow, and you can even ride the streetcars for free. Perhaps you should take a trip to Canada or Mexico before you relocate, enjoy a change of scenery." His words shook me fully awake, for surely I had heard wrong. Al wanted me to move to *Russia*, a land where I didn't even properly speak the language? I was as American as the Declaration of Independence—my ancestor had signed alongside Jefferson and Washington. I wasn't going anywhere.

But I'd learned it wasn't a good idea to contradict a member of the NKVD. At least not out loud.

"Also," Al continued, "I have more fortuitous news."

He said it strangely: *for-tu-ee-tous*. I almost laughed—I wasn't sure I could handle any more of his particular brand of news. *What game are they playing?* "What might that be?"

"The NKVD wishes to offer you a salary, plus a Persian lamb coat. And an air conditioner. In recognition for your years of loyal service."

Now I knew for certain . . . I was being bribed.

"To what end?"

"Excuse me?"

"The NKVD is trying to sweeten me up." My arms went akimbo. "So, I repeat, to what end?"

Al avoided my gaze by flipping through a pile of Russian travel leaflets. "You're being taken out of circulation, Elizabeth, from all your contacts and USS&S. This is *not* up for negotiation. However, this should tide you over until you're able to move to Russia."

My jaw dropped as he tossed an open envelope onto the table, its white mouth yawning open to expose a fan of crisp twenty-dollar bills.

"Two thousand US dollars," he said. "As a gratuity for past services and a token of friendship."

(What I should have done then was take the money and grovel at his feet for his magnanimity and that of Mother Russia before taking a page from Mary Tenney's book and hightailing it as far from Al and the Center as I could manage. But I didn't do any of that, because I was an idiot. And let's be honest, Catherine, also because I was fueled by my breakfast of courage-inducing cognac.)

Instead, I placed both my hands on Al's lapels and pushed. *Hard.*

Al stumbled from the edge of my desk and, like a walrus flopping on an ice floe (a scene I'd have given my imaginary Order of the Red Star to see), would have fallen to the floor had the wall not stopped him. "*Chert*, Elizabeth! What is wrong with you?"

I lunged toward Al with a prizefighter stance. Something irreparable had snapped inside me. "What's wrong is that you tell me in one breath that I'm getting an award, then that I'm being taken out of circulation from both the company and the rings of contacts I built from the bottom up. And that I'm supposed to be thankful because the Center wants to buy me out with some cash and a *god-*

damned air conditioner." I shook a livid finger in his face. "If I'm so valuable, then why the hell are you making demands, taking away my livelihood, and destroying my freedom?" I snorted when he didn't respond. "That's what I thought. You tell your bosses back home that Elizabeth Bentley can't be bought. And I'm *not* leaving America *or* giving up USS&S, damn it."

Al straightened to his full height, his chest heaving as he glared down at me. "You smell as if you've been drinking, which is entirely unacceptable. I am disappointed and disgusted at your reaction, Elizabeth, but I already anticipated this. To that end, I have recommended that the Party pair you with someone from home, perhaps a man posing as a Polish or Baltic refugee."

I pivoted to face Al, my eyebrows arched like deadly Cossack scimitars. "Pair me? As in reassign me to a new handler? Because I accept that wholeheartedly."

"Not as your handler." He brushed the wrinkles from his lapels, sniffed as if he wished he could brush me away so easily. "As your *husband.* The current arrangement is not working. You are an American woman, officially untrained, and you don't play by the rule book—there's no precedent. A Party husband will be able to guide you once you are back in Russia, as did Jacob here."

Except Yasha wasn't my husband. He was my *partner.* My *equal.*

I leaned forward, my fingers tented on the desk and my hackles up. Since when did I take orders from the Party? (In retrospect, Catherine, I now realize this might have been part of our problem, given that the Communists expected to be obeyed or they'd book you a pissed-on bunk at the nearest Siberian gulag.)

"If you refuse to move to Russia, I'm recommending you and your husband be posted outside of America, probably to Canada or South America." Al rubbed his jowls. "Of course, if such an arrangement is disagreeable to you, I would be amenable to persuading the powers that be *not* to match you with someone. *If* you resign from USS&S this instant, that is."

"Get out." I pointed to the door, opened the damned thing my-self when Al didn't move. "I never want to deal with you Russians again. You're all gangsters who care only about Russia, and the American Communist Party is a gang of foreigners. As of this day, I'm through with you."

"No, as of this day, Elizabeth Bentley, you are through having any further contacts with your operatives. And you will follow all of my further instructions *to the letter*." A vein pulsed at Al's tem-ple, and it occurred to me that this former NKVD agent was much larger than me and that all I had in the way of protection was Ya-sha's old switchblade, which was tucked into my purse. "You have become a serious and hazardous burden for us." His eyes narrowed dangerously. "By now, I'm sure you understand how the Center deals with burdens."

I recalled Yasha's worries before his death, magnified a thou-sandfold as Al halted on the threshold to issue one final ultimatum.

"Miss Bentley, do not step out of line again. Do not forget that we have the power to make you"—he snapped two fat fingers—"disappear."

I stared after him, the cash he'd left on my desk a cold parting gift.

IN RUSSIAN FOLKTALES, there is a story of a peasant who comes upon a sleeping bear in the winter forest and cuts off the creature's paw, then takes it home and gives it to his wife to boil soup from the flesh and make gloves from the fur. The bear wakes with a single-minded focus—to hunt down the peasant and find his lost paw.

I was the idiot peasant who had woken the bear that was the NKVD and, in refusing to hand over Muse and then insulting Al, had stolen its damnable paw and boiled it into a soup. There was no doubt in my mind that the NKVD was now going to be dogging my every step.

And they wouldn't fail to exact their retribution.

Al's further instructions arrived the next day typed and coded, commanding in his typical dictatorial fashion that I move into Hotel St. George in Brooklyn Heights—my brownstone was deemed too risky since it was likely being surveilled by the FBI and several of my contacts knew my address. I'd prodded the bear, and now the bear commanded that I leave behind the only home I'd ever made for myself, the very space where Yasha had died and where I'd always felt at peace.

There was no peace now, only shame. Everywhere I looked, I saw evidence of my failures staring me in the face. Everything I touched had turned to ash—even Coriolanus in his place on the windowsill had withered and died, a victim of my negligence after so many years of diligent care. Hennessy's cognac failed to soothe, since its very taste reminded me of Yasha and how I'd botched everything he'd so carefully built. So I'd poured the last of the Hennessy down the drain along with a vow to stick to gin when I needed to drown my sorrows.

To prepare myself and Vlad to move, I was packing up the last of Yasha's clothes to donate to the Russian War Relief (as stipulated in his final wishes—I hadn't been able to bring myself to box them up until they'd lost his smell) when a knock at my door startled me out of my sadness and anger. At least I had the sense to keep the door chained, especially considering that Vlad could hardly be bothered to pick his head up from his paws and snuffle the air before either ignoring a visitor entirely or rolling over for a belly rub. I was glad for the chain when I saw the unfamiliar man lurking in the hallway.

"Excuse me, ma'am." He stared at me intently, as if memorizing every detail of my appearance. "But I think my aunt used to live in this apartment."

Only a few days ago, my landlady had informed me on the stairwell that someone matching this man's exact description had been asking about me—what my schedule was, where I worked, how long I'd lived on Barrow Street. Was I being paranoid? Was I becoming one of those contacts who went off their rails and started seeing shadows in the dark?

Always trust your gut, Umnitsa. If something feels wrong, it is.

If this suit wasn't tracing me, then I wasn't a Communist spy queen.

Well. A *former* Communist spy queen.

I kept the chain on the door, closed it until I could see only one of the man's eyes. Was he FBI? Or NKVD, as Al had threatened?

"No one else has lived in this apartment for years." I willed my heart to stop fluttering within the cage of my ribs. If he was NKVD, I could expect the barrel of a pistol at any moment. "You have the wrong apartment."

Then I slammed the door in his face, flipped the dead bolt, and snapped shut all my curtains.

"Some help you are," I said to Vlad when he padded toward the window and nosed at my leg.

This man's visit was a warning. By being in New York—or anywhere in America, really—I was too close to the FBI while not far enough from the NKVD. I certainly wasn't going to take a vacation to Mexico or Canada as Al had suggested—we'd all seen how well that worked for Leon Trotsky.

Something had to give, and soon. Or I might well end up one of those women found dead in her apartment, undiscovered for weeks until the smell got too bad.

ııııııııııııııı

NOVEMBER 23, 1963
6:37 P.M.

Cat noticed how slowly Elizabeth moved while they ate the lackluster tuna casserole—the ancient peas were freezer burned, and apparently Elizabeth didn't believe in fresh produce, so Cat had substituted onion powder for real onion. Elizabeth's same hands that had gestured so animatedly when talking about her sources now fell limply at her sides between bites. Under normal circumstances, Cat would have felt guilty for making Elizabeth relive all these terrible experiences, as if she was forcing an exhausted, aging woman on some terrible Bataan Death March down memory lane.

But these weren't normal circumstances. And if anyone could survive a death march, it was Elizabeth Bentley. Hell, the woman hadn't even asked for a bathroom break since she'd started talking this afternoon.

Cat set down her fork and asked the question that had been niggling at her since Elizabeth's story went south. "Did you ever blame yourself for your fallout with Al and the NKVD?"

She expected Elizabeth to snarl like the semi-feral beast she was, but the former Soviet spy merely brought out that golden lighter, gave it three damnably annoying clicks. Cat had recognized it the moment it showed up in Elizabeth's reminiscences, wondered how it came to be in Elizabeth's possession given her falling-out with Al. "It's difficult to feel responsible considering Earl Browder intercepted one particularly long and chilling memo in which Al went through all the viable options of eliminating yours truly."

"No. Really?"

"Hmm." Elizabeth raised both eyebrows. "That would have saved you a lot of trouble, now wouldn't it, Catherine? The report was actually terribly unimaginative and by the book: Al deemed shooting would draw too much attention, faking my suicide was too problematic, and arranging an accident was judged too risky." Her tone was carefully measured, but Cat caught the way she shivered despite the heat of the casserole-scented kitchen. "But the clever mouse—or the Clever *Girl* in this case—gets the cheese. Or at least avoids the cheese laced with nerve poison."

"Meaning?"

"Meaning I beat them to the punch so the NKVD couldn't assassinate me without causing an international incident."

"*You* outmaneuvered the NKVD? Really?" This time it was Cat's turn to snort. "I think you're full of shit, Elizabeth. That's like outsmarting the FBI."

Cat didn't know what she said that was so funny, but Elizabeth doubled over in sudden laughter that quickly turned into a choking fit that had Cat thumping her on the back. It occurred to Cat that while Elizabeth wasn't that old, she also wasn't in the best of health. *Smoking, spying, and drinking will kill you early*, Cat mused. Although at the rate she was going, if Elizabeth's liver hadn't failed yet, Cat suspected it was pickled well enough to last at least two lifetimes.

Not that any of that mattered, given that Elizabeth might still wind up with a bullet between the eyes.

"I'm all right," Elizabeth finally rasped out, waved off Cat's assistance as she righted herself, cheeks flushed with color that made her suddenly seem younger and full of life. "Catherine, if your college major or being an assassin doesn't pan out, you may have a career waiting as a stand-up comedienne."

Cat frowned. "So, you're telling me you outsmarted the FBI?"

Elizabeth crossed her heels beneath her in one of those jarring mannerisms so at odds with her tarnished appearance, a glimpse into one of the many more elegant personas she had once played. That was, until she removed a small flask from her dress pocket. "Catherine, there's a saying that a jealous woman does better research than the FBI—it doesn't take much to outthink them. But after my falling-out with Al and knowing that the NKVD was ready to slip a noose around my neck, I was sick of jumping at every motorcycle engine that backfired and hiding from each strange bump in the night. A person can only be besieged from so many sides before they lose it."

All right, Cat thought. *I'll humor the old bat. For a while longer at least.* "So, what did you do?"

"Well, according to *Out of Bondage*, I went into a white-steepled

Congregational church on Long Island Sound and had a religious epiphany." The smile that slid onto Elizabeth's lips could only be described as *sly*. "There was a deep voice saying *You must make amends* before I walked out into blinding summer sunshine."

"I call utter bullshit. Don't tell me people actually bought that."

Elizabeth chortled. "Honestly, Catherine, that priceless anecdote was some of my best work. People lapped it up. And I *did* convert to Catholicism later." She gestured to the wooden crucifix nailed to her kitchen wall. "Although that was mostly strategic. As well as being a good way to hedge my bets for the inevitable day when I cash in all my chips."

"All right. We've come this far—you may as well tell me the rest." Cat picked up her empty plate and ran water for the dishes. *Am I really washing up for this woman?* She put the plate in the sink, refusing to go that far. "What's the real story?"

"There's that old Russian saying Yasha taught me: the best defense is an attack. The real story is that I did the last thing any of them expected—I attacked. And I did it *because* it was the last thing anyone expected." Elizabeth removed the stopper from the flask, kicked back God only knew what proof. "Pick your poison, so they say. To which *I* always say, choose the poison you know best."

ИЗМЕННИК
THE INFORMER

||||||||||||||||||||||||||||||||||||||||||||||||||||||||||||||||||||||||||||||||||||||||||

With a pang of nostalgia, I realized that the good old days were over. Now I was one of the hunted and no matter where I went, the footsteps of the hunters would be hot behind me.

—Elizabeth Bentley, *Out of Bondage*

14

NOVEMBER 1945

I recalled the old Lithuanian gentleman who had come into World Tourists and told of the Nazis killing his family during the war, my disbelief at his warning that the Soviets had been even more ruthless when they'd come under the guise of liberation. How Americans like me didn't realize what a paradise we were living in.

How could I have been so blind?

I'd hoped to take down Hitler, but in doing so, I had thrown my lot in with the wolf in sheep's clothing, just as America had done when getting into bed with Stalin. In trying to buy me off and then planning to have me killed when I wouldn't cooperate, the Party had become anathema to me. I now understood how much Yasha had shielded me from the dark machine that mangled decent human beings, whored out women like Mary Tenney, and ordered their own agents liquidated.

With what I knew of the Center's network here in America and what I'd done, I could never return to a regular life. Not because I maintained any delusions of grandeur about my own self-worth, mind you, but because neither the Russians nor the Americans would allow me to fade into the background. Not when I understood both their strengths and weaknesses.

If I gave in to the NKVD, I'd end up shivering in a gray and drafty Communist apartment in Siberia during a December snowstorm, sharing a package of crackers with my Party-mandated husband whose real name I would probably never learn. And that's if I was lucky. The more likely scenario was that they'd put a convenient bullet in my head.

If I threw my lot in with the FBI, my fellow Americans would shun me as a traitor and a leper.

Pick your poison, indeed.

But the FBI wasn't likely to murder me, so I'd just have to take the shunning on the chin. Hell, maybe I even deserved it for being so blind and idealistic. The school of hard knocks and all of that.

The New Haven FBI office I arrived at was an ordinary business building where the danger of detection was minimal, especially after I took the elevator to the third floor and backtracked down the fire stairs. Beyond the receptionist's partition was an office in a drab shade of puce, its linoleum peeling off the floor and water stains marring the ceiling. Was this room with its government-issue metal desk and two uncomfortable office chairs where I would slide out of this ugly mess?

I almost bolted when the secretary asked me to wait in the interrogation room, fell back on the old Party maxim of my revolutionary days: when you're in a tight spot and want to keep calm, think of a group of words—it doesn't matter whether they make sense or not—and repeat them over and over to yourself until you have drowned out everything else.

Safety. Freedom. America. George Washington. Crossing the Delaware.

This was my Delaware. And there was no turning back.

"I'm Agent Buckley, and this is Agent Jardine, our specialist on the New York Communist scene." Buckley, in his double-breasted wool tweed suit, was the New Haven office's Soviet expert; I'd asked for him specifically. "I want Agent Jardine to sit in on our interview today."

Interview . . . Interrogation . . .

My pulse was thrumming in my fingertips, and I was already perspiring beneath my dark wool suit. I kept on my kid leather gloves as we shook hands so the agents wouldn't notice my sweating palms. "Thank you for seeing me today, gentlemen." I kept my voice level, bored even. I was struck by both men's faces: lined with fatigue but lacking the superficial arrogance and underlying fear that I'd seen on so many Communist faces over the years. "I hope I'll have some information that's helpful to you."

Helpful while also loosening this double noose around my neck.

"Why don't you start by telling us a little about yourself?" Buckley prompted. "Explain how a woman like you got mixed up in Party business."

And that's how it went, these two FBI agents in their striped ties tossing me softball questions while I cherry-picked which tidbits to tell them. I spoke of my desire to see America awash in economic equality during the Depression and how I wanted Hitler to fail during the war. I chose each word wisely, knowing that this first impression meant everything, thankful that I'd been able to resist a drink that morning. I must come across as well educated and eloquent, well-intentioned, and above all, *stable*.

And I could tell they were biting; hook, line, and sinker.

The agents scribbled on yellow legal pads, filling the pages until they had to call for more when I started speaking of Yasha, World Tourists, and even USS&S.

All the while, I was the perfect idealist. I'd just wanted to see a better world.

I didn't tell Agents Buckley and Jardine *everything*, but I sprinkled in enough chicken feed to make them *believe*. That was the key—that they accept this version of my story as ironclad truth.

Which was also tricky, given that I had absolutely no documentation of anything, which also meant they weren't likely to arrest me. All my evidence was gone, either passed along to the Soviets or turned to ash in my Barrow Street fireplace. Yasha and I had broken many cardinal rules of spycraft, but never had I *ever* kept a single page of incriminating material. And now I was kicking myself for a month of Sundays because of it.

All I had was my memory and my word. It would have to be enough.

Even if what I gave them wasn't quite the *whole* truth.

I dropped names; I had to. Not all of them—certainly not Mary Tenney or Earl Browder (who couldn't help me, given that after intercepting the memo about my possible execution he had been expelled from the Party for his public views concerning postwar harmony between the US and USSR), or even William Remington—I focused on those who had already been outed or lost to me, including the Silvermasters and Perlo group. I wasn't endangering the Perlo group by naming them, given that the letter by Perlo's ex-wife had already landed them on the FBI's watch list. I hoped that perhaps the Silvermasters would come to see the truth as I had, that the Party they served wasn't the savior we'd been led to believe.

I talked all afternoon and long after the sun set. Told Agents Buckley and Jardine of microfilm carried in my knitting bag (which included specs on American military strength), which Whelan's Drug Store I'd met Mary Tenney at once three years before (without naming her, of course—the one on Vanderbilt Avenue, with the sign for a dance studio on the second floor that read *Guaranteed $5 Course: If you can walk, we can teach you to dance*), what shoe size Helen Silvermaster wore (size 11 wide—the woman might have passed for a Hollywood starlet, but her feet were boats—which I knew after tracking down a pair of stunning black slingbacks for her as a Christmas gift in 1942). Buckley sent out for sandwiches, but neither FBI agent touched theirs. Finally, when it was over and

I'd given them my new contact information at the Hotel St. George, they both stood, their metal chairs scraping against the linoleum.

"We'll be in touch, Miss Bentley." Which meant they weren't going to arrest me, at least not today. Of course, on the other end, they couldn't offer more than that, not until they'd verified that this wasn't a trap set by the Russian Secret Police.

I accepted their handshakes, gloves still on. "I certainly hope so."

My ears perked to hear their excited murmurs that started before I'd even left the office.

I think we've got something here, Buckley.

You're damn right. This goes straight to Hoover's desk.

I was now a defector.

TWO DAYS AFTER my initial interview, FBI's Manhattan office on Foley Square called me in to corroborate my claims (if they thought I'd waver, they were wrong), and the day after that I met two new agents—Spencer and Kelly—at a hotel near USS&S.

"Do you recognize this one?" Spencer showed me FBI surveillance photographs of known Russian operatives, trying to link my information to existing files. Oftentimes, the shots were too grainy or taken from too far away to make a positive identification.

Not so today.

Because the jowly face of the man ducking out of a Woolworth's in grainy black and white . . .

. . . was Al's.

I wanted to shout his name from the rooftops, but instead . . . I faltered. Here was something concrete I could give the FBI, a direction I could point them that they could verify and confirm. It also meant I was blowing wide open the cover of my direct superior.

This was a dangerous game of Russian roulette I was playing. One I would be lucky to escape from unscathed. Then again, Al had considered how best to execute me.

I glanced up to see both FBI agents staring at me expectantly.

Without realizing it, I'd starting working one of their pencils between my fingers.

"I know him." I set the pencil down, heart thudding. "His code name is Al—I was never given his real name, of course. He told me he's a Czech businessman working in Washington, DC. That's just a cover story, of course."

"You're sure this is him?" Kelly fixed me with a gimlet eye, the barely leashed eagerness in his stare akin to one of Pavlov's dogs just before the bell rang. "You're one hundred percent sure?"

"I'd swear it on my father's grave. Why?"

Spencer rubbed his forehead, his eyes wide. "That's Anatoly Gorsky, Soviet *rezident* here in America, head of the NKVD in America and first secretary at the Soviet Embassy. We think he's responsible for sending ten thousand documents from London to Moscow during the war."

Shit. Holy shit. *And a fuck or two for good measure.*

As it turned out, it was a day made for cursing.

"We just intercepted a coded memo from Gorsky to Russia last week, outlining specific liquidation plans for one of his contacts. Ruthless, really, either faking her suicide or dribbling a little agent X on a handkerchief and, how did he put it . . . ?" Spencer's eyes narrowed, and he flipped through his notes. ". . . *hoping for the best.*"

I'd already been told by Browder that Al had been brainstorming ways to eliminate me, but I thought the plans had all been rejected. Some invisible hand closed around my throat. "What was her name?"

"Myrna."

I shall refer to you as Myrna in all my correspondence with the Center, although you shall remain known as Miss Wise to your contacts.

Shit, shit, shit. I was definitely *not* feeling very wise or clever right now.

Buckley glanced at me, must have caught the way the blood had drained from my face. "That's not you, is it?"

"Myrna is one of my code names." I was sure Spencer—and probably the secretary in the room next door—could hear the tremor in my voice. I'd known when I'd joined the underground that I was swimming with sharks—Yasha had helped coordinate Trotsky's assassination, for crying out loud—but it was a different thing entirely to hear that you might soon be twitching on the floor while foaming at the mouth from nerve agent.

"I'm going to need some sort of protection from the FBI." The room was suddenly hotter than the flames of hell as I decided to leapfrog a few steps of my plan. "Surely, you can see that."

"We understand the predicament you're in, Miss Bentley, but I'm afraid that in order for us to guarantee your safety, we're going to need proof of your claims."

I could tell from the gleam in both Agent Spencer's and Agent Kelly's eyes that they *wanted* to believe me—desperately, fervently desired nothing more—but also that they needed more from me.

UPON UNLOCKING MY apartment door, I froze when I retrieved the slips of paper from where I'd hidden them between the door and the frame. The numbers were out of order, no longer arranged to the day of Yasha's death. My room had been tampered with, no doubt about it.

The switchblade came out of my purse, blade drawn. I slowly opened the door the rest of the way, left it open as I threw on the lights.

Everything else was in its place, just as I'd left it that morning. *Almost.*

"Who was here, Vlad?" I asked my dog, but he only followed me from room to room, inscrutable. Why, oh why, hadn't I gotten myself a fearsome guard dog instead of this charming pile of fleas who had probably begged for an ear rub from the masked intruder?

The dark strands of my hair that I'd strategically placed atop my folded linens, along my shelf of books, and even in my sock drawer had all been disturbed. All the pieces of Scotch tape I'd attached to dresser drawers and even the bathroom medicine cabinet had been broken.

"Not the NKVD, then," I murmured to Vlad. "Right, boy?"

For if the NKVD had visited my room, they'd never have left so blatant a calling card. No, if they'd been here I'd never have known until a garrote was around my throat.

This was the work of the FBI, a black bag job to see if there was anything that would prove or disprove the claims I'd made to Agents Buckley and Jardine.

Unfortunately for them, there was nothing to find, no bona fides. Fortunately, they'd missed the proof I planned to show the FBI, hidden away beneath a floorboard I'd jimmied loose beneath the bed.

THE NEXT DAY as I strode down the corridor of the Manhattan hotel where I'd agreed to meet the FBI, it was reassuring to feel Yasha's switchblade, which I'd taken to tucking into the strap of my brassiere; I also had the proof the FBI sought hidden in the deepest cavern of my knitting bag. I knocked on the door—three times, as agreed—then ironed out my features to discover that a man in his late thirties draped in an ill-fitting brown suit and a well-worn fedora had joined Spencer and Kelly.

"I'm Thomas J. Donegan," said the fedora agent. "Head of the Major Case Squad."

Major Case Squad . . . I liked the sound of that. High enough on the ladder to be worth my attention. And high enough to show that the FBI was taking me seriously. *Very* seriously.

"Everyone in the office calls him the Hat," Spencer piped up. "Because he's always coming or going, no time to take off that godawful fedora."

I merely removed my coat and a fabulous new angora hat I'd treated myself to. I nearly confronted these agents with their messy ransacking of my room, then thought better of it. Let them think they had the upper hand. Instead, out came my proof, which I tossed onto the hotel bed.

"Here's some Moscow gold," I said by way of greeting. "Two thousand dollars." I affected a perfect mask of insouciance as Spencer thumbed through the crisp bills with bulging fly-eyes. (Still a hefty sum today, back then it was nearly three times a working man's yearly wage.) "A gift to me from Al, or Anatoly Gorsky, as you know him."

Donegan—the Hat—ignored his junior colleague. "One question, Miss Bentley: Why would the Russian *rezident* give you two thousand dollars?"

His accusation hung in the air. There were many reasons why the NKVD might give someone that much cash, none of them good.

"It was a thinly veiled bribe meant to buy my loyalty. And potentially entice me into accepting a Russian husband who would take me back to the motherland and spy on me until one of us offed the other."

"I assume the bribe didn't work?"

I fluttered my left hand at him, where Yasha's gold-and-ruby ring glinted. "I'm here, aren't I?"

"Well, Miss Bentley." Donegan cracked a smile that didn't reach his eyes. "If this is indeed from the Russians, it's the only money we've ever gotten back from the Lend-Lease program."

I smiled at the agent's little joke. "Keep it as evidence if you want. Also, do you want me to keep or cancel the meeting I have scheduled with Gorsky? It's four days from now."

I desperately wanted to cancel, hoped never to see Anatoly Gorsky again.

"Don't change anything about your regular schedule." Donegan pocketed the envelope of cash, which left a telltale bulge beneath his jacket. I felt a sudden pang at its loss, my worry about the future increasing with every moment. "We need evidence, and we don't want to tip our hand—or yours—to the Russians."

"So, act natural?"

He patted his pocket. "It's as if you've done this spy bit before."

"Once or twice." I waited for him to give me further instructions.

Unfortunately, his directions were the last thing I wanted to hear. "Well, Miss Bentley, I'm here to ask you to do something else for us. You see, we'd like you to play double agent."

I couldn't help myself—I balked. "You want me to spy for you? On the Russians?"

"Think of it as a little reconnaissance to ferret out the full extent of the relationship between the CPUSA and the USS&S, the Party here and the NKVD. That sort of thing."

Everything went cold. I may as well have marched myself into Stalin's office and announced my betrayal. Booked myself passage to the nearest gulag and shot myself in the head. "I can tell you most of that."

"But without any proof. We need details—offices with clear paper trails that we can get warrants for, that sort of thing. Remember, Miss Bentley, we're a democratic country that operates under the stance of 'innocent until proven guilty.' We want to believe you, truly, but we need *more*."

When a rat is on a sinking ship, it has no choice but to claw its way out of the waters. And my ship was sinking, compliments of the torpedo that I'd sent careening straight into its bulwarks. I'd cut my ties with the Center when I'd crossed the threshold of the FBI's New Haven office and spilled my story.

I couldn't go back, only forward. I needed the FBI and they needed me.

"Now that you mention it . . ." I swallowed hard, wondering how much I was going to regret these words. My tongue felt like a heap of gristle and my voice came out in a minor key, flat and dull. "I've always been interested in a career in counterespionage."

About as interested as I'd always been in drinking cyanide or driving myself off the Brooklyn Bridge in Yasha's LaSalle. Unfortunately, I didn't have much of a choice.

FOUR DAYS LATER, I found myself waiting outside Bickford's restaurant on Twenty-Third Street for Gorsky, drilling myself to call him *Al* and not *Anatoly*, my mind skimming through the litany of information the FBI agents wanted me to glean from Russia's most senior operative in America. The FBI and I had pieced together Al's routine, that he'd fly to New York on Eastern Air Lines from Washington National. From there, he'd take the subway and then arrive on foot at Bickford's. It didn't escape my notice when Agents Kelly and Spencer—dressed in civilian-grade khaki and nondescript button-down shirts—passed by on the opposite street as Al approached. I, on the other hand, had no disguise, had merely made liberal use of my Victory Red Bésame lipstick.

Its shock of color on my otherwise pale face was violent and brutal. Savage, even.

My battle paint. For after all, this was war. And I intended to win.

"You seem well, Comrade Bentley." Al's oily voice shook me from my reverie as we walked away from Bickford's. To my surprise, he started off the interview by presenting me with a gift box—no fur coats or air conditioners this time, just a lovely red flowered silk scarf from Saks Fifth Avenue that I looped around my neck. Following the war with its silk rations, the gift felt beyond decadent. "Think of it as an early Christmas present," he said as he cupped a hand around a cigarette and lit it with that golden lighter of his. I'd finally realized its double-headed eagle emblem was from Russia's coat of arms—and the damned thing's sharp-eyed stare seemed honed on me tonight. Something told me if I failed tonight, I'd find something more akin to a vulture picking the meat from my ribs. "And who is this?"

I had Vlad on a leash, had decided to bring him as a way to focus on something other than my nerves. And perhaps also to keep from picking a fight with my handler as I had last time.

"This is Vlad." I was surprised when Al reached down and ruffled my dog's fluffy ears. "He's kept me company since Yasha's death. If you have a stick in one of those pockets, he'll be your new best friend."

"Then I shall have to remember a stick. For next time." Al straightened and we continued walking, appearing to anyone who cared to look like two old friends enjoying an evening stroll. "I presume you are recovered from last week's unpleasantries?"

Recovered enough to turn defector. "As well as can be expected."

"Good. I wanted to talk about USS&S, Elizabeth." No beating around the bush, then. "It appears you have yet to vacate your position at USS&S. Do you not understand the problems with retaining your place there?"

"I also wanted to discuss USS&S." My palms were clammy, my mouth filled with cotton. When had I become so nervous? "You know, I've never really understood the relationship between our enterprise and the CPUSA. I assume we're a cobbler of sorts—accepting false passports, diplomas, other official papers. We're a front for the Party, but Yasha never went into the exact details—he focused on everything behind the scenes while I ran everything up front."

It wasn't exactly a lie, but it wasn't the truth either. And I was talking too damn fast. Even Vlad seemed to notice my discomfort, glanced up and cocked his head at me in question.

I continued, slower this time. "I've been wondering, how much money do we make for the Party? Does that all funnel back to the NKVD? Or does it go elsewhere?"

Gorsky looked askance, studied me just a little too long. I was rambling, which was out of character. "What brought all this about?"

Too much, Elizabeth. I was nervous at playing the double agent, and it showed. *Change the subject, and fast.*

"You know what they say about idle hands . . ."

"I'm afraid I don't."

"They're the devil's tools—you've really never heard that?" I needed to soften my cadence and inflection. "Al, I'll be honest . . ." (For what it's worth, Catherine, when you hear someone utter those words, assume they're lying. Or hiding something.) ". . . I have no intention of leaving USS&S. You forced me to break off contact with all my old sources, and now I have nothing else left to do."

"As I said, perhaps after your year is up, you might receive contacts. Until then, Moscow needs to know that you'll play by the rules."

Oh, I'm already playing by the rules, Anatoly Gorsky. My rules.

"Patience has never been my strong suit." I kept my voice light, but Gorsky didn't seem to catch the inflection.

"As you've demonstrated many times." Al cleared his throat, glanced down the next street. "I'm afraid we must part ways here— I have another contact to meet. *Proshchay,* Miss Bentley. Good-bye, Vlad. Until we meet again."

I returned the farewell, inwardly fuming that this meeting had been an utter waste of time—I hadn't gotten a scrap of real intelligence to give to the FBI. Now I knew how my own contacts felt when they had nothing of substance to report, could finally empathize with Bill Remington and his recipe for rubber made from garbage. *Next time . . .*

Except there wouldn't be a next time.

I SHOWED UP at the FBI office the following Friday morning to sign the manifesto that Kelly and Spencer had written up based on my full testimony. It was a colossal 107 pages—no light reading there—

which I'd been informed J. Edgar Hoover himself would use to create a report about Soviet espionage in the United States. I'd unleashed something huge at the FBI, something they were planning to run with.

And that meant I had something to bargain with, even if I'd failed to gather any fresh intelligence last week.

"I don't have anything to report from Al. Anatoly Gorsky, I mean." I tugged at my scarf, the same Al had given me. It really was lovely *and* it matched my Victory Red lipstick, a combination that made me feel like I could conquer the world. "Our meeting last week was unproductive. Also, it's odd—I haven't heard from him this week. He's usually more punctual than Greenwich time."

Spencer gestured me to a metal chair across from his desk. We were in the interrogation room, the double glass at my back. I preferred it that way, liked to see who was entering without having to turn around. "That's because there's a mole." Spencer ran a hand over his balding pate. "Someone may have exposed you."

That didn't make sense—not when *I* was the mole. "The Soviets couldn't possibly know anything—I've been careful."

"It's possible one of the British intelligence birdwatchers may have gone rogue."

"Wait, what?"

Spencer sighed. "The FBI shares frequent reports with the Brits—it's a professional courtesy, since we're longtime allies chasing the same bad guys. The leak about you isn't on our end, which means it must be on theirs."

"And what information about me did you share with them?"

"Summaries of your interviews, mostly."

I gaped and bolted upright in my chair, suddenly electrified for all the wrong reasons. "That means they know everything."

Spencer winced, ran a hand over his forehead. "It's possible one of their operatives alerted Moscow."

Terror squeezed at my throat. "The Center could come after me, you know. For retribution. Gorsky already threatened as much."

"True, but that would be out of character even for the NKVD, given that you're American, not Russian. Not even Stalin wants the headache of an international incident, and harming you would simply validate the importance of your claims. Plus, you're now worthless to Russia since you've already told us everything you know. Don't worry—we have an agent posted at your building, and we're wiretapping the phones of everyone you named in your interviews. If one of them so much as sneezes wrong, we'll hear. Plus, all Soviet transmissions dried up as of last week. It's damn near impossible to pass out liquidation orders when you're operating under radio silence. We'd know if they sent any orders about you."

Liquidation. Spencer used the word so casually, but he wasn't the one potentially being liquidated. Then I realized what Spencer had said, probably without even meaning to.

We'd know if they sent any orders about you.

I leaned forward, both hands splayed on the table. "Soviet codes are impossible to crack—I've burned through enough one-time pads to know." Agent Spencer actually squirmed in his seat. "Do you mean to tell me that the same organization that just leaked the entirety of my interviews to Stalin has somehow managed to decrypt Russia's code? How is that possible?"

Spencer didn't get to answer—the office door opened and in walked a stocky agent in a department store suit, his neck almost as thick as his skull, hair close cut in a military shave. I knew him from his portrait that hung downstairs in the FBI office. In every FBI office, actually.

J. Edgar Hoover.

His face might have been that of a schoolyard bully in his youth and now belonged to a man who wouldn't blink when ordering illegal wiretapping or flinch when interrogating members of the Mafia. Hoover would have made a formidable enemy; thank God and all the angels he was on America's side.

Which meant he was on *my* side. For now, at least.

"Thank you, Agent Spencer," Hoover said. "I'll take it from here with Miss Bentley. Or should I call you Gregory?"

Gregory . . .

Umnitsa, Miss Wise, Myrna . . . and now Gregory.

Confidential Agent Gregory was my gift from the FBI in what was becoming an ever-lengthening list of my code names. The FBI had determined that giving me a man's name would provide me an added layer of protection, but I wondered if this was just another sign that they—like the rest of the world—didn't quite know what to do with a female spy.

I wondered what had prompted this appearance of the head of the FBI, how long Hoover had been waiting on the other side of the double glass.

I expected the red-blooded head of America's intelligence agency to be contemptuous of a mere woman who had spied for our current enemy, but Hoover only straightened the knot of his striped tie before he sat in the too-small metal chair Spencer had just vacated. "I wanted to introduce myself personally and convey my gratitude to you for enlightening us about what was going on beneath our noses. Allying with Stalin was a necessary evil during the war, but now we need to look after our own interests. That means hunting down every Communist in America who sympathizes with the sickle and hammer. Miss Bentley, by informing on the Soviets, you single-handedly ended the golden age of Soviet espionage here in America."

Well. I rather liked the sound of that. Except . . .

"Except I'm afraid you still don't have any proof. *I* don't have any proof."

Hoover waved an unconcerned hand. "I'm confident we'll be able to get the proof we need when we go to a grand jury."

"Grand jury?" My throat suddenly constricted; I remembered the hell Yasha had endured when he'd been indicted. Was I doomed to follow in his footsteps? "May I ask who will be on the stand?"

Hoover steepled his fingers, leaned forward over them. "Let me assuage your fears, Miss Bentley. You came to us of your own volition and proved with your interviews precisely what I've feared would come of Truman's laxity in the Oval Office: that our government has been infiltrated from within. Now, with your assistance— and I'm sure you'd be willing to help us by testifying, perhaps even before the Senate—we're going to root out the slimy Soviet bastards once and for all."

I was most certainly *not* thrilled at the idea of testifying before grand juries *or* the Senate, but I still heaved an inward sigh of relief, given the fact that *I* wouldn't be the one squirming under the microscope. "So, I'll have immunity from prosecution?"

"Provided that your testimony helps us put away other Communist spies, yes. The problem is, Miss Bentley, that you've provided us with plenty of information but no documentation. However, we believe every word of your story. *I* believe you."

"Why?" It didn't make sense that the FBI would just believe me out of the goodness of their hearts, even after they had ransacked my apartment and found nothing to contradict my statements. Hell, even Hoover's appearance and his countenance toward me right now were a conundrum. I'd given them everything, including my honesty—now I wanted their side of the story. Because I knew deep in my gut that they'd been keeping something from me. Something critical.

Hoover sighed. "I believe you because we have Russia's decrypted messages to prove everything you've told us. To answer your earlier question of how such a thing is even possible, it's called Project VENONA. You see, our agency figured out a few years ago—right around the time of the German advance on Moscow— that the Soviet company manufacturing one-time pads made the critical error of producing around thirty-five thousand pages of duplicated key numbers."

I gasped. "Meaning none of those keys were secure."

Hoover nodded. "Apparently, the company had a hard time scrambling to keep up production, and they panicked, deciding to repeat keys. Of course, that duplication undermined the security of the one-time system that protected every Soviet transmission."

I wanted to groan at the idiocy, but I held myself perfectly still, my very breath poised at the rest of Hoover's story. At how this verified *my* story.

"I can't go into its details, but our cryptanalysts noticed the re-uses and decided to crack them—we believed Stalin might be undermining our interests by attempting to negotiate a separate peace with Germany. What we found instead was a detailed chronology of Russian espionage here in the United States, all encrypted by the NKVD." He raised his eyebrows. "And by you. Umnitsa was by far the most prolific handler here in America—your fingerprints are all over those transmissions."

I bowed my head in a rare flush of pride at the recognition of my work, and he continued. "I'm telling you all this so you know that we believe you, that we *need* you. We have information that at least three hundred of our own citizens have been supplying the Soviets with intelligence throughout the war."

"Does that include my contacts?"

Hoover seemed to be choosing his words wisely. "Based on your statement, we've been able to comb Bureau files and corroborate code names with people using mainly personnel and travel documents. Perlo is Eck, Nathan Silvermaster is Robert, and so on."

Part of me wanted to collapse with relief; the other wanted to rock on my heels with excitement. "Then you have all the evidence you need, wrapped up with a shiny bow by none other than Mother Russia herself."

Hoover frowned, tapped the knuckle of his forefinger on the table. "Unfortunately, it's a gift we can't unwrap for a grand jury. Project VENONA isn't for public consumption. Not even the new Central Intelligence Agency knows about it. Hell, I even thought about keeping it secret from President Truman. One thing's for sure: we don't want Russia to know that we spent years during the war decrypting their diplomatic cables. We want Russia to continue using the same codes they believe to be unbreakable. So even though revealing Project VENONA would result in convictions for a good many American traitors, we cannot use this evidence. You see the problem?"

"You have no proof. Other than me."

"Correct."

I weighed my options, saw only one clear path. "Well." I straightened my spine, lifted my chin as I leveled my gaze at J. Edgar Hoover. "Then I'd better prepare my testimony for your grand juries."

THE SUBWAY STOPS passed in quick succession, but I was too busy mulling over my conversation with J. Edgar Hoover to notice any of them. A grand jury . . .

Dear God . . . What am I getting myself into?

I did everything right that evening.

On high alert, I paid extra attention to every grandmother, businessman, and child who passed me on their way to a seat. Scanned every man—and woman—who stood and swayed with the motion of the metro car.

I double-, then triple-checked that I wasn't being followed when I finally got off at Clark Street station.

Even walked all the way down Henry Street and back up Monroe Place before heading toward the Hotel St. George, where Al had insisted I relocate. I'd wanted to move after going to the FBI, but that would have been a red flag.

It wasn't enough. Not when I approached my room to find the door ajar.

As if whoever had broken in wanted me to know that they'd paid me a visit.

I should have turned back around, called the cops. Or the FBI.

Except . . .

"Vlad?" I left the door open behind me as I removed the switchblade from where I'd hidden it in my brassiere. Flipped it open. Usually Vlad was waiting at the threshold with his raggedy terrier tail thumping against the carpet, eager to remind me where his treat jar was hiding. I knew I should leave, but this was *Vlad*. I couldn't—*wouldn't*—abandon him, was suddenly kicking myself for not taking him with me today.

The hair on the back of my neck prickled the instant I turned on the lights.

A dark and sickly fear pooled in the space between my shoulder blades when I spied Al's cigarette lighter standing upright on my kitchen table, its golden eagle glinting starkly in the weak light. A gift, a calling card . . .

"Vlad?"

My voice took on a higher pitch. Panicked.

"Vlad? *Vlad?*"

And then I screamed.

My loyal companion lay sprawled on the kitchen linoleum in an ocean of his own blood, the gaping mouth of a death-red wound slashed across his furry throat.

An animal sob of pain erupted from deep in my soul as I crumpled to my knees beside him, dropped the switchblade, and pressed my hands against the bloody gash in a vain, hopeless, *desperate* attempt to staunch the life that was spilling out of him. Vlad's eyes fluttered open, and he lifted his head as if he could still rise to greet me. His tail thumped. Only once.

As if he'd been waiting for me.

"Oh, Vlad . . . Vlad, Vlad, *Vlad* . . ." Heedless of the still-warm blood, I gathered my beautiful, loyal dog into my arms as if he were my child, pressed my forehead to his as another sob wracked my body. "You're my good boy, aren't you? You've always been my good boy . . ."

I felt him wiggle as he always did when I picked him up, moaned in horror when the fresh spray of his blood fauceted into my lap.

And then Vlad, the last of my dear loyal wonderful friends, was gone.

I didn't even have a chance to scream when a man's gloved hand clamped down on my mouth and shoved me hard against the hotel wall. A white sunburst of pain exploded against my forehead and left me gasping and my ears ringing.

"Not so clever now, are you, Miss Wise?" With my arms pinned behind me, my attacker's free arm pressed painfully into the back of my neck. Unable to see his face, I recognized the guttural Russian cadence that no number of years living abroad could fully erase.

Al had found me out. And now, in this soulless hotel room, he was going to kill me.

Keep calm, Elizabeth. Remember your training.

Adrenaline hummed through my veins, and every fiber of my heart and lungs stretched taut with panic. My face pressed into the cold wall, no switchblade within reach, no opportunity to stomp his instep with my heels or even gouge my thumbs into his eyes. My options had become very limited, very quickly.

The man gave a low rumble deep in his chest. "You know, I wanted to kill you and so did the Center. They sent the instructions, told me to review the prospects and choose the method. I had it all planned out, you see. It was going to be a sublime death . . . painful, but glorious."

My bladder threatened to release from fear.

"But it's your lucky day, Elizabeth Bentley. AKA Clever Girl, Miss Wise, Myrna." He paused, his breath hot on my ear before his next words. "AKA Gregory . . ."

Shit, shit, shit.

"After such a betrayal, it would be so very satisfying to leave you here in this room, next to your dead dog, with your lifeless eyes staring up at the ceiling." His extra pressure on my neck elicited a desperate whimper from me. "Unfortunately, the Center reconsidered and determined that your heart in a box is more trouble than it's worth. The ramifications of spilling American blood on American soil and all that."

"Then why are you here?" I gasped out. "To scare me?"

I waited for the hammer that would crush my skull, the mallet that would mangle my fingers, the knife that would sever my hamstrings. Instead, Al only pressed me further into the wall.

"This is your message, Elizabeth: we're always watching." His murmur in my ear was a caress, a guarantee. "The NKVD has a long memory. You so much as take a lover, have a child, make a new friend . . . You can be sure that relationship—and that person you care about—will be short-lived. Do you understand?"

Somehow, I nodded. Then he wrapped his fingers in my hair and gave a sudden jerk of his hand that smashed my head into the wall anew. I slid to the ground as if in slow motion, landing with a thud that jarred my skull.

There was the sound of Al's footfalls receding down the corridor.

After that, only darkness.

JULY 1948

I'd failed Vlad, just as I'd failed Mary and Yasha.

Al's golden lighter was a brutal reminder that I didn't dare endanger anyone else with my incompetence.

Fighting red-hot tears every time I expected to see Vlad wagging his scraggly tail at me, I'd moved to the Commodore Hotel, where I'd hoped it would be harder for the Center to find me, even as I'd learned from the FBI that Al had returned home to Russia and was due to receive the Order of the Red Star he'd so craved.

And at night . . .

No matter how much time passed, I always woke from the same nightmare. A firing squad faced a blindfolded prisoner—sometimes Yasha, other times Mary Tenney, sometimes Nathan Silvermaster, other times myself—and the prisoner would point a finger at me and yell, "Traitor! It's you who killed me!" Shots would ring, the prisoner would die. And I'd look down to find Vlad lapping up the pool of their blood, his innocent eyes still so trusting and his furry muzzle wet with crimson droplets.

I knew what it was to hate then. The only question was who I hated more: The NKVD? Or myself?

I grew thin and pale and more exhausted than ever, jumped at every loud noise and checked and rechecked the new locks installed on my hotel door, wore my nails to the bone by chewing on them. I couldn't keep living like this.

But the NKVD kept their word even as the months turned into years. So long as I remained a solitary soldier—one whose ammunition was already spent—I no longer posed a threat to them. I'd traded my soul, and now I needed to prove my worth to the FBI.

That was the deal I'd made with the devil.

It took two weeks to retell my story behind closed doors at the US Courthouse in Foley Square, this time under oath as the FBI's star witness in front of a panel of twenty-three balding and white-haired men. I'd already given the FBI everything I knew, but even I could see as I looked around that without proof, the grand jury was unlikely to hand down a single indictment. Everyone I'd named was going to walk free; I'd believed I'd had a choice and had sacrificed everything—my life, my livelihood, *Vlad*. But, in hindsight, I'd never *really* had a choice; I'd sacrificed it all for *nothing*.

The NKVD, the Center, Moscow . . . they would all win.

Unless . . .

I had to blow this thing wide open, shock the hell out of America and terrify them into believing that the entire government had been infiltrated with Communists. And if I could do it while protecting myself at the same time?

I was ready to take matters into my own hands.

Against the FBI's strict admonitions that I avoid the media like a biblical plague of locusts, I did the exact opposite. Because honestly, sometimes a woman really does know how to run her own life.

I needed to go big. *Really* big.

"Hello, is Nelson Frank available?" I asked the *New York World-Telegram* secretary across the crackling line. Old habits meant I covered my mouth with one hand so that no one outside the telephone booth across from the Foley Square courthouse could read my lips. "Please tell him that Miss Elizabeth Bentley is calling—he once interviewed me for a story on the customs duties Russia charges on relief packages sent by Americans. I think he'd want to know that I have on-the-ground information on the government boom and sizzle going on at Foley Square."

It took exactly fifteen seconds before I was patched through to Nelson Frank.

"Miss Bentley, so good to hear from you again." Nelson's hungry voice was piranha-sharp over the line. "What's this Patty tells me about you having some juicy tidbits?"

"Can you clear your schedule tomorrow?" I fiddled with the coin return and held my breath, heaved a silent sigh of relief when he affirmed his day was open. "Oh, and why don't you invite that colleague of yours—what's his name, Woltman? The one who just won the Pulitzer after writing all those articles about Communism?"

I hung up with an appointment for noon the next day.

One thing was certain: I was going to need to stock up on Victory Red lipstick.

"WHAT THE HELL were you thinking?" J. Edgar Hoover was livid as he shook the morning issue of the *World-Telegram* at my face a mere two days later. Something told me the sweat stains in the armpits of his button-down shirt weren't due to the July heat. "'Red Ring Bared by Blond Queen'?" he read. "'The sparks that touched off yesterday's indictments originated in the gnawing pangs of conscience suffered by a svelte striking blonde from an old American family'?"

Those indictments he mentioned had been a shock yesterday; a grand jury had handed down indictments against the eleven Communists who composed the so-called politburo of the American Communist Party. I'd managed to box away my guilt at seeing former comrades charged with crimes that I, too, had committed—

they'd have their chance in court to prove their patriotism, just as I was having mine—while I read the triumphant article on my subway ride to the FBI office. I'd smiled for the first time since Vlad's death at Frank's portrayal of me as a mysterious blond naïf who hightailed it back to the US government once my small service—in the name of my country—to the Soviets had "mushroomed into a gigantic, treasonable assignment." I also appreciated the way Nelson had hyped the value of the first plans of the B-29 and the almost-daily airplane production numbers I'd secreted away in my knitting bag.

The story made me out to be a patriotic young woman who'd gotten in over her head and recanted everything Communist the moment she'd realized things had gone wrong. It was absolutely, positively pitch-perfect.

(Even if it turned out that I hadn't needed to go public to land the hunt for Communists on the front pages. Better to beg forgiveness than to ask permission, right?)

Hoover threw the offending paper on the metal table, his chest heaving while an electric fan sputtered and rearranged the hot air in the room.

I pursed my lips, shook my head. "I know," I conceded. "It's preposterous."

Except it wasn't, given that I'd told the FBI about Al killing my dog and threatening me. And they'd still insisted that their hands were tied until my testimony could garner the guilty verdicts they sought.

"Did you give them all this information?" Hoover's face turned an alarming shade of purple. My fingers itched to wipe the offending spot on the table where his spittle had just landed, too close for comfort. "On purpose?"

Time to change tactics. Scratch the confidence and verve . . . J. Edgar Hoover prefers his witnesses pliant and demure.

"I'm terribly sorry." I let my eyes flicker from my purse to Hoover and back as I dug for a handkerchief. "I didn't know what to do, what with the NKVD coming after me, and everything I've done going to waste. Nelson Frank just asked me a few questions . . ." I held Hoover's gaze for a moment with limpid eyes I let fill with tears, some of which were real when I thought of Vlad. Let Hoover think me hysteric and repentant. "I've ruined everything, haven't I?"

Hoover looked for a moment like he'd love nothing more than to throttle me, his fingers going white around the edge of the table instead. "Frank makes the entire agency look like saps by waxing poetic about how gobsmacked we were by your sudden defection. It's as if we didn't know there were Russian spies operating in this country. At least the indictments were handed down yesterday, before we were made to look like fools."

Except you didn't *know where the spies were in this country,* I wanted to add. *Not until I told you who they were.*

Hoover continued his tirade. "And where the hell did the blond bit come from? If you're blond, then I'm seven feet tall."

In fact, I'd suggested to Nelson that a blond bombshell would make better headlines. And it wasn't really a lie—after all, I'd worn a blond wig to meet my contacts. Once or twice.

"Who knows?" I merely shrugged. "Whatever sells papers, right?"

Or whatever would sell enough papers to make a woman so high-profile that the NKVD would never dream of offing her and outing themselves in the process. So high-profile, in fact, that her story would never, *ever* die.

I'd gone to the FBI for protection, but it hadn't been enough. Going to the press now had served a double purpose: lock down the indictments while also providing me with a bulletproof layer of security.

"So, what does this mean?" I asked Hoover. "Are you ordering me not to speak to the press anymore? To cease and desist?"

Hoover rose and pushed in his chair, leaned toward me with

two hands gripping the chair back. "You, Miss Bentley, are going to keep your mouth shut. Especially now that the Senate is gearing up for hearings. You're going to promise not to make any more unauthorized contacts and swear that you'll testify in front of the House Un-American Activities Committee."

"You have my word, Mr. Hoover."

The half lie was forged before those words even left my red-rimmed lips.

|||||||||||||||||

NOVEMBER 23, 1963
7:19 P.M.

Cat was still blinking back tears for the dead dog—faithful little Vlad reminded her of a cocker spaniel she'd had as a young girl—when Elizabeth got up and went to the kitchen sink, scraped her plate into the trash. It wasn't lost on Cat that Elizabeth had declared herself full after only a few bites, although she wasn't sure if that was due to the quality of the casserole or the turmoil at the story she was reliving. Cat expected her to start a fresh pot of coffee—Elizabeth Bentley seemed like the sort of woman to drink the stuff until she finally collapsed into bed at some godforsaken hour—but was surprised when she instead popped two Alka-Seltzer tablets into a glass. "Are you feeling all right?"

An admittedly incongruous question, given that Cat had come here to kill her. At this point, Cat wouldn't have been surprised if Elizabeth still kept Yasha's switchblade in her brassiere. She was far less helpless than she looked.

Elizabeth shrugged. "Close enough. Stop treating me like an old woman."

Except this time, instead of assuming her usual place at the kitchen table, Elizabeth folded herself onto the couch, an old green-and-white granny square afghan that had seen far better days spread across her lap. She looked as tired and frayed around the edges as the blanket—which Cat realized might well be from Yasha's death—especially with the remnants of that signature scarlet lipstick now ossified into the lines that radiated from her lips. Still, there was almost something regal about Elizabeth Bentley as she leaned back against the couch pillows and sighed. "We're getting closer to the important bits. Of course, after that, you're free to kill me."

Is she purposefully making herself look pitiful? In the hopes that I won't kill her?

Which, honestly, Cat was having a harder and harder time even imagining doing. Not that it was impossible. "You sold people out, Elizabeth. People who had made the exact choices you had. Tell me about your testimony before the House Un-American Activities Committee."

Because Cat had read just enough before she came here to know that was when Elizabeth *really* went off the rails. And she knew that was intricately tied up with her mother's story.

Elizabeth nodded, her lips curled into a sinful sort of smile. "Ah yes, my role as the Red Spy Queen." She paused long enough that Cat could tell she was remembering the past in all its Technicolor glory. "Did you know an actual *hush* fell over the chambers when I walked in—the galleries were packed tighter than sardines. I still remember the stunning white gabardine suit I wore, accented with the most perfect jaunty navy blue beret. Mary Tenney herself would have been proud."

Irritated, Cat shook her head, even banged her open palm on the table. So much for feeling sympathetic toward Elizabeth Bentley. "That's not what you wore, Elizabeth. I saw the photograph in the library. You were sitting in front of all the microphones, testifying. You wore a plain black dress, no hat. With understated earrings."

Elizabeth had appeared calm and collected in the photograph, but Cat had wondered whether her armpits were sticky or her palms damp with sweat from nerves that roiled deep within as she testified toward charges of subversion in the federal government.

Elizabeth shrugged. "Does it really matter what I wore?"

Cat exhaled a puff of exasperation. "Yes, damn it. If you can't tell the truth about something as small as what outfit you wore, then why the hell am I listening to you? Are you trying to convince me that you deserve to die?"

"Oh, I definitely deserve to die, but time will take care of that even if you don't. And what if I *have* been lying all this time, Catherine?" She crossed her arms before her chest, leaned forward. "What if I've been lying about very important things?"

Cat's frown deepened. "Then you're an even more worthless woman than I suspected."

Elizabeth looked infinitely sad then, but her expression was wiped clean before Cat could blink. Turned playful, even. "My dearest Catherine, no one cares if I wore a white suit or a black dress, so long as I wasn't naked in the Senate chambers. Remember what I told you about the truth?"

"That there's shades of truth? I say that's bullshit."

Elizabeth reached for the yellow glass ashtray from the end table behind her. "*Shades of Truth.* Now that would have made an excellent name for my memoir."

"Or *Clever Girl.*"

She smiled at that—a real smile this time. "I *was* a most Clever Girl. Perhaps Shades of Truth could be a lipstick instead. Speaking of which, did you check your photograph for my lip color?"

Cat wasn't sure what bearing her shade of lipstick had on anything. "Black-and-white, I'm afraid."

"Grayscale again." She fluttered a hand. "For what it's worth, I was wearing Victory Red. It's unsportsmanlike to attack them unprepared, you know."

"What? Attack who?"

"My enemies. Red lips always lie, Catherine. At least, mine certainly do."

Cat slanted her eyes at the remnants of that Victory Red lipstick. *Has she been lying all this time?* Instinctively, her hand sought out the revolver, its coldness grounding her burgeoning anger. *God help her if she has . . .*

"Don't say you weren't warned." It was as if Elizabeth could read Cat's mind as she smirked, struck a match, and lit the Lucky. Then she shifted on the couch and tucked the ratty afghan around her legs, reminding Cat of a much older woman. "Now are you going to let me tell my story, or not?"

Cat waved a hand, her eyebrows lifted expectantly.

|||||||||||||||||

I wore a simple black dress accessorized by fabulous silver earrings from Bermuda that Mary Tenney had once given me for Christmas. (At least that matches the description you gave me, Catherine.)

And, of course, a flagrant slash of Bésame Victory Red lipstick.

After all, this was war.

A savage murmur spread like a tidal wave throughout the room at the fact that the woman who had sounded the warning cry against Communists was neither svelte nor blond, but instead a nondescript brunette of a certain age. "Why, she's not beautiful at all," one senator muttered to another. I leveled an obsidian-sharp glare at them, rather enjoyed the way they shrank back.

(Don't judge them too harshly, Catherine. I'd guess you felt the same way after you first saw me. Most people do.)

I didn't mind the hurt feelings over my underwhelming appearance—I'd been playing parts and wearing a multitude of different faces since almost the day I'd become a card-carrying Party member. The important thing was that everyone, including the media and the public, kept coming back for more. Not only that, but I knew popular opinion would be on my side.

Just today, the front pages on my way to Capitol Hill had been packed with photographs of downtrodden Germans standing atop the rubble of Berlin with arms open as American planes dropped humanitarian relief packages to them, compliments of the Berlin Blockade in which Stalin had effectively cut off the city from all food and medical supplies. Once again, it fell to America to resist oppression and injustice, and I would do my part by exposing the crimes of the USSR here within our own borders. This testimony— my fait accompli—would ensure that no other Americans would be tempted to enter Communism's candy-covered house and find themselves pushed into its burning-hot oven.

I would stop Communism here in America in its tracks.

The Senate hearing room was closed to the media once my testimony began. Blinking hard against the klieg lights, I took my place at the witness table alongside the stenographer, a half dozen clunky microphones waiting to capture my every word. It was a sweltering summer afternoon outside in Washington, DC, but inside, under those lights and facing the glares of the Silvermasters, Lud Ullmann, and Bill Remington, I felt pearls of sweat rill down my back, my palm slick as I stroked the golden cigarette lighter. I removed it from my pocket in an attempt to gain resolve from it.

Click click click.

Never again would I be a victim. Never again would I be weak.

To start, bulldog Joseph McCarthy threw me a surprisingly gentle round of questions. "Miss Bentley," he began, "how old are you?" His timorous grin didn't fool me. This spineless little man was an insipid impresario—no more than a performing monkey, really—who had nothing more than hot air to back up his list of 205 supposedly card-carrying members of the Communist Party in the State Department. Unlike *my* testimony, which would prove once and for all that there certainly *were* card-carrying, Stalin-loving Communists hidden deep within the US government. "Of course, if you don't want to answer that question," McCarthy continued, "it's all right. That's a woman's privilege."

Was it possible to roll my eyes so hard they hit the ceiling?

"The Red Spy Queen drops her mask today." I may as well have hand-fed the newspapers their headline for tomorrow's edition. "I'm forty years old."

After that, McCarthy moved straight to my education and time in Italy before asking me to explain how I'd fallen out with Fascism before returning to America and getting mixed up in the CPUSA. During the hours that followed, I had no notes nor the benefit of any lawyers, relied on only my memories and recollections.

"Miss Bentley, while you were an underground agent, did documentary evidence exist verifying the fact that you were such an agent?"

I merely stared straight ahead, wiped my expression clean in order to protect the FBI. You scratch my back and all of that. "None, except in Moscow."

Unless, of course, you ask Hoover about the VENONA Project . . .

"Did you feel that it was your business to make sure there was no documentary evidence?"

"Of course. I took every possible precaution."

"It is common practice in all underground organizations to avoid documentation, is it not?"

"It very definitely is."

This line of questioning worked out neatly for me, establishing that there would be no paper trail of anything I had to say, while proving that such a lack of evidence was actually a testimony to my superior ability as a spy and courier.

"And can you explain how you were pulled into this particular underground organization? The Communist Party of America?"

I folded my hands on the table before me, a coolness settling over me as I repeated the truths I'd rehearsed in my mind so many times. "We poor devils were a bunch of misguided idealists led astray by the cheap little men who run the Party."

"And when did you find yourself fully in the Party's clutches?"

"The point of no return was when the Party realized I had important access at the Italian Library. They turned me over to Jacob Golos—the perfect Communist with his selfless devotion to humanity." I hesitated over the painful truth, plunged ahead. "I fell in love with him, couldn't have backed out then even if I'd tried."

A congressman from Louisiana leaned forward. "How old were you when you started this maneuvering, this espionage?" he asked.

"That was nearly a decade ago."

His fingers drummed against his table. "I want to know whether or not you were a mature individual."

Of course I was mature, you addlepated ninny. I was a grown woman in full possession of her faculties. Yet, I weighed my response carefully, sensed the sharp teeth hiding in the trap of his words. It was important that *I* remain in control of this interview, not allow them to turn this into an ad hoc trial about my activities. "I think you may be physically mature, but many times you are not mentally mature."

"Didn't it ever dawn on you during these secret meetings that you were doing a disservice to your country?"

My stomach curdled with fear. Disservice was a synonym for treason. The punishment for treason was the electric chair or firing squad.

It was up to me to avoid this trap, to sidestep the quicksand that threatened to engulf me.

"I did not think it was betraying my own government," I said. "Communism is virtually a religion—one does not question, only follows."

"Was it this Golos who spurred such emotionalism in you?"

Emotionalism . . . For God's sake, I dare you to ask that question to any man in this seat.

That was what I wanted to say, but I could hear Yasha's reprimand in my head. *Don't you dare, Elizabeth. Do what you must in order to survive . . .*

"Yes." I forced myself to scramble toward the path to solid ground they were offering, even if it somehow made me feel like I was cheapening my love for Yasha. "It was Golos."

"Was it that you were devoted to him so much that you followed him and were blind to everything else?"

"Yes," I replied, my voice hushed. Stepped more firmly onto bedrock. "Yes, it was."

Please forgive me, Yasha, I thought, my eyes stinging with the blasphemy of painting the only man I'd ever loved as the villain of my life's story. For I loved him and had loved what we had done together to help our country. *Forgive me for my lies.*

I'd escaped the trap that had been set for me. But my ordeal wasn't over.

After that, I was forced to listen to the other subpoenaed witnesses cast me as both a liar and a fool. All the players of this comedic tragedy were there—William Remington, the Silvermasters, Lud Ullmann, the entire Perlo group. All save Mary Tenney.

Everyone except Remington invoked the Fifth Amendment. And every single one of them looked at me as if they wished they could disembowel me then and there.

"You understand that if you are not a Communist, there is no need for you to invoke the Fifth Amendment?" McCarthy asked Nathan Silvermaster at one point. His Russian battle-ax of a wife sat across the way; Helen leveled at me a glare that would have cut glass.

"I refuse to answer the question," came Silvermaster's reply. "I continue to invoke my right to refuse to answer the question posed to me by this witch hunt."

He was smart, damn him. I clenched my fists, wondering if it was worth risking contempt of court to lash out at him. Fortunately, the Senate had the last word. "This committee isn't so much interested in witch hunts as it is in rat hunts."

Lud Ullmann looked straight through me when it was his turn. "The woman I knew as Myrna, or Miss Wise as she preferred to be called, was a neurotic nuisance of a woman. Helen, Nathan, and I wanted her to stop coming around, but she was like a stray puppy that we'd made the mistake of feeding."

I understood that my former contacts were trying to run to higher ground to save themselves. Hell, I'd just done the same thing myself. But still, lonely and broken as I was, I found myself pitying each and every one of them. That they could no longer see that Russia was the enemy, that we had been *wrong* to stay with them once they became America's Cold War adversary.

Then William Remington took the stand.

William Remington, my former problem child with the specs for rubber made from garbage, was now chairman of the Commerce Department committee that allocated exports to the Soviet Union and had access to all manner of secret military information including airplanes, armaments, radar, and the Manhattan Project that had built the atomic bombs. That contact of mine who was redder than a red herring told the jury the bold-faced whopper that he had no idea I was connected to the Party.

"I never knew Miss Bentley was a Communist," he lied. "Yes, I gave her money, but I thought she was Jacob Golos's research assistant, and that Golos was a Dutch journalist interested in my work. I truly believed the money I'd given in exchange for Party literature was so I might examine it for myself—I was curious about the Party's beliefs, you see."

McCarthy had caught his scent. "Didn't you find it odd that Golos and Bentley always met you somewhere different?"

"Why, yes, in retrospect, that was odd, but Miss Bentley always claimed to be hungry before she set up the meetings. You see, she worked uptown, far from my office, so we always met somewhere in the middle. I thought she just liked trying new places."

"So, you're telling me you never grew suspicious?"

Remington actually pulled at his shirt collar, a dead giveaway that he was nervous. And lying through his perfect teeth. "I did become suspicious of Miss Bentley's motivations, which is why I fed her a crackpot scheme to make rubber out of garbage, as if I were some sort of mediocre alchemist. Honestly, I had no idea what she was up to—I suppose I was quite the gullible fool in those days."

If there was any justice in the world, William Remington would have burst into flames there on the stand. As it was, the handsome, all-American would-be linebacker just strode back to his seat unscathed.

And I was recalled.

Feeling the threat of that quicksand again, I elaborated on my story, gave the Senate everything I had about Remington, even upped the ante of the synthetic rubber formula he'd given me—which I'd told the FBI was probably of no value even to a chemist—into quite a complicated thing that could have been used to build entire atom bombs.

(Catherine, my degree is in fourteenth-century Florentine poetry; I have no idea if rubber is even used to make atom bombs. But I held those salivating senators in the palm of my hand, and that was all that mattered. Because Remington *was* a Communist, and there was no way I was going to allow him to keep feeding the Center American secrets.)

From the way those men balanced on the edges of their seats, I might have told them Remington had given me instructions on how to make a hydrogen bomb from a paper clip and a helium balloon. And they'd have believed me.

Perhaps it was a bit of smoke and mirrors. But I'll go to my grave maintaining I did what I had to in order to protect myself. And my country.

THE NBC SECRETARY for *Meet the Press* cleared her throat, peered at me through severe horn-rimmed glasses that contrasted with her good looks. "May I help you?"

"I'm Elizabeth Bentley, here for my interview." I gave what I hoped passed for a sunny smile, suddenly wished I'd had more than the two martinis I'd downed at the bar across the street. I'd agreed to this interview to keep my profile high, but the knot of nerves in my belly suggested I'd made a mistake. "Where shall I sit?"

The secretary gestured to the couch opposite four chairs. As usual, I'd arrived early—seventeen minutes this time—so I could be prepared. Unfortunately, the martinis had done little to soothe the jangle of nerves in my stomach before I appeared on national television.

Correction: on *live* national television.

I watched with rising hackles as the four renowned *Meet the Press* journalists wandered in, heads bent together over disposable coffee cups and looking like the walking definition of a good old boys' club. Well, except for Inez Robb, world-famous and eminently fashionable press juggernaut who eschewed slacks (she claimed women in slacks looked like the back ends of hacks) and had left off her infamous white kid gloves today.

Nelson Frank (writer for the *World-Telegram* and anti-Communist special agent with US Naval Intelligence), Inez Robb (World War II correspondent and one of the world's top newspaperwomen), Cecil Brown (CBS war correspondent and Peabody Award winner), and Lawrence Spivak (cofounder and producer of *Meet the Press*). Their credentials were enough to float an entire newspaper.

These were the big guns. Which meant they'd be able to smell a lie a mile away.

"For weeks, the front pages have been full of stories of two congressional investigations." Lawrence Spivak addressed Camera 1 once we were seated and the cameras were rolling. (None of the journalists had so much as offered to shake my hand, which told me we were in for rough sailing. Or at least I was.) "Names were printed in bold type that shocked the nation. And at the roaring center of all this was one American woman. Is her fantastic story true? Could all this be a figment of her imagination?" He looked at me. "Only Elizabeth Bentley can answer these questions."

Don't react, I told myself, but it was difficult not to grind my teeth or flick the double-headed eagle lighter hidden under the table. *Of course my story is true, you nitwit. The important parts, anyway.*

"Miss Bentley, these are pretty exciting times," said Nelson Frank. "Are you scared?"

My eyes narrowed as I tried to glean the meaning from his question. Finally, I asked, "Scared of what?"

"Of suffering reprisals from the Communists. Scared of publicity, scared of anything?"

Scared of everything, you mean?

"I think you rather get accustomed to it." I supposed that wasn't a lie. Despite my fears, I was so accustomed to portraying myself as calm and collected, but a little vulnerability—no acting required—might counteract the slurs of my being a neurotic and menopausal woman with delusions of grandeur. "Although there are moments when you get a little shaky."

"Elizabeth, every American now knows you as the Red Spy Queen from the recent House Un-American Activities hearings." Inez Robb folded one impossibly long leg over the other. "We can see with our own eyes that the stories of the sultry blonde are utter fabrications. After those lies, is there anything we should know about you? Anything that's true?"

I winced. The juggernaut's white kid gloves might be off, but they'd been replaced by boxing gloves.

"It's true I've been unmasked," I said, "but in my line of work, you become accustomed to wearing disguises. I think of those newspaper descriptions as simply another disguise." I paused, then smiled, remembering to look at the camera. "My life is now an open book, which is fitting as I've recently begun planning my memoirs. I hope to have them serialized soon."

So far, no lies. *The truth will set you free*, and all that, right?

Brown had the next question. "We understand you've testified against several highly placed government officials. Would you be willing to repeat those accusations tonight?"

I tilted my head, wishing the lights weren't so bright. Or so hot.

"Well, I'm afraid none of those people are in the audience tonight." My attempt at a joke fell flat. It was one thing to accuse my former comrades from the Senate stand, where I was protected from libel suits, quite another to denounce those same comrades on live television. "And unfortunately, my transactional immunity expired the moment I left Capitol Hill."

Something told me my dodge and weave wasn't going to work. Not with these four inquisitors.

Inez smiled, but Brown just leaned forward, stabbing the air with his cigarette. "So, without your immunity, are you still willing to name William Remington as a Communist?"

No, I'm absolutely not willing to point fingers publicly. Not when I have no desire to face the consequences.

If I'd been wiser, perhaps I would have said that out loud. Even after Brown asked me the same question a total of three times.

Instead, after the third time, I gave an exasperated statement that I immediately wished I could rescind. "Certainly. I testified before the committee that William Remington was a Communist."

And now I had said it in front of all of America. On public television.

I wish I could blame the martinis. But I had only myself to

blame the moment those words left my mouth. Because you can't go slinging accusations of treason at fellow Americans, certainly not on a live national broadcast. So much for being clever.

Spivak interjected again. "It's obvious from the testimony I've listened to that someone is lying—either you or Remington. Isn't there some way that you can present intelligence that would prove beyond a doubt that the people you say are Communists really are, or is there no way, and is that the reason the grand jury was unable to take action against some of these people?"

Now I was getting annoyed. "I'm afraid I wouldn't know, Mr. Spivak," I said. "I only know that there are my facts, which I have, and that the FBI itself made a complete investigation."

"And having been a Communist, what do you think of the US government now?"

No hesitation. "I think its freedoms and democracy make it the best government in the world." I pivoted to face the camera, ignoring Spivak and the rest of this panel of harpies so I might appeal directly to the American people in their living rooms. "In fact, I hope the current members of the Communist Party will leave it and come forward to help. It isn't enough to quit being a Communist, as I know hundreds have. Come forward now and tell what you know while there's still time to undo the damage we have so foolishly done."

Yes, I might have originally gone to the FBI in order to save my own hide, but in that moment, I fervently wanted what was best for America too.

We were enemies with Russia. We had atomic bombs and other secrets those same Russians would have loved to steal. And I knew without a doubt that America was rife with Soviet secret agents working for the same organization that had thrown Yasha to the wolves, had threatened to kill me, and had slaughtered my own innocent dog in cold blood.

Now if only I could get America to believe me.

|||||||||||||||||

NOVEMBER 23, 1963
7:36 P.M.

Cat cleared her throat, halting Elizabeth's reminiscences. "Bullshit."

Elizabeth blinked, taken aback at the interruption. "Excuse me?"

"You wanted what was best for America?" Cat pulled a sour face like she'd eaten something far worse than bland tuna casserole. She wasn't mad, more annoyed. "Please, Elizabeth—it's obvious that you only wanted revenge against the NKVD and anyone who still worked for them. Not only that, you're a hypocrite who accused William Remington of treason on national television. And you lied. *On the stand.*"

Elizabeth held up a hand. "Don't start with all that talk of truth again, Catherine. I told the truth while on the stand. Mostly, at least."

"No, you didn't. According to what you told me only a few hours ago, you practically begged the Party to take you on once you began working at the Italian Library. And Yasha didn't even care when you were fired from the library. I don't think you were quite as important there—or maybe anywhere—as you like to think."

It was a low blow, but Cat didn't care. She'd agreed to listen to Elizabeth and had been waiting half a day for a confession, perhaps even some regret or remorse . . .

Only to find out that Elizabeth really *was* a despicable specimen of humanity.

Her finger itched for the trigger of the revolver, but Elizabeth kept talking. "It's a game of semantics, Catherine. I was Yasha's contact by then, and I couldn't have backed out even if I'd wanted to."

"Because you fell in love with him."

Elizabeth's love for Yasha was the only pure part of this story, but that certainly wasn't enough to excuse her crimes after he was gone.

"I told the truth there, now didn't I? Twisted it up a little, but I was under oath. Under the right circumstances, espionage and perhaps even treason can be acceptable behaviors. McCarthy and the rest of them wanted to paint me as a naive, star-crossed young woman. So, I let them."

Cat scoffed at her insouciance. "No, you put on a show. And allowed innocent people to get caught in the cross fire."

"Innocent? *Please.* The Silvermasters and Remington and every member of the Perlo group knew exactly what they were getting into—we all did. And I put on a show for a good reason—the FBI informed me in no uncertain terms that my testimony had to result in at least one guilty verdict. I thought it would come from the Silvermasters or the Perlo group—aside from Mary Tenney, they'd been my most important contacts. They all pleaded the Fifth, which told the world they had something to hide but also meant the Senate's hands were tied. Never in a year of Sundays would I have guessed it would be Remington who would become our focus."

"Meaning you were willing to let Remington take the fall. For you. For all of you."

"I'm not sure I'd put it that way, but yes, Remington was the only source I knew personally who was still working for the feds by then. If we wanted to take down Soviet espionage in America, *someone* had to take the fall in order to prove that a vast network of spies had infiltrated the highest levels of American government. And Remington was the only one foolish enough not to plead the Fifth—he was young and intelligent and good-looking and thought he'd outsmart us another way and come away scot-free."

"Just like you."

"I can see I'm not going to convince you." Elizabeth got up and began to pace, but the effort seemed to cost her. "You'll be happy to know the rat got off without even a slap on the wrist. This time, at least. Had I kept any evidence on him, he would have gone down in flames then and there."

"Lucky for him. Unlucky for you."

"Luck is a fickle bitch," Elizabeth practically spat out. "And as you're about to see, she's never cared for me." Her impatient flick at the golden cigarette lighter caused a fine spray of angry sparks. "We don't have much time left, Catherine, and I'm sick of hearing myself talk. Consider yourself my priest, for this next part contains all my darkest sins and secrets—the lies I told, the lives I upended, the people who died because of me. And after we're done here, you're welcome to kill me. And even if you don't, I'm going to find the deepest, darkest hole I can hide in. And I'm never, *ever* going to tell this story again."

16

With Remington and all my other contacts allowed to walk free, the press, who I'd hoped to control, suddenly turned on me like a many-headed Hydra.

Not a blonde at all . . . Elizabeth Bentley is a nutmeg Mata Hari.

(Nutmeg because I was from Connecticut, which was the Nutmeg State. You'd think they'd have worked a little harder at that one, although I *was* brown haired and, compliments of a steady diet of hot dogs and martinis, getting rounder by the day.)

That was relatively harmless, but many of the things they said struck deep. Others had me seeing red.

A sex-starved man-eating temptress. Or perhaps a sex-starved, man-hating spinster.

Her charges are those of a neurotic spinster . . . Joined the Party in a pathetic attempt to meet men.

Elizabeth Bentley is no more than an old biddy with delusions of grandeur who listens at keyholes.

The story—*my* story—had gotten away from me. And I had no idea how to rein it back in.

"We're not sure that Congress can continue to use you," Hoover said one day before the committee planned to resume. "We might have to put you on ice."

"We?" I stopped riffling through my handbag at that. This morning I'd downed a martini breakfast to steady my nerves and needed mints to cover my breath. However, Hoover's pronouncement meant my alcohol-soaked breath could wait. "As in . . . ?"

"As in the FBI. You've started this train down the tracks, Elizabeth, but it's not going anywhere. You and I both need this investigation to gain traction. Congress appreciates your service thus far, but they need *more*."

So, I'll have immunity from prosecution?

Provided that your testimony helps us put away other Communist spies.

The insinuation was clear. I was the only spy who had confessed my crimes. Which meant it was only the American government's good graces that were keeping me on this side of a jail cell.

I had to produce. Or else.

"I still have a few tricks up my sleeve, Mr. Hoover." The reel of my mind cast ahead to what I could possibly mean by that. I'd told the FBI everything I knew, had pointed them straight at Remington. How was it my fault that they—and Congress—were failing to put away card-carrying Party members who would potentially continue to betray America?

We were deeply entrenched in what was being called a Cold War against Russia. Just as I had during World War II, I wanted to help my country, but now I had an even greater motivation: to prove my own patriotism. (Catherine, that meant I unwittingly played right into the hands of the GOP, who wanted me to name names in order to discredit President Truman before the next election and give their Republican candidate the keys to the front door of the White House. But I didn't know any of that—I thought I was putting away people who would double-cross the United States.) Only I had nothing else, and not a shred of proof of any of it.

Worry about that later. Don't let Hoover cut you loose.

"You just wait until my testimony today, Mr. Director," I said.

"Good." He adjusted his narrow tie so I wondered if it felt as tight as my buttoned-up collar. "After all, there's no point in raising hell and then not being successful, right?"

That day in the Ways and Means Committee room with its banks of auditorium seats on either side of a central aisle, blinded by more klieg lights and on edge from the steady rattle of newsreel cameras—unlike the Senate, these proceedings were open to the media—I became the most important person in the room.

I *began* with the truth. I recited the familiar list of names, my voice cool and clinical.

Remington.

Silvermaster.

Perlo.

Ullmann.

All the usual suspects.

"Can you name any other individuals, Miss Bentley?" interrupted the junior representative from California. Behind his bronze nameplate, Richard Nixon sat like a young monarch on the raised platform for committee members in the front of the room. He had recently been elected after a smear campaign against his Democratic opponent, had been active in the HUAC hearings against the Hollywood Ten. A force to be reckoned with, that one.

Nixon and his colleagues would only stay on my side so long as I produced for them.

(I'm not proud of what followed, Catherine. People say to live a life with no regrets, but sometimes fear makes us do terrible things. And God, was I ever fearful in those days.)

So, like the coward I was, I caved. And I'd regret it for the rest of my life.

I watered down the truth until it was barely recognizable as the afternoon progressed, named at least a dozen names and alluded to perhaps another hundred in order to buy myself time and save my own reptilian skin. None of it could be backed up by a shred of truth. And none could ever be corroborated by another spy.

Brothman.

White.

Currie.

Miller.

Adler.

Halperin.

Collins.

People I'd only heard of in passing who happened to work for the government . . . I named them all. (Little did I know, but one of them was the great white whale the FBI was searching for. Words are bullets, Catherine, or in this case, one name was a giant harpoon.)

"Elizabeth Bentley, you are a reformed saint," said a Louisiana congressman once we'd finished for the day. Except I didn't *feel* like a saint, quite the opposite. "You are an American citizen who has had the courage to put herself in a highly dangerous position."

Nixon added his two cents, no flimflam about it. "I commend you highly for coming here, for having had such a grueling time. Your ability to stand up the way you have is something to be proud of. In fact, I wish the entire country could hear what you have to say."

I felt filthy dirty in more ways than one. And in terrible need of a martini.

I got that martini as soon as I left Capitol Hill, darted into the first corner bar I saw. And then I downed another one. And another.

Sometimes, not even an ocean of alcohol is enough to drown out your misery.

IN THE MIDST of all the grand juries and press interviews, I'd thought that the Center had forgotten me.

God in heaven, was I ever wrong.

Upon removing the wooden chair I always rigged beneath the hotel door handle, I found a fresh copy of the *Daily Worker* sitting atop my usual editions of the *World-Telegram* and the *New York Tribune*.

Once again, their headlines screamed my name. Only this time, I'd had no part in creating them.

FAUX SPY QUEEN ELIZABETH BENTLEY
SPENT TIME IN MENTAL INSTITUTION:
Neurotic Pathological Liar &
HUAC Informer Spins Web of Lies

Someone had wanted me to see this. And first thing in the morning too.

The following story was patently false—the dates I was supposedly in a mental institution (the NKVD insinuated several institutions, among them New York's Payne Whitney Clinic) coincided with when I began my interviews with the FBI—and was obviously a fancy bit of malicious defamation. Still, there it was in print. It was likely that Al had started those wheels turning as soon as I'd named all my sources and before he'd even left the country, but now that I was testifying in public—as opposed to within the safety and security of the Senate or grand jury chambers—I was back on the Center's radar.

Reeling from this new slander (Catherine, don't you dare quibble that I actually *had* spun a web of lies), I locked myself inside my hotel room that day and ordered room service, including several martinis I'd certainly earned, even if I wasn't exactly sure how I was going to pay for them when the bills came due.

I'd thought the day couldn't get much worse until a uniformed hotel attendant showed up with more bad news.

"Miss Bentley, the front desk asked me to bring up your mail." He offered me a silver plate laden with several envelopes. "I hope you don't mind the intrusion."

I certainly *did* mind—I scowled at both him and the letters as if they might contain plague, then shut and bolted the door. Only when the chair was firmly wedged back under the doorknob did I tear open the envelopes.

The first was a hotel bill in a modest dollar amount that still had me wincing given that I was currently unemployed and no longer collecting a paycheck.

The next was a plain white envelope addressed from Massachusetts, a piece of yellow foolscap paper with pristine folds tucked inside.

Dear Betty, it read in a heavy-handed scrawl written in pencil, one that looked entirely male and left-handed. I scowled. I'd never allowed anyone to call me *Betty* without correcting them; my name was Elizabeth. One didn't just go around amending people's names, certainly not without permission.

> *Congratulations on your spy story. It will be the last story you
> will ever write. We will wright the last chapter.*

Misspelling notwithstanding, the letter sent chills down my spine.

Death threats . . . What kind of person sends death threats to a woman they've never met?

The last was a letter from a law firm representing William Remington, informing me that he was suing me for libel. To the tune of one hundred thousand dollars in damages.

Shit, shit, shit.

I stopped opening the letters after that. Built up a fire in the fireplace and watched the flames devour them as I knocked back one straight shot of gin after another.

I was a target now, besieged by all corners of the board.

The least I could do was be a *moving* target.

IT WAS A relief when the DC Police Department asked me to visit their headquarters the next morning. Perhaps they could provide me some protection; at the very least I could be relatively sure no one would try to harm me while I was surrounded by armed officers.

Except I left my hotel only to be confronted by an angry-faced mob who had apparently tuned in to my interview on *Meet the Press*. It was a small group—thank providence—but pockmarked with familiar faces.

Lee and her daughter, now grown.

Harold Patch. Marcel.

And several other people I recalled from my days with the Party. Before I'd met Yasha. Before everything had fallen apart.

"There she is!" Patch's angry sneer branded itself onto my heart. I suddenly knew how women throughout history had felt, condemned by an angry crowd before being dragged to waiting pyres and scaffolds. "Traitor! Liar!"

Panic fisted my throat as the mob's tidal wave surged toward me, one woman—perhaps Lee's daughter—grabbed my hair and tried to pull me down the stairs. I tumbled to my knees, scraped the heels of my palms, and felt something warm on my face. Until I was yanked backward by another set of hands.

"For Christ's sake, leave Miss Bentley alone!" The bellhop's voice bellowed out over the mob's angry cacophony. "This is America, not some Fascist state where thugs terrorize people on the streets!"

He tugged me back inside, where I collapsed into a chair while he secured the door, then handed me a starched handkerchief from his pocket while fists pounded on the glass. "For your cheek."

I dabbed my face, expecting the handkerchief to come away bloodied. Instead, it came away clean, save for a patina of saliva. Hysterical laughter bubbled in my chest.

Not blood. Just spit. I'd been *spit* upon.

I felt like the central figure in Edvard Munch's *The Scream*, my world melting out of control around me while my sanity slipped through my fingers. Perhaps I *was* as neurotic and deranged as the papers claimed. "Thank you, Sam. Unfortunately, this isn't the first time I've been attacked." I recalled Al's ambush in my hotel room, felt the familiar sharp stab of guilt at the remembrance of Vlad. "And that's not counting the death threats."

Once, a lifetime ago, my younger, lonely self had no one to talk to except an African violet, had recited a line from *Coriolanus. Thus I turn my back. There is a world elsewhere.*

Except this time, the world had turned its back on me.

"I hate to say it—the staff here appreciates what you've done for our country"—the bellhop lifted his hat, rubbed a hand over his slicked-back hair—"but perhaps it would be better if you left the hotel? And moved somewhere safer?"

When I left the Commodore Hotel an hour later for my meeting with the DC police, it was with my brown leather suitcase in hand, through the back door, down a narrow alley where a taxi was waiting. All my belongings—my entire *life*—fit in that one bag as I fled into the unknown. I didn't know where I'd sleep tonight, but I couldn't worry about that now.

One minute, one hour at a time.

"Thank you for coming down to the precinct, Miss Bentley." The DC police lieutenant and detective had been waiting when I entered the conference room. "We wanted to inform you of a situation in San Francisco before it hits tomorrow's news."

"San Francisco?" My mind was still a whirlpool of worries from this morning. It took a moment to paddle out of those turbid waters and decipher what he was saying.

The lieutenant perused his notes in front of him. "A San Francisco highway patrolman made a discovery this morning on the Golden Gate Bridge. A pile of women's clothing . . . and a red handbag."

The detective clasped his hands in front of him. "Inside the handbag was a letter. It was addressed to you."

Words I hadn't heard in a long time haunted me. *I swear I'd sooner jump off the Golden Gate Bridge than allow anything to happen to the child.*

My voice suddenly didn't work; I had to clear my throat—once, twice—to form the words properly. "What did it say?"

He glanced at a steno pad in front of him. "The letter wasn't signed, just stated that no one would care about the writer's name. Except you. The writer said she had suffered and that she didn't want her baby girl to suffer with her so she'd taken her daughter with her." He looked up at me, his voice softer. "Presumably off the bridge."

"Do you have any details on the handbag?" I closed my eyes, not wanting him to read anything there. "You said it was red?"

He glanced at the pad again. "Reddish, scallop-shaped. Calfskin."

I knew the rest without needing to see the bag.

Ruched. Louis Vuitton. Coral-toned, not red. With kitten heels to match.

When I opened my eyes, it was to find the detective studying me. *Nothing fazes you, Elizabeth,* I thought to myself. *A nuclear bomb could detonate next door and you wouldn't flinch.*

"The San Francisco police believe this might be a hoax," the lieutenant continued. "But it's also possible that the writer jumped off the bridge. Along with her child. Authorities are searching for bodies now."

I wanted to scream in panic but somehow forced myself not to react, allowing the silence to stretch until it became so taut that the detective felt the need to slice through it. "Unfortunately," he said, "the story is already flying across the country via the wire service. Including the letter's connection to you."

From unknown spy to famous and *infamous . . . How many mobs shall I expect tomorrow?*

"Thank you for apprising me of the situation, officers. Please send word when you receive the verdict on the investigation."

I left the precinct with my lone suitcase in tow, somehow kept my worries from clawing their way up my throat during what felt like the longest taxi ride of my life. To another new hotel, where I immediately locked the door and placed a call to the FBI. Demanded to speak to the director, and only the director. "I need you to investigate a possible suicide at the Golden Gate Bridge this morning," I said once I'd finally been patched through to J. Edgar Hoover. "And I need to see the letter with my own eyes."

Words, I thought when I finally hung up. I needed words to keep the monsters at bay.

Safety. Hiding. Bridge. Survival. Suicide. Death.

This time, the words failed to calm me.

|||||||||||||||

NOVEMBER 23, 1963
8:22 P.M.

"Was it Mary Tenney?" Cat asked Elizabeth. If anyone else had just told her that story, she'd have immediately offered her sincerest condolences—hoax or suicide, it was an awful situation—but Elizabeth was a woman whose need for lies bordered on the pathological. And she had a feeling—what Elizabeth surely would have called a *gut feeling*—that Mary's story was critical to her own. "With the handbag?"

"Of course, you daft girl," Elizabeth snapped. "Who else would it be?"

"But Mary's earlier letter said she had a *son*, and you said she named him Jacob after Yasha. Now she had a daughter?"

Elizabeth frowned, shot Cat a disappointed stare. *Click click click* went the golden lighter. "That was code, my dear, to keep the Soviet apparatus from piecing anything together. Mary's main concern was that the Russian secret police never find her and, more importantly, that they never track down her illegitimate child to use as leverage against her. Her *son*. She covered her tracks. Multiple times, in fact. And then circled around again, just to be sure."

Cat folded her arms, trying to think several moves ahead like a chess player. That would be rather smart, *if* it were true. Mary's first accomplishment was hiding the existence of her child, making everyone think she'd had an abortion. Next came abandoning her position as a honey trap when it became clear Elizabeth was no longer a smoke screen against the Center. Moving cross-country and going deep into hiding, followed by faking her death and that of her child. Finally, a red herring regarding the child's sex.

Layers upon layers. Cat wondered if Mary learned that from Elizabeth.

"I kept hoping she'd contact me," Elizabeth continued, "but Mary was smart. She'd have known the Russians were watching my every move, that they'd likely be tracking down each of my contacts even just to deactivate them." Elizabeth set down the lighter, folded her hands over it. "She wouldn't have wanted the chance that she was going to be liquidated, or worse, that they'd use her child as collateral to keep her quiet. Remember, she'd slept with virtually every spy and Party member during the war. Also, there was the possibility that the FBI would have deciphered the much-sought-after identity of Muse and come pounding on her door."

Cat winced, imagining what a life on the run would have been like. It made her childhood look downright rosy in comparison, despite her parents' deaths.

"So . . ." Cat drew the word out, hoped Elizabeth would throw her a bone and not force her to ask the question. Of course, that hope was in vain. "Did Mary kill herself?"

The golden lighter clicked at a steady tempo. *Click click click.* "The FBI did their due diligence, even procured the suicide note that was found on the Golden Gate Bridge and sent it my way."

"And?"

This time Elizabeth produced an envelope from inside a hollow book. Not *War and Peace* this time, but *Anna Karenina*. Apparently, Elizabeth really did have a vendetta against Tolstoy. The paper she held out was stamped with Elizabeth's name in willowy handwriting. Inside, the note's text repeated what Elizabeth had already told her. "I'm missing something, aren't I?" Cat asked.

"Mary was a consummate spy. Anything strike you as odd?"

Cat frowned, turned the letter over and over. "No invisible ink, I assume?"

"No. Although I was ready to run it through lime juice before I figured out the solution."

Cat's attention returned to the envelope. And then she realized . . .

"It's stamped." Cat felt a rush of exhilaration, knew she was on the right track from the way Elizabeth's lips quirked up. "But there's no address. And this was found on a bridge; it was never going to be mailed."

"Check the back. Carefully."

Cat did as Elizabeth commanded, gently lifted up the stamp with her thumbnail. On its adhesive side was a hidden swirl of numbers written in pencil, a tiny universe of information.

"It's coded."

To which Elizabeth held up a finger, scrawled something on a scrap of paper before handing it to Cat. Just the letters of the alphabet with an assortment of out-of-order numbers beneath them.

"This was the code Mary and I had agreed to use when we initially set up our plans," Elizabeth informed her. "Mary kept the original one-time pad—I memorized it."

It didn't take Cat long to decipher the simple code in front of her—it was just a matter of matching the numbers of the stamp with their coordinated letters. Although she could see how it would have been impossible to decode without the key.

THQUNISTHMOSTPOWRFULPICINTHGAM.

Cat frowned. "This doesn't make sense."

"Remember my Royal typewriter? From my days at that wretched insurance office?"

"The one with the fiddly *E*?"

Another few moments and Cat had it.

"The queen is the most powerful piece in the game."

"I should have burned the thing, but I wanted to keep it," Elizabeth admitted, "to hold proof in my hand that my friend was still alive. That I hadn't dreamed the whole thing."

"But this is nebulous." Cat had been hoping for some message that Mary was alive and happy, preferably somewhere tropical. "Did she survive? She didn't actually commit suicide, did she?"

"She wrote the suicide note, obviously, but no bodies washed ashore in San Francisco Bay. No, I assumed—as did the FBI—that this suicide note was a message meant to throw certain people off her scent, to keep them from putting together too many pieces of her puzzle. Just in case."

"Those certain people being NKVD."

Elizabeth's eyes, usually so shuttered, flared with emotion for a moment. In those twin whirlpools, Cat glimpsed pain and perhaps guilt. Remorse too. "Hearing from Mary reminded me that I'd ruined more than my own life. That I hadn't done enough to protect her."

"Now you're being dramatic, Elizabeth. Mary survived. Unlike everyone else that you sold downriver to the FBI."

"Oh, the folly of youth." This time Elizabeth's expression was downright condescending as she snarled at Cat. "Remember, I told you there are worse things than dying. But here's a little secret: there are different ways a person can die, Catherine, yet still remain breathing."

17

All of America was sweltering in the grip of summer's heat when there came the terrible headline that slipped the noose from my neck and simultaneously terrified the rest of the world: *TRUMAN SAYS RUSSIA SET OFF ATOM BLAST.*

It was impossible that the Soviets could have created their own bomb so quickly following the destruction of Hiroshima and Nagasaki. Which led the entire globe to the one inevitable conclusion: American atomic secrets from the Manhattan Project had, without a doubt, been leaked to the USSR.

There was a spy in our midst, someone who was willing to sell our most important secret to our enemy.

I told myself I would never have done such a thing, that I'd only shared intelligence with our wartime ally. (Of course, now that I'd been threatened by the Soviets and knew their true colors, I'd never share even the lyrics for "The Star-Spangled Banner" with them.) Still, my conscience needled me every time my thoughts wandered in that direction. If I'd been given the blueprints to Fat Man and Little Boy, what would I have done?

None of my philosophical angst mattered, only that we'd been betrayed. I'd have bet money it was William Remington—my lone contact who still worked for the federal government—who had done it. That is, until I woke up one morning to headlines blaring that Julius and Ethel Rosenberg—a quiet and unassuming Jewish couple from New York—had committed the crime of the century. That *they* were underground Communists who had supplied Russians with schematics for the atomic bomb.

Suddenly, the FBI was once again desperate for counsel from their top expert on Communists and the Party underground. *Me.*

"We have irrefutable proof from VENONA cables that Julius *was* a courier and recruiter for the Soviets, that he was actually the kingpin of an entire ring of spies and received payments from the Russians for his work," Hoover informed me after I'd answered a summons to the New York field office. "Actually, without you, we never would have gotten to Julius Rosenberg. Or his wife, Ethel."

"Oh?" In all my years of spying I'd known only one Julius, from that time just after Pearl Harbor when Yasha made a drop during the wartime dark-out and then when I'd answered the man's poorly timed calls. I'd never even known his full name.

Hoover enlightened me. "You named that Long Island city chemist—Abraham Brothman—in your earlier testimony to the HUAC, and that led us to his Soviet courier, Harry Gold. One of Gold's other contacts, David Greenglass, was Ethel's brother. Julius recruited him, but he cracked open like a walnut when we questioned him about the leaking of atomic secrets to the Soviets. Told us everything about Julius and Ethel."

What a tangled web we weave. Still, at least something good had come from perjuring myself on the stand. Something *big.* Perhaps the ends really did justify the means.

"Ethel is a bit trickier," Hoover continued, "but she clearly hid money and espionage materials for her husband, typed and relayed her own evaluations of sources Julius was recruiting. But as you know about VENONA . . ."

"You can't use any of it."

"That's my Clever Girl." Hoover pointed his steepled fingers at me. "That's where *you* come in, Agent Gregory. It's up to you to convince the jury that the Rosenbergs were traitors to their country. After all, if it wasn't for you, we never would have found the trail of bread crumbs that led us straight to Julius . . ."

Upon entering the courtroom that afternoon, I felt a flicker of recognition as I passed tall and reedy Julius Rosenberg, the pencil mustache and round eyeglasses that made him look every bit the withdrawn engineer that he was. However, it wasn't lost on me that Ethel Rosenberg and I might have passed for sisters. Both of us were of a certain age, our dark hair curled and lipstick carefully drawn on pursed lips (Victory Red for me, something akin to Persian Melon for Ethel), both our jawlines starting to go soft with middle age. How had *her* choices led her to being on trial for treason alongside her husband? How had *my* choices led me to testifying against her?

Several twists of fate, I supposed.

Just like an atomic bomb, I'd started a chain reaction without even realizing it. And now, with VENONA verifying the Rosenbergs' guilt, it was my responsibility to finish the job.

"Miss Bentley," asked the prosecution once I'd taken the witness stand, "during your time as a spy, had you learned what the relation of the Communist Party was to the Communist International?"

I'd already been briefed on the prosecution's line of questioning and understood that my job as a star witness was to establish that the CPUSA was *always* a springboard for spies. The Rosenbergs had been verified as Party members—all that was required was that I cast them under a darker cloud of suspicion. Julius Rosenberg was no misguided American hoping to better his country; no, he had stolen classified details from America's most carefully guarded military secret and ferried that information to our greatest enemy. And his wife had been his accomplice through it all.

"The Communist Party of America only served the interests of Moscow, be it propaganda or espionage or sabotage," I answered.

(At least that's what I think I said. Damn difficult to remember through the four-alarm hangover I had at the time.)

"And did you ever come into contact with Julius or Ethel Rosenberg?"

I recalled that night in New York spent sitting in the LaSalle while Yasha met with a shadowy man in spectacles. Named Julius.

A man the same height and build as the Julius in front of me now. With the same spectacles.

So that's what I told the prosecutor. I resisted the urge to embellish as I'd once done on the stand. *Nothing but the truth, Elizabeth. Let the jury decide.*

Then I looked directly at the defendants. Julius's eyes were partially hidden behind the glare of his glasses, but his guilt hung about him like a shroud in the way his gaze suddenly slid away from mine like oil on water. It was Ethel who made me pause, Ethel who had either blindly followed Julius out of love or might have known exactly the treason she committed when typing up top secret notes to be passed to the Soviets.

Her story was too close to mine for comfort.

Except Ethel had made her choices, just as I had mine. We both had to face the consequences of those decisions.

The prosecutor ceased his pacing, looked at me. "We've been informed of your impressive feats of memory regarding your contacts, Miss Bentley. What do you remember of this Julius?"

Not just Julius, *this* Julius. Leading the jury to draw the inevitable conclusion that this thin man wearing round eyeglasses and sitting in front of them was one and the same.

Was it possible that Yasha had been speaking to a different Julius? Possible, but not probable. In my heart, and knowing what I knew about VENONA and what Hoover had told me about Ethel's brother, I fully believed that the man sitting a mere twenty feet away from me had leaked critical secrets to Russia after they'd become our enemy again.

There was nothing good or noble in Julius Rosenberg. If I could bring him down, perhaps I could redeem myself from all my other failed attempts.

I turned my gaze to stare directly at Julius. I would look him in the eyes, even as I condemned him. "Julius called several times, always in the early hours of the morning, and he always wanted to speak with Yasha. He refused to speak with me, only claimed he had information that would benefit the Party to pass along."

It was flimsy evidence, circumstantial at best, but this truth of mine corroborated what Harry Gold and David and Ruth Greenglass had already testified. It was enough for the jury.

Less than two weeks later, the court—and the country—had its verdict.

Guilty.

The Rosenbergs were sentenced to die via the electric chair.

||||||||||||||||||||

NOVEMBER 23, 1963
8:40 P.M.

Cat didn't give Elizabeth time to regain her composure. "You sent the Rosenbergs to Old Sparky? Even if they were guilty, how do you live with yourself?"

"It's not easy." Elizabeth shifted in her seat. On the surface she appeared relaxed, nonplussed, but Cat had caught the way her voice trembled with that last sentence. *Electric chair.* "It's something you can never outrun, knowing that you doomed someone to die."

"There were protests, too, people who believed the Rosenbergs weren't guilty. Especially Ethel." Cat kept prodding, wasn't about to let Elizabeth off the hook for this. Or for anything. "Wasn't there a chance she was innocent? At least partially?"

Elizabeth gave that trademark snort of hers and crossed her arms over her chest. And leveled a glare at Cat that would make the devil cringe. "You won't accept shades of truth, but now there's shades of guilt, eh, Catherine? I'm afraid that's not how the justice system works. No, according to VENONA, Julius and Ethel were both guiltier than cats with canary feathers in their teeth, but the FBI needed me to connect the dots for the jury. So, I did. And, as my reward, half of America turned against me." She rapped her knuckles against the Formica table. "Once again, I couldn't even leave my hotel room to buy a loaf of bread without getting spit on by people who believed I'd sent an innocent man and woman to Sing Sing."

"Was it worth it? Would you do it again if you had the choice?"

Elizabeth blinked, let her eyes lift to the crucifix on the wall, then her gaze snared Cat's. "I don't know . . . Ask me again if you ever run into me in hell."

"You told me that you were responsible for three deaths. Now I know about the Rosenbergs. I've been patient—it's time you tell me about my mother."

That damned lighter started up again. *Click click click.* "Unfortunately, if you include your mother, it's actually *four* deaths."

"What—"

"All I wanted was peace," Elizabeth interjected, lifting her chin. As if going into battle, one she knew she wouldn't win. "Instead, after the Rosenbergs, everything really went to hell."

IIIIIIIIIIIIIIII

MAY 1950

Compliments of my comments on *Meet the Press*, William Remington sued both me and NBC for libel, to the tune of one hundred thousand dollars. If the courts decided he had a case, it would be *Elizabeth Bentley v. William Remington* all over again. Only this time, I would be in the defendant's box, the very thing I'd made Hoover swear would never happen.

Of course, Hoover hadn't made me point the finger at William

Remington from the studio of *Meet the Press*. That had been my own special brand of idiocy. Still, I had no desire to set foot in that courtroom and defend myself.

So, I disappeared.

A judge had yet to decide whether Remington even had a case, but my vanishing act was akin to waving a red matador's cloak at the ravening beast that was the press. There were all sorts of headlines: *RED WITNESS MISSING AT 100-G SLANDER SUIT* was the first one, from the *New York Daily Mirror*.

Well, I couldn't have that, so I planted a story of my own.

The *World-Telegram* complied nicely with my wishes by running a story that I was sequestered at a Catholic retreat in the Bronx. Patently false, of course, but the story made all the newspapers in New York and Washington, DC. (I recall their exact words that I was "quietly pursuing religious meditations while the US Marshals, attorneys, and process servers were frantically seeking me." I *was* praying, but let's be honest—manipulating the truth that time bought me some much-needed breathing room.)

I eventually made good on part of the story, returned to New York and had myself baptized as a God-fearing Catholic. Some thought the conversion far too convenient, but there was something inherently reassuring about shutting the confessional door and pouring out all my sins to a priest. Wiping my conscience clean.

If only it were that easy.

No matter how many Hail Marys or Our Fathers I said, I never felt entirely pure.

Hail Mary, full of Grace . . .

Yasha, Mary Tenney, Julius and Ethel Rosenberg, Vlad . . .

My prayers and meditations always brought me back to all the mistakes I'd made, those who had suffered because of me. Until I realized my penance would be to carry with me the terrible weight of what I'd done. Always.

I supposed I could live with that, could shoulder the added burden of Al's promise that the NKVD would hunt me down the instant I forged a bond with anyone else. I would never hurt anyone again. *Ever.*

I resurfaced after a brief—and strategic—disappearance, accepted a position as a political science teacher at the prestigious Mundelein College on Lake Shore Drive in Chicago.

Between courtroom appearances, I'd given a few paid lectures about the Communist menace that was stalking America, but this new position would be permanent. I'd be surrounded by good, honest people, all of my coworkers nuns and all of my students bright-eyed and Catholic.

Catholics hated Communists, you know. So, we had that much in common.

Keeping everyone at arm's length, I found myself filled with hope for the first time in a long, long while. That I could live some semblance of a normal life. Hold down a normal job. Pay my bills.

Until a Manhattan judge decided that William Remington had a basis for his libel case against me. Which meant months of traveling back and forth between Chicago and New York, conferring with lawyers, and giving my deposition to Remington's legal team, facing grueling examinations and cross-examinations.

Things got uglier when I received word that Remington's lawyers had dug up information—or more likely, fabricated it out of thin air—that in my youth I was admitted to Yale University's psychiatric ward. "Right," I said over the telephone line to my lawyer, so livid I could scarcely think straight. "Because the NKVD was going to put a certified nutjob in charge of couriering sensitive information back to Stalin."

One phone call to the FBI and they dug up evidence that the psych ward rumors were untrue. Still, I had no choice. I resigned from my new position before it even started.

Just like that, my hopes of peace and happiness were slipping through my fingers.

I remember picking up a newspaper before I boarded the train that would take me to New York for another deposition, how the paper felt as I crumpled and hurled the ineffective, lie-laden projectile against the carriage's dull gray wall.

Miss Bentley claims that her frequent subpoenas did not help class morale, and she is afraid the libel suit would embarrass the school. But, according to sources in Chicago, Bentley has been living openly and notoriously with a man. Sister Mary Joseph of Mundelein College believed it best that Bentley left.

It didn't help that the final line read, *"It was very hard to replace her."*

Meaning I'd already been replaced.

I should have just sipped malted milk on the rest of the train ride, but instead I guzzled one martini after another. (Some people chain-smoke; I suppose I chain-*drank*.) I pulled into Grand Central Station irate and ready to flay the very skin from anyone in my way.

And that was *before* I learned that NBC had settled my case out of court.

"What do you mean, they *settled*?" I gripped the chair in front of me and faced off against my lawyer.

"They negotiated an offer to settle for nine thousand dollars. Apparently, the insurance company believed that was a better deal than taking the chance that they'd have to pay one hundred thousand dollars instead."

"I thought that the witness from Knoxville planned to testify that he knew Remington was a Communist? And the eighteen others who worked with him on the Tennessee Valley Authority? You said with a list like that, we were guaranteed to win. Incontrovertible proof and all that."

"Yes, but winning the case would have cost more than settling," my lawyer said. "I'm not happy about it, either, but NBC's insurance company wouldn't cover the expense."

"So, they settle and I wind up looking like a liar?"

(Yes, Catherine, I know I *was* a liar, but it's more irritating than someone chewing with their mouth open to be accused of a particular falsehood when you're telling the honest-to-God truth.)

"I'm sorry, Elizabeth, really I am. I've had complete confidence all along that you would be vindicated if we went to trial. Unfortunately, we're not going to be given that chance. I issued a statement that you will not be issuing a retraction, which is usually part of a libel case. I'm afraid that's the best we can do."

Instead of being exonerated, I was vilified as a liar when I was actually the one telling the truth. Meanwhile, the man who had lied and perjured himself would go free. Again.

I slammed my hand on the table, barely feeling the pain that lanced up my arm.

I'd put my name and reputation on the line, had cooperated fully with the FBI and told nothing but the truth on *Meet the Press*. I'd quit my job in order to cooperate.

All for nothing.

I WAS A woman with a bachelor's degree, two master's degrees, and years of real-life experience. I had proven my poise and my worth through countless courtroom and congressional testimonies. However, I still lacked the two main avenues women typically took to support themselves: family money or a well-connected spouse.

Sometimes it felt not much had changed since my years of heating beans over a hot plate during the Depression. No teaching position meant that I needed to find a source of income, and fast.

Unfortunately, not even my Catholic connections could locate a teaching position in the middle of the school year.

Which meant I had to get serious about writing my memoirs.

Devin-Adair Publishing offered me a three-thousand-dollar advance, which was close to a year's wages, but the bigger carrot was the possibility that I might get my life story serialized before publication. That's where the real money was.

It had been nearly four years since my defection from the NKVD, and I hoped that putting my story to the page would offer me a fresh chance at redemption, that my life's story might persuade America that when I started down this path, I had been just a naive student unaware of the perils and pitfalls of Communism. (I don't mind saying that Mussolini himself could have learned a thing or two from my propaganda skills.) The reality was somewhat cruder—I hoped to save myself from vitriol hurled my way by the American public following the mess of the Rosenberg and Remington trials. I was weary of being public enemy number one. (Or maybe number two, after failed witch-hunter Joseph McCarthy tumbled from grace. And let me make the distinction between myself and McCarthy crystal clear, Catherine, once and for all. Yes, we both hunted Communist spies, but that man was nothing but a snake oil–selling charlatan who foamed at the mouth with his conspiracy theories and smear tactics. Whereas I was an authentic handler who actually had firsthand knowledge of the NKVD and its contacts, all backed up by Project VENONA. So, don't you *dare* ever compare us.)

Unfortunately, writing my memoir proved more difficult than I thought.

If I learned anything from the experience during those five months of coffee-driven mornings and martini-infused nights (sometimes it went the other way, guzzling martinis to fend off a hangover and slugging back Folgers to keep myself awake long into the nights) spent slaving away over my typewriter, it was this: I was *not* a writer.

My chair and my typewriter were my thumbscrews, my iron maiden, my rack.

My penance.

Retelling the stories of my past was invisible self-flagellation as I was forced to relive Yasha's death—both its real and imagined forms—and the terror that I might be liquidated by the NKVD, the betrayal of my former contacts. In an attempt to heal myself, I forced myself to live out each horrible detail.

I wrote of meeting Lee Fuhr and taking my first tentative steps into the Party.

Of encountering my contacts and promising to protect them.

Of the room swirling around me when Yasha died in my arms.

Of listening to my former sources slither around the questions posed to them by the HUAC.

I told my truths, even admitted in black and white that Yasha and I had been lovers, something I'd never dared say out loud while on the stand.

Page by page the stories added up. Until, eventually, I had an entire manuscript.

And I wanted every American to read it, to appreciate my sacrifices and patriotism, especially when *McCall's* magazine picked it up for serialization shortly before its release.

Unfortunately, the book I'd thought would be the key to my salvation became another weapon to use against me.

"Miss Bentley," said one veteran reporter at the press conference *McCall's* arranged, "you speak of the Great Depression in your book. Yet, a lot of us went through the Depression, too, and we didn't turn Communist."

Another hand shot up. "Do you think this exposé of yours will help America just as much as your spying hurt it?"

How dare you little press rats question me? I wanted to yell in their faces. *When have you ever faced down the NKVD or put your life on the line for your country? Or dreamed of a better world only to have it crash and burn all around you?*

Instead, I managed the disguise of a smile. "That's for the government to decide, I suppose."

I hoped critics—and readers—would be kinder than the media, but that was further proof of my delusions. Sales were sluggish when the book finally released. And I'd met more warmhearted NKVD agents than some reviewers who pilloried the book.

Joseph Alsop claimed that "a deep strain of phoniness" ran

through my story, and *Commonweal* wasn't sure whether to find my book "tragic, ludicrous, terrifying, or pathetic," written by an "obviously unstable author, at once so vulgar, so girlish, and so portentous."

The *New Yorker* was even crueler, claiming I wrote in a fashion that suggested I'd had almost as grievous a tussle with freshman English at Vassar as I had later with my New England conscience.

Why again did I decide to write a book?

Still, I'd written *Out of Bondage* to free me from my constant financial strains. In that regard, at least, the book delivered, for I was finally able to buy myself a house.

A *real* house.

Not a room in someone else's house. Not a hotel suite. Not an apartment. No more hiding like a rat in hidey-holes all over New York City.

It was an honest-to-God *house*. In Connecticut. With a garden.

I went home. I bought myself a new African violet, named it Coriolanus in a self-indulgent nod toward both simpler days that were long gone and Shakespeare's tragic hero whose attempts to build a better world ultimately led to his own downfall. It felt so good to have something that was living and growing, some harmless thing that I could never hurt. And yes, sometimes I even talked to him.

Better than talking to myself, I supposed.

I intended to stay there and live a quiet life away from the glare of the klieg lights of the press and Senate. (Well, after I posed for reporters on move-in day, that is. With the bossy and demanding ginger cat who somehow came with the house.)

I wish I could say that's where my story ends, that I lived happily ever after and all that. Except I already warned you . . . this was never going to be that sort of story.

Not for a sinner like me.

18

I put out at an advertisement for a caretaker, wound up with a man in my bed that night.

I wasn't too picky anymore, found myself willing to take someone a little past his expiration date. I was nearly forty-five and figured that at that age you have to seize your happiness—and especially your chances at romance—with both hands. His name was John Wright. Which is funny now, because John *Wright* couldn't have possibly been any more *wrong*.

I kept the lights off, mortified at what time and all those martinis had done to my waist, which while never all that trim had always at least been identifiable.

Of course, John didn't seem to care. It's taken me this long to realize no man really does.

I once heard someone say it's impossible to understand the cul-de-sacs of the human heart. It seems pretty straightforward to me—it was nice having someone next to me in the dark that night. So nice, in fact, that I found my spine pressed up against John's side when I woke the next morning. Sometime during the night my unconscious body had sought out the warmth of human touch I'd gone without for so long.

(I missed Yasha then, Catherine. So much it was physically painful.)

"I'll just work on the hedges this afternoon," John said when I tried to slip out of bed unnoticed. Of course, I'd given him the job as caretaker. I wondered how long he'd been awake, was grateful I'd slipped back into my cotton nightgown before we'd fallen asleep.

"That sounds good," I said. "And tonight?"

John's face was as interesting as a blank wall, and I'd soon discover that there wasn't an original thought in that head of his, but just then I wondered what he was thinking as he viewed me in the unforgiving morning light. No lipstick or rouge, my hair pressed down on the side where I'd slept. Did I actually hold my breath, waiting for his response?

"I'll be right here." He pressed a kiss onto my shoulder blade, just above my nightgown's modest neckline. "If you want me, that is."

"Right here would be nice."

And suddenly, I had a new routine. One that included a man fixing my leaky faucets and the back door that wouldn't quite shut right, then taking care of me at night. Except I knew not to make the mistake I had that first night and made a point to send him home before each morning. I kept John at arm's length for my own protection and his, since I didn't care to find him bleeding out on my kitchen floor as a fresh calling card from the NKVD.

So what if John and I sometimes went to Joe's Bar and drank too much, or that the bartender often had to cut us off? Or that we sometimes stumbled home after Joe's closed at midnight before tripping our way upstairs and into my bed?

I wasn't happy per se—those days were over—but I was *satisfied* for the first time in a long time. So much so, in fact, that I scarcely cared when I was subpoenaed for Remington's perjury trial. I only wished they could replay the newsreels from the first trial: I'd take the stand, repeat the same tired—and true—story about Remington's contributions to the Party. Remington would give his wide-eyed story about having no idea that I'd been a Communist, that he'd only felt sorry for me and humored me by giving me money for Communist newspapers. The jury would never recognize the Pinocchio sitting before them.

Remington would go free, and I'd become America's punching bag. Again.

"Same story, different day," I said when John dropped me off at the New Haven train station the morning of the trial. It was a guilt-laden punch to the gut to let him behind the LaSalle's wheel—Yasha's car—but I'd braced myself against that particular pain before the blow could fully land.

"Doesn't the trial start at noon?" John asked when I closed the passenger door. He held a pack of cigarettes in his hand—I'd forbidden him to smoke in Yasha's car. *Ever.* "I still don't understand why you had to catch the first train, Lizzy. I could've gotten two more hours of sleep if you'd gone in later."

"I have some other business in DC." I ignored the way he shortened my name. "Nothing to worry about. You'll pick me up tonight?"

John frowned, chewed on the toothpick pursed between his lips. He was *always* chewing toothpicks. "I told you I would. Swing by Joe's afterward?"

"Not tonight."

John frowned, but I ignored him—my mind was already on the certain something else I needed to attend to in DC.

Suffice to say, it's true what they say about death and taxes. None of us will escape either of them, at least not alive.

BEFORE REMINGTON'S TRIAL, I stopped by the FBI headquarters in Washington, DC.

They had something I wanted, something I *needed*.

Yes, a phone call would have been easier, but I suspected Remington's lawyers had tapped my phone and been tailing me the past few days. I could never prove it, but I was better off safe than sorry.

The more immediate problem was that, while the serialization of *Out of Bondage* had afforded me the means to purchase my house, John had been extremely helpful in burning through my entire advance. There had been plenty of shared booze in addition to an impromptu weekend getaway to the Bahamas. My mortgage was due (all right, several months *over*due), and the revenue and royalties from my book meant I had to pay taxes for the first time in a long while. The situation had gotten so desperate that I'd taken to hiding my mail in a kitchen drawer in order to make the entire humiliating problem disappear.

The truth was, I was flat broke, and I needed an infusion of cash. *Now.*

"I hope you all know how highly I regard the FBI," I said to its assistant director, Alan Belmont, after I'd been shown into his corner office. It always helped to butter a man up before you asked that he give you something; I could only assume an entire bureaucracy filled with men operated the same way. "It's the only government agency that can't be bought these days."

Yes, I laid it on thick, but it seemed to be working—I'd interrupted Belmont's morning, but he became friendly and deferential. "Thank you for the compliment, Miss Bentley," he said. "What brings you to our office?"

"Two things, actually. First, I was wondering if the Bureau had made any progress into the investigation of the woman who reputedly jumped off the Golden Gate Bridge. The one who left a note addressed to me?"

Belmont scratched his chin. "I'm familiar with the case. Unfortunately, nothing new has turned up."

That was disappointing while also reassuring. It had been nearly four years since that mysterious note had been left for me, but I still liked to check on occasion to see if the FBI had heard anything new. No news was good news—Mary was likely sunning herself on a beach in Barbados, living incognito under a different name. God, I wished I could join her.

Belmont cleared his throat. "And the second reason you're visiting today?"

"I'm afraid it's a little embarrassing." I fiddled with my purse, glanced at him through my lashes. "You see, I'm very interested in what the FBI is planning to do with the two thousand dollars I handed over to the Bureau back in 1945."

That was the Moscow gold Al had given me in recognition of my services to the Party, which I'd then used to prove my story to the FBI. It had been just a pretty prop back then, and I'd never had any intention of laying claim to the money. Except now that cash was the easiest way I could think of bringing my bank account back into the black.

I waited for Belmont to laugh me out of his office, but he took a harsher stance.

"I'm aware of the cash, Miss Bentley." He frowned—so much for friendly and deferential. "Unfortunately, our agency deemed it to be espionage money, which means that it should be handed over to the Treasury Department."

I tilted my head. "*Should* be? Or has it already been handed over?"

Belmont rubbed the back of his neck, which was peppered with hairs and in need of a shave. "To my knowledge, the money you speak of is still in a safe-deposit box in Manhattan. The New York office recommended that it not be returned due to the manner in which you obtained it."

A fact that I was well aware of. It was a decision that made sense and that I had agreed with back when I was still living off my savings from USS&S. Except now I was drowning in bills and had no hope of any real income for the foreseeable future.

"Well, I regret to inform you that my current indebtedness to the IRS will interfere with my usefulness as a witness." I stood, brushed invisible lint from my sensible wool skirt. "Including that of Remington's trial today."

(Was I threatening the FBI, you ask, Catherine? You're damn right I was.)

"Miss Bentley, please wait." The worry in Belmont's tone nearly made me smile. "I'm sure the Bureau doesn't want you fretting over something as mundane as financial woes. I'll speak to Hoover about this immediately and do my utmost to expedite the process of getting those funds returned to you. If you'll just wait outside my office? I know they're expecting you at the courthouse in a few hours."

I let my smile crease the corners of my eyes. "Of course. Your help is much appreciated, Mr. Belmont. I'm eager to hear what Director Hoover says—I'm afraid my mind won't be at ease until I hear that this fine agency will do right by one of their most helpful witnesses."

And wouldn't you know it? Within the hour, Hoover himself authorized the return of my Moscow gold.

SORDID MONEY WOES now assuaged, there was nothing new to tell in my testimony against Remington that afternoon, but the federal government had impaneled another grand jury and indicted our star boy on five new counts of perjury, including his denial of passing secret information to yours truly.

I didn't expect a different verdict this time, not with Remington's duck-like ability to let all charges and accusations roll off him like water.

Still, I did my duty as an American citizen and smoothed the hem of my several-years-out-of-fashion black suit jacket as I took the stand. Then I repeated my previous testimony, conducting myself in a credible fashion. Unlike before, today Remington seemed a little frayed around the edges. He and his wife, Ann—she of the babies and doilies—had divorced recently, so I wondered if it was the strain of a broken relationship or that of carrying around his lies for so long that weighed upon him. (I understood both, given that the same expression and worry lines greeted me each morning in the bathroom mirror.)

Finally, it was Remington's turn on the stand.

"I admit I was a philosophical but not a card-carrying Communist." My former problem child lacked the cocksure air he'd once emanated. I wondered how often he rued the day he'd decided not to plead the Fifth. "I realize now that I was very indiscreet in having any contact at all with Miss Bentley. But I maintain that I didn't know she was a Communist and that I certainly never passed her any sensitive information."

And if you believe that, then I'm the tooth fairy.

The surprise came when the prosecution called Ann Moos Remington to the stand.

Remington's now *ex*-wife.

I leaned forward. I knew Ann—Bing, as Remington had called her—from that first meeting with Remington. I wondered how she'd fared during their separation; the papers had reported adultery on Remington's side as the official cause of the divorce and that there were two children involved. Now Ann had been called upon to testify against her former husband, something that had never happened in any of Remington's prior trials.

Called by the prosecution, I'd mostly expected a bitter harangue from the woman Remington had wronged. Instead, it became readily apparent that she wasn't here to vilify him.

No, she was here to *support* him.

Smart, I thought as I ticked through the list of possibilities of why Ann was dancing nimbly around the questions posed to her. Never incriminating, always sticking to the story that Remington had been a naive idealist. *A housewife with no skills and two children to raise. Without Bill, she loses her only source of income. If he's convicted, her monthly alimony and child support checks dry up. Not to mention her children's father gets branded as a traitor.*

But this was a grand jury case, meaning Ann was without legal counsel. On her own and, honestly, not faring well. It didn't help that the prosecution kept the poor woman on the stand all morning and into the afternoon, without food or water.

"May we have a recess? I'm afraid I'm getting fuzzy," she said as the sun sank toward the winter horizon. "I haven't eaten in so long that I doubt I'm coherent anymore."

"The truth waits for no man. Or woman." Donegan had taken off his trademark fedora and his suit jacket lay draped over his chair; sweat stained the armpits of his white collared shirt. "We must continue, Mrs. Remington."

I frowned. Denying the woman sustenance seemed cruel and unusual punishment, but the counsel for the US government were bloodhounds on the scent. They weren't about to let this woman escape.

Donegan continued. "I need you to replay for me whether Mr. Remington told you that he was paying party dues. To the Communist Party."

"I've already told you." Mrs. Remington's cheeks were flushed, and tiny tendrils of hair had escaped from their perfectly set waves, giving her the air of a frazzled housewife. "Can't we continue another day?"

"We're right down to the issue. I need your answer. Now."

"Well, I don't want to answer." Ann's gaze flicked to the courtroom's wood-paneled exit, and I could just imagine what mental gymnastics it took to tamp down the urge to flee. I'd felt it myself on occasion in court and before the House Un-American Activities Committee, but I'd willingly led myself to the slaughter. Remington's wife was an innocent lamb. Or at least she was *very* convincing playing one.

Donegan towered over her on the witness stand. I eyeballed the judge, willed him to put a stop to this, but . . . nothing. Instead, the men in suits continued to batter this woman—wife and mother—on the stand.

"You have been asked a question, and you must answer it," Donegan commanded. "You have no privilege to refuse to answer the question."

Liar . . .

I stood, the word on my lips.

"Miss Bentley, sit *down*." The judge lifted two bushy gray brows in my direction, gavel poised like a bludgeon. "You've had your turn on the witness stand."

"Yes, but—"

This time it was Donegan who leveled a glare at me. "The Honorable Judge Leibell told you to sit down, Miss Bentley. You don't wish to be found in contempt, do you?"

The message was clear. *Sit down and shut up.*

So, I forced my knees to bend, swallowed the argument on my lips. (Catherine, I regret that decision to this very damned day. Not that it would have made a difference, but honestly, sometimes a person has to *try*, especially when they have nightmares about the other people they've sentenced to die. Doomed causes and all that.)

A wife couldn't be forced to testify against her husband, and even though the Remingtons were divorced *now*, they'd been married during the period in question, which should have given Ann some immunity. Of course, without counsel, Ann had no way of knowing that.

"Please answer the question, Mrs. Remington," said Donegan, his back to me as he circled around to his prey. "We haven't shown our teeth yet, and I don't want to have to bite you. Did William Remington tell you he was paying dues to the Communist Party?"

It was a meager threat, but I could see the last frazzled nerve that Ann possessed stretched to its breaking point. Perhaps she was thinking of getting home to the children and the sitter, or wondering if they'd remembered to let the dog out. Hunger and dehydration might have been setting in as she thought of the dinner she still had to cook when she got home. Or perhaps it was one of a hundred other worries that plagued a single mother on any given day. Hell, maybe she simply lost the fight against her baser nature, had wanted to turn William in all this time in revenge but forced herself to take the high road until she simply couldn't stand it anymore.

Whatever it was, that last nerve snapped with an audible *twang*.

"Yes." Ann's confession came out in a gust. "William told me he was paying dues. He was a Communist from my earliest acquaintance of him and the entire time he worked with Miss Elizabeth Bentley."

In those two sentences, Ann proved her ex-husband's perjury, confirmed every single thing I'd ever said about William Remington.

I should have been jubilant. Instead, I felt only a pickax of bone-deep guilt lodged in my lungs. That pickax lodged even deeper when the judge found Remington guilty of two counts of perjury and sentenced him to three years in prison at Lewisburg Penitentiary in Pennsylvania.

With my testimony, I'd helped deprive a man of his liberty, a wife of her livelihood, two children of their father.

For what?

William Remington wasn't the most important spy in my once-golden arsenal, and it wasn't as if he'd ever have been trusted again—either by America or the Soviets—after all these trials. The poor idiot just happened to be in the wrong place at the wrong time, the only spy who still worked for the US government after everyone else had quit their positions and had the good sense to plead the Fifth.

A scapegoat.

An idiotic scapegoat who had made his own bed—and had

caused me the added irritation of that obnoxious libel civil suit—
but a scapegoat nonetheless. Yes, I'd wanted to take down the
Communists who had infiltrated the American government, but
now all was said and done, I knew justice hadn't truly been served
with Remington's verdict.

I felt ill when I left the courthouse that afternoon. And the
queasy feeling only intensified as I took the train back to Connecticut that evening.

I'D BECOME A weapon the US government could point at anyone
they wished. And if I wanted to keep my house and my livelihood,
I had to perform.

This new and uncomfortable truth about my life plagued me on
my way home to Connecticut that night until it was all I could
think about. So, I did what I always did to drown out my guilt and
discomfort and worries: I ordered a martini. Hell, I had two thousand dollars burning a hole in my pocket, so I ordered another.
And another.

Three martinis that night was three martinis too many.

When I arrived at the New Haven station—whose brickwork
floor seemed suddenly rather uneven—on the last train of the evening, it became apparent that John had forgotten to pick me up. I
waited until the station had emptied and the parking lot too. And
another twenty minutes after that.

Was it so damn difficult to be on time?

A pair of yellow headlights finally weaved toward me as I was
stumbling my way on foot down the dark road. I could make out
John behind the driver's wheel of Yasha's LaSalle. *Yasha . . . Hellfire
and damnation, I miss you.* "Evening, Lizbeth," John said when I
opened the passenger door. "Sorry I'm late. I heard on the radio
they're locking away that Remington snake. Serves him right, the
liberal lyin' Commie."

John's insults toward Bill Remington—after all, I had been a

Commie too—and the sour tidal wave of whiskey on his breath would have been enough to repulse me, but what had me near apoplectic with rage was the acrid scent of cigarette smoke that billowed out the car door. Inside, a glass ashtray perched on the seat with a still-glowing cigarette. And there were fresh burn marks on the leather that Yasha had painstakingly oiled.

John had defaced Yasha's car, had been *smoking* in it, which Yasha had never allowed. After I'd forbidden it.

"There's no goddamned smoking in my *goddamned* car." I reached in, picked up the ashtray, and flung it across the road, heard it shatter with a satisfying crack.

"What the hell is wrong with you?"

"It's my car, which means I'm driving. So, unless you want to walk home, you'd better get out. *Now.*"

I slid across the bench seat, peeled out in sheer frustration just as John sat down and before he'd even slammed shut the passenger door. I drove in enraged silence, my mind reeling from one problem to another with each mile that passed. I needed to stop drinking and get my finances in order. I sure as hell couldn't do any of that with John around. "It's time we end things." My pronouncement fell like a gavel. "We've had a good run, but I want you out of my house by morning."

"You don't mean that, Lizzy."

"I *do* mean it, John. It's over between us."

"Like hell it is."

The next thing I knew, his fist connected with my jaw. The right side of my face erupted in a white-hot streak of pain, and the car veered off the road, sending me careening into the driver's door. A second explosion of jagged whiteness went off like a sonic boom in the lower half of my face. (Later, I realized it must have been the steering wheel. Or perhaps the dashboard. Thankfully, not the windshield.) I can't remember the rest—I blacked out and woke to find the car tipped into an embankment, the front end slightly crumpled around the driver's side wheel well. The passenger door was open, and John . . . ?

. . . was gone.

Something hot and wet streamed down my chin; my lower lip felt loose and terribly *wrong*. Numb fingers that probed my chin came away slicked with ruby-red blood as I tried to make sense of the new geography of my face.

Two teeth had punctured my lower lip. *That's going to leave a scar* . . . Probing with my tongue, I discovered several of my teeth—top and bottom—were also loose.

A sound caught my attention, a low animal sort of moaning I was surprised to find coming from my own throat. It took me a while before I could will my teeth to stop chattering, mostly out of fear that they might fall out of my mouth entirely.

Somehow, I managed to back up onto the deserted street and reversed the battered LaSalle out of the ditch, prayed that Yasha's beloved car would hold together long enough to see me home. I also prayed that I'd see John walking along the road.

The better that I might run the son of a bitch over.

Unfortunately, a woman can't get everything she asks for.

|||||||||||||||||

NOVEMBER 23, 1963
9:02 P.M.

"I can't believe John *punched* you." Despite herself, Cat felt angry for Elizabeth, wished she'd killed the man in the crash. She thought of her best friend Shirley and the bruises she sometimes sported, and found herself wishing that Shirley had enough gumption to cut loose her worthless husband like Elizabeth had done. Of course, Elizabeth hadn't married the man. "That dirty, rotten piece of garbage."

Elizabeth's meager smile drew taut the ugly scar below her lips.

Cat realized that the thick line did indeed match the size of her two front teeth. "It would have been better if I'd gotten this taken care of right away." She gestured to the scar. "I waited too long, let it get infected. There's a metaphor in that, you know."

"What happened with John?"

"He disappeared for a few days. I came home after finally going to the hospital—nursing a whopper of a bruise and a bandaged chin—to find him sitting in my armchair, watching *The Lone Ranger* with an open bottle of my favorite gin in one hand."

"Please tell me that you called the cops and had him thrown him out."

"How mundane, Catherine. No, I did far better than that." A grin that could only be called diabolical crawled its way across Elizabeth's face. "I marched myself to the nearest pay phone and called the FBI to go after him. They subpoenaed John and threatened him with federal charges for interfering with a government witness. I swear I've never seen a man disappear so fast."

Cat gave a high yip of laughter before she could stop herself. "Elizabeth Bentley, you are an evil genius. Brilliant, even."

Maybe I'll have you talk to Shirley one of these days, teach her a thing or two.

Since causing a scene at her mother's funeral and demanding that Shirley leave her husband hadn't gone so well.

"Oh, Catherine." Elizabeth looked at her sadly. "If only you knew." Her chair scraped across the linoleum as she went to stand at the darkened kitchen window, chin drooping and elbows tucked in toward her ribs as if to take up as little space as possible. As if she was defeated. Or was trying to keep herself from flying apart.

And her final tell: fingers flicking that golden cigarette lighter in a manner Cat had come to recognize. Only faster, the tempo allegro.

Click click click. Click click click.

Elizabeth Bentley was *nervous.* Worse than nervous—terrified.

"What is it now? Spit it out, Elizabeth."

The lighter fell silent, and she clutched it between both hands, knuckles gone white. "A doctor recognized my name when I was at New York Hospital getting my chin patched up, a psychiatrist from the Payne Whitney Clinic. He wanted me to see someone, someone who would change everything . . ." She stopped, shook herself. "No, there's a proper order for everything. I'll save that for the very end."

"The Payne Whitney?"

Cat was entirely confused as to how that psychiatric ward fit into Elizabeth's story. However, her confusion never seemed to matter, at least not to Elizabeth.

"Do you have a pen and paper?" She plowed forward. "Because this is the last bit I have to tell you, about your mother. And you're going to want to remember every word."

19

JUNE 1953

They say there's no rest for the wicked. Well, there I was, case in point.

Some weeks after I'd sent John packing, I sat unwashed and undressed on the creaky bed of my spartan roach-motel room—my Moscow gold was gone, and I'd been forced to sell my Connecticut house to pay off mounting bills and those crippling back taxes—and listened to the evening radio broadcast that informed me that I was now an accessory to murder.

"We interrupt this broadcast to bring you breaking news that the US Supreme Court has overturned a stay of execution for both Julius and Ethel Rosenberg. The husband and wife are the first US citizens to be executed for espionage following their conviction for transmitting atomic bomb secrets to the Soviet Union. While both continue to maintain their innocence, their execution via electric chair at Sing Sing Prison in Ossining, New York, is scheduled for fifteen minutes from this moment. This is a developing story and we will return with updates."

Deep down, I knew that both Julius and Ethel were as guilty as I was. Guiltier, even. Yet, as I listened to the oaken mantel clock tick down the Rosenbergs' final minutes, I was seized with icy cold dread.

What if I was wrong? What if it wasn't Rosenberg that Yasha had met, but some other Julius? Why do they deserve to die and I don't?

I was shivering and covered in gooseflesh by the time the radio announcer interrupted the broadcast again.

"Julius and Ethel Rosenberg were executed in the electric chair at Sing Sing Prison tonight. Neither husband nor wife spoke before they died."

President Eisenhower then made an official statement over the crackling receiver, of which few words registered in my mind. Something about the Rosenbergs receiving every safeguard of justice that America could provide.

Perhaps they had, but perhaps not. So many other spies had gone free (yes, Catherine, including me, thank you for pointing that out); maybe the Rosenbergs were simply unfortunate enough to be in the wrong place at the wrong time, a scapegoat of sorts.

If so, they weren't the only ones.

Bad news comes in threes. This time, so did deaths.

The headline of the *New York Times* delivered word of the final death I was responsible for.

REMINGTON DIES IN PRISON

Not executed—no, unlike the Rosenbergs, William Remington had the misfortune to be bludgeoned to death by a fellow inmate with an IQ of 61. What was left of my heart blackened into nothing when I read that the killer had confessed to murdering Remington because he was a *damned Communist who wanted to sell us all out.*

Still holding the newspaper, I fingered the red floral scarf Al had once given me and that I kept but no longer wore. *Too flimsy.* Instead, I eyed first the leather belt discarded from one of my dresses and then the light fixture studded into the ceiling. The belt was thin, but the fixture appeared sturdy enough to hold a woman my size for a few minutes. Long enough to do the job, at least.

Death by hanging was surely better than a botched execution by electric chair such as Ethel Rosenberg had endured. They'd said she'd endured three electric shocks on Sing Sing's Old Sparky before the prison officials ascertained that her heart was still beating. It had taken two more shocks to finally kill her, and by then, smoke was rising from her head.

It was a scene I relived in full gory detail in my newest nightmares.

I tried to escape it then, really I did. I paced my tiny motel room and thought of words, any words.

Yasha. Vlad. Mary Tenney. Ethel and Julius Rosenberg. William Remington.

The nightmare wouldn't stop, this time made worse by the names running through my mind. I could end this. In a world where I'd lost all power, that was the only thing I could still control.

When I tested the light fixture while standing atop the only chair in the room, the damned thing came off the ceiling.

I left it dangling from its wires, grabbed my bottle of gin, and found myself behind the LaSalle's wheel. I'm not proud of it, but that's what happened.

An endless sky of gray and uncaring trees and old dilapidated barns sped by on Route 79 as I pressed the pedal of Yasha's old LaSalle to the floor while sipping liberally from the gin bottle until the nightmare that was my life started to fade around its edges. "You know, old girl," I said to no one in particular, to the car, "I first spoke to Yasha in this very spot. Our first kiss happened after we dug you out of the snow. And I was sitting right here when he met with Julius." I snorted. "Look at me now, a drunken old woman talking to an old heap of dented metal and rubber as if it was my only friend."

I don't know how the tears started, but once they began, they wouldn't stop.

Unseeing, did I drift into the other lane? Or was it the other car that was somehow in my lane?

I suppose we'll never know.

What I do know is that when the black blur of a car came barreling toward me, it was all I could do to swerve out of the way.

I've often thought that I should have let it hit me. Except I didn't want to hurt anyone else. Never again.

As it was, I veered that beautiful LaSalle I'd inherited from Yasha off the road and down a rocky embankment, tossed about in the cab like an unwanted rag doll as it careened toward destruction.

The last thing I remember was the gigantic boulder barreling at me from the other side of the windshield.

"Ma'am, are you all right?"

"Careful, I think she's coming to."

"We need to get you out of the car, ma'am. Hold on."

I wanted to open my eyes, really I did, but they refused to cooperate as concerned voices floated toward me. Part of me wanted to respond, but another part—the jagged pieces that were exhausted after being alone so long—was perfectly content to remain in the darkness. That is, until sensation flooded back into my body.

The feeling of being in a position that wasn't quite right.

The wet stickiness that itched down my face.

The *pain.*

It came from so many directions that I couldn't pinpoint the cause, just the general sensation that I shouldn't move.

A bark of pain escaped my lips when firm hands moved me. Only when I felt solid ground did I crack open my eyelids and blink away a blur of anxious faces that took longer than normal to focus.

"You've had a bit of an accident." A kindly older woman frowned down on me. She dabbed something soft on my forehead. "This looks worse than it is—a head wound always gushes like a geyser. Harry and I here were headed toward New Haven when we saw your car smoking and stopped to help. Do you remember what happened?"

My groan was inconclusive.

"Well, if there was another car," said the man—Harry, presumably—"it's long gone."

Even in my battered state, I tried hard to remember if there even *had* been another car. Had my mind concocted that bit?

"Is there anyone we can call for you?" the woman asked. "Someone to pick you up?"

The world was solidifying; I could shake my head and even sit up. The ground's dampness from recent rains seeped through my skirt and my teeth started to chatter. Or was that the shock of it all? "There's no one," I whispered. "Just me."

My shivering prompted the woman to retrieve a musty blanket from the trunk of her car. I was probably going into shock, a state that only worsened when I caught sight of Yasha's old LaSalle.

What was left of her, at least. Which wasn't much.

I moaned again, clamping my eyes shut against the carnage. The poor girl was absolutely decimated, her face and front wheels crumpled in a protective hug around the boulder that had aimed for me, the driver's side door an open maw from where these kindly strangers had dragged me out. The car that Yasha had so adored—my last connection to him save the gold-and-ruby ring that never left my finger—was now destroyed. By my hand.

I was a reverse-Midas, doomed to destroy everything I touched.

The kindly bystanders loaded me into their car and drove me back to the motel, even helped me trundle into bed and called their own doctor to come examine me.

I didn't protest when he flicked my vein and filled it with a syringe of something sweet.

If only those Good Samaritans had known what manner of demon I really was. They'd have let me bleed out on the side of the road.

* * *

My LIFE DURING that time has always felt a bit like Picasso's *Guernica*, a black-and-white charnel house of all-encompassing gore and destruction. That last car accident was my final wail of agony; I was the screaming woman surrounded by the flames of dismembered, shattered pieces of my life.

Except if you look closely at that painting, there's something few ever notice: a dove scribed on the wall behind the bull. Part of its body comprises a crack in the wall, through which the brightest of light shines.

A symbol of hope, even in the darkest of times.

My hope came in the form of a letter, delivered by an eager young bellhop.

"Miss Bentley, it's Jack from the front desk," he announced through my hotel door one day. I had physically recovered from my last car accident but was lost in a dangerous malaise. "Your mail is piling up, and one letter is stamped FBI. I brought it up just in case it was important."

"Slide it under the door."

"But I have something for you from the kitchen. It won't fit under the door."

I considered ignoring Jack and staying in bed, but then he'd probably return with a key to make sure everything was all right. Apparently, he'd never heard the nursery rhyme—not even all the king's horses and all the king's men could put back the pieces of my life.

I trudged to the door and cracked it open enough to poke my face through. To his credit, young Jack didn't blanch at the sight of such a terrifying old woman. Well, at least not too much.

"Here's your mail." He handed me a stack of envelopes. "And I took the liberty of bringing you tomato soup from the kitchen—I thought you might be sick since you haven't left your room in so long."

Damn it all if my stomach didn't give a banshee growl at the aromatic steam wafting from that tomato soup. My mind might be weary of living, but my body hadn't yet received the self-destruct message.

"Thank you, Jack," I said. "That's very kind of you."

After he departed with a tarnished quarter's tip, I closed the door and tossed most of the meager pile of mail on the bedside table, settling in to sip my soup while opening the letter from the FBI, dreading another subpoena or court summons. I was blowing on a bite when my eyebrows hit my hairline.

It was from J. Edgar Hoover himself, in response to the message I'd sent him several weeks ago. *Before* I'd destroyed the LaSalle.

I scarcely remembered what I'd written, only that I'd sent it out the same day I'd received a rejection for a teaching position at a Catholic girls' school. The school superintendent had claimed that my loyalty was still in question, that she couldn't hire someone who might not be a dutiful and patriotic American.

Essentially, she'd thought I was a *liar*.

Well, I might have been drunk or crazy—let's be honest, probably both—but I'd done the only thing I could think of then: I'd written directly to Hoover and asked if he might write a recommendation on my behalf.

To my shock, he had.

Dear Miss Bentley,

Your cooperation with this Bureau is a matter of public record and a commendable service to your country. I am happy to provide the same statement that I made before Congress in 1953: All information furnished by Miss Bentley, which was susceptible to check, has been proven to be correct. She has been subjected to the most searching of cross-examination, her

testimony has been evaluated by juries and reviewed by courts
and has been found to be accurate.

Sincerely yours,
J. Edgar Hoover

I traced a finger over the words, imagined him writing them.
A commendable service to your country.
Commendable instead of *condemnable.*

That short and serviceable note on official FBI letterhead was nota-
rized proof that the director of the FBI believed in my loyalty. It wasn't
enough to stop the torrential floodwaters of guilt that had been
drowning me, but Hoover's tiny buoy bobbing valiantly against the
storm was something to cling to: the possibility that maybe now, with
proof of my patriotism, I might find a headmaster willing to hire me.

To start anew.

I considered waiting to open the rest of the mail—most was
likely rejection letters—that is, until I saw the Manhattan address
poking out of the pile.

The Payne Whitney Clinic.

I don't know what I was expecting—the Payne Whitney was the
mental institution housed inside New York Hospital where I'd gotten my chin patched up—but I certainly wasn't anticipating the
handwritten message that followed.

(Brace yourself, Catherine. I told you I'd tell you about all this at
the end. Well, here we are, as promised. Don't you dare interrupt
until I'm done.)

Dear Miss Bentley,

I've been meaning to write you since that serendipitous day you
visited New York Hospital. I'm so glad I was able to connect

*you with our patient Mary Tenney at the Payne Whitney
Clinic. However, I must apologize—I should have done more to
prepare you for the fragile state of her mind following her
suicide attempt. Oftentimes, family and friends expect a full
recovery of their loved ones, but unfortunately, such a
transformation wasn't possible in Miss Tenney's situation. I
truly believe the fine staff here at Payne Whitney did our best
to provide for her comfort and treated her as well as we could.*

*Regrettably, I write to inform you that Miss Tenney is to be
transferred at the end of the month from our facility to the
state-run Willowbrook State School. Unfortunately, although
Miss Tenney arrived at our state-of-the-art institution with the
means to finance her stay, her funds ran out some months ago.
I hid this unfortunate situation from the hospital's board for as
long as I could—I find it detrimental to remove a patient from
their routines and familiar surroundings—but a recent audit
brought the situation to light and has forced her relocation.*

*As you seemed to care about Miss Tenney very much, I
thought it pertinent to inform you that Willowbrook is well
over capacity and there have been recent reports of physical
and sexual abuse of patients. When I visited some months
ago, I was shocked to find the majority of patients naked and
covered in bedsores while wallowing in their own feces. I
worry for Miss Tenney's safety if she is moved to such a
facility and hoped that by alerting you, you might find some
solution that would spare her these potential horrors.*

Yours,
Dr. Richard Johnson

I was shaking by the time I finished reading. Terrified that perhaps Mary had already been moved, that in my malaise this letter
had languished downstairs for too long. I nearly cried out in relief

to find that it was only postmarked five days ago. There were still two weeks left until the end of the month. Two weeks to find a solution.

And absolution.

I'd lied and committed treason against my country, ratted out my fellow spies and let them die. Yet, my greatest sin was neglecting my sacred promise made to my best friend.

Sinners make the best saints.

It had been Mary's mantra. And now? Well, now it would be mine.

I knew then that I had to pick myself up. To keep my promise to Mary.

And her daughter.

NOVEMBER 23, 1963
10:01 P.M.

"Mary Tenney was in a mental institution?" Cat gaped, feeling as if the wind had been knocked out of her. Elizabeth merely stared at her with the same expression Cat had seen in the black-and-white photographs of her facing off against the House Un-American Activities Committee. "And she had a *daughter*? But you said she had a son—"

"I *lied*." Elizabeth shuffled to the kitchen, retrieved a file from a drawer. Her voice was fragile and brittle, and there was no color to her face at all. It was as if telling these final pieces of her narrative had leeched something vital from her. "You are Mary Tenney's daughter. And I met you for the first time in 1942. On the day you were born."

This was what Cat had been waiting for, and she thought she'd been ready for it. Except now she struggled to keep the panic from rising in her throat. "But I was born in 1943, not 1942 . . ."

It was a small detail, trivial really. Reading her mother's letter had rewritten everything she'd ever believed about herself. Learning that her birthday wasn't even correct shouldn't have been a surprise, but for some reason, that was what her stubborn mind snagged on.

"I changed your birthday when I forged your birth certificate,"

Elizabeth proclaimed, as if forging documents were an everyday occurrence. "You were born in Nashville General Hospital on December 30, 1942, *not* January 7, 1943. You were born to Mary Tenney, father unknown. I was there the moment you entered this world and gave your first red-faced squall against this unfair life. Then I watched your mother—my best and only friend—hold you. For the first and last time."

She passed Cat something from inside the file. The certificate was yellowing with age and stamped *Bureau of Vital Statistics— Certificate of Live Birth*. Listed was all of Mary Tenney's information, albeit with her occupation listed as beekeeper, which Cat assumed was a sly reference to her real position as a honeytrap. Cat traced her finger over the signature. Her *mother's* signature.

Followed by the information about her newborn daughter.

> *Catherine Louise Tenney. 6 pounds, 8 ounces.*
> *Born December 30, 1942.*

Cat thought that was all, until Elizabeth passed her another aging paper.

She read, then reread the words there, struggling to make sense of them.

OFFICE OF VITAL STATISTICS—CERTIFIED COPY
CERTIFICATE OF DEATH

> *Name: Catherine Louise Tenney*
> *Date of Death: January 1, 1943*

Cat didn't know what elaborate scheme Elizabeth was playing at, but she was sick of the games. "What the hell is this?"

"Well, Catherine, I'm afraid that, at least according to the state of Tennessee, you died two short days after your birth." She sniffed.

"Which also meant that you were dead to the NKVD and any other Russian organization that might have come looking for you during the last twenty years. You were safe."

Cat's anger reared its Gorgon head; before she knew it, the gun was out of her purse and pointed at Elizabeth. "Tell me the god-damned truth."

Elizabeth's hands lifted, this time as if in surrender. "Just keep that gun pointed at me, Cat, not at yourself. I've grown rather fond of you, you know."

Cat's growl was guttural. "The *truth*."

"I traveled with Mary to Tennessee when she was pregnant, not to help her through an abortion but to hold her hand while she gave birth to you. Mary wanted you, but even more, she wanted you safe from the life she led. It wasn't difficult to find a sympathetic social worker who was willing to help, for a price. Baby brokering was a booming black market business then—still is—with far more adoptive families than there were babies."

Every nerve stretched taut as piano wire, Cat motioned with the gun for her to continue. Elizabeth plunged on.

"With the social worker's help, I forged your death certificate to snuff out any trail to you, just in case the NKVD ever came sniffing. With the very same pen, I wrote out a new birth certificate—the one that was given to your adoptive parents—with a false birthday."

"Did my mother—did *Joan Gray*—know? Did Mary know what you did?"

"Suspicions aren't the same as knowing." Elizabeth scrabbled for Cat's hands, but she threw her off, stood so fast her chair knocked over. "I killed three people," Elizabeth said, a frantic, *desperate* note to her voice. "But worse, I made a baby disappear and landed my best friend in a mental institution. After my first car accident, Dr. Johnson heard that I was at New York Hospital and sought me out because he'd once heard Mary utter my name amid her disordered ramblings about being a Russian spy. He asked me to visit Mary, and

I did, thinking I could take her home with me, but she was too far gone, had tried to kill herself by mixing alcohol with an overdose of phenobarbital. She was unconscious for five days and had been in a severe hallucinatory psychotic state ever since."

Cat stopped, perfectly motionless. "Where is she now?"

"My Mary?" Something in Elizabeth's face fractured then. "I should have burned her as a spy the moment she asked for my help, saved her from herself. Because I didn't, she's dead and gone, I'm afraid."

And just like that, the rest of Cat's world dropped out from under her. She'd come here armed with her mother's letter, thinking to end the woman who had tried to play God—and perhaps even herself—yet, still hoping to find answers. And perhaps to discover that there was still someone to tether her to this life.

Only to have Elizabeth blow the fuse on a cache of dynamite she hadn't even known existed.

"You should die for what you've done." Cat pointed the gun straight at Elizabeth, one cold finger on the trigger. The ringing in her ears grew louder until it drowned out everything else; the scope of her sight narrowed to Elizabeth's bloodless face. "A hundred deaths aren't enough for you."

Elizabeth merely squared her shoulders. "Trust me, Catherine, *I know*."

In one swift movement, Cat aimed, exhaled.

And squeezed the trigger.

THE SHOT REVERBERATED down Cat's arm, and she flinched as white ceiling plaster rained down. At the last moment, she had raised the gun.

Elizabeth lurched forward. "I have more, Catherine." She didn't try to grab the gun, but instead clasped Cat's wrist. "So much more."

Again, Cat shook her off, began backing toward the door. "I've heard enough. If I don't get out of here, my last bullet will wind up lodged between your eyes."

This time, she meant it.

But Elizabeth shoved the manila file at her. "Here's the adoption contract—the Grays were desperate to be your parents, just as Mary Tenney was desperate to protect you. Everything checks out; the contract even stipulated that you keep your name. I've included the card for the New Haven FBI office. They'll confirm everything I've said— they're the ones who helped me track you down three years ago."

Cat slammed the door behind her, but Elizabeth's words chased her down the darkened front steps of the building. Cat didn't look back, but she swore she could feel Elizabeth's gaze hot on her neck.

Stunned and shocked, Cat pulled up her collar against the night's chill before she broke into a run, needing to outpace the jagged teeth of Elizabeth's words that nipped at her heels.

They'll confirm everything I've said.

Except, there was more.

They're the ones who helped me track you down three years ago.

Three years ago? But the first Cat had heard of Elizabeth had been mere days ago, when she read her mother's letter.

Some of her shock fragmented, its pieces slowly metamorphizing to disbelief. And consternation.

There was more to Elizabeth's story, Cat knew it.

Just what are you playing at, Elizabeth?

UNABLE TO RAGE at her dead mother or the woman who had birthed her, Cat spent the next three days swinging between angry incredulity toward the Communist spy who had directed the circus that was her life and being mired in fresh waves of grief as America laid President John F. Kennedy to rest. It was too much, all at once: her mother's death—for no matter what, Joan Gray would always be the mother who hid nickels under her pillow from the tooth fairy and plied her with an endless supply of Mallomars when her high school boyfriend broke her heart—followed by the discovery of her adoption, tracking down Elizabeth, the death of a president . . .

It was more than any one person should be asked to endure. But, just as America and the president's family were being forced to endure too much, so, too, would Cat. Simply because there was no other choice—she'd already come to the realization that she was no murderer, that she never could have pulled the trigger on either Elizabeth or herself, no matter how much she was hurting.

She'd walked through hell and she'd survived. That was something.

Uncertain about what she should do next, Cat took to listening to the radio—the Beatles' "Love Me Do" and the Beach Boys' "Surfin' U.S.A." seemed to be every deejay's latest favorites—while sitting in the plastic shell chair her mother had bought for her last birthday, reading and rereading her mother's final letter, that lone piece of paper that had started this entire avalanche she'd been powerless to stop.

My darling Cathy,

This is a letter I never wanted to write—I refused to once, in fact—but after telling myself for years that I'd wait until the time was right, well . . . now I'm out of time and I can't find the courage to have this conversation, not when I'd have to tell you about the cancer too. Maybe if your father were still here, but I'm not strong enough on my own. I hope you can forgive me for that.

Your father and I loved you, Cathy, so very much. We wanted you for so long, prayed for you, moved heaven and earth to have you. You were our miracle.

One minute your father and I were convinced that we'd never have a child, and the next we received a phone call that there was a baby whose mother had died while giving birth and who now needed a family.

Little did I know, the woman who made that phone call— and later placed you in my arms—was a crook and a liar and God only knows what else.

I recognized her—Elizabeth Bentley, down to the very same mole on her cheek—when I saw her in 1948 on a Meet the Press *interview, wondered how the hell a Communist spy, and not a social worker as she'd claimed, had facilitated an adoption. You were lying on the living room floor, chin propped in your hands, and your feet in their Mary Janes kicked up behind you while you read* Black Beauty, *and I had a terrible feeling then that things hadn't been aboveboard. I never knew the details of where or how Bentley found you—it was cowardly of me, Cathy, but I suspected that this traitor had somehow made a criminal of me, and I didn't want to know the truth.*

When Bentley showed up on my doorstep a few months ago—just after my diagnosis—demanding that you be told the circumstances of your birth, I slammed the door in her face. She kept coming back, but I was so exhausted—I told her to go to hell each time, prayed to Almighty God she wouldn't contact you herself.

It was selfish of me to keep the truth from you all these years, I know, but you were all I had after your father's death, and I wasn't willing to lose you. That's something I hope you can forgive me for too.

I can't burden you with watching me die, Cathy, but I realize I'm leaving you alone in this world. Now it's up to you to decide whether you want to talk to this Bentley woman. She's the only one who has the answers about your real mother, although I suspect you may not want to hear them.

I hope you can find it in your heart to forgive me.

I will always, always *love you.*
Your mother

Sometimes when she finished, Cat contemplated burning her mother's letter and pretending Joan Gray had never left her that damned piece of paper so she could just get on with her life. Other times she thought of storming her way back to Elizabeth Bentley's apartment and demanding the answers to fresh questions that sprouted like poison ivy in her mind.

The New Haven FBI card taunted Cat from where she'd dropped it by her dormitory's rotary telephone. She had finals to study for, not to mention she still needed to figure out how to pay for her room and the tuition for the last semester of her journalism degree. Given that she had hardly a penny to her name, the very thought should have sent her into a tailspin of panic, but she couldn't seem to function, couldn't do anything except stare at that card and re-play Elizabeth's story in her head. Calling the FBI felt like admit-ting there was a possibility Elizabeth was telling the truth. And that simply wasn't possible.

So, instead of calling the FBI, Cat did something she'd been put-ting off for a while. She pulled the rotary phone onto her lap and dialed Shirley, her best friend since they'd Hula-Hooped them-selves silly and swooned over Elvis on the radio.

"It's good to hear your voice," Shirley answered after the fifth ring. Cat could hear baby Maggie gurgling in the background and suddenly wished she was at Shirley's cozy house, imagined her wearing a freshly starched apron over her fashionable circle skirt, probably something with cherries or flowers on it. "I was begin-ning to think you'd fallen off the face of the earth."

"I wish."

"What's going on? You don't sound like yourself."

Shirley knows me, Cat thought to herself. *She's the closest thing I have left to family. And I need to tell* someone *about this entire mess with Elizabeth . . .*

First things first.

"Shirley, I called to apologize. I was out of line at the funeral. That wasn't the right time or place to talk to you about Eddie—"

"You were right, Cat."

"What?"

Shirley gave a wry sort of chuckle, so Cat could imagine the twist of her lips. "I'm not as smart as you, Cat, but even I know that Eddie shouldn't treat me the way he does."

Some of the tension melted from Cat's shoulders. *Thank God.* Cat cleared her throat. "So, what does that mean? For you and Eddie?"

"Eddie's gone to stay with his parents for a while. He's going to find someone who can help him. With his anger, I mean. The YMCA might have classes that can help."

Cat wished she could hug Shirley right then, said as much. "I'm glad for you, Shirley, really, I am." She took a deep breath. "So, can you forgive me?"

This time Shirley's chuckle was light and airy. "Always. Unless you become a serial killer. Then I'll pretend I never knew you." Her voice grew muffled as she said something to little Maggie. "Sorry, the baby was dropping peas on the floor for the dog. It's their favorite game. So . . ." A long pause. "How are things with you, Cat? And don't just say *fine*. I want the truth."

Cat had never spent so much time thinking about the truth as she had in the past few days. "Well." She took a deep breath. "I found out I'm adopted."

"*What?*"

Cat found herself spilling the entire sordid story to Shirley. Everything—her mother's letter, even going to Elizabeth's house to kill her, and Elizabeth's entire revelation.

When Cat finished, it was if all the words and emotions had been wrung out of her until she felt hollow. Empty. "Now I don't know what to do," she managed to say, fiddling with the New Haven FBI card that had been taunting her.

There was a long silence on Shirley's end—she'd put baby Maggie down for a nap sometime during Cat's recitation. "The real question is: When are you going to talk to Elizabeth and find out the rest of your story?"

"It's *not* my story," Cat barely managed to grind out. She set the FBI card on the side table so she wouldn't shred it out of anger. "Elizabeth Bentley is a consummate liar, has been from the first day I met her. This is all some colossal joke to her."

"Maybe. But what if it's not? Don't you owe it to yourself to find out?"

That was *not* the answer Cat wanted to hear. And Shirley wasn't done.

"You need to call the FBI to verify part of Elizabeth's story," she commanded. "As soon as you hang up with me. And then you need to talk to Elizabeth again."

"You're a good friend, Shirley."

"Thanks, Kit Kat. So are you." The old nickname meant Cat knew she'd truly been forgiven. "Let me know how things go, okay?"

"Pinky swear."

Cat stared at the FBI's card long enough that she half expected it to burst into flames. She didn't want to open a new chapter in this sordid story Elizabeth had told her, but knew she'd regret it if she didn't—the FBI could at least corroborate what Elizabeth had said.

She forced herself to dial, each spinning number on the rotary phone tempting her to hang up.

When the FBI secretary answered, Cat informed her in a level voice that she was seeking to verify Elizabeth Bentley's claims of her work with the FBI and even her working relationship with J. Edgar Hoover.

"I'll forward your request, Miss Gray," the secretary said in a manner that made Cat wonder how many strange telephone calls their field office received every week. "But I'm not sure when an officer will be able to answer your inquiry."

It's the best I can do, Cat told herself, *save showing up at the New*

Haven office and demanding answers. Which is precisely something Elizabeth Bentley would do.

Cat wondered if she should borrow a page from Elizabeth's playbook.

She'd almost convinced herself to do precisely that—while pondering what long-term impacts her interview with Elizabeth Bentley had on not just her entire worldview but also the very marrow of her personality—when the telephone rang.

That was fast.

"Hello, Miss Gray, this is the registrar's office at Trinity Washington University. I was calling to inform you that, as of today, we processed payment for your final semester. Your balance is now paid in full, for both tuition and housing."

Cat stood holding the phone, utterly dumbfounded. "Wait . . . What?"

"The payment arrived yesterday via a wire transfer."

"From whom? Was it a bequest from my mother's estate?"

Not that there had *been* an estate, given that her mother had even reverse mortgaged their very home.

"It appears to have been a scholarship. I'm afraid I don't know more than that."

Her mind awhirl, Cat hung up, sat dumbstruck with the phone in her lap. *Surely, there's been some mistake?* She nearly didn't answer when it jangled to life a moment later, feared the registrar's office was calling to confirm her suspicions.

"I'd like to speak with Miss Catherine Gray," said a gravelly male voice on the other end. "This is J. Edgar Hoover."

The phone receiver might have become a Burmese python for how fast Cat almost dropped it.

"Excuse me?" she managed to say once the receiver was in hand again.

His chuckle was raspy with decades of cigarette smoke. "The

New Haven FBI office has long been instructed to inform me of any queries regarding Miss Bentley."

Cat could only imagine that Hoover would have wanted to be apprised of Elizabeth's comings and goings, especially during her rough years. Still, it struck her as incongruous that the director of the FBI would be paying a college student a personal call.

Unless everything Elizabeth said was true. All the important parts, anyway . . .

"It seems that you're seeking to validate Elizabeth's story, including her contact with me and also her involvement with the Rosenberg and Remington cases. I can assure you those are factual instances of her loyalty to her country."

"And what about her assertion that the FBI helped track me down?" The words spilled out before Cat could stop them. "Or that she helped my mother—another Russian spy—arrange for my adoption?"

The pause was longer this time. "If you're referring to Elizabeth Bentley's request that we locate one Catherine Louise Gray, biological daughter of Mary Tenney, I authorized that fieldwork myself."

"And when was that?"

A pause. "Three years ago. Seeing as how the FBI never paid Elizabeth Bentley for her services, that one favor seemed like the least I could do." Papers rustled on the other end. "Miss Gray, I'm afraid that's all I have to say on the matter. If you require further verification, my secretary will send you a signed affidavit of what I just told you."

Cat stared blindly at the *Vogue* covers she'd taped to the wall back when her life was simpler, when her biggest concern was whether to wear a box dress or an A-line to her journalism class. Now she just felt numb. "That would be acceptable, thank you."

She was telling the truth. And she's known where to find me for three years and never lifted a finger. The bitch.

Yet, Hoover wasn't quite done. "Miss Gray, we both know that

Elizabeth Bentley can be an extremely trying individual." His understatement nearly made Cat snort in disbelief. "However, her motives are generally altruistic. She told me her part in your story to convince me to sign off on tracking you down. I suspect she'd appreciate your forgiveness before it's too late."

"What do you mean, too late? It's already too late—I have no desire to see that meddlesome woman ever again."

Another pause, longer this time. "I take it she didn't tell you about the cancer?"

Cancer.

The same disease that killed Cat's mother.

This was a scene Cat had played before, except this time the director of the FBI was breaking the bad news instead of her mother's doctor. This time she managed to keep breathing. "No," she finally said. "She didn't tell me about any cancer."

It must have slipped her mind. Just like so many other truths.

"It's abdominal, I'm afraid. A terribly painful disease that doesn't often end well." Hoover's voice became muffled, and Cat could imagine him covering the receiver on the other end as he spoke to his secretary. Then he was back. "There's something terribly tragic about a woman who has no one to call about such a diagnosis save an office of FBI agents. Anything you want to say to—or ask—Elizabeth Bentley, I'd suggest you do it soon. Just in case. Good-bye, Miss Gray."

The line went dead then, leaving Cat staring at the receiver and wondering if she had imagined the entire conversation.

Except the revelation of Elizabeth's cancer answered so many questions. Including why she felt the need to reveal everything to Cat when she did. Hell, even why she dared to open the door to her in the first place. And why she'd sometimes almost seemed to goad Cat into shooting her—a gunshot was certainly a more merciful way to go than slowly wasting away from tumors in your belly.

But why did she track me down so long ago and then never contact me? Why, why, why?

Elizabeth Bentley was the last person on earth who had known Mary Tenney. And she was the only one who could answer Cat's questions.

Cat gave a resigned sigh. That meant Shirley was right. She was going to have to go see the lying old harpy one last time.

CAT POUNDED ON Elizabeth's door so hard the bones in her hand threatened to fracture. There was no way Elizabeth could pretend she simply hadn't heard Cat.

I want answers, goddammit, Cat wanted to demand. *And I want to know why you didn't tell me that you're dying from cancer.*

Still, no answer.

She tried the door. Locked.

"Elizabeth." Cat raised her voice. Barring childhood outbursts, this was the only time she could remember raising her voice to an adult, and she was prepared to do it all day. "There's no point in ignoring me. You owe me answers, and I'm not leaving until I get them."

And I don't have a gun, she nearly added. *Not this time.*

Instead, she'd lugged along the reel-to-reel tape recorder she'd used for interviews in her investigative journalism class. She wondered whether it might be handy in breaking down Elizabeth's door.

Until the door to the apartment below creaked open.

"Miss?" questioned the frowning neighbor, a snowy-haired elderly woman. "Is there something I can help you with?"

"Do you know where Elizabeth Bentley is?" Cat realized she must look like an inmate from Bedlam, did her best to at least smooth the flip of her bob. "I'm an old friend." It was amazing how easily the lie pirouetted off her tongue. "I need to speak to her."

"Oh dear. I'm afraid you won't be able to catch her. It's a pity, really . . . Harold and I were hoping to invite her to join us for Thanksgiving again this year."

Ice replaced Cat's bones. "What do you mean?"

"You know she was ill, dear. Very ill."

No, I didn't know. Not until today. Elizabeth can't weasel her way out of this. Not this way.

The old lady looked at Cat kindly, but it was a version of kindness mixed with pity. "It's not the worst, at least not yet. But I'm afraid Elizabeth found a new lump in her abdomen, checked herself into Grace-New Haven Hospital." The neighbor took off her cat-eye glasses and polished them with her sweater, then replaced them on her nose to peer back up at Cat. "I know she'd love to have visitors to keep her spirits up—she told me on the phone this morning that it's nothing but an armada of tests at that hospital."

Cat must have nodded, because the neighbor motioned for her to wait and returned with a key. And a plant. Not just any plant—an African violet Cat recognized as the newest iteration of Coriolanus. "Elizabeth left me her spare, asked if I could water her plant and check on her cat. I would, except Harold and I are headed upstate to spend Thanksgiving with our daughter. Would you mind doing it, just until we get back?"

Cat wanted to say no, to *scream* the word, but the old woman was already pressing Coriolanus and the key into her hand. "That darned cat surely does work himself into a frenzy if you don't feed him on time," she muttered.

Cat had spent only a single day in Elizabeth's apartment, but this time when she pushed open the door, time slowed and she found herself setting down the bag with her tape recorder and gulping great, huge breaths as history repeated itself.

Everything was orderly. Not just orderly. *Empty.*

This is not my childhood home, she had to repeat to herself. *This is* Elizabeth's *home.*

Except everything was gone, and each surface and square of linoleum scrubbed until it shone. All the furniture was gone—including the couch with its tattered crocheted eyesore of a green-and-white throw—leaving only vague outlines on the shag carpet. Yasha's portrait on the mantel and even the crucifix were gone.

The single spark of life in the entire apartment was the oversize ginger cat that threaded his way through Cat's legs on dainty white paws, mewing plaintively.

She set down the violet, scooped up George Washington, and flung open kitchen cabinets, dismayed to see them all empty save one with a perfect pyramid of canned cat food. The can opener was still in its drawer, and an open tin placated George Washington even as Cat became more and more alarmed.

The apartment could have easily belonged to someone who knew—had *known* for a long time—that she was dying.

In an apartment swept completely empty, the cardboard box on the kitchen counter stood out.

Inside, Cat discovered a hand-carved wooden cross she recognized from Elizabeth's talc, its gleaming vines and flowers smooth to the touch. Attached was a simple note in handwriting she recognized from the bottom of the birth certificate Elizabeth had given her: *A blessing for Catherine, from her mother.*

Eyes stinging, beneath the cross, Cat dug through the layers of detritus from Elizabeth's life. There was a lavender journal with the words *Human Behavior* painstakingly stenciled on the cover, its pages crammed to the margins with Elizabeth's notes and sketches. And a yellowing paper pad about the size of Cat's palm that was riddled with numbers that she recognized as an unused one-time pad. She hadn't realized Elizabeth was sentimental enough to keep such mementos.

The framed photo of Yasha was surprisingly missing from the box, but Cat found a different photograph, one of Elizabeth wearing a plain fitted suit standing next to a stunning blonde in a stylish floral shadow dress with wrist-high black gloves, the Grand Ole Opry behind them. The woman could have passed as Cat's older sister.

Or her mother, which Elizabeth's scrawl on the back of the photo confirmed.

With Mary Tenney. October 1941.

Flipping it over, Cat took in Mary's hand resting on her stomach, which was rounded in the late stages of her pregnancy. *With me*, Cat thought before she could shake the words from her mind.

She slipped the photograph into her pocket and rummaged through the rest of the box, found J. Edgar Hoover's letters to Elizabeth that she had initially showed Cat and a near-empty tube of Bésame lipstick. Victory Red, of course. Near the very bottom, Cat almost ignored what appeared to be a stack of checking account ledgers. Except . . .

Elizabeth was a woman who kept no records. So, why had she kept these?

As she skimmed the pages, Cat realized the records began in September 1959. However, from that point, Elizabeth had kept meticulous—albeit somewhat coded—records, including regular deposits that were made from Long Lane School for Girls, which must have been where Elizabeth had been working. Apparently, her dream of being a teacher had finally come true.

Yet, money appeared to have always been a crux for the self-proclaimed sinner who never really reformed her ways. According to the ledger, Elizabeth managed to spend every last penny of every single paycheck.

Cat almost tossed aside the ledgers. That was, until two entries caught her eye. They read:

October 1, 1959	*P.W.Clinic*	*$500*
December 1, 1959	*Bing Moos Remington*	*$125*

It didn't take a spy to decode that P.W.Clinic was the Payne Whitney Clinic. Or that Bing Moos Remington was Ann Remington née Moos, also known as Bing to her now-dead husband.

Why would Elizabeth make payments to the asylum that housed her friend? Or the wife of a man she sent to prison?

Cat cautiously flipped through the rest of the ledger while scrutinizing its lines. The small amounts she ignored—they were all labeled with standard and unsurprising titles: several dollars for groceries at Grand Union, the monthly electric bill, an occasional check to a local veterinary clinic for George Washington. It was the large ones she sought.

And she found them.

The payments to the Payne Whitney Clinic were paid every three months on the first of the month, as were those to Ann Remington. It was the next huge sum listed that stunned her.

August 1, 1961   *TWU.21346*   *$ 564.28*

That entry repeated itself like clockwork every August and January afterward until the most recent payment on August 1, 1963.

Cat sat down, hard.

The number 21346 was her student account at Trinity Washington University. She'd received a notice from the school before her sophomore year that her semester's tuition was overdue. When she'd informed her mother, Joan Gray had gone extremely quiet, finally informing Cat in a tight voice that they might not be able to cover the cost. Miraculously, Catherine received word just three weeks later that she'd been awarded an academic scholarship.

In the exact amount of $564.28.

Just like the one I received today.

As Cat delved further, she found familiar infusions of cash that she remembered as pleasant surprises. One had arrived on her twentieth birthday; she remembered thanking her mother for the extra spending money, had been puzzled when she'd only laughed.

"Right," her mother had chuckled as she mixed Cat's favorite cranberry banana Jell-O, a birthday staple as far back as she could remember. "I just pruned the money tree growing out back." Cat had thought she was joking, had laughed along with her.

Now, sitting in Elizabeth's apartment, Cat ran her hands through George Washington's thick fur, her mind jumping from one shocking conclusion to the next while the cat purred on her lap. It was no wonder Elizabeth was always broke, given that she was hemorrhaging cash all these years.

All the better to alleviate her conscience?

And it seemed self-proclaimed sinner and villain Elizabeth Bentley had also been playing another role all this time.

Cat's dirty-winged guardian angel.

One question remained: *Why?*

Cat picked up Elizabeth's telephone, half expecting that the line might be disconnected. To Cat's relief, there was a dial tone.

"Are you family?" the Grace-New Haven Hospital switchboard operator asked when Cat inquired after their visiting hours. "Visiting hours are only for family."

"I'm the patient's niece." *You'd be proud of me, Elizabeth,* Cat thought to herself. *I could fool even you with my lies.*

"I'll be back tonight to take you to my place," Cat informed George Washington after she hung up. "Wish me luck." Like a normal cat, he barely looked up from his nap.

IT WAS A short bus ride to Grace-New Haven Hospital, not nearly long enough to work out in Cat's mind all the ways this conversation might go. She was still angry and confused at Elizabeth, but another part of her—the logical part—knew that, due to the cancer, she may not have another opportunity to confront her.

To make Elizabeth Bentley, pathological liar and spy extraordinaire, answer her questions.

When Cat asked for Elizabeth's room at the front desk, the grizzled, white-clad nurse scarcely glanced up from her paperwork, didn't even bother to ask how Cat was related. "Bentley? She's in room 185. Down the hall."

The hospital was eerily quiet as Cat made her way to Elizabeth's room, as if the entire building was holding its breath. She peered through the slim window on the door to room 185. Elizabeth was sitting up in the hospital bed, her dark hair wilted and the unattractive blue johnny making her seem paler than before. Not pale . . . *ill.*

How did I not notice the sickly hue of her skin before? Or the way she shifts in her seat so often, as if suffering some silent sort of pain? Now that Cat knew there was cancer eating away at her, it seemed impossible not to see it.

After being so angry at her, Cat was surprised to experience a new emotion toward Elizabeth: sympathy. There was no denying the feeling, especially when she spied the one lonely item Elizabeth had brought from home that now sat on her bedside table: Yasha's black-and-white photograph. Of course, there were so many other complicated layers of emotion atop the sympathy that its surprising ember was nearly buried.

Cat had no choice. The only way to get through this . . . was to get through it.

She didn't wait for Elizabeth to answer her knock before pushing through the door.

"Murder on your mind again?" Elizabeth's arms hung at her sides like sticks, but it almost seemed as if her eyes lit up when she saw Cat. Or maybe that was a side effect of whatever drugs she was on. "I'll have you know it's poor form to kill a woman in her hospital bed," she announced.

"You have cancer. And you didn't tell me."

"Pah. It's nothing. I'm just here for routine tests."

"Really? Is that why you emptied your apartment?" Cat unpacked the clunky reel-to-reel recorder, forced Elizabeth to crane her neck to look at her. It was a petty victory over this woman who had apparently pulled the strings of Cat's life for so long.

"Merely a precaution," Elizabeth answered. "Having cleared out both my father's and Yasha's things after they died, I thought to spare my landlord the trouble. Just in case." She shifted in her hospital bed, frowned, and adjusted the short sleeves of her hospital gown. "But I'm guessing you didn't come here to talk about my health."

"I want to know how Mary Tenney died. How her story ended. And I want to know why you tracked me down. *Three years ago.*"

Elizabeth's smirk surprised her. "And what if I don't want to tell you?"

Her flippancy should have offended Cat, but she'd learned to decode Elizabeth's tells. Realized that her bold stare was really a cover. That her fingers fiddling with the thin hospital blanket were searching for the comfort of her golden cigarette lighter.

I'm scared, her body language screamed at Cat. *My bluster is all a cover, can't you see that?*

Cat *did* see. But she wasn't willing to let her off the hook.

"You're the only person who can answer all my questions." Cat leveled a frosty stare at Elizabeth to let her know this was no joke. No games. "This time you're going to tell the truth. The *absolute* truth. And I'm not leaving until you do."

"Fine." Elizabeth waved Cat to the metal folding chair. "One last sordid tale. This will be downright pleasant compared to our last interview, given that I won't have a gun staring me in the face."

Cat ignored the dig as she pressed play on the recorder. She sat across from Elizabeth and crossed her ankles, forced herself into a relaxed position even though her first inclination was to start barking questions and demanding answers. "You told me the last time you saw Mary Tenney, she was in the Payne Whitney Clinic following a complete mental breakdown. Is that true—yes or no?"

It was a carefully crafted question, so airtight that even the liar extraordinaire Elizabeth Bentley couldn't weasel her way out of it.

"I did see her in the Payne Whitney Clinic, yes." She responded so calmly that Cat could easily envision her sitting placidly across from Joseph McCarthy and Richard Nixon, the klieg lights glaring down at her. Cat wondered briefly which was the more difficult interview for her—*that or this?* "Following my car accident. And after Mary's suicide attempt and breakdown."

"Was this before or after you were hired by Long Lane School for Girls and used your salary to pay the Payne Whitney Clinic?" Cat folded her arms over her chest. "I saw your account ledgers, so don't bother trying to make something up. Why did you save those ledgers? And then leave them so you knew I would see them?"

Elizabeth winced. "I saved them precisely so you *would* see them. I've done terrible things, Catherine, things I'm not proud of—"

"Like always putting yourself first? Did you ever think that maybe if you'd tried harder, you could have helped Mary Tenney more, kept her from harming herself?"

Cat knew the questions were unfair the moment they left her mouth, but then, nothing about Mary's life—or Cat's—seemed terribly fair, even if that hadn't all been Elizabeth Bentley's fault. Elizabeth just happened to be the easiest and most accessible punching bag available.

Except, this punching bag punched back.

Elizabeth's eyes crackled with sudden rage, and she leaned forward. "Now you listen here, Catherine, and you listen well. I've made many mistakes in this life of mine, but the one person I never, *ever* wanted to hurt was Mary Tenney. I did everything in my power to protect her. And once she was gone, I did everything I could to protect *you*." She sighed, seemed to deflate again. "I left the ledgers because I once made the mistake of destroying every scrap of evidence that would prove my story. I wasn't about to do that again. I visited Mary—your mother—three years ago, after the FBI located you for me. I wanted to tell her that the queen was still on the board and that I was going to protect you. However, the first day I visited her at Payne Whitney was after my car accident with John."

"Tell me," Cat commanded.

And so, Elizabeth did.

MARCH 1952

I was in the hospital, the skin in my lower lip numbed and crammed with stitches following my fight with John Wright and my subsequent car crash. The physician at New York Hospital told me that the wound had gotten infected and could have turned to blood poisoning if I'd waited another day. He'd stitched me up and pumped me full of antibiotics, wanted to keep me overnight for observation.

I wasn't keen on the idea, but also wasn't thrilled with the idea of going home to Connecticut and dealing with John. So, I stayed, drifting in and out of sleep until I had an unexpected visitor. Another doctor, slim and wearing delicate wire spectacles. The sort of man you imagine poring over books, not slicing into humans in a surgical amphitheater.

"Hello, Miss Bentley." His diminutive appearance belied an authoritative voice that reminded me of the many FBI agents and senators I'd spoken to over the years, someone accustomed to being listened to. "I'm Dr. Johnson of the Payne Whitney Clinic, the psychiatric unit of the New York Hospital."

The Payne Whitney Clinic was one of those things people joked about sometimes—*If I have to listen to that song one more time, you'll have to lock me up in Payne Whitney.* Or, *One of these days I might check myself into a rubber room at Payne Whitney.* Why on earth would Dr. Johnson be visiting me?

Unless . . .

"I've never spent time in Psycho," I said defensively. "The FBI proved that definitively. I'm only here because of an injury from a car accident—"

"I'm not here for you, Miss Bentley," Dr. Johnson informed me in a kindly voice. "Actually, I overheard another physician mention that you were here in the hospital and I recognized your name from your *Meet the Press* interview. I'm here on behalf of a patient, someone I believe was your acquaintance at one time. Are you familiar with a woman named Mary Tenney?"

Every bit of me was suddenly electrified, and gooseflesh rolled down my arms and legs. When I answered, my voice was small, shrunken. "There was a time when I knew her very well."

"I'm relieved to hear it. Unfortunately, Miss Tenney suffered some years ago from a complete mental breakdown."

His voice disappeared down a distant tunnel, replaced by a loud ringing in my ears. I didn't want to hear more, preferred to freeze this moment like a fly in amber, keep its secrets forever locked away. *I did everything I could to protect her . . .* "A breakdown?" I managed to ask. "What do you mean?"

Dr. Johnson leaned against the counter, arms crossed against his chest. "Almost four years ago, Mary attempted suicide by mixing alcohol with an overdose of phenobarbital. She was unconscious for five days and has been in a severe hallucinatory psychotic state ever since."

Four years?

Four years ago, I'd received word that a woman had tried to commit suicide with her infant off the Golden Gate Bridge. And then she'd disappeared.

I pressed a fist into my lips, closing my eyes in a vain attempt to shut out the pain. Mary hadn't jumped, but she'd attempted to kill herself all the same, had even faked the death of her child as an added layer of protection after I'd defected just in case the Center ever got wind of what we'd done to hide her baby. And she had been in a psychiatric unit for *four* years?

I hadn't been here for her. Not for *four* goddamned years.

Dr. Johnson continued, oblivious to my turmoil. "Miss Tenney has been with Payne Whitney since her incident. I'm afraid that throughout the entirety of her breakdown, Miss Tenney has maintained some very detrimental hallucinations."

I had to force myself to release the bedsheets that were twisted in my hands. "What sort of hallucinations?"

"Well, Miss Tenney claims that she is a Russian spy."

Oh, Mary. Sweet mother of God.

I tried to imagine our roles switched, the FBI laughing at me after I'd become an informer and locking me up simply for the crime of telling the truth. It wasn't the first time I'd marveled at how closely I'd walked a similar path to the women I'd encountered during my time as a handler, how our lives had diverged in such different ways. How I'd somehow been the lucky one.

"Miss Tenney is one of our long-term patients," Dr. Johnson continued. "She is mostly mute now, but maintains a violent phobia against everything Russian. A few weeks ago, one of our orderlies mentioned something about a Russian bank, which sent Miss Tenney into hysterics. By the time I got to her, she was screaming over and over again, 'I never talked. I never talked!'" A pause. "Then she said your name. It wasn't the first time. I assumed she'd simply heard of you from the news, but when I heard you were at the hospital . . . Well, I had to see if you knew her."

I cradled my head in my hands, couldn't seem to gather the words to respond. Fortunately, Dr. Johnson didn't seem to expect an answer.

"My social call today is of a more personal nature," he said. "You see, in the four years she's been with us, Miss Tenney has never had a single friend or family member visit her. I believe some time with an old acquaintance might provide the balm she needs to soothe her troubled mind."

I'd felt guilt before—guilt at spying on my country, guilt that I hadn't been able to save Yasha or his legacy, guilt at pointing the FBI toward the Rosenbergs. More recently, a crushing sort of guilt when William Remington was convicted and killed in prison.

This was far worse. But also, better in one critical way.

Hidden deep within Dr. Johnson's offer was a second chance. Perhaps I could set right one damned thing in this entire broken life of mine.

I could help my best friend. The woman I'd once called my sister.

I threaded my hands in my lap. "When are visiting hours?"

"You can come any day, Monday through Friday. Only—"

I didn't want to hear another word that might dissuade me. "I'll be there. Tomorrow after I'm discharged. Thank you, Doctor."

Dr. Johnson recognized the dismissal, nodded his good-bye. I stared at the pale-yellow hospital wall for a long time after he left.

I was going to make this right. If it was the last goddamned thing I did.

I HAD GOOD intentions, I swear I did.

I was going to corroborate Mary's story. I was going to give up booze and bring her home to live with me in Connecticut. I alone knew her story; I alone could rehabilitate her. And I would, no matter what it took.

No longer would I be lonely *Whistler's Mother* with her shades of black and white and gray; no, together Mary and I would be more akin to Klimt's *The Women Friends*, with its phoenix rising from the ashes. She and I would sit on my front porch and grow old together, paint our nails while she bested me at chess and we reminisced about the old days.

Not the *good* old days. For while I'd had some good days—good *years*—with Yasha, I knew that Mary's life, especially these past years, had been quite the opposite.

And then there had been that other business with the baby. Which was also my fault. Things might have been fine for Mary had I not defected and forced her to live with the terror that the NKVD—now transformed into the KGB—would hunt her down. Not just her but her child too.

I was going to right those past wrongs.

The only problem was, those intentions become more and more terrifying with each step that led me deeper into the hospital wing that housed the Payne Whitney Clinic. Twice I retreated back the way I'd come, had to force myself to plunge forward. For Mary.

I would *not* be a coward. Not this time.

The psychiatric hospital that had sheltered my friend these past years was nothing at all what I'd imagined. Perhaps I'd read too many novels, but I'd envisioned walls spattered with week-old oatmeal and numbed-out patients with dirty feet staring at Popsicle stick sculptures. Instead, a hospital wing of gleaming marble and polished oak greeted me, accentuated by arched doorways and smiling nurses in starched uniforms.

"Hello." I preened at the way I didn't slur my greeting. (I'd brought a flask of gin to the hospital with me, had drained it dry this morning when the nurses weren't looking.) "I'm here to see Mary Tenney. She's expecting me."

"Of course," the starched nurse answered. "Please wait here."

I did, sitting in one of the velvet upholstered settees with curved feet until Dr. Johnson appeared. "I'm so pleased you're here, Miss Bentley," he said. "Miss Tenney is waiting in our patients' lounge. She's having an exceptional morning."

An exceptional morning for me to pack her up and move her to Connecticut, you mean.

"Here she is," Dr. Johnson said as we entered an open room that overlooked the hospital's small courtyard. Patients—many dressed in soft cotton bathrobes—were gathered around tables, some stacking blocks, others constructing small arts and crafts projects. A thin woman with a perfect bob of blond hair was seated at the nearest table with her back to us, hunched over a half-finished oil painting of what appeared to be a vase of sunflowers. "Mary, you have a visitor."

The blond woman might have been a papier-mâché statue made by one of the patients for all she moved. Warning bells went off in my head, commanding me to turn tail and run.

But Mary was my oldest friend.

Sinners make the best saints, she'd once said to me. And today I would be less sinner, more saint.

I would make this right. Mary and I would have the happy ending we deserved.

"Mary." I ignored the doctor's raised hand of warning as I came around the table. "It's been so long—"

"Actually, Miss Bentley"—the doctor gestured to a second woman hunched over a stack of maps at the next table—"*this* is Miss Tenney."

I stopped, frozen as I stared at the woman who hadn't so much as lifted her head to acknowledge me. She remained absorbed in a flat image of what appeared to be a map of Manhattan. I sank into the chair across from her, tried to peer into eyes that wouldn't lift to mine. Reared back when those watered-down blue eyes finally glanced up.

This woman wasn't Mary.

Her face was slack. Blank. *Lifeless.*

Yet, somehow, she *was* still Mary.

She had gained weight in the intervening years—my friend had always possessed just the right curves to snag men's attention—but now she appeared pale and puffy, as if she never left the chair she'd been planted in. Those dull eyes had once sparkled; waves of blond hair now hung limp around her face. Only one thing was untouched by the ravages of time: the pale bands of puckered scar tissue at her wrists peeked out from the sleeves of her bathrobe, with many more slashes added since I'd seen her last.

"Mary." This time I reached out to touch her hand. I willed that bit of human touch to be the flint that would light some spark in her. She only stared at me.

Lifeless.

Until she twitched.

Not a twitch so much as a convulsion, followed by another. The involuntary emotion seemed to radiate out from her heart until her entire body shook. Over and over again.

Panic reared its ugly basilisk head; nowhere in my imaginings had Mary been truly ill, merely *mistaken* for a madwoman. Dr. Johnson merely observed my friend, scratched a note in the journal taken from his pocket before sitting in the empty chair next to her.

"Her convulsions are normal," he assured me, "following her attempt to take her own life a few years ago. I promise she's much improved since when she first came to us."

I stared at Mary's hollowed-out eyes and her once-beautiful body. It was as if her mind had been scooped out with a melon spoon, leaving behind only a hollow shell that had once laughed and danced, cried and made love.

"When will her treatment be finished?" My voice came out tinny, bile rising in my throat as the room tilted dangerously beneath me. "When can Mary leave and go home?"

The sad shake of the doctor's head confirmed my panicked suspicions. "With her history of suicide attempts, I'm afraid Miss Tenney will remain a resident here at Payne Whitney for perpetuity. However, as you can see, she's safe and well cared for, spending her free time between treatments with flower arranging and map reading, just as is recommended by preeminent psychiatrists in the field of schizophrenia."

Mary had always been fragile, but now, according to the doctor, she was beyond repair. And I couldn't handle this terrible new reality.

(Catherine, I've lingered on the stoops of hell more than once in my life and tried to be brave—the moment when I protected Yasha and his contacts while his body lay on my sofa, the day I defied the NKVD to turn myself in to the FBI, even when I stared down Joseph McCarthy and Richard Nixon at the HUAC trials—but in my heart of hearts, I am a coward. And cowards run. So, that's what I did. I ran.)

Clutching my handbag tight to my chest, I ignored Dr. Johnson's startled shouts and fled from that hospital as fast as my utilitarian black heels would take me. I didn't stop running until I reached Central Park, my hair whipped into a Medusa-worthy frenzy and the armpits of my blouse stained with foul-smelling sweat.

I wandered blindly past the fountain where Yasha and I had once thrown sticks for Vlad, somehow found myself at the bar of the Hotel Abbey.

I tried to drink myself into oblivion that night. Maybe into the next world.

As you know, I failed even in that.

||||||||||||||||

NOVEMBER 26, 1963

Elizabeth rubbed her temples. "I've already told you what happened after that, Catherine. I took the train home, failed to hang myself, and got myself into yet another car accident."

Cat struggled to remain objective, to simply gather the facts. Difficult to do when there were a thousand questions stinging the tip of her tongue. "When did you next see her?"

"After the last car crash. It was Dr. Johnson's letter that did it. I certainly wasn't going to send my best friend to the notorious hell-hole of Willowbrook."

Cat lifted her chin, sifting through the questions that tumbled through her mind for just the right one.

"Had her condition changed?" Cat forced herself to keep breathing, her heart to keep beating. "Or was it still the same?"

Some of the light winked out of Elizabeth's eyes. "She was the same. I cleaned myself up before that next visit—stopped drinking and, with Hoover's affidavit, convinced Long Lane School for Girls to hire me. I went to Payne Whitney still hoping I could take Mary home with me. But she wasn't lucid—far from it, in fact—and I realized the clinic was the best place for her. The only place, really." She lifted her gaze to Cat. "That's when I realized I couldn't do right by Mary—except keep her safe at Payne Whitney—but I could do right by her daughter. By you."

Which explained all the payments to Cat's student account at Trinity. But she wasn't ready to let Elizabeth off the hook, not even if she had been playing a guardian angel with dirty wings all this time.

"Why didn't you tell me you have cancer?"

"Simple: I don't need you feeling sorry for me."

Or apparently, even *liking* her. Cat suspected this was Elizabeth's way of protecting herself. After all, it was easier to lose someone if you never became attached to them in the first place. Or let them get attached to you.

Still, Cat was weary of Elizabeth's games. It was time to get everything on the table.

"You sent money to Trinity. For me. Why?"

Elizabeth's gaze dropped. Silence.

This woman across from me is a human Enigma machine. Cat couldn't for the life of her understand why she would rather own up to being a spy and Communist, a drunk and a liar, than admit to the kindness discovered when she left her accounts in that box. Cat still wasn't sure if she'd even really wanted them to be found.

Finally: "It was the least I could do," Elizabeth ground out. "I called Trinity once back in 1961 and pretended to be your mother—to be Joan Gray, that is—claiming I wanted to deposit money into your account. They told me I was just in time since your account was overdue. I did a little digging, had the FBI confirm that your mother had reverse mortgaged her house to cover your tuition. That the money had run out."

Cat gaped. Since her mother's death, she'd thought the house had been reverse mortgaged to pay for her mother's medical bills and that it hadn't been enough, hadn't realized their home had been sacrificed even before the cancer. For *her*. Of course, Joan Gray likely hadn't planned on coming down with cancer when she'd mortgaged everything. Which had meant she'd had to sell the house to pay her own medical bills.

Elizabeth sniffed. "I certainly couldn't have you being thrown out of college."

Cat shook herself, would deal with this new shock later. "And I assume you just wired more money to Trinity to cover my final semester? And my housing?"

Elizabeth shifted again, winced. "I did what I could. I should have done more."

"Why, Elizabeth? *Why?*" Cat demanded. She thought she was done being mad, but her anger was a slumbering giant that was beginning to wake again. "Why not just invite me for coffee after you had the FBI track me down instead of making me come to you? I wanted to *kill* you, for God's sake. Why all the grandstanding and all the goddamned *lies*? For crying out loud, you even told me Mary Tenney had a *boy*."

"That was survival, said for the same reason Scheherazade made up stories: to buy myself—and you—more time, to convince you to keep listening. I lied when things got hard because that's what I've always done." She lifted her shoulders—fragile as a bird's wings—in a pitiful shrug. "You're my priest, Catherine, and I'm dying—I needed you to hear my full confession. And now you have." Her hand fluttered alongside her leg on the hospital blanket, and Cat caught the flash of gold that she knew was a cigarette lighter inscribed with a double-headed eagle. *How she got that past the nurses and doctors is beyond me.*

Cat was so exhausted, so wrung out from all of this, that she rose, ready to leave. Except Elizabeth stopped her.

"There's one more thing I must confess to." Elizabeth's tone was tortured, stripped of the armor of her usual bluster and bravado. She closed her eyes, as if that somehow made it easier to speak. "Mary Tenney isn't dead. Your mother is still very much alive."

"What?"

"She's not the Mary I once knew—it's an incontrovertible truth that Mary Tenney is dead and gone—but the woman who carried you for nine months and nearly broke my hand giving birth to you still lives and breathes. I thought I was protecting you—it will be damn hard for you to meet her, but you deserve to know. Deserve the *choice*."

"Is she at the Payne Whitney Clinic?"

At Elizabeth's nod, something unfurled deep in Cat's chest. *Hope.*

That Cat might not be totally alone.

But she'd gotten everything she needed from Elizabeth. That much was certain.

"I know I don't deserve any favors from you, but will you do one last thing?" Elizabeth asked as Cat rubbed the tension from her temples, turned off the recorder, and started packing it into her bag. Cat almost pointed out the utter audacity of her question until she saw the golden cigarette lighter cradled in Elizabeth's hand. "Get rid of this for me?"

Cat's fingers closed around the cold metal, and she flicked it once. *Click.* Somehow, the sound was comforting. "Why did you keep it all these years?"

"As a reminder to stand up to my monsters." Elizabeth's broken voice made Cat wonder which monsters she was thinking of: Al and the Russians, Elizabeth and her own vices, or perhaps the mountain of lies she'd told? Cat tucked the lighter into her pocket and slung the heavy recorder bag over her shoulder, resolving not to care. "I have exploratory surgery scheduled sometime after Thanksgiving," Elizabeth announced. "Will you visit me again, Catherine? After the surgery?"

Cat thought of offering her some platitude or perhaps even a lie, but her own world had spun off its axis and she needed to catch her breath. There was only one thing she could say as she left the tomblike quiet of that sterile hospital room.

"I'll take care of your cat until you're back on your feet."

PART OF CAT wanted to wait to visit the Payne Whitney Clinic, to make a plan.

I've always made plans—graduating high school early, the ideal White House internship, the perfect journalism degree—and look where it's left me. To hell with plans.

"What a special treat for Miss Tenney to have a visitor." The white-garbed nurse ushered Cat from the main lobby with its chandeliers and wingback chaise lounges down a well-lit corridor. They stopped outside a patient's room, and Cat caught a whiff of peppermint. The door was open, but the nurse gave a little knock anyway. "It's been a while."

Since the last time Elizabeth visited, Cat was willing to bet. Yet she didn't say anything as they entered. She was hardly expecting this cozy room with cheery primary color canvases on the walls. A woman sat with her back to the door as she stared out the window at the gloom of the November-draped city beyond. The perfect French braid down her back was the same shade as Cat's honeyblond, gleaming beneath the fluorescent overhead lights.

Catherine, I've always believed hair to be a person's unofficial résumé—critical to dating and romance, used to inform, adorn, or shock.

Mary's hair informed Cat that she was well cared for here at Payne Whitney, but Cat couldn't help wondering what her hair would look like if Elizabeth Bentley hadn't moved heaven and earth to keep her at this facility. The tangled rat's nest of the mentally disturbed? Shorn close to her skull to keep the lice at bay? It was too much to imagine for any human, much less the woman Cat now knew gave birth to her.

"Mary, someone is here to see you," the nurse crooned as she turned the blond woman's chair. *Wheelchair*, Cat realized with a start. "Her name is Catherine."

Cat searched for a spark of recognition at her name, but the only movement her birth mother made was to cock her head like an inquisitive and terribly fragile bird. Cat strained forward, eagerly waiting—hoping—for more, but it didn't come. The nurse motioned her to a polished wooden chair next to the bed. "I'll check back in a half hour. You have a nice visit, all right?"

Her staccato footsteps echoed on the marble. Then it was just Cat and her mother.

I'm in a mental institution, meeting my birth mother for the first time, and I have no earthly idea what to say. Mary sat in her wheelchair, hands mostly still save for the occasional flutter of one of her pinkies. Cat wondered what she was like when she was younger, when Cat was a child, whether different choices would have led her down a path that hadn't ended in this psychiatric clinic.

"We don't know each other, Mary, but we have a mutual friend." Cat realized the fragile truth of the statement only after the words had left her mouth. Elizabeth's methods left much to be desired, but without her tarnished efforts at playing Cat's protector, Cat would likely have had to drop out of college, certainly would never have found herself sitting across from her birth mother. "Her name is Elizabeth Bentley, and she's told me so much about you. However, I wanted to meet you for myself."

Mary lifted ocean-blue eyes to Cat's, but they were flat, hollow even. Cat knew she shouldn't expect a response, that she should be content just sitting here with the woman who'd sacrificed her own sanity to keep her safe.

But Cat wanted *more*. So . . . she began to talk.

"My name is Catherine," she said, "but everyone calls me Cat. I'm due to graduate from Trinity this spring, but I've hit a rough patch I'm trying to overcome. You see, my mother died of cancer." It felt like a sort of betrayal—to both Mary *and* to Joan Gray—to be here, to call one woman her mother and not the other, but it was the truth. Cat now had two mothers, and she realized she wouldn't be where she was today were it not for both of them. "Then I met Elizabeth Bentley." She gave a low sort of chuckle. "I actually wanted to kill her the first time I met her—you might be able to relate. Her life story would make a quite a book."

Cat paused then, realized the truth of that statement. Elizabeth's story had been rattling around in her head since she'd recited it. A Communist spy turned FBI informer turned lying guardian angel? A writer—or a journalism student—would be hard-pressed to make that up.

Cat continued talking, weaving the story of the past few days—everything from President Kennedy's tragic death to her subsequent interviews with Elizabeth, of learning of her life as a spy, all the while omitting mention of Mary herself or Elizabeth's revelations that Mary was her mother. *After all, this will likely be the first of many visits*, Cat mused to herself, *which means there will be plenty of time for me to tell her everything.*

Cat talked for half an hour, pausing every so often to see if Mary would interject. She never did, of course, but Cat had listened to Elizabeth for so long, it was refreshing to be able to share her own story—and Elizabeth's—with this woman who shared her blood.

Because Cat realized now that Elizabeth's story and her own . . . their sinews were woven together tightly enough that it would be impossible to separate them. And wrapped around Elizabeth's and Cat's threads were Mary Tenney's.

"It's been nice visiting you," Cat said when the nurse returned and gave Cat a cue by gently tapping her watch. "I'll be back every weekend, all right?"

It was as she brushed Mary's shoulder, a gentle touch meant to convey good-bye, that Mary reached up to touch Cat's fingers. Their gazes snagged, and Cat read the confusion there, saw clouds trying to break as if the madness that was wrapped around Mary's mind had loosened. "Catherine," she whispered.

That was it.

Just one word—one name—whispered by a woman whose connection to her Cat hadn't known about until a few days ago.

Yet, that one word filled Cat's heart.

22

Cat had to find the courage to forgive Elizabeth.

"I'm here to see Elizabeth Bentley." Cat juggled the paper bag with what were hopefully still-warm hot dogs—extra ketchup—in one hand while dusting the early-December snow from her coat with the other. The nurse on duty at Grace-New Haven's inpatient desk today was young—not the grizzled veteran from the first time she'd come to visit Elizabeth—and Cat expected to be waved through just like before.

It had been more than a week since she'd met Mary Tenney, and she'd planned to visit Elizabeth sooner, but then Shirley had invited her to spend Thanksgiving with her and Maggie, and the visit stretched out longer than she'd planned. Not only that, today's world was unrecognizable from that of just two weeks ago following the assassination of Lee Harvey Oswald by nightclub owner Jack Ruby and headlines about potential further Communist assassination plots. All of which reminded Cat of Elizabeth.

Where does America go from here? Where do I go?

Cat didn't have all the answers, but she knew she couldn't put this off any longer. Her anger had been a heavy burden to bear—too heavy—and she'd decided it was time to set it aside. To let bygones be bygones.

Hell, she'd even brought hot dogs for Elizabeth. A peace offering of sorts.

The New Haven nurse's brow furrowed. "I'm afraid Miss Bentley is no longer here."

Cat frowned. It would be just like Elizabeth not to bother to call—if she'd traced Cat's address and school account info, surely she had her telephone number—to tell Cat she was returning home, even if Cat *was* taking care of her persnickety cat who refused to eat anything that wasn't tuna. "When did she leave?"

"I'm sorry, Miss—?"

"Gray."

The nurse perked up at that. "As in Catherine Gray? We've been trying to reach you. Miss Bentley listed you as her next of kin."

Next of kin . . .

There were very few scenarios that required contacting next of kin. Cat didn't want to hear any of them, found herself clutching the Formica counter and fervently wishing she could write herself out of this scene.

No more death, for God's sake. No more sickness and cancer and pain and suffering.

But the nurse continued, oblivious to Cat's distress. "I'm afraid Miss Bentley went in for exploratory surgery yesterday. Unfortunately, the cancer had spread to her entire abdominal cavity."

Cancer . . .

Entire abdominal cavity.

Cat closed her eyes, recognized this moment from one she'd acted out mere weeks ago. History did indeed seem to repeat itself. "And?"

The nurse's eyes went soft—she was young but had likely witnessed this moment dozens of times, knew her part to play. "Miss Gray, there was so much cancer that the doctors couldn't remove it all, couldn't even tell where it had originated. The operation was too much of a shock for Miss Bentley's system."

Cat held up her hands, as if those frail webs of flesh and splinters of bone could stop the blow she knew was coming.

And then it landed.

"I'm afraid she didn't make it. Elizabeth Bentley is dead."

23

Elizabeth Bentley—AKA Clever Girl, Red Spy Queen, Miss Wise . . . whatever people wanted to call her—made headlines one last time. Cat made sure of it.

In a country still reeling from the death of President Kennedy and unconvinced of the veracity of Elizabeth's testimony during the Red Scare, *Time* magazine only allotted her a two-sentence mention in its "Milestones" section. However, the *New York Times* found room to print the twenty-nine-paragraph obituary that Cat submitted.

> ELIZABETH BENTLEY IS DEAD AT 55;
> SOVIET SPY LATER AIDED U.S., TESTIFIED AT
> TRIAL OF ROSENBERGS . . .

The spy who inadvertently started the Red Scare, she was the woman whose revelations helped set the tone of American political life for nearly a decade . . .

A naive young woman who unmasked a web of wartime red treachery in this country . . .

She made the kind of sacrifice that can be necessary to preserve the country . . .

Condemned in life, Elizabeth was finally exonerated in death.

"It's not her whole story, I know," Cat said to Shirley from where they stood at the edge of the cemetery's lake. Her best friend had insisted on coming, had even found a sitter for Maggie for the day. Cat flicked a black-gloved finger over the rolled-up obituary. She was only a budding journalism student, but fortunately, not many journalists were interested in writing obituaries, especially in the melee following a presidential assassination and its aftermath. Which meant that Cat's freelance submission on Elizabeth's behalf was picked up. And by the *New York Times*, no less. "But it's a start."

"A damned good start," Shirley said. "I wish I'd had a chance to meet her. She sounds like one hell of a woman."

Cat watched in silence as the Cedar Hill Cemetery gravediggers dropped the final shovelfuls of dirt that would tuck Elizabeth's gleaming mahogany casket into the earth.

Of course, Cat shouldn't have been surprised that the woman the Russians dubbed Clever Girl had already made all her final plans—outlined in meticulous handwriting in a folder the nurse from Grace-New Haven gave Cat along with Yasha's framed photograph. Hell, Elizabeth had spent the last of her savings to prepay a year of Mary Tenney's bills at the Payne Whitney and then spent her last check from Long Lane School for Girls to finance the plot nestled among her Connecticut family members. Elizabeth Bentley would finally have the peace she once claimed she sought, resting for all eternity at the base of a forty-foot sugar maple. Cat expected it would turn a spectacular shade of red next autumn.

Victory Red, even.

As she stared at that bare scar of earth among the dead winter grass, she wondered what secrets the Russian spy turned informer had taken with her to her grave. Except Cat felt she knew the answer to that, that Elizabeth had finally told the truth when she claimed that Cat knew the entirety of her past.

Elizabeth might not have had any family, but there was still a steady trickle of people filtering back to their waiting cars now that her funeral was over. A handful of FBI agents, several teachers from Long Lane School for Girls, and even her elderly neighbors from the downstairs apartment.

And there were students. Dozens of them.

Teaching at a school for troubled girls was a part of her life that Elizabeth hadn't gotten around to telling Cat about, but she liked to think they would have gotten to it had the damned cancer not stepped in the way. Still, the shining eyes and sniffling into handkerchiefs from the girls told Cat that Elizabeth had touched their lives too.

Much as she would have once balked to hear it, there was no denying that Elizabeth Bentley had touched Cat's life.

She had chosen Cat's adoptive mother. Revealed her birth mother. Financed her education. Entrusted Cat with her life's story.

Thank you, Elizabeth, Cat thought to herself as a gentle patter of rain started. *For picking me to tell your story. And for pushing me into the sunlight when I needed it most.*

It was bad form to hold a grudge against a dead woman, so Cat had finally done what she'd wanted that last time she'd gone to the hospital, had found the courage to forgive Elizabeth. And while Cat wished they'd had the chance to speak one last time, she was thankful she'd had the chance to excavate the many layers of Elizabeth's life.

"I'm going to write her story," Cat finally admitted out loud. "The whole damned thing."

Shirley merely looped her arm through Cat's as they walked back to her waiting car. "I think that's a bang-up idea. You need something to do with all that free time you'll have after you graduate this spring."

It would be a story of spies and two wars—one with the world and one at home—and also of love and sacrifice. But it would also be a tale of loneliness and courage, a starkly honest portrayal of the terrible and amazing feats a single woman was capable of. Cat would let readers be their own judge of Elizabeth, of her triumphs and missteps.

After all, sinners sometimes do *make the best saints.*

EPILOGUE

In front of her typewriter, her journalism textbooks for her last semester stacked neatly on her windowsill, Cat flexed her fingers and rolled out the stiffness in her neck. She took a deep breath and steeled herself for the Rumpelstiltskin process of transforming Elizabeth's story into the first typed pages of a manuscript.

Of a *book*.

Elizabeth's book. And her own.

For further inspiration, she'd arranged on the desk in front of her Yasha's framed photograph—she'd found some of his *I love you* notes to Elizabeth tucked into the back—plus the carved wooden cross Mary handed down to Cat and even Al's double-headed eagle lighter. Elizabeth's lavender journal on human behavior—now faded and fragile—was there for handy reference, a tube of Bésame Victory Red lipstick next to it. Of course, the scene wouldn't have been complete without a certain fluffy orange cat curled next to the typewriter, occasionally flicking the keys with his tail.

At one edge of the desk was Coriolanus, well pruned and with fresh violet buds on the cusp of bursting open, sitting on the hollow copy of Tolstoy's *War and Peace*. The other side of the desk held a vase crammed with fragrant lilies and pink carnations from the FBI, the typeset signature on the card from J. Edgar Hoover himself. The flowers had arrived scarcely an hour after Cat had returned from the hospital following Elizabeth's death. Now, a week later, they'd wilted and dropped the first of their petals, leaving a dusting of vivid orange pollen on what would become the first page of Elizabeth's story.

Of our *story,* Cat thought to herself.

She pressed play on the reel-to-reel recorder, let the confidence of Elizabeth's raspy New England finishing school voice from their last interview fill the room. If Cat closed her eyes, she could almost imagine that Elizabeth was in the room, that they were sitting at her wobbly kitchen table again.

And so . . .

Cat began typing.

The gun in Catherine's Pucci handbag bumped reassuringly against her hip as she double-checked the address of the Connecticut apartment building . . .

AUTHOR'S NOTE

People often ask how I choose which historical women to write about, and the answer is different for every book. In Elizabeth Bentley's case, my aim has been to shed light on her forgotten story and also, to a lesser extent, to polish away some of the tarnish on her legacy.

Elizabeth Bentley has been mostly ignored by history, and when she *is* remembered, it's often in the same vilified breath as Senator Joseph McCarthy and the Red Scare. However, Elizabeth Bentley didn't resort to smoke screens and scare tactics; she went to the FBI in private long before McCarthy began waving around his list of supposed Communists. Not only that, but Elizabeth's list of names was based on her real list of contacts. (The one she kept memorized—Elizabeth was never so inept as to write down anything incriminating.) Elizabeth Bentley named over one hundred names of those either engaged in Soviet espionage or connected to Communist activities. Fifty-one were investigated by the FBI, and twenty-seven were employed by the US government on November 7, 1945, when she first spoke to the FBI. As a result of Elizabeth Bentley's allegations and the fact that she exposed practically all the agents the NKVD had been using during World War II, the Russians were faced with the task of completely rebuilding the agent network in the United States. Since then, the Soviet intelligence services have learned that one spy turned informer can cause the entire house of cards to come crashing down and have rarely recruited American citizens.

However, unlike other Soviet spies turned informers—namely Whittaker Chambers, who was posthumously awarded the Presidential Medal of Freedom—who were lauded for doing their patriotic duty and informing on the Russians, Elizabeth was often vilified, and the veracity of her story was constantly in doubt. At the same time, the FBI was caught in a catch-22—their top secret Project VENONA proved Bentley was telling the truth, but America couldn't broadcast that information and expose that they'd been spying on their allies during World War II. (Plus, they wanted the Soviets to keep using the code they'd cracked for as long as possible.) Unfortunately, Project VENONA wasn't declassified until 1995, several years after the fall of the Soviet Union, which means Bentley didn't live to see her own vindication. Among all of her contacts, only William Remington would be convicted—for perjury, not for treason—but her testimony against the Rosenbergs also helped produce a guilty verdict for both Julius and Ethel. And while Americans at the time of their execution believed the Rosenbergs might have been innocent, Project VENONA detailed Julius's role as a Soviet courier, and as his accessory, Ethel had full knowledge of her husband's espionage activities.

While I aimed to keep my fictionalized version of Elizabeth's story as close to the truth as possible, this author's note will serve as my confessional for instances when I had to tweak things to better fit the narrative.

With the exception of Cat, who is entirely fictional, the characters you've read about in these pages are all based on real people. However, in order to streamline the cast list, there were several historical characters that I merged and some names I changed for the sake of clarity. For example, I combined Lee Fuhr with Hallie Flanagan, Elizabeth's former drama teacher at Vassar, who was apparently one of her first introductions to Communism. During Elizabeth's days with the Party, she worked with many Communist officers, whom I chose to condense. For example, I gave Juliet Glazer some of a certain Comrade Brown's responsibilities, such as introducing Elizabeth to Yasha, because honestly, I could only keep track of so many comrades. Nathan Gregory Silvermaster became just Nathan Silvermaster in order to avoid confusion with Elizabeth's FBI name of Agent Gregory, and I also omitted one of Elizabeth's code names—Helen Johnson—given that the name Helen was already claimed by both Helen Silvermaster and Mary Tenney's alter ego Helen Price.

The most important merging of characters is that of my combination of two of Elizabeth's contacts—Mary Price and Helen Tenney—into the composite character of Mary Tenney, whom I gave the code name of Helen Price. In reality, both women shared many connections. For example, Helen Tenney moved into Mary Price's old DC apartment, and Mary Price was passed over for an OSS job while Helen Tenney worked in the Spanish sector of the OSS, a job she took at the suggestion of Jacob Golos. Elizabeth Bentley did try to protect both women—following Yasha's death, she told Earl Browder that Helen Tenney was psychologically unfit for clandestine work, and he had her released from service. Unfortunately, Helen Tenney suffered a nervous breakdown in 1947 and was institutionalized following a suicide attempt. She developed a violent phobia against everything Russian and was deemed delusional due to her claims that her telephone was tapped and that she had once been a Russian spy. Mary Price was known as Dir in coded messages, but Tenney's code name in Project VENONA was Muse, which seemed apropos for a character working as a honey trap. While there's no evidence that either historical woman was a honey trap to the extent of my fictional Mary Tenney, Iskhak Akhmerov, chief of the NKGB illegal station in the US, hoped to establish Mary Price in an apartment in Georgetown for the sexual entrapment of blackmail victims, and sources claim she did have an affair with one contact.

Elizabeth actually had at least three handlers after Jacob Golos died (and I've found three possible dates for Golos's death—November 25, 26, or 27, 1943); the first being Iskhak Akhmerov (code name Bill), and the last of whom was Anatoly Gorsky (code name Al). (As a side note, some of Elizabeth's contacts appear to have had multiple code names; in that instance I chose the more common version.) I combined Akhmerov and Gorsky into one central character and stuck with Al, as Elizabeth had more contact with him for a longer period. Plus, he was the one who penned the memo about all the possible ways to liquidate her. Soviet-savvy readers will also notice that I stuck with the NKVD designation instead of also using the NKGB. The Soviet secret police really was an alphabet soup that changed every few years—the GPU became the OGPU, which was part of the NKVD (which was around from 1934 through the end of WWII), then the NKGB (the counterintelligence force, which lasted from February to July 1941 and was re-instituted temporarily in 1943), and then the KGB, which lasted until the end of the Cold War. To keep from making readers' eyes bleed, I decided to simplify and just use the NKVD.

The FBI didn't become aware of the British intelligence leak to Moscow regarding Elizabeth's defection for some time and continued sending reports. On November 24, three days after her final meeting with Al, the People's Commissar for State Security notified Stalin and Molotov of Bentley's defection. Gorsky did have plans to kill Elizabeth, including shooting, poisoning, or faking her suicide, but rather than do the deed himself, he would likely have assigned this task to Soviet agent Joseph Katz, whom Elizabeth knew as Jack. It was eventually decided that a slow-acting poison should be administered to Elizabeth, something Katz could place on a pillow or handkerchief or in her food. Luckily for Elizabeth Bentley, the plan was aborted at the last minute.

In the interest of avoiding penning a thousand-page novel, there are a few instances where I tweaked how Elizabeth's history unfolded. For example, the timeline regarding Elizabeth's early relationship with Golos and work at the Italian Library is unclear, so I chose to arrange events in the way that made the most narrative sense. I also compressed the timeline regarding Trotsky's assassination. Stalin apparently ordered his assassination in 1939, but it took until August 1940 to orchestrate.

One of the greatest liberties I took was pulling J. Edgar Hoover onto these pages. It's unlikely that J. Edgar Hoover would have shared any information about Project VENONA with Bentley, and she probably never met Hoover—there's certainly no documentation that they did meet—but he and Elizabeth *did* exchange letters, including the one I incorporated here verifying the contents of her testimony. Elizabeth actually met with Donegan after the *World-Telegram* Blond Spy Queen story came out, but Hoover was reputedly furious and called her contact with the press "outrageous."

Elizabeth did *so much* testifying that I suspected readers would lose patience with constant scenes in front of grand juries and the House Un-American Activities Committee. I combined some of her grand jury testimony and the Ferguson committee testimony with that of the HUAC to avoid repetition (and to allow notorious Joseph McCarthy an appearance, although it was actually Senator Ferguson who questioned Elizabeth), and I also combined *Meet the Press* radio and television appearances, of which she had several. In a further attempt to whittle down her volume of courtroom appearances, I combined two Remington perjury trials into one. William Remington was convicted of perjury in 1951 and sentenced to five years in prison, but his lawyer appealed. The first trial was in 1951, the second in 1953. I had the perjury trial in this novel take place before Elizabeth's car accidents and before she split with John Wright, but with the resulting outcome of the second trial. Also, readers of any biography on Elizabeth Bentley will note that she also had a minor hit-and-run car accident that took place when she was driving a neighbor to the train station. I decided two car accidents was enough for the reader to understand that Elizabeth was falling apart and omitted the hit-and-run.

In regards to Catherine's story, she is entirely a figment of my imagination—there is absolutely nothing to suggest that either Mary Price or Helen Tenney had a secret child or that Elizabeth Bentley ever helped arrange an adoption. This bit of the novel was actually very loosely inspired by my own family history—my mother was an infant who was "brokered" during the 1960s and whose biological parents were told that she had died at birth. During the postwar years, there were actually many child traffickers— the most notable is Georgia Tann—who sought to profit via black market baby adoption schemes from the fact that there were more prospective adoptive parents than there were children who needed adopting. At the time of her death, Elizabeth Bentley left behind no family, but I thought it would be kinder for my fictionalized versions of Elizabeth and Mary Tenney to end their stories with some bit of human connection, while also casting a spotlight on a forgotten aspect of American social history.

ACKNOWLEDGMENTS

There are so many wonderful people I have to thank for helping shape this story into the book that you hold in your hands today. Most especially to my intrepid first readers—Stephanie Dray and Kate Quinn—who read the first cringeworthy draft and then waved their magic wands to fix all the plot holes and broken character arcs that were making me tear my hair out. You ladies are goddesses of the written word, seriously. Also, I owe debts of eternal gratitude to Kristin Beck, Eliza Knight, and Christine Wells for jumping to my rescue and helping fine-tune this beast of a manuscript. I owe all of you ladies a drink at the next Historical Novel Society Conference!

A big thank-you also goes out to loyal reader Esther Dale for connecting me with Eric Dale, who kindly checked my Russian phrases and saved me from a huge gaffe when it came to Russian curse words. *Spasibo!*

Of course, this book never would have made it past the idea stage had it not been for my agent extraordinaire, Kevan Lyon, who I am convinced could have stared down the NKVD without batting an eye. And thank you to her fearsome crew of Lyonesses, who have been such great wells of support and strength, especially Renée Rosen, Chanel Cleeton, Janie Chang, Laura Kamoie, Jennifer Robson, and Bryn Turnbull. Also, to my editor, Kate Seaver, for helping me sift through so many story ideas that eventually led me to telling Elizabeth Bentley's unexpected tale. And to the entire talented crew at Berkley who made this book into a reality: Mary Geren, Fareeda Bullert, Claire Zion, Tara O'Connor, and especially Katie Anderson, who designed the gorgeous cover.

Writing can be a lonely business, so thank you to my amazing tribe of teachers who have had my back since my very first book was published: Kristi Senden, Claire Torbensen, Megan Williams, and Cindy Davis.

Family is everything, and I have so many family members cheering me to the finish line with every book. Thank you to Hollie Dunn and Heather Harris, Kerry and Ray Flynn, Christine and Jonathan Carrasco, Johnie Thornton, Steve and Margo Thornton, Tim and Daine Crowley, Don and Billie Paulson, and Carolyn Christler.

Of course, my final thanks go to Stephen and Isabella Thornton. None of this would have been possible without the two of you. I love you both to Jupiter and back.

ADDITIONAL READING

NONFICTION

Bentley, Elizabeth. *Out of Bondage, KGB Target: Washington, DC.* New York: Ivy Books, 1988.

Chambers, Whittaker. *Witness: A True Story of Soviet Spies in America and the Trial That Captivated the Nation.* Washington, DC: Regnery Publishing, 1952.

Fox, Amaryllis. *Life Undercover: Coming of Age in the CIA.* New York: Alfred A. Knopf, 2019.

Kessler, Lauren. *Clever Girl: Elizabeth Bentley, the Spy Who Ushered in the McCarthy Era.* New York: HarperCollins, 2003.

Mitchell, Marcia, and Thomas Mitchell. *The Spy Who Seduced America: Lies and Betrayal in the Heat of the Cold War, The Judith Coplon Story.* Montpelier: Invisible Cities Press, 2002.

Olmstead, Kathryn. *Red Spy Queen: A Biography of Elizabeth Bentley.* Chapel Hill: University of North Carolina Press, 2002.

Romerstein, Herbert, and Eric Breindel. *The Venona Secrets: Exposing Soviet Espionage and America's Traitors.* Washington, DC: Regnery Publishing, 2000.

FICTION

Eliasberg, Jan. *Hannah's War.* New York: Back Bay Books, 2020.

Prescott, Lara. *The Secrets We Kept.* New York: Alfred A. Knopf, 2019.

Quinn, Kate. *The Rose Code.* New York: William Morrow, 2021.

Robuck, Erika. *The Invisible Woman.* New York: Berkley, 2021.

Wilkinson, Lauren. *American Spy.* New York: Random House, 2019.

A NOVEL OF AN AMERICAN SPY

STEPHANIE MARIE THORNTON

INTERVIEW WITH THE AUTHOR

You've written so many wonderful novels based on the lives of real women. How did you discover Elizabeth Bentley's story? How was it similar and different from writing about Alice Roosevelt in *American Princess* and Jacqueline Bouvier Kennedy Onassis in *And They Called It Camelot?*

I actually came across a reference to Elizabeth Bentley when I was researching Cold War spies and was intrigued by this woman whose story is virtually unknown today. What was interesting to me was that everyone knows about Joseph McCarthy, but his accusations regarding Communists infiltrating the US government were based on hot air. Elizabeth Bentley—whose many testimonies were secretly confirmed by the FBI via Project VENONA—was vilified and then forgotten due to the fact that no one could corroborate her accusations, and because she was seen as a hysterical, menopausal woman. Project VENONA was declassified in 1995, and now we know the truth of Bentley's story, which I felt needed to be told.

Elizabeth Bentley's story was similar to that of Alice Roosevelt and Jackie Kennedy's in that they were all American women who deeply loved their country. The big difference was that Bentley made many choices that at first glance appear the opposite of patriotic—she was an American spying for Russia during World War II, after all!

In *A Most Clever Girl* you created an entirely fictional narrator in Catherine Gray. That's different than in your previous novels, in which there was only one heroine and she was based on a real person. How did that change your writing process? How did you weave together the stories of two women and two time periods?

All of my six prior novels are narrated by real women from history, but including Catherine Gray in this book allowed me to weave in more of Bentley's redemption at the end. The real Elizabeth Bentley had a rough time in her last final years, given that her testimonies brought about few convictions and those that did—William Remington's and the Rosenbergs'—didn't end as planned. Cat's storyline also allowed me the opportunity to interject with questions that might mirror readers' questions as they followed the story. Elizabeth Bentley was a complicated woman—being able to see her making the choices she did during World War II and the Cold War and then hear the older version of her character justify those decisions was a good way to really get inside her head.

What's your research process like? Do you start by reading biographies? In general, what are usually the most effective sources for informing your novel? How much of your research do you finish before you start writing the novel?

I always start with reading biographies about my narrators—this time it was Lauren Kessler's *Clever Girl* and Kathryn S. Olmsted's *Red Spy Queen*—to figure out the foundations of the plot and characters. My aim after that is to read anything written by my subject. In this case I was lucky that Elizabeth Bentley wrote her own memoir, *Out of Bondage*, which I was able to track down. Once I have all that research under my belt, I start writing. As I continue to revise the story, I'm constantly layering information from additional primary sources—for example, transcripts of Bentley's House and Senate testimonies—and also any nonfiction about the general subject, which in this case meant learning about spy tools and what it's like to be an undercover spy. Finally, I try to search out any related museums or historical sites to really immerse myself in the material. The International Spy Museum in Washington, DC, was an invaluable source for this book!

Elizabeth Bentley was such a complicated woman. Did anything surprise you in writing her story?

Shockingly, Elizabeth Bentley's story has been so nearly forgotten. Here's a woman who ran the largest Soviet spy ring in America, ended the golden age of Soviet espionage in the US by informing to the FBI, and testified repeatedly about actual spies in the highest tiers of American government. However, Bentley was vilified and then forgotten, mostly because the FBI's hands were tied with the secrets of Project VENONA. At the same time, you have Whittaker Chambers—whose story is very similar to Bentley's—who received a posthumous Presidential Medal of Freedom in 1984 for his contributions to "the century's epic struggle between freedom and totalitarianism." While Elizabeth Bentley was an incredibly complicated woman—and she sometimes made terrible decisions—I felt people needed to hear her story again, especially now that we know she was telling the truth all those years ago.

Your love for history and historical fiction shines through in your novels. What intrigues you about history? Have you always loved studying it? Are there historical novels that you first fell in love with?

I have loved studying history since I was in first grade. I remember watching a documentary on the *Titanic* and gaping at the image of the underwater chandelier and grand staircase, realizing that people decades prior would have seen those same items as they walked into dinner decked out in their tuxedos and evening gowns. In high school, I devoured *The Red Tent* by Anita Diamant and *Memoirs of a Geisha* by Arthur Golden, finding myself transported to biblical times and wartime Japan. History—be it in a classroom lecture or a historical novel—is really about the stories and human emotions that link us together. That's what I love about historical fiction—its ability to let readers experience history as it unfolded and feel what it was like to be a First Lady, a president's daughter, or even a spy during World War II.

QUESTIONS FOR DISCUSSION

1. Throughout this story, Elizabeth Bentley is an unreliable narrator as well as an antihero. At what points did you cheer for her? When did you condemn her? What do you think she should have done differently in her life?

2. Elizabeth calls herself a villain and tells Cat that even the most heinous villain has reasons that let them rationalize their wrongdoing. How did Elizabeth rationalize the many wrongs she committed?

3. Many of the characters in this book—Elizabeth, Yasha, Mary Tenney, and even Cat—go by multiple names. What is the power of a name? What role did code names play throughout the novel?

4. When he recruits her, Yasha tells Elizabeth that he needs operatives who trust him implicitly and who will report any mistakes they have made even if it's the dead of night. Was there

anything that surprised you throughout the story about the relationships between Russian handlers and their contacts?

5. The life of a spy is often portrayed as exciting and glamorous—complete with dazzling spy gadgets and high-speed chases. What parts of Elizabeth Bentley's life as a spy fit that stereotype and what parts were entirely the opposite? Did Elizabeth's life remind you of any other spy stories you've read or seen on television or in movies?

6. Mary Tenney says to Elizabeth at one point, "There's a saying my father often said: Sinners make the best saints. I know what I'm doing isn't strictly right, but it's not wrong either. Because it's for a good cause." Do you think her work as a honeytrap and Elizabeth's spy work were more right or wrong? Did the ends truly justify their means?

7. Following the end of the war and Yasha's death, Elizabeth decides to go to the FBI with her insider knowledge of the Russian spy rings in America. Do you think she made the right decision?

8. Early on in the story, Elizabeth tells Cat, "That's the problem with being an accomplished liar—no one believes you even when you're telling the truth." At what points in the story did you suspect Elizabeth was lying? When did you think she was telling the truth?

9. The adoption scam Elizabeth speaks of was a real phenomenon in America, especially in the 1950s. (The author's own mother was adopted this way.) Were you surprised to hear of such illicit adoptions taking place?

10. Elizabeth's work as a Soviet spy and FBI informer spanned both World War II and the Cold War. What did you know about spying during these eras before reading this book? Had you heard of William Remington and the Rosenbergs, Joseph Mc-Carthy, and the House Un-American Activities Committee?

ABOUT THE AUTHOR

Photo by Katherine Schmeling Photography

Stephanie Marie Thornton is a high school history teacher and the *USA Today* bestselling author of *And They Called It Camelot* and *American Princess*. She is also the author of four novels about women in the ancient world. She lives in Alaska with her husband and daughter.